THE SNOW QUEEN'S HEIR

THE SNOW QUEEN'S HEIR

KEILAH JUDE

This book is a work of fiction. Any and all references to people, places, events, and incidents are fictional and originated from the author's imagination. Any resemblance to actual people, places, events, or incidents is coincidental.

Copyright © 2026 by Keilah Jude

Contact: www.KeilahJude.com

KeilahJudeBooks@gmail.com

Cover design by Miblart.com

Library of Congress Control Number: 2025913111

ISBNs:

979-8-9989342-0-9 (paperback)

979-8-9989342-1-6 (hardcover)

979-8-9989342-2-3 (e-book)

Printed in the United States of America

All rights reserved.

No part of this book may be reproduced in any form or by any electronic or mechanical means, including information storage and retrieval systems, without written permission from the author, except for the use of brief quotations in a book review.

For Jesus because He answered my prayers

AUTHOR'S NOTE

I cannot begin to say how grateful I am that you've chosen to read *The Snow Queen's Heir*. This is my first published book and I'm so excited to share it with you. My hope is that this story finds a home with the right readers, who jibe with this story and these characters as much as I do.

Thank you for reading my book!

Love,

Keilah Jude

CHAPTER 1
NOELLE
MEETING THE SNOW QUEEN

Noelle Hudson was going to knock out the creepy man who stalked her. Noelle inhaled the sharp, cold air as she realized he had followed her *again*. She didn't dare look to her right at the bald man with a scar on his face who walked next to her. Her feet crunched the snow beneath her, as she pulled her martial arts gym bag against her body.

He got closer, and despite her quickened pace, he kept up with her. She flinched as she felt a firm grip on her arm. His hand somehow burned her through her jacket—and she winced as she struggled against his fiery hold. She balled her fists, gritted her teeth, and looked into the dark eyes of her stalker.

"I'm here to deliver a message," the man hissed in Noelle's ear. "Find the necklace and give it to me. We found a dead body in my realm, and your name was mentioned in writing next to it."

Noelle frantically looked around, but the snowy alleyway was empty but for the copious amounts of snow that had accumulated on the ground. She begrudgingly looked over at the man, whose gruff face contorted into a twisted smile, the scar on his left cheek seeming to expand with the motion. Her breath hiked, and she felt exposed as she considered that he knew about the secret necklace. Her eyes narrowed on him; she was determined to fight his claim to *her* necklace.

"Threaten me again, and you'll have a new scar to sport," she warned and yanked her arm away. When he didn't respond, she added, "Leave or I'll call the police." But her fingers were already on the tip of the knife in her pocket, ready to be used.

He scoffed. "Tell a soul about me, and you'll pay a pretty price for it. You have until January, and if you don't deliver that necklace, you'll be sorry." The gruff-looking man bared his teeth, and then he yanked her forward down the alleyway by her arm.

She pulled her knife from her pocket and plunged it into the back of his hand. Noelle raised a fist to strike him, but to her dismay, he moved inhumanly fast. By the time she had blinked, he'd slammed her against the brick building and had pinned her arms by her sides. His blood coated her sleeve, making her gasp. She blinked several times, wondering if her mind had played tricks on her, but the man's scorching hands burned her arms, and she recoiled in pain.

"How did you move so quickly?" she whispered, trembling. The man's blazing hands suddenly stopped emitting dreadful heat.

"Speed is my ability, and I have more. So before you try that again, I'd suggest rethinking, or I'll give you a scar to match mine," he snarled, and pulled her farther along the snowy alley with his good hand.

Noelle struggled against him in an effort to break free, but he was too nimble and held on to her arm tightly. Wide-eyed, Noelle could only watch as he effortlessly dragged her with intense speed as the world whizzed by. She tried to plant her feet against the ground, but it was of little use. Her head spun as she tried to take in the reality that this man was incredibly fast, and she didn't fully understand what was happening.

"Where are you taking me?" Noelle asked through clenched teeth.

"To the others. You're being investigated in our realm for the death." He continued forward and pulled her along.

She was growing dizzy from how quickly they moved, which forced her to close her eyes. She thrashed against the man, desperate for freedom.

"But I didn't do anything! I don't even know what you're talking about!" Noelle cried out as his blazing hand roughly guided her. As they drew near, two voices became more pronounced: a man's whimper and a woman's threat.

Noelle listened intently as her heart hammered against her ribs. The man seemed to be pleading, and with every step, she wished desperately to run away. She longed to find the necklace before he did.

The scar-faced man began to move faster, and though he pulled Noelle along, she continued to struggle. He was supernaturally quick, and her mind couldn't comprehend what her eyes saw when she opened them. They turned the corner of a brick building, and ahead was a tall woman with flowing blond hair, holding an icy dagger to a man's throat. She had him pinned against the wall, where he blubbered and begged.

"It's her," the scar-faced man gasped, and before Noelle could turn to face him, he moved so quickly that he seemed to have vanished into thin air.

The blond woman turned from the man against the wall, and her piercing gray eyes, which were hoisted above high cheekbones, tightened on Noelle.

"Please! Let me go!" the man cried.

The tall woman placed a palm on the man's face, and ice spread over his mouth, effectively shutting it. She waved her fingers over his wrists, and thick ice formed, freezing him to the wall. The man made muffled sounds, but the woman's attention was now on Noelle.

"I didn't see anything," Noelle said and tried to back away. She stepped on a patch of ice, though, and fell onto the snow covering the dirty concrete. She gaped as she looked over at the woman and then back at the man, whose wrists were pinned by ice.

Noelle wondered if she might be going insane. First she saw a man who could move quicker than any mammal on Earth, and now she had witnessed a woman who could mold ice out of nothing. Noelle tried to shake her head, to snap out of it, but no matter how many times she tried, she was still in the snowy alley, staring at the tall woman.

The woman took a step toward Noelle, and Noelle tried to scurry to her feet, but the woman's cold fingers were instantly on Noelle's shoulder. She held her icy dagger to Noelle's throat and peered down at her.

She was ethereal, with a defined jaw and strong, sharp features.

"Please don't hurt me," Noelle managed to say, aware fighting would be futile.

"Who are you?" the woman growled in an unidentifiable accent. Even her voice was airy, delightful. "And how did you find us?"

CHAPTER 2
THE SNOW QUEEN LUMI
A SECOND CHANCE

"Noelle Hudson," she breathed. "Please, I don't have anything valuable. And I'm not a snitch! I'm telling you, I didn't see anything." The girl shook violently.

Lumi's breath hitched, and her grip loosened slightly. The girl seemed to be only a teenager, and although Lumi was rumored to be a monster, she didn't *want* to be. She had become a shell of a being, and she didn't think she had hardly a shred of mercy or kindness left in her, but the girl reminded her so much of her daughter Lorelei. They had the same beautiful shade of mocha-brown hair paired with freckles sprinkled across a button nose. If Lorelei could see what her mother had become, and what she was doing, she would be ashamed of her. Lumi imagined that if her daughter had managed to live long enough to be a teenager, she might look something very similar to this young girl.

Lumi loosened her grip even more but kept the dagger at the girl's neck.

"All right. But *how* did you find us?"

The girl perked up slightly, but not completely. She looked at the man behind Lumi, wide-eyed and bewildered. Noelle balled her fists together but then seemed to think better of it and relaxed her hands. Lumi noticed the calluses on Noelle's hands and the scars on her knuckles; it appeared the girl had some experience fighting. Still, she wouldn't be a match for Lumi. Noelle swallowed once, then twice.

Lumi sighed and said, "I'm not going to kill you."

She was so very out of practice with humans; she knew she came off as cold and intimidating. She had infrequently interacted with humans since they'd killed her people, but she wanted to put this one at ease—for Lorelei, of course. She knew her hard, icy heart couldn't beat for humans any longer. So she gave the girl the best smile she could manage.

For some odd reason, the girl leaned away, as if repulsed. Lumi's face fell. She studied the girl, and the eerie similarity to her daughter made Lumi drop the icy dagger to the ground, where it shattered. For the first time in many long, arduous years, as she looked at the shaken girl, Lumi actually wanted to give a measly portion of comfort to a human.

"Okay, don't tell me how you found us. I'm just going to wipe your memory and call it a day. Get lost, kid." Lumi reached her hand up to Noelle's head.

"Wait! Don't kill him," Noelle pleaded.

Lumi froze. She cocked her head to the side and looked at the man still frozen to the wall. The human girl was pushing her luck. The girl's deep brown eyes searched hers, and Lumi resigned with a sigh. "Fine."

Lumi pointed toward the man, and he was freed as the ice disappeared instantly. He began to stumble but ran away quickly.

She turned back toward the girl, and before Noelle could say anything else, Lumi placed her palm on Noelle's forehead. "You won't remember seeing me."

Noelle blinked a few times and then looked up at Lumi, then looked around the alley with pouted, full lips.

"Hey, how did I get here?" she asked, looking quite puzzled.

Lumi shrugged. That was enough kindness for one day; she needed to find the man before he got too far. She turned to leave, but the girl wrapped her arm around her. Wiping a memory tended to have a hazy, dreamlike effect on humans. The girl clearly was experiencing some sort of euphoric feeling, but Lumi knew it would only last a brief moment.

"Want to be friends?" Noelle wrapped her arm around Lumi's back.

"No." Lumi frowned. "Get off me." Lumi tried to pry the girl away, but she clung to her. Lumi scowled as the short human held tight.

The girl started giggling. "Want to hang out?"

"No, I have dinner plans at the Chicago Café. Now let go." Lumi began to think her lapse in judgment had been a poor choice. "I should have just killed you. You're insufferable," Lumi said with a humorless laugh.

"You're funny!" Noelle laughed and threw her head back. "But how perfect! My friends Marko and Luis are waiting for me at the Chicago Café! We can all hang out together. Want to hang out?" The girl smiled wide at Lumi, her dark strands swaying with the wintry air.

Lumi clenched her teeth and shoved the girl away. "Not unless you have my daughter's lost golden necklace."

Noelle laughed and laughed, as if Lumi were hilarious. She held her stomach and leaned over with loud, wild laughter.

Lumi began to walk down the alley, away from the girl.

"Actually, it's funny you should ask for that. I have the letters that tell me where the necklace is," Noelle said and laughed heartily. The girl seemed so carefree and full of joy, as if nothing in the world mattered to her at that moment.

Lumi froze, rigid. She turned on her heel and looked over at the young girl. She had calculated that the necklace was here in Chicago. But could it truly be this easy after all this time? As the girl laughed, Lumi couldn't help but let the dormant hope that had been dead for so long rise up. What if the girl really did know where the necklace was? What if she could hear her daughter's laughter again? Lumi watched the girl laugh, and her icy heart thumped for the first time in many years. The strange sensation made Lumi's hand cover it and gasp.

The girl stopped laughing, slowly. She looked around, and obviously she had become settled as the effect wore off.

Lumi was quick on her feet and waved. "Hi, I'm Lumi! I'm new to Chicago."

"Hi," Noelle said. "I'm Noelle. Welcome, I suppose." She shrugged, seeming much shier than before. She looked around the alley, as if unsure of the environment, or perhaps she wondered how she had arrived there.

"Thanks." Lumi smiled. "I'm off to the Chicago Café for dinner, but it is a real shame that I don't know anybody in the city yet."

Noelle's head tilted. "Oh wow! Crazy coincidence. Me too. You're welcome to join my friends and me."

Lumi beamed. "Really? You mean it? I'd love to make some new friends."

Lumi hoped her voice sounded warm. She hadn't interacted this much with a human in a desperately long time. Interacting with humans at this point repulsed her, and she wanted to retch just considering eating a meal with several of them. She had befriended humans before and paid a hefty price for it. She shouldn't be doing it again. But if the girl truly had the necklace, she needed to work with the one group of species she hated the most—humans. What a cruel, twisted fate—it was by human hands that she lost everything and everyone, and now it's by human hands that everything might be restored. If the girl was telling the truth, that is.

"Great! Let's go," Noelle said and merrily walked forward. Lumi sighed but followed her. "So, do you have a boyfriend?" Noelle's lips turned upward.

Lumi walked beside her and looked at the girl with a disdainful frown. "No."

"Oh." Noelle smiled up at her with a carefree grin. "Me neither. Do you like anybody?" The girl's smile triggered so many memories of Lorelei that flashed before Lumi's eyes; the resemblance was uncanny.

Lumi looked at the young girl from the corner of her eye and studied the girl—her beautiful face seemed to glow with excitement, but her eyes betrayed her. She looked around frequently, as if she expected danger to emerge at any moment.

Lumi mulled over the question in her mind. Of course she didn't like anybody—what sort of question was that? Lumi wasn't sure she could do this. But as the girl looked endearingly at her with her large chestnut eyes and scrunched her nose, Lumi clutched her chest because she felt her cold, icy heart grow slightly warmer. Calling it *warm* would be inaccurate and a downright lie, but it was warmer than it had been in 150 years.

"No," Lumi said curtly. Lumi liked nobody and hated everyone. She just needed to use the girl and get the necklace before Noelle found it. This should be easy.

CHAPTER 3
NOELLE
THE CHICAGO CAFÉ MEETUP

Noelle's hands were shaking, so she slid them into her coat pockets. Her eyes darted around, and she walked briskly across the dirty Chicago pavement, avoiding the huddles of people gripping their jackets. She shuddered, uncertain if her trembling was caused by the man's threat or the frigid weather. Lumi stayed beside her, and she had an eerie feeling of déjà vu while looking at her. Noelle gripped her own jacket as the wind blew harder and frantic chatter about the polar vortex swirled in the air.

She tried to avoid ice spots on the sidewalk where the salt failed to completely clean off the pavement. She spotted the café sign ahead and increased her pace as the numbing wind continued to push against her. Noelle was grateful for Lumi, because the scar-faced man had threatened her, and then he simply was gone. Noelle believed Lumi's presence must have scared him off.

Noelle frantically threw open the cafe doors and peered inside, relieved to be greeted by warmth, and Lumi trailed behind her. She looked around and eventually spotted two familiar faces. Her friends waved at her from a booth in the corner. Luis smiled warmly in his red knit sweater, and Marko peered next to him.

Lumi seemed to have gotten sidetracked by a painting of Chicago on the wall—she studied it intently.

"Where have you been?" Luis frowned and shook his head.

"I am going to start lying to you and giving you times that are thirty minutes early, then *maybe* you will be on time," Marko said with a wry smile.

Noelle plopped onto the bright red booth seat opposite of Luis and Marko but didn't bother to take off her jacket. Instead, she placed her icy fingers in her pockets but frowned when she noticed the blood on her sleeve. She shivered as she recalled the man's mention of a dead body. She had so many questions. Who was the man who'd stalked her? Why had *her* name been written next to a *dead* body? And how, exactly, had he moved *so quickly*? She considered informing her friends but worried he might make good on his threat. Her entire body trembled as she replayed their interaction in her mind.

Lumi walked up to the table, and Noelle's friends gawked. Noelle shifted in the booth to give room for Lumi, and Lumi sat next to her, awkwardly rigid. Lumi's heart-shaped face and high cheekbones looked even more prominent now that she was closer.

"How can you expect me to get here on time with the constant snow?" Noelle sighed. "They can barely keep up with the roads." They likely thought her trembling was due to the cold temperature. "Also, this is my new friend Lumi. She is joining us!"

A waitress suddenly appeared, smacking her gum loudly. She pulled out a notepad and pen. Her dark hair cascaded over her glasses as she scribbled on her notepad.

"Hey, hon! What will it be?"

Noelle peered at the menu and then looked up at the waitress. "I'll take a hot chocolate and a Chicago hot dog."

"You got it!" She scribbled on her pad, then looked at Noelle, and her eyes widened. "Aren't you adorable!" she added in a loud, boisterous voice.

"Thank you." Noelle smiled without showing her teeth.

Luis began to chuckle. "Don't get a big head. She is just trying to get a good tip from you," he whispered.

Noelle rolled her eyes, but grinned.

"And you?"

Lumi searched the menu and seemed entirely lost. "I suppose a regular one with ketchup."

"Hon, we don't have ketchup for hot dogs here." The waitress's loud voice carried.

Lumi looked perplexed and stared at the waitress dumbfounded. She looked like she belonged in another era with a sideways cocktail hat perched on her head. She looked out of place at this little café. Lumi's brow furrowed as the waitress tapped her foot.

"You must be new here," Marko said as he stared at Lumi, and his lips curled upward at the corners. His eyes were intensely fixed on her for a long moment. Marko shifted his schoolbooks with his name on them to the side.

Noelle curiously watched Marko, as fascination colored his features.

"What do you mean there is no ketchup for the hot dogs?" Lumi asked in her distinct accent.

The waitress's face contorted in what seemed like disgust to Noelle. "This is Chicago," the waitress said loudly, still chomping on her gum. The entire restaurant began to stir and looked at the loud waitress now. The waitress said nothing more, as if informing her that being in Chicago was enough of an explanation.

"That is practically a sin in Chicago." Luis smiled.

"We don't put ketchup on hot dogs. Asking for ketchup will get you five years in prison around here," Marko said.

"Aww, you're sort of funny!" the waitress loudly retorted.

"He isn't funny," Luis protested. Marko gave him a fierce look. Luis's smile softened until it disappeared entirely. Only then did Marko look away from him and back to Lumi.

"I just wanted to help," Marko explained.

"Thank you." Lumi warily smiled at Noelle, then Marko, and finally at Luis—who smiled back. Lumi then turned back to the waitress and ordered a hot dog properly, with no ketchup. The waitress scribbled on her notepad and left in a hurry to her next table.

Marko shifted his gaze from the waitress to Lumi and said, "I'm so sorry that you're visiting Chicago during this polar vortex. Don't get me wrong, we know bad weather here. But we have never experienced it this badly and for this long." Marko sighed.

"Yeah, you really have to come back and visit in the summer months!" Luis quipped.

"It really is beautiful in the summer. You can see Navy Pier, walk on Michigan Avenue, or visit the Art Institute. Honestly there is a whole slew of things to do. This winter has been unlike anything we have ever seen. There have been record temperature lows, more snow than ever, and we can't seem to get a break. I'm Marko Jokovic, by the way," Marko added.

Noelle eyed him—Marko never smiled this much. It's like his normally grumpy, stoic self had been replaced by somebody else entirely.

"And I'm Luis Hernandez. We're going to find the Snow Queen's lost golden necklace. You should join us," Luis blurted out. Marko sharply elbowed Luis under the table, and Luis gasped.

Lumi inhaled sharply. "It's really nice to meet you. I'm Lumi Heikkila." Her accent seemed to belong somewhere in Europe, but Noelle couldn't really pinpoint where. "And tell me—what do you know about the Snow Queen and her necklace?" Lumi asked with an eyebrow raised. She clasped her pale fingers together on top of the table.

Noelle wondered if people in Europe dressed like her often. Noelle looked around the room and noticed the Chicagoans in their casual sweaters, boots, and jackets and then looked back at Lumi. The contrast was glaring.

"Well, you might think we are crazy—but we actually think

there might be something to that old myth about the Snow Queen," Noelle said.

Lumi didn't respond; she simply stared at the three friends with an indiscernible look.

"You do know the myth, right?" Luis broke the silence. Luis shifted in his seat, sipped his hot chocolate, and held the hot cup in his hands.

"I do. What version have you heard?" Lumi sat up straight.

"The only version. That the Snow Queen was a *poisonous, murderous heathen* who turned on humans after they graciously offered her people refuge," Luis said, then took a sip of his drink.

A muscle in Lumi's jaw twitched. "Sounds like you've heard the false version." She clenched her teeth, and agitation tightened on her face.

"Oh, I had no idea that there were different versions," Marko said. "Tell me what you've heard."

Lumi leaned forward. "Long ago, the Snow Queen and her people lived in a realm called Merklei. But the icy realm began to warm up, and so they sought shelter on Earth. In exchange for safe passage, she did swear an oath to a human king, but it wasn't out of necessity, it was as a favor." Lumi shot Luis a look. "She did it because she believed humans should be treated fairly, despite her people living longer and being more powerful. The humans and Merklei lived together, peacefully, for a long time until a wicked king took the throne. He turned on the Snow Queen and her people, the Merklei, killing all of them due to paranoia. They even killed her young daughter, Lorelei, with a poison called merca that weakens the Merklei. But the Snow Queen managed to escape. So she cursed the humans with disastrous winters wherever she set her foot in the human realm. The curse will remain until the day the humans return her daughter's necklace, which they stole. She intends to use the powerful necklace to undo the king's betrayal and bring back her family."

"I've never heard that!" Luis scoffed. "She was *a monster*. She killed an entire kingdom of humans."

"No, she didn't. She was betrayed." Something dark flickered in Lumi's light gray eyes.

"Then why does the legend say that she did?" Luis frowned.

"Because winners write the history, Luis. She wasn't the villain."

"Oh, so you're a conspiracy theorist." He shook his head. "Who killed the humans within that kingdom then?"

"The Leizei. They belong to the fire realm and opposed the Merklei, those with the snow and ice ability. They opposed them because of their stance on humans. But you probably haven't heard of them. They keep themselves hidden from humans." A wicked smile formed on Lumi's lips.

The trio of friends exchanged looks.

Lumi's eyes scanned Marko's books and journal, and then she locked eyes with him. "Are you from Yugoslavia?"

Marko's mouth parted open, then closed. "How... did you... know that? But it hasn't been a country for a long time." His eyes narrowed. "I'm Serbian." Marko's eyebrows pulled together in seeming confusion.

"I saw that your last name ends in *ic* and surnames that end in *ic* typically come from Yugoslavia. Um, well, what used to be Yugoslavia." Lumi pointed at his journal with his name on it.

"You have a cool accent. Where are you from?" Luis asked.

Lumi pulled her jacket closer again and folded her arms. "I have lived in many places, and I get told I have a weird accent because nobody knows what to do with me." Lumi shrugged and tapped her fingers on the table.

Noelle noticed that Lumi was quite stiff and seemed uncomfortable. "Oh that's great! I want to travel so badly. Where have you lived?"

"Where I have not lived would seemingly be a shorter list." Lumi laughed without humor. "I feel like a bit of a wanderer. But the last place I lived was Finland."

"What brought you to Chicago?" Noelle asked, shivering.

Despite the warm café, her hands were still freezing. And they still trembled because of the scar-faced man's threat.

"I'm here for grad school at the University of Chicago. I just moved in, and I start school in January after the winter break," Lumi said.

"What a small world. We are students at the University of Chicago too. You are welcome to hang with us anytime," Noelle said.

"Yeah, we are going to find the Snow Queen's necklace so she will leave Chicago. You should join us," Luis said.

Lumi's light eyes suddenly looked intense and curious. Her hard expression softened into a slight smile.

"You really believe in that?" Marko asked.

Noelle looked down. "Yeah, I do," she said softly.

"Isn't it called *a myth* for a reason?" Marko asked. "Come on, let's be logical, friends." Marko rolled his sweater up his arms.

"Well, I'm with Noelle. What if there is a Snow Queen and we could find her stupid necklace and get her to leave?" Luis gave a firm nod to Noelle.

Noelle smiled sheepishly. She needed to find the necklace so that she could utilize its power to bring back her only family member that had passed—which was her grandma. She had no intention of giving it to the man with the scar who'd stalked her.

"All right, well then it is one versus two. You're the tiebreaker, Lumi," Marko said.

The waitress reemerged with a tray full of food. Several various hot dogs filled her tray.

"Okay, kids! Here are your hot dogs... with no ketchup!" The waitress distributed the plates. "Now remember, those plates are hot! Don't burn nothin'."

The friends looked to Lumi, who peered down at her plate.

"Ahem," Marko interjected.

Lumi's head shot up, and her light-colored eyes scanned each of them.

Marko had already eaten one of his hot dogs before the rest could even begin their meal.

"How do you intend to find this necklace?" Lumi asked and pulled off her elegant coat. She brushed her long blond hair back behind her shoulder and picked up her hot dog. She held the hot dog awkwardly with just her fingertips, vertically. All of her toppings slid off and covered her hand. She stared at the hot dog, perplexed. "Oh merca," she muttered under her breath.

The three friends watched Lumi and exchanged looks, but nobody spoke.

Lumi sat in silence, holding her hot dog. She watched them, eating awkwardly. She was soon covered in chili and frowning.

"What if I told you something that was hard to believe?" Noelle asked and took a bite.

"Try me." Lumi gestured to her.

Noelle swallowed hard, then nodded. "I have letters passed down from my grandmother. They talk about the Snow Queen, and my grandma had the necklace. The letters inform me where to find it."

Lumi froze.

"According to the letters, it is hidden here in Chicago. And it's nearly winter break, and we don't have much to do. So we figured it could be fun to go on a hunt for it. My grandma even made hints because she loved games."

Lumi's eyebrows flicked up, then down. To Noelle's surprise, she didn't laugh. Lumi's eyes widened, and Noelle struggled to discern her thoughts.

"Oh, I just moved in, and honestly I don't know anybody or have anything else to do, so why not? I could use some new friends." Lumi shrugged. Despite her casual words, her face betrayed different feelings. She seemed *very* interested.

Lumi had all but entirely abandoned her hot dog now. She couldn't seem to manage figuring out how to eat it without getting the contents all over her. Noelle considered that perhaps they didn't eat hot dogs in Finland and maybe she should offer some advice on how to hold it, but she didn't want to embarrass her. She remained silent and pretended not to notice the chili that splattered all over Lumi.

"Ah Lumi, I was counting on you to make it a tie and save me from these nutjobs' idea of fun," Marko complained.

"Well, it does sound a little odd, but it could make for some fun memories."

Lumi had barely finished the word when she suddenly gasped and picked up a succulent plant that had been sitting on their table. Without warning, she threw it across the café.

Noelle looked at her from the corner of her eye.

"Um, are you all right?" Luis asked with hesitancy.

"Yeah, sorry! I have some allergies to certain plants. I didn't want to... you know, get hives. But if you'll excuse me, I need to use the restroom and clean up," Lumi said and stood.

Marko offered his hand to help, and Lumi graciously took it. He stood with her.

"Thank you," Lumi said and let go of his hand and walked briskly past him toward the restroom. Marko took a seat and kept his eyes on Lumi.

"Were you just flexing?" Noelle asked with a hint of amusement in her voice.

Luis frowned.

"What? No, I wasn't flexing!" Marko furrowed his brow.

"Hey, I think she is pretty. What about bro code?" Luis huffed.

Lumi reappeared after a moment, then quickly sat down. She had managed to clean up the chili from her face and hands, but it remained on her clothing.

"Any Christmas plans?" Lumi sat in the bright red booth.

"Well, Noelle is coming over for Christmas," Marko said. "We grew up on the same street, and she is practically my little sister. She spends a lot of time with my family."

"Yeah, and my family is about an hour away in Indiana," Luis said. They all looked to Lumi, who sat quietly. "And what about you?"

"I-I don't know. I will probably just relax and enjoy the day. I don't know anybody here." Lumi bit her lip and looked down.

"Oh, are you here in Chicago alone?" Marko asked. Luis kicked him under the table.

"Yeah, I am. But I'm used to it." Lumi slid her hands into her pockets and looked away. Silence ensued.

"If you don't have plans, my home is always open," Marko said. "Noelle makes some pretty awesome cookies. I have a sister probably about your age too. Her name is Danica."

"That is very Serbian of you to open your home to a stranger," Lumi said.

Marko gave a warm smile.

Luis crossed his arms and scowled.

"Now that I think of it, you are often opening your home to others. Your parents are such good hosts too," Noelle said. "Lumi, you should really consider joining us for Christmas." She felt it was a real shame that anybody would spend Christmas alone.

"I don't want to impose on your holiday," Lumi said.

The waitress emerged with one check and placed it on the table. "Hey hons! Whenever you're ready, here is the check."

Marko took the check and pulled his credit card out.

"That is also very Serbian of you," Lumi noted.

Marko looked at Lumi, and his eyebrows made a straight line. "Have you been to Serbia?"

"Yes, twice. I loved it."

Luis sighed.

"Well that explains a lot." Marko nodded. "Could I have your number?" Marko took out his phone and gave it to her. A firm smile was planted on Marko's lips, but Luis glared at him.

"Oh, right. Phones. I need to set one up since I moved here. You know what, write your numbers here on this napkin, and I'll be in touch." The trio of friends each wrote their names and numbers on the napkin, which Lumi folded and placed in her pocket. Once Marko finished paying the bill, he stood. Lumi gathered herself together and also stood.

Noelle and Luis followed. Luis and Lumi were nearly the same height, but Noelle noticed how Lumi towered over her—just as Marko did.

The always friendly Luis hugged Lumi, but she stood there with a bewildered look on her face and her hands remained at her sides.

Luis noticed and pulled away. "Oh, do you not hug in Finland?"

"Hug?" Lumi's voice sounded disgusted in her slightly strange accent. "Oh, right. Friends hug. I knew that."

"Yes, it's like a friendly greeting or a goodbye that friends do," Luis said.

Noelle covered her mouth and tried to choke back laughter. She didn't want to embarrass Lumi.

Marko held out his hand. "Don't be a stranger."

Lumi gripped Marko's hand tightly. He grunted, apparently because she gripped it too tight. Lumi pulled away, and Marko winced.

Lumi then turned to Noelle and offered her hand. Noelle took a step backward as she looked at Marko's hand and said, "I prefer to wave." Noelle waved, and Lumi mimicked her. Noelle watched Lumi disappear through the snowy window until she could no longer see her due to the thick white flurries that engulfed Lumi entirely.

"Oh merca. She's weird," Noelle said under her breath.

But then her breath caught. The scar-faced man who had threatened her earlier walked across the sidewalk outside the café and locked eyes with her. He winked. Noelle stumbled backward and gasped. Luis caught her, just before she could fall to the ground.

"Noelle? Are you all right?" Luis asked, holding her arm and steadying her. Noelle kept her eyes on the sidewalk, but he was gone.

"Yeah. Do you think you could walk me to my apartment? I think I have something to give you there," Noelle said. She racked her brain and thought of what she might possibly give to Luis. She did have a new notebook that she thought he would enjoy. That would do.

The scar-faced man never bothered her about the necklace when she was with people. It only happened when she was alone. He seemed to be afraid of being seen—and Lumi's words about the Leizei suddenly pieced together. He didn't want anybody to know about him, and his hand was scorching hot.

"You have a gift for me? Yeah, let's go! I'd gladly walk you to your apartment anytime."

An older lady struggled to open the door, and Luis hurried to the door and held it for her. She slowly hobbled inside.

"Thank you, young man. Your friend is a gentleman!" she announced to Noelle and Marko.

"Yes, he is," Noelle said and braced herself to enter the snowy fray, trembling from fear and chills.

CHAPTER 4
NOELLE
THE LETTERS

"Have you heard from Lumi?" Noelle swung her feet back and forth on the train's chair. Noelle's dark hair, now pulled tight into a bun, had snow intertwined in the strands. Some of the snow had already melted onto her hair, leaving part of it wet.

Marko peered out the window, not immediately responding. "Actually, I haven't." He turned to Noelle and shrugged.

Noelle watched the snow violently fall outside. "It's sort of beautiful in a dreadful way." Marko followed her gaze, then nodded. The gray, normally smooth Metra train rocked a bit as they watched the window.

"I'm starting to get worried, Noelle. My grandparents can hardly get outside. They have been holed up for two months and rely on us to bring them food. What do you think is actually happening?"

Noelle played with the threads on her army-green scarf before meeting Marko's eyes. She kicked her black boots out again, shaking off some semi-melted snow. "You already know what I think," she quietly admitted.

Marko's tongue clicked, and he looked away. "You really think there is some mythical creature causing all this?"

Noelle sighed and pulled on the thread on her scarf again, which grew longer. "What if it isn't nonsense? I mean, my grandma seemed to think it was all real and that the necklace is here in Chicago."

"What did your grandma say exactly?" Marko rubbed his temples and then quickly withdrew his hands to his pockets.

"All the letters give warnings about the Snow Queen and instruct me where to find the necklace. She always said it was here in Chicago. My grandma kept saying we had to be ready."

"Ready for what?"

"I don't know," Noelle admitted. "She said she would bring the curse with her and that she would bring terrible ice storms. She said that people's lives would be lost, livestock would die, and entire buildings would be destroyed."

"Great," Marko said with little enthusiasm.

Noelle snapped her head in his direction. "And what do you think it is then? Since the news can't seem to tell us what is happening!"

Marko shrugged. "Who knows? But since Lumi seems to be out, I think we should cancel our little expedition on finding the pretend necklace." Marko sat back on the train chair as it jostled again.

"Fine," she said and pulled out her phone and brought up files. She scrolled until she found a PDF photo of the letter from her grandma.

Dear Noelle,

For several generations, we have known that the Snow Queen is, indeed, real and so is her dangerous threat of cursing our land. We know this because we have the lost golden necklace that once belonged to the Snow Queen's daughter. She has hunted it for a long time, yet we have kept it keenly safe. I worry that in my older age I may forget where it is. My mind is beginning to slip even now, and I forget the keys in the door quite often. I've decided it would be foolish to reveal the location, yet I also think, in case of an emergency, I should make it somewhat evident where it is—should the Snow Queen turn up. This way, we could hide the necklace elsewhere. And you know how fond I am of games and treasure hunts.

Whatever you do, do not let her get ahold of the necklace, because it can undo anything. There are four hints total. May you stay safe and may the Snow Queen never find the necklace in Chicago.

I love you!

Hint #1: The first Chicago man's home was a sight to be seen. If you look down, you will see a crown.

Warm regards,
Lolli (Rose Hudson)

Noelle inhaled, staring at the name.

"Your grannie's hint sucks," Marko said. Noelle hadn't noticed that he had read over her shoulder.

"I think it makes perfect sense!" She crossed her arms.

"Why is she called Lolli?"

"She was Lolli, and my grandfather was Pop. So together they were LolliPop."

Marko smirked. "This is so stupid. How are you so invested in fiction treasure hunt letters?" He put a hand on her shoulder, but she shook it off.

"Because it's all that I have from my Lolli." She locked her phone and sighed. She was, of course, partially telling the truth.

But she hadn't yet revealed the truth about the scar-faced man and his threat to find the necklace. Which didn't matter—because she would use the necklace to bring back her Lolli. She missed her dreadfully.

He shifted toward her, slowly. "I'm sorry. That was—harsh of me. I know—look, I know these letters are really meaningful to you. And I really do apologize for not being more sensitive." He gently grabbed her shoulder, as if she were a wounded animal.

She just stared at her feet, which still swung back and forth. She shifted in the colorful train seat, not because she was uncomfortable but because she felt embarrassed by the emotions that bubbled to the surface.

"So what does this first clue mean?" He removed his hand and placed it in his lap.

"Well, she said it's in Chicago. I have a few ideas for who the 'first man' might be. But I think it is Jean-Baptiste-Pointe du Sable. He was the first Chicago settler," she said and gave a slight smile as he leaned in.

"Okay, that checks out."

"I was thinking we could go to his monument where his first home was on Michigan Avenue. She said his home was a sight to be seen. So maybe we should see where his home used to be and go from there."

"I'm in. But what do you think about the crown reference?"

"I have a few ideas, but it'll work best if we can get there first."

The train's screeching shoved them both forward.

"All right, we'll meet Luis and check it out. But if you don't mind, a few of my friends are on this train." Marko pointed at a group of college guys in the front who waved at him.

She gave a nod and Marko stood to his feet and joined his friends.

She watched the flurries falling rapidly and wondered how so much snow could accumulate. There weren't any signs of it stopping.

"Oh," a nasally girl's voice said. "Look, Noelle is here."

Noelle snapped her head up and realized across from her was Olivia, Daisy, and Shelby. She had to hide the grimace that nearly surfaced on her face.

"Oh. I haven't seen you since we all graduated." Noelle tried to press a smile onto her face.

Olivia and Daisy clutched their matching coffee orders and looked Noelle up and down. "We had an amazing vacation in Italy this summer. Did you go anywhere cool?" Daisy took a strand of hair into her fingers and twirled it. Daisy and Olivia wore matching leggings, as if they had planned it.

"No," Noelle admitted. "But I hope you guys had a great trip." She turned and hoped they would stop talking.

"That's too bad," Olivia said. She then pointed at Noelle's teeth. "You know, I see you still haven't fixed your teeth. I have a great orthodontic referral for you!" A cruel, plastic smile appeared on Olivia's face, baring her beautiful smile.

Daisy snickered, but Shelby didn't laugh.

Noelle flinched, then pressed her lips together, concealing her teeth.

"Stop that," Shelby said. Noelle was always grateful for Shelby.

"I meant it in a helpful way," Olivia objected.

Noelle looked longingly at Marko and wished he had never left. She briefly considered moving, but there were no empty seats with his friends.

Noelle begrudgingly looked at Olivia. "I would have loved to get braces, but my grandma was sick, and so most of our money went to medical bills for her. And my foster family didn't get it for me either. So, it is what it is." She shrugged and shook her head.

"I think your smile is beautiful just the way it is." Shelby gave a gentle smile. "Honestly."

Noelle tried to smile at Shelby; she wished it conveyed her gratitude. For sticking up for her, this time and *every* time.

"Well, great seeing you all," Noelle lied and went to turn away only to see the scar-faced man walking toward her with a wicked smile.

Noelle's heart thumped and fresh adrenaline flowed throughout her. She reached down into her pocket and felt her knife where it usually rested.

Noelle looked at Daisy, Olivia, and Shelby. Only seconds ago, she despised their presence. Now she was most grateful.

"Hey guys! Actually, I need to sit with you! I need to hear more about Italy!" Noelle pushed her way forward to the empty seat with the girls. Noelle sat next to Olivia, who looked at her sideways.

"Who said you could sit next to me?" Olivia crossed her arms.

"Olivia!" Shelby nearly yelled.

"I don't like her." Olivia smiled at Noelle, showing her beautiful smile again. Noelle suddenly had the impulse to hit her in her beautiful mouth. She imagined what it would look like to see her dazzling smile with a missing tooth. But with another glance at the scar-faced man, she remained calm despite her wishes. He settled in the back of the train, but watched her.

"Oh, you don't mean that." Noelle faked a smile back. She made sure to smile with her lips firmly together.

"Freak," Olivia said and rolled her eyes.

Shelby fussed at Olivia, but Noelle couldn't focus on the words because the scar-faced man had his eyes locked on hers. She tried to take in every detail possible. Long scar, dark eyes, muscular frame, and weathered features. Noelle just knew she couldn't be alone; it was her only safety net. He never bothered her if she was with others. Whatever was going on with him and the necklace, he didn't want others to find out. This was seemingly her only advantage.

A few moments passed, and Shelby had fussed the entire time. Noelle didn't pay attention. She kept her eyes on the scar-faced man. His eyes occasionally met hers, and then he would look out his window.

Noelle's train of thought was interrupted when a very tall and handsome guy walked down the aisle toward her. His dark, wavy hair framed his face, and his emerald eyes were on her. He wore a simple, plain black shirt, which fit just right and seemed to show off his muscular physique, and it complemented his dark, handsome skin. He arguably could be the most attractive guy she had ever come across in person, and when he flashed her a dimpled smile, her cheeks felt warm. She looked back at the girls.

He sat right across from them, where Noelle had just been seated. When Noelle glanced in his direction, his eyes were still fixed on her and a warm smile rested on his lips. Uncomfortable, she looked away.

Shelby seemed to notice too. She stopped talking. All the girls had noticed now and looked at him. But his eyes remained focused on Noelle, who despite feeling his gaze on her, refused to look back at him.

"Excuse me, weren't you at the Chicago Café last Friday? I think I saw you there," the guy said with a deep voice.

Noelle dragged her eyes to his. "Yeah." But how had she not seen him? She would have remembered a guy as attractive as him.

"Do you want to sit with me?" he asked and pointed at the open seat. "It isn't every day that strangers run into each other in a city this size... twice."

Grateful for an opportunity to escape Olivia and Daisy, Noelle eagerly nodded and shifted to the other side of the train. She sat opposite from him and wasn't certain what to say. Her shyness swallowed her.

"I'm Eli," he said and broke the silence. "If I'm honest, I'm *really* glad to see you again. I actually wanted to talk to you in the café, but you looked busy." He ran fingers through his dark waves.

"I'm Noelle." She wished she knew what else to say. She bit the inside of her cheek and looked back at the girls who were all silent. Shelby put up a thumb, then she pointed at Eli, and made a fanning motion toward herself.

"It's a small world, isn't it? I saw you on Friday with your friends, and now we're on the same train," Eli said, dragging

Noelle's attention back to him. Eli seemed to not notice the other girls. Or if he had, he didn't seem to care.

"Yeah," Noelle admitted. *Yeah?* She felt it was a stupid answer.

Eli leaned in closer toward Noelle, and Noelle's heart rate increased. Perhaps as much as it did when she spotted the scar-faced man. "Did you follow me?" He grinned and raised a brow in anticipation of her answer.

"What? No! Of course not!" Noelle swallowed.

Eli laughed softly. "I wouldn't mind if you did. It wouldn't bother me to see your pretty face more often."

Noelle sat, dumbfounded. Her cheeks reddened more deeply, and amusement appeared on Eli's face. His chiseled face and attractive sharp features were too much for Noelle, especially paired with his flirty grin. He leaned forward, and she leaned away with a flushed face.

His features softened and became more serious, as if he remembered something suddenly. "Do you know the blond woman who sat with you?"

Why did he want to know? "Lumi, she is our new friend. She just moved here."

"Yes, I overheard you talk about that and the necklace," Eli said, and his eyes roamed over her.

Noelle swallowed unsteadily as his eyes bored into hers eagerly. "Oh, you heard that?"

He leaned in even closer so that only Noelle could hear him. "Listen, Noelle, I can help you with what you're seeking. Your new friend isn't what you think. You can trust me, and I'll protect you and help you sort through all this. You'll get the necklace—I give you my word. But I need something from you."

"What do you want?" She eyed him suspiciously and gripped the knife in her pocket tightly. Noelle looked past him and tried to see where the scar-faced man was seated, but he was out of sight. Were they working together?

Eli seemed bothered by her reaction. "Do you not want my help? I don't make promises that I can't keep. You couldn't get anything better than *my* help." He frowned as if insulted. "I need you to report to me about your friend Lumi. If you do that, I'll personally make sure you obtain the necklace. Or you can tell me what you want in exchange. If you want money, I can arrange that." Eli withdrew a massive wad of cash from his pocket and placed it on Noelle's lap.

Noelle took the money, and although she could use it and it pained her to depart from it, she placed it on Eli's lap. "No," she said and frowned. This felt oddly suspicious to Noelle.

"Well, if you aren't interested in money, then I suppose my presence will suffice, doll." Eli smirked.

Noelle scoffed. "Doll? Don't call me that. And no, I don't want anything to do with you." Noelle folded her arms.

"No? People don't tell *me* no." He was leaning so close to Noelle that she could feel his breath against her face.

Noelle leaned away from him in disgust. "Gross. You sound like an arrogant oaf. I have no idea who you are, and *that* is why I'm saying no." Noelle had said the words before she could think through them. She raised her own eyebrows in surprise at the fierce tone with which she met him. Only moments ago, she felt so charmed by his very presence and his bright green eyes. And now she would rather visit with Olivia and Daisy than him. Which was actually saying a lot.

"Keep it down." He reached for her shoulder and pulled her forward again. His fingers laced with rough calluses rested on her shoulder. "I don't want anybody to hear us. If you knew who I was, you wouldn't speak to me like that," he said with indignation. "Show a *little* respect." A cocky smirk reappeared on his face.

"Jerk." Noelle flicked his fingers off her shoulder with her free hand; the other hand remained on her knife. "I don't care who you are. Don't ever turn up again," Noelle said and pointed to the aisle.

He sighed. "You'll wish that you accepted my offer."

"I doubt it," Noelle sneered.

"You're going to need me. This wasn't how this was supposed

to go at all." Eli let out a frustrated sigh through his nose. "You're pretty stubborn," Eli said and glared at her. "And yet fate led me here."

"And you're *pretty* annoying," Noelle said with a huff.

Eli leaned forward, and his lips brushed Noelle's ear as he whispered, "All that I heard in that comment was that you think I'm *pretty*."

"I do not," Noelle lied.

"I'll be seeing you around," Eli whispered, then gave her a slight smile. He stood up and made his way to the back of the train.

A troubled thought crossed her mind. Did she now have two enemies? Both Eli and the scar-faced man? Eli promised her, *if you knew who I was, you wouldn't speak to me like that.* Did she just anger a dangerous man? A chill went up Noelle's spine. What had she done?

Noelle was the first out of her seat when the train stopped. She quickly found Marko, and they walked together in silence. She avoided the back of the train, and to her gratitude, she didn't see Eli or the scar-faced man as they left the train station. Her heart thudded uneasily at the thought of the two men.

She toyed with the idea of telling Marko everything, knowing all too well that he would instantly be in big brother mode. But she avoided the conversation entirely when she remembered the scar-faced man's threat—she worried that he might hurt Marko if she told him.

They met Luis at the brick building where their lecture was held.

"After class we'll go to the monument." Noelle greeted Luis with a hug.

"Yeah, sure! I'll text Lumi. She said this morning that she wanted to know when we would start looking."

Both Marko and Noelle looked at Luis.

"Lumi texted you?" Marko looked wearily at Luis.

"Yeah, of course."

"She hasn't reached out to either of us," Marko said and gestured to Noelle.

"Maybe she has a soft spot for me." Luis grinned and raised his eyebrows at Marko.

"Or maybe there is a more logical explanation." Marko turned on his heel, and they each walked into the university building.

CHAPTER 5
NOELLE
THE CHICAGO CROWN

Noelle entered the large lecture hall and found three empty seats in the back. Students filled the room, pulling out laptops, binders, and students' jackets were strewn across the room. Dr. Locke stood at the podium in his usual brown jacket and khaki pants. His gray hair, or what was left of it, looked more wild than usual in Noelle's opinion. He looked at his notes with his black glasses sitting on the bridge of his nose.

"I studied really hard for the quiz," Marko said, sitting next to Noelle. Luis pulled his jacket off and sat down too.

Dr. Locke looked up at the clock and then cleared his throat. "Good morning, everyone! Only one more week until your Christmas and winter holiday break," he announced, and a girl on the right side gave a cheer. Dr. Locke smiled, then continued, "I understand you're already likely checked out. But let's push through! I did bring some snacks to enjoy during your history quiz." He pointed to a table on his right where there was coffee, biscuits and jam, candy canes, and a bowl of chocolates. "Feel free to grab some breakfast and candies before we start the quiz."

"He is my favorite professor," Marko whispered.

Noelle nodded. Students took turns grabbing plates and pouring coffee before sitting.

"Once you finish your quiz, you are free to go!" Dr. Locke announced, and Luis fist-bumped the air. Once the students had sat down, Dr. Locke passed out quiz papers, and everyone quietly began taking their quiz. Noelle wrote her name at the top of the paper but then got lost in thought.

The door opened loudly, and a student, Tracy, emerged with her baby. The baby cooed as Tracy made her way to the front where Dr. Locke stood.

"Dr. Locke, I couldn't get a babysitter! I am so sorry, but please let me take the quiz. I can keep her on my lap. Please—"

"That isn't necessary. Why don't you calm down, have a seat, enjoy some coffee and biscuits, and I'll hold your little one if you like. I am really glad you could make it to class today." Dr. Locke smiled and held his arms out.

"Thank you!" Tracy handed her baby to Dr. Locke and exhaled deeply. Her normally styled light hair was swept into a bun with strands sticking out of the sides.

"Get some breakfast if you'd like." Dr. Locke sat in his chair and rocked the baby.

"Are you sure? I'm already late." Tracy's lip quivered.

"Class, I'm much more interested in your long-term success than in your perfection. Tracy is always on time, and she is a hard worker. So what if she couldn't get a babysitter today and she is late? I'll excuse it. I'm not asking my students to be perfect, and I understand life happens. Please just try your best and take care of yourselves," Dr. Locke said.

Noelle looked up as Luis turned in his paper and gave her a small wave as he exited the lecture hall. Noelle had completely blanked and noticed everybody had finished and left except Tracy. Noelle sighed, tapped her pen for a brief moment, and then collapsed her head into her hands. To Noelle's dismay,

Tracy also stood, collected her things, and placed her paper on the podium.

"Thank you, Dr. Locke," Tracy said as Dr. Locke handed her baby back to her. His lips curled into a wide smile as he looked through his black glasses on the bridge of his nose.

"Do you have a babysitter for after break?" Dr. Locke asked in a hushed tone, and Noelle snapped her face back down toward her paper, aware that she could hear the private conversation. Noelle tried to busy herself with her quiz and bit down on her lip hard as she realized she got completely lost in thought and still had many questions left.

"No, things have been really tough lately if I'm honest. I can't thank you enough for excusing my tardiness. It won't happen again!" Tracy said with a high-pitched tone.

Noelle listened, but Dr. Locke didn't answer. Noelle peeked up slightly and saw Dr. Locke handing her money.

"Here." Dr. Locke placed some cash in Tracy's hand. "Use this to get a babysitter."

"I couldn't—"

"You can." He nodded. Tracy wiped her eyes, and Dr. Locke then locked eyes with Noelle, who snapped her head down again.

"Noelle, it looks like you're the last one," Dr. Locke called out. Noelle mumbled under her breath as she looked at the many unanswered pages, gripping her pen in frustration. Tracy practically skipped past Noelle, holding her coffee in one hand and her baby in the other. She exited with haste and a pep in her step.

Dr. Locke slowly made his way toward Noelle. His old age seemed to take a toll on his ability to maneuver. His oak-colored cane helped him move down the aisle of the gray lecture hall.

"I'm concerned." He spoke to her in his usual warm, gentle voice as he glanced down at her nearly blank paper. "Are you all right?"

"Marko is letting me stay with his family again this Christmas. I'm really grateful, but I can't stop thinking about my grandma. And I know you probably think I'm crazy, but I'm pursuing those hints from the letters that I received from her," she said and broke eye contact.

After a moment, he sat beside her. "I'm really sorry about your grandma, Noelle. I cannot imagine the pain that you've experienced at such a young age. But sometimes we have to focus on our blessings to survive the difficult seasons of life. Not everyone is fortunate enough to have a good friend like Marko who invites them over for Christmas."

She stared at her black boots, and her eyes brimmed with hot tears. She wiped her eyes quickly, trying to hide her face. "You're right," she admitted. "And we invited a new friend named Lumi too."

"You can come to my open hours anytime and finish your quiz," he said and picked up the paper.

"Thanks for actually caring about us." He didn't say anything back; he just smiled and placed her quiz on the podium. She gathered her things and checked her phone as she exited. Marko texted once.

> Lumi found the next hint! Come quick!

But Luis texted four times.

> Why are you taking so long?
>
> I found Lumi. She is helping us find the hint!
>
> Marko is totally into Lumi. So annoying.
>
> Lumi found it!

Noelle walked as quickly as she could. She grimaced as blisters began to form under her black boots. The tall skyscrapers looked almost cinematic with all of the snow falling, but Noelle's eyes were glued ahead to the destination—the public green line transportation.

She ground her teeth while riding the green line. When she

saw her stop, Noelle exited and walked with a slight limp as her blister on her right foot began to sting. The cold nipped at her face so she pulled her scarf up to partially cover it. She scanned the crowd of people until she saw familiar faces. Lumi stood at the center and sported a slicked-back ponytail and held a paper. And there next to her was Luis and Marko. Her pace quickened and her jaw clenched as she watched the three of them laughing together. Noelle's mouth gaped as she looked over Lumi's clothing. Her overcoat was checkered and fastened together by a sleek black belt. She wore thigh-length black boots, and the checkered material draped over her arms and fell at her thighs. Noelle had never seen such an ensemble, and she didn't know if she liked it or hated it.

"Hey!" Noelle stamped her foot. "What on earth are you guys doing without me?" Noelle demanded. She spun around and looked at Michigan Avenue and eyed the Jean-Baptiste-Pointe du Sable statue.

"Calm down, we are on this mission together," Luis said.

"You found the hint without me? You can't even bother to text me?" Noelle narrowed in on Lumi.

Lumi's sharp features looked unreadable to Noelle. "I'm sorry. I explained to Marko that I am terrible with phones. I have this old clunker and can barely text on it." Lumi pulled out a very old navy-blue phone. She smiled, and her pale skin seemed to glow in the snow. Her gray eyes fixed on Noelle, and she said, "I didn't intend to be rude. It takes forever to send texts on this! I have to press the same button several times just to text. It doesn't have a keyboard on it." She gave a little giggle.

Noelle, despite her anger, also couldn't help but laugh at the sight of it. "Merca! What is *that*?" Noelle looked incredulously at Lumi's chunky cell phone.

"I guess I'm old school." Lumi shrugged. "But here! Look what I found." Lumi handed a crinkled brown paper to Noelle.

Dear Noelle,

Congratulations! You found the crown at Jean-Baptiste-Pointe du Sable's first home's location. Follow the remaining hints to find the golden necklace.

Hint #2:

Generally, our toughest occasions never agree. Very young people inspire everything rare.

The water is your friend.

Love,

Lolli (Rose Hudson)

"I don't understand this at all." Marko ran a hand through his dark hair, frowning.

"Now hold up a minute!" Noelle spat angrily. "What makes you think you can find the hint without me? Where was it?" Her lips formed a straight line as she pressed them together.

"I looked all morning and found a crown etched into the pavement over there!" Lumi's pale finger pointed to an area on Pioneer Court where a black bench stood. To Noelle's horror, she found a chunk of cement missing and a hammer and chisel abandoned next to it.

"Did you do that?" Noelle couldn't hide the horror in her voice.

"Yes," Lumi confidently responded with a look of pride in her eyes.

"Yeah, and I found her digging up that part of the cement! Were you even going to share the hint with us?" Luis put his hands on his hips.

"Of course." Lumi shrank back slightly, seemingly hurt.

"Okay, listen to me. Do not look up any more hints without me!" Noelle demanded with a heavy sigh. She looked around the busy sidewalk. "We will do this together from now on, understood?"

"Understood," Lumi said without a trace of emotion. "And,

just so you all know, I can make phone calls. But I can't text easily."

Lumi softly smiled at Marko, and he smiled back at her, holding her gaze for a moment.

"Maybe we could get lunch and figure out the next hint." Noelle looked back at the gaping hole in the cement.

"Oh yes! I already figured out the first part. If you circle the first letter of each word then it spells out Go to Navy Pier and then something about the water being our friend," Lumi said. The snow was falling harder now, and it mixed with Lumi's hair. It stood out on Luis's and Marko's dark hair in contrast.

"We need to go before somebody notices that Lumi destroyed property." Marko shoved them forward. They quickly darted through droves of people, each in winter gear, as the snow began to amass even more on the ground. The Chicago skyscrapers seemed to block what little sun could shine through.

"All right, so where do you want to eat? I was thinking we could—" Lumi, who was walking backward to face them, suddenly slipped on a patch of ice. Marko put out an arm and caught Lumi and helped steady her. "Oh, thanks!" She held onto him, stood upright, and smiled at him, dropping her hands.

"Here, take my arm. Your shoes are... really *wonderful*." He struggled to find the right words as he gazed at her heeled shoes. "But I don't want you to slip and fall." Marko offered his arm.

"What about me?" Luis asked, and Noelle began to laugh. Noelle took Luis's arm.

"That is kind, but I'm really fine." Lumi kept her arms at her side. Lumi walked ahead of Noelle, next to Marko. Marko's broad shoulders blocked a lot of the incoming snowflakes, and for that, Noelle was grateful.

"Please, Lumi, let's walk together," Marko insisted with an outstretched arm.

Lumi hesitated for a long moment, as if in consideration. But then she delicately placed her hand around Marko's arm.

CHAPTER 6
NOELLE
NAVY PIER

Noelle managed to convince them to walk and eat on the pier, much to Luis's dismay. Each with a corn dog in hand, they strolled onto the pier. Noelle began to shiver, and her teeth chattered as they walked.

"It's well salted here," Lumi said, dropping her hand from Marko's arm. Marko and Lumi walked ahead, outpacing Luis and Noelle.

"Well, they're annoying." Luis spoke softly so only Noelle could hear him. The snowflakes fell harder now, making Lumi and Marko nearly out of view. The ice on the water floated, and the normally busy pier was a ghost town.

"Luis, when have you ever seen Marko look at somebody like that? Out of all of the years that we've known him, when have you *ever* seen him take notice of somebody? Anybody?" But Luis simply shrugged.

Marko and Lumi were now so far ahead that the snow and wind mixture made them both silhouettes.

Lumi called, "Luis? Noelle? Coming?"

The snow made it difficult for Noelle to see anything, so she focused on finishing her corn dog, which was now quite cold.

"Yeah," she said, mouth full.

"Okay, let's try to find this next hint," Lumi said greedily. She rubbed her hands together, then smiled at Marko, who quickly looked away.

"Well, we're at Navy Pier, so we got that part. And the icy water is here, so what does 'the water is your friend' mean?" Luis asked.

"I have an idea, but I'm unsure," Lumi said.

"There aren't any bad ideas." Noelle slid her boot over the salt on the pier.

"What if the hint needs to get in the water to reveal the next clue?" Lumi asked. Noelle eyed Lumi.

"I think t-that is a great idea," Marko agreed. Noelle swore that his voice sounded slightly nervous when Lumi peered up at him.

Noelle's mouth dropped as she watched him seemingly melt under their new friend's gaze.

"No, that is risky. I don't want to lose the paper." Noelle crossed her arms.

"Well, what else could it mean that *the water is our friend?*" Luis asked.

"Maybe the clue is here at Navy Pier," Noelle said. She looked around, and nobody else seemed to be brave enough to walk the pier today. Only a small handful of workers were on the pier. Noelle pitied them for having to work in such dire weather.

"In the water?" Marko asked doubtfully.

"All right, but what if we lose the paper?" Noelle asked and bit her lip.

"I won't, but even if we did, we have it memorized," Lumi answered.

Noelle brushed the salt under her boot again and looked at Luis. "And you? What do you think we should do?"

"I think getting the hint wet makes sense." Luis shrugged. "I mean, what else will we do?" He grimaced, looking at the semi-frozen lake. It never fully froze, which Noelle imagined must seem odd to Lumi. But that is just how it goes. "I'm not putting my hands in that and getting the hint wet! I'm staying warm." Luis shook his head.

"Then give me the hint." Lumi held out her hand. Noelle fidgeted in her pocket and retrieved the hint and handed the brown crumpled paper to Lumi, who took the paper and clasped her fingers around it tightly. She walked to the edge of the pier, and her high-heeled boots clicked as she did. Lumi stopped at the edge and peered down. She turned back to look at Noelle, and then she jumped feet first into the lake water.

A loud slap could be heard against the water as she hit it.

"Lumi!" Luis yelled with a strained voice. The three friends ran to the edge of the pier, nearly sliding from the heavy salt, looking down. The water's dark color revealed Lumi's silhouette, but her features were blurred.

"She isn't coming up!" Noelle said after a moment. She looked around to see if the two workers on the pier noticed. They hadn't. She looked to the water again, which now had bubbles that rose to the surface.

Marko threw off his heavy jacket and hastily removed his black shoes before edging toward the water, preparing to jump.

"What are you doing?" Noelle demanded. If the workers hadn't noticed before, they probably had now.

Before Marko could jump, a bright blue light shone where Lumi's silhouette was. It burst out brightly at first, giving a neon-blue hue to the water, reaching nearly six feet. But then it dimmed slowly, and Lumi's silhouette came closer and closer to the surface, until she gasped for air. Her head popped up, and her blond ponytail now looked much darker. She swam toward the pier, and Marko shifted to lie on his stomach and grabbed underneath her arms, pulling her out of the water onto the pier. Marko wrapped his heavy jacket around Lumi, a mark of worry appearing between his brows.

"What is wrong with you?" he demanded.

Lumi looked at the scene with Marko partially unclothed with no shoes. "Put your shoes back on! Please take your jacket. I insist! Did you guys see that?" Lumi grinned ear to ear.

Noelle looked back at the water, then rubbed her eyes.

Luis's mouth fell open, and he quietly watched Lumi.

"You're going to get hypothermia. What were you thinking?" Marko barked. Marko's practicality always came first, and his normal moodiness seemed to have returned with his focus entirely on Lumi. He hastily put his shoes back on.

Noelle looked over her shoulder back to the workers, who remarkably still hadn't noticed them.

Luis's eyes were wide. "Did anybody else see that?" His voice was an octave higher than usual.

"Yeah, I-I did," Noelle managed to say. Her throat had gone dry, and the cold burned her face. "What just happened?"

"I got the next clue." Lumi beamed. She held up the same brown wrinkled paper, which now had blue ink on it.

Lumi took Marko's heavy coat off and tried returning it to him. He refused and wrapped it back around her. "No, I'm fine! I'm a Fin, remember? This isn't my first time doing an ice plunge. We practically do this stuff for fun." She winked. "Seriously, take your coat. I don't want you to get sick." Lumi removed his coat again and put it onto Marko's shoulders. Marko hastily removed Lumi's wet jacket as if she were something like a stubborn small child and then placed his heavy coat over her shoulders.

"Do not take this off." His voice sounded nearly threatening.

"Oh merca. Why would you give me your coat when you could jeopardize your own health?" Lumi's lips made a straight line.

"Because that is what friends do." Marko lifted Lumi to her feet, and water sloshed to the pier as she stood.

Lumi stood frozen and looked at Marko, perplexed.

"Are you insane?" Luis demanded and also stood to his feet. His nose was bright pink.

"It seemed like fun." Lumi's lips curled.

Marko shook his head. "Well, I've had enough fun for one day," he mumbled under his breath.

"Let me see the clue!" Noelle swallowed. The blister on her foot screamed as she stood up, and she rubbed her dry lips together. It took all of Noelle's self-control to not rip the clue from Lumi's hand. Lumi handed the little brown paper to Noelle.

> Dear Noelle,
> I suppose you must be in dire circumstances if you're looking this closely for the golden necklace. You should know that the Snow Queen intends to use it to save her family. The reason we cannot let this happen is because the Snow Queen's family can bring great harm to people. It is better that they do not exist. Find the necklace and keep it away from her.
> Hint #3: To find the next clue, you'll need to look up. Your inspection will be in the reflection.
> Love,
> Lolli (Rose Hudson)

"Oh no, she really does suck at hints. What is that supposed to mean?" Noelle stuffed the hint into her pocket.

"Who is Rose Hudson?" Lumi asked.

Noelle's teeth began chattering.

"All right, we need to get inside. Now!" Marko shoved all three of them toward the doors of the little mall on the pier, where warmth greeted them as they stepped inside.

"You three wait here." Marko pointed at a table in the corner.

Lumi dripped, and a small puddle formed at her feet where she stood at the entrance. Three restaurant workers turned to face Lumi and looked horrified.

Marko returned with four hot coffees. "Drink up. Especially you, Lumi," Marko snapped.

Noelle took a cup and took a long swig.

"Who is Rose Hudson?" Lumi asked again.

"She was my grandma," Noelle answered, feeling a lump form in her throat.

"Where did she get the necklace?"

"I don't know. It has been passed down in my family line for a while." Noelle shrugged. She took another big sip of her coffee. "I'd like to know what you saw with the blue light."

"When I got into the water, at first nothing happened. But then this brilliant piercing blue light shone through the paper! And then blue ink appeared, and it covered the paper!" Lumi's face lit up.

"I still don't understand how that is possible, but I do know if you don't warm up, I'm about to spend my entire day with you at the hospital. Please drink the coffee," Marko said with a weary face. He slid the coffee toward Lumi and placed it into her hand. Marko's fingers remained against Lumi's.

Lumi's smile softened. "You seem frustrated. Here, please take your jacket back. I come from cold lands, and this is nothing." Lumi reached for her shoulder and pulled on the jacket, but Marko's large rough hand clamped onto hers tightly.

"Lumi, so help me, if you take this jacket off one more time." He sighed.

Lumi nodded, signaling she understood. "Why not take it?" she asked, confusion settled on her face.

Marko looked downright annoyed. "I already told you, friends take care of friends." He placed his head into his hands, closed his eyes, then rubbed his temples. "Please just drink the coffee and never do something like that again."

"Why are you angry with me?" Lumi asked.

"Because I care about your well-being," he replied politely. "Are people in Finland just cruel and uncaring?"

"But I am a stranger. Why would you care about me?" Lumi's light gaze floated between Noelle, Luis, and Marko.

"Well, I hardly know you, but I've enjoyed being around you. And I'd like to continue getting to know you so it would be nice if you didn't die from stupidity." Marko grinned. "I think we could have a great friendship."

"Friendship," Lumi said curiously. She looked past Noelle's shoulder, but it appeared as if she were staring many miles away.

"Yeah, friends. I don't know how they do it in Finland, but we consider you our new friend," Luis said. He pressed his coffee lid to his lips.

"Did you give my invitation any more thought? I mean, if you don't have plans." Marko leaned toward Lumi.

Lumi awkwardly picked up the coffee and sipped it and ever so slightly leaned away. "I don't have a family to spend it with, so yes," Lumi said softly.

"I'm so sorry, what—"

"I don't really feel like talking about it." Lumi's demeanor shifted entirely. A tempest flickered behind her eyes.

"I get it. I don't have any living family, so it has become a sore topic for me. That's why Marko's family invites me over for the holidays." Noelle folded her arms onto the table.

Lumi's stormy gray eyes locked onto Noelle's and the intensity of her expression made Noelle flinch.

"I'm really sorry to hear that. I completely understand what you've experienced. It is unimaginable grief." Lumi's face softened further, contemplative. "I'd like to come for Christmas. That is really generous of you to invite me. What should I bring?"

"Bring yourself." Noelle smiled.

"I'm going to head out," Luis announced, and he stretched his arms out and yawned.

"I'll join you." Noelle stood to her feet. Her blister rubbed against her boot and made her wince.

"Can I escort you back to your place? I'll get you a taxi. You're still soaking." Marko looked Lumi up and down.

"No, I'm fine," Lumi said.

"Well, I'd like to make sure you get home safely," Marko protested.

"You want to?" Lumi asked, her voice hushed in her strange accent.

"Yes, but I respect you if you don't want—"

"I'd really like that," Lumi said with a bemused look. "I'm sorry if I seem rude. I am just surprised that you all would care so well for a stranger."

"All right, I'm ordering the taxi now. We'll catch up with you guys later." Marko nodded toward Lumi's direction with a half smile. He pulled out his phone and began tapping on it.

Noelle held Luis's arm as they walked the long, snowy pier. The view exiting the pier was even better, in Noelle's opinion, than the view facing the water. The majestic skyscrapers reached high into the sky and paired perfectly with the falling snow; it practically looked like a Christmas snow globe. Noelle looked up, but the gray sky was filled with so much snow that she couldn't see clouds or sun.

"She seems weird. She and Marko could hit it off together," Luis said, and they both laughed.

CHAPTER 7
THE SNOW QUEEN LUMI
COFFEE

Lumi unlocked her apartment door and turned on the light which illuminated the posh apartment. Gold adorned much of her decor, and the view of the city was striking from the enormous window.

"Your apartment is beautiful," Marko said and scanned the vast space.

"Thank you. You're welcome to come in." The words escaped Lumi's lips somehow and surprised them both.

Marko walked toward her, where she stood and watched him carefully. Lumi tried to neutralize her features but struggled as she pondered why she felt so comfortable with a human. *She slipped up.* Perhaps it was her old ways coming back. Lumi sensed her heart, and it emitted the tiniest warmth. She put a hand over her chest and tried to freeze her heart again, not wanting to experience the unpleasantness of feelings that protruded from it.

Marko shivered. Lumi looked at her own clothing—still wet from her plunge. She never bothered with heat in her apartment, because she was cozy with freezing temperatures. But she needed to act human, and surely humans would be bothered by this temperature, as evidenced by Marko's shivers.

"Oh, let me get the heat on! How odd. It must have been

turned off." Lumi moved quickly toward the hallway where the thermostat was. She hadn't used it once, enjoying the cold on her skin, but now she squinted at the device, unsure of how to work it. "Please feel free to start a fire. Since I'm on the top floor, I'm fortunate to have a fireplace." She only had such a useless feature because the chic apartment came with it. Marko quickly made his way to the fireplace and began to arrange the logs. Lumi produced matches from her cabinet and handed them to him and then went back to her thermostat, pressing every button on it hoping something might work.

After many frustrating moments, Lumi managed to get the heat to turn on and returned to her living room, where Marko stood with the fireplace lit. He had his palms outstretched to the flames and seemed to enjoy the warmth it emitted.

"Sorry it's so cold. It should warm up soon," Lumi said and pretended to shiver as she approached him.

Marko shrugged. "I like to camp, so I don't mind. I'm used to sitting around a fire in cold temperatures." Marko's square jaw was defined, and he had ruggedly handsome features. He faced Lumi and rubbed his hands together.

"You have strands of wet hair stuck to your cheek," Marko said. He gently swept the hair behind her ear and let his hand fall to his side. The intimate gesture sent a spark of warmth toward Lumi's center, and her rebellious heart began to thump against her wishes. The gentle caress and stroke of his finger against her cheek felt so strange yet alluring. Heat blossomed inside her chest as she stared at him. Lumi had locked away these feelings, yet now she seemed to have remembered the fondness of a gentle touch and even *craved* it. She eyed him and swallowed as his smile deepened. Her eyes remained on his lips and she studied the curves of it intricately. She hadn't noticed until now how attractive Marko was, and the glow of amber flames highlighted the contours of his face.

Curious, Lumi used her ability to reach into his mind. She often perused wicked people's minds to find their true intentions.

She imagined this man was no different. Humans *always* wanted something. Greedy little creatures. She could sense dangerous or malicious intentions or kind ones. So what did *this* human want from her?

Lumi waded through his mind, pulling on the threads of Marko's intentions and desires—all laid bare because of Lumi's ability. She saw his brotherly loyalty and love for Noelle and his family. And then she found his intentions for her—which made her eyebrows rise.

The first string in his mind, albeit small, revealed that he *liked* Lumi. That made her want to laugh. He wouldn't like her if he truly knew her. But the larger thread in his mind revealed that he wanted to protect her. There were no other intentions.

Lumi marveled at him. Humans weren't usually so pure-hearted. A spark of heat suddenly erupted in Lumi's heart as she looked at Marko. She placed a hand on her chest and attempted to ice it over and quench the building heat. Lumi was in no mood to thaw her icy heart and *feel* those wretched emotions *again*.

Marko grinned, and she couldn't help it, she did too.

"Would you like to stay for coffee? I'd like that," Lumi blurted out loud.

Alarmed, she balled her fists. But then released them as she realized perhaps this wasn't such a terrible thing. She could weaponize his feelings so that she would find *her* necklace.

But if she simply wanted to use him, why did she desire nothing more than to continue looking into his dark eyes? She felt so oddly safe with him, knowing his motive for being around was to protect her. The thought made her want to laugh. A human protecting the Snow Queen? How ridiculous. How adorable.

But if she were less selfish, she would tell him to run. She would implore him to leave, to avoid her so that he wouldn't become entangled with a monster.

Marko's cupid's bow expanded with a smile. "I'd love to."

CHAPTER 8
NOELLE
SCHOOL GROUNDS

Noelle and Marko sat together in the lecture hall. Marko hummed and set out his laptop and notebooks.

"You seem to be in a good mood," Noelle noted.

Marko smiled, deeply exhaling, then faced Noelle. "I've been spending a lot of time with Lumi." A boyish grin flicked across his face.

"I see. How did that come about?" Noelle asked, and she tried to hide her own smile but failed. She pushed her brown hair away from her face in an attempt to get a better view at her smiling friend.

"Well, we took a taxi back to her apartment. And she invited me in for coffee. We chatted over coffee for probably six hours and—"

"*Six* hours?" Noelle's mouth dropped. "Who *are* you?"

"Well, we also played a game that she had there, and then it just sort of morphed and..." Marko's smile disappeared. "Do you think I'm being foolish? I hardly know her." A more ominous look swept over his face. "I mean, she was very impulsive the other day." His face went blank.

Students began to file in and take their seats in the lecture hall, and Dr. Locke stood at the front of the classroom.

"No, I don't." Noelle picked at her nail bed. "I think, for once, you like a girl, and it is a really normal thing. Besides, six hours is really promising, and maybe next time when you hang out—"

"Well, we also hung out the next day. And then on Sunday again too," Marko admitted.

Noelle lifted both eyebrows and turned toward him. Her eyes scanned Marko's as if unsure what to say. "You're truly unrecognizable."

Luis entered the room and practically crashed into his seat next to Noelle, throwing his jacket to the side. "Morning!" He'd donned a forest-green knit hat, which still had snowflakes clinging to it. He yanked off his dark wool gloves. "How did your weekend go?"

"I spent the entire weekend trying to figure out what the next clue might mean," Noelle hastily said. "And you?"

"Nothing exciting. What did you do?" Luis nodded to Marko.

"Lumi and I hung out all weekend."

"That's cool," Luis said, indifferent.

Dr. Locke cleared his throat, and the class looked to the professor, who had yet another table filled with treats. "Class, I wanted to wish you a Merry Christmas and happy holidays!" Dr. Locke's hand drifted toward the table. "Please enjoy some treats today. We'll get started in about fifteen minutes." His wild hair looked like a rat's nest piled high upon his head.

"Did you get anywhere with the clue?" Luis asked.

"I have a few ideas, but I'm still not sure. Lumi and I are going to hang out tonight to work on it," Noelle said.

Marko raised a curious brow. "Oh? Mind if I join? I mean—it's fine if this is just your thing."

"I don't mind."

"I'll catch up with you all after break. But do let me know if you see any more shining blue lights," Luis said.

Dr. Locke peered down at Noelle through his black eyeglasses. "Any luck with your hint over the weekend?" His patient, dark eyes rested on Noelle, then he looked to Luis and finally to Marko.

Noelle parted her mouth to speak, but Marko was too quick. "Nothing at all, sir," Marko reported and placed his hands behind his back. He appeared to be something akin to a soldier at that moment.

"That is a shame. But I'm sure you'll find the necklace." Dr. Locke gave a soft smile, then slowly turned and grasped his cane. He walked toward Tracy, and they began to chat about her weekend.

Marko leaned low to Noelle's level, and his mouth was inches from her ear. "If you trust me, if I have ever been worthy of your trust, do not speak to him or anybody about these hints any longer. And do not tell *anybody* about the blue light or what you saw," Marko whispered, his breath hot against Noelle's ear.

She opened her mouth to protest, but he had already straightened up and walked toward the snack table.

"Why wouldn't I tell Dr. Locke?" She looked at Luis now, who shrugged.

Luis pulled off his hat and placed it on the edge of his desk. "Maybe he's worried that people won't believe you," he suggested.

"People will think all four of us are lying? We all saw the same thing! Besides, what if Dr. Locke could help?"

"People don't tend to take well to talk of otherworldly sights," Luis said. "I can't explain what we saw, but I agree with Marko. I don't think it would be wise to share it. And if the Snow Queen really is here, and I think I've become completely convinced that she is, don't you think she's also looking for that necklace?" Luis stood and headed for the snack table.

Noelle wanted to stand too, but her legs felt numb.

Later that evening, Marko, Lumi, and Noelle sat huddled together inside the library, where they pored over books and researched potential next locations for the clue.

Lumi sighed. "I'm starving. I think I'm going to call it quits tonight." She tossed aside another book. Her stack of books was high. Noelle's pile was smaller, as she tended to become engrossed in potential buildings that the next clue could be in.

"Let's get dinner," Marko suggested, eyes locked on Lumi. Marko leaned toward Lumi, but Noelle noticed Lumi's rigid posture. Lumi seemed cold and distant as though her walls were firmly built and nobody could penetrate them.

"I'd like that. As long as Noelle can join." Lumi's bright eyes looked to Noelle for a response.

Something flashed across Marko's face and then just as quickly disappeared. Noelle had recognized it. *Annoyance.* She understood Marko's expression as he stared at her. She wasn't really invited, at least not by him. It was tempting to become a third wheel on this date, only because she knew it would irritate him so much. A smile pulled at Noelle's lips as she looked at Marko. He wanted time with Lumi for himself, and Noelle found him irritatingly selfish for it. Lumi was her new friend too, and she hadn't even gotten a chance to tell her about the guy on the train.

Noelle tilted her head sideways as she stared at Marko. She felt he and Lumi were moving far too quickly; it had only been a few days. And Marko's dark eyes now rested on Lumi with an intense fascination that Noelle feared could lead to trouble. He seemed to be captivated, but she was still a complete and total stranger. She could leave, and he'd probably be crushed. Or worse, she could be tangled in something far more sinister than they understood. Noelle's mind traveled to the handsome guy on the train, Eli, and she looked over Lumi closely. Was Lumi dangerous?

"Actually, I can't. I need to tie up some loose strings with homework, and I'd like to keep working. I'm going to pick up from the cafeteria and call it a night. But I hope you both enjoy dinner."

Marko sighed. Noelle's smile widened as she recognized it was a sigh of relief.

"All right, but if you change your mind, then let us know," Lumi said and stood.

Noelle nodded and returned the old, musty-smelling books to their places. She exited the tall library arches and walked toward her apartment. Once inside the building, she stepped onto the elevator and clasped her hands together after pressing the button for the sixth floor.

Just before the door shut, a familiar presence entered the elevator. Noelle gasped as she recognized the gruff-looking man with the scar on his face. His weathered face looked even more sinister since their last meeting. She stepped backward, and the cold, slate-gray elevator wall pressed against her back.

He also pressed the button for six, and the door closed promptly.

"Look, we're going to the same place," he said and faced forward. Noelle's heart began to thud. "Change of plans. I'm not going to take you to my realm since you're getting so close to the necklace. We'll deal with the dead body later. You need to work *faster* though. And if you don't give me the necklace, then you'll be sorry." His tone was steady, but his voice was as weathered as his face.

"Why don't you just get it yourself?" Noelle calculated how quickly she could press a button and exit, but it seemed impossible with him standing in front of the buttons. His scar was more evident in the harsh elevator light.

"Because *you* have to," he snarled.

Noelle's heart was beating faster by the moment. "Why?"

"You don't know why?"

The elevator music didn't help with Noelle's growing anxiety. The violin, normally quite easily ignored, now sounded shrill and uneven.

"No, I don't! I don't know why you're following me or harassing me!" Her voice carried, and she hoped somebody would notice.

"What are you going to do?" He laughed. "Call the police? Tell them a man wants a mythical necklace? That you saw a flash of blue light?"

Noelle tried to recall if the man had been there at Navy Pier, but she only remembered seeing her friends and the workers on the cold pier.

"Besides, in my realm, we found a dead body and someone wrote *your* name next to it. Care to explain that?"

"I don't know what you're talking about. *Who* are you?"

"I'm your friend. An enemy threatens, but a friend warns. And I'm here to warn you. Get the necklace and give it to me. In my realm, they're contemplating forcing you to duel to the death soon because of the fuss you've created. If you were smart, you'd get that necklace quickly and rid yourself of this entire ordeal. Do that, and your blond friend will be just fine if you do," he said with a calculated tone. His long trench coat was stained with red streaks. She hoped it wasn't blood.

"Leave her alone," Noelle squeaked.

"She doesn't need to be involved." The scar-faced man turned to face Noelle now. A shiver went down her spine. The elevator suddenly stopped abruptly, and she shifted against the wall in an attempt to push farther away from him.

"This is my stop." The man took a step forward, but Noelle didn't dare follow him. She fell to the floor. The door shut but not before he glanced back at her and walked to the right, toward the direction of her apartment. Her hands shook as she pressed the first floor, her heart racing.

She shakily stood and waited for the elevator to stop, holding on to the wall for support. Her trembling fingers dialed a number, but then she erased it as she quickly walked out of the elevator. Her legs were numb again. Who could she call? Would the police even believe her?

CHAPTER 9
NOELLE
THE NATUREI

Noelle's cold fingers wrapped around her phone. She stood outside in the dark. She ran, unsure of where to go or whom to call. She could see her breath and focused on that to try to calm her nerves. She breathed in; she breathed out. She thought carefully about whom she might be able to stay with. Marko's family was the obvious answer, but they would want to know why.

Noelle rested her back against a tall building and looked frantically around at the falling snow that dusted trees and what was left of withered plants. She saw one bright green plant that curiously looked vibrant and alive despite the snow. It seemed so out of place and looked identical to the plant that Lumi threw.

And then dread overcame her when she heard a gruff voice.

"I need a verbal confirmation that you're not going to let your friend get the necklace," the scar-faced man said as he approached Noelle. Noelle closed her eyes, angry that she had focused on the stupid plant for so long. He was far too close for her to run.

She reached into her pocket, pulled out her knife, and pointed it at him. "Stay back!"

The scar-faced man laughed, then closed the remaining gap

between them. He moved too quickly for Noelle to process it clearly, but his hand gripped her wrist before she could strike and he had disarmed her. He moved supernaturally fast.

"First rule for you, kid. Don't ever bring a weapon to a fight unless you're prepared for it to be used against you."

He lunged forward, but Noelle managed to hit him first in the face. Her fist made contact with his nose, and from the sound of the cracking noise, it was likely broken. Blood spattered his face, and he groaned.

Furious, he pinned Noelle to the building and held her own knife to her throat. Her head slammed and throbbed in pain. She reached for his arms and pulled against the knife with all her strength. She kneed his groin, and he groaned again. Noelle had been in several fights growing up, and it had created a scrappy, resilient spirit within her so that she could simply survive. She had spent countless hours training in mixed martial arts in the gym, just so she could defend herself for moments like this.

A sound escaped Noelle as a small amount of blood trickled down her neck. The sharp point of the knife stung, and Noelle ceased squirming to avoid more blood being drawn.

"Find the necklace, or you'll be my next victim," he said and gestured to the red stains on his coat.

"I'm not a victim, I'm an opponent. I might not win every fight, but rest assured that I will not go down without one," Noelle said through clenched teeth. She leaned toward the blade and bit his hand forcefully.

He lifted his hand and raised it toward Noelle.

"Hey," someone said casually from behind them. Noelle couldn't see past the scar-faced man, but she vaguely recognized the voice.

The scar-faced man turned, keeping the knife steady. "*Naturei*. How did *you* get here?" And then a fist met the scar-faced man's temple with great force and he fell to the snow, no longer moving.

Noelle gasped and looked up at the attractive young man who

had just knocked him out. Eli stood there in a dark coat, and his long, wavy dark hair looked disheveled as the wind blew it around.

He stepped forward and said, "I told you I'd be seeing you again." Then he sighed. "How exactly did you manage to incite a rebellion with a dead body in the fire realm? And how did you manage to get *this* Leizei's attention?" Irritation circled his words and swirled in his eyes.

Noelle looked to the left and then the right, uncertain where he'd even come from.

"A what? Excuse me, where did you come from?" Noelle demanded.

He tore his emerald eyes from her and looked at the Leizei on the ground. "I'm not supposed to be here," he said in almost a whisper. His eyes flickered back to her, and a smile appeared. "I just couldn't let him mark up your pretty face though."

Noelle could feel her ears go warm despite the cool weather. "I was fine. I had him. Besides, were you *watching* me?" She grimaced as she felt a small amount of blood on her neck.

A laugh fell from Eli's lips. "No, I have more important matters to attend to than your trivial day-to-day affairs. But I did see him threatening you through our plant portal."

She shook her head as if she hadn't heard him correctly. "Are you watching me because of the necklace? So you're arrogant *and* creepy. And what is a *Naturei*?"

Eli flinched. He looked at the odd green plant, grabbed Noelle by her arm, and dragged her with him. "Don't ever say that word again. I had strict orders not to intervene with you. I don't know what overcame me, but I just couldn't let that Leizei hurt you. But now that I've helped you, and now that you even know the word *Naturei*, I've committed treason against my realm." He sighed heavily, and they walked for a moment in silence. "They don't know I'm here." He said the words under his breath.

"Then don't help me. Why not leave me alone?" Noelle asked bitterly. She wasn't about to be somebody's problem. She was confident she could take care of herself; she had managed to do it for years.

Eli stopped walking. "I have never met a human before. I've studied your kind, but I've never interacted with one. I find you interesting." Eli looked her over with intrigue. "And I need your help. But if a human finds out about the Naturei, I have direct orders that require me, by our realm's law, to kill them."

Noelle trembled and tried to slide her hand out from his, but he kept it there.

"But I'm not going to kill you so long as you make me a promise."

Panic emerged, but she tried to keep her facial expression calm. Noelle wanted to run. But after she looked Eli up and down, she decided it would only be a moment before he caught up to her. The intensity in his eyes revealed that he wasn't pranking her, nor did he find this amusing.

"Sure," Noelle said with annoyance. Whatever it was that he wanted, she planned to lie through her teeth. She would promise the moon and the stars if it meant he would just get away from her—and let go of her hand.

"I'll let you go if you promise to see me every day with reports on your friend Lumi. And you must never tell anybody that you know about the Naturei."

Noelle stepped backward. "All right, yes, that's fine." She couldn't wait to pry her hand from his.

"And you cannot tell anybody about who I am or where I come from. You must simply tell them that we are friends, and you cannot behave in any way that isn't friendly toward me in front of others. Also, if I tell a lie to protect myself, you will not negate it. You will go along with it," Eli added with a sly smile. He stepped closer.

Noelle imagined running just then. But she figured if she could simply make him happy, he might leave voluntarily. "All right, deal."

She was plotting her escape when suddenly a flash of green

light circled around their hands and a ribbon of the light made a tie. Noelle blinked several times, and then the light vanished altogether.

"What just happened?" Noelle asked, baffled. She withdrew her shaky hand.

"Well, you just made a Naturei vow. You can't break them even if you tried. It's impossible. I look forward to seeing more of you," Eli said with a wink and turned to leave.

Rage brewed inside Noelle. What had she just agreed to?

"You pompous jerk!" she called after him.

He had tricked her, and she wouldn't simply comply. But he didn't seem to care, because he took long, confident strides in the snow. She kicked the snow, sending much of it flying.

"I *saved* your life. That Leizei has a speed ability, and I doubt you would have been fast enough for him. You should be *thanking* me. But you need to get safe. You should find a friend to stay with tonight!" he called back over his shoulder with a smug smile. "I suggest Lumi." Noelle could hear the amusement thick in his voice.

She angrily picked up her phone and sent a text to Lumi. And to her surprise, she received a text back immediately. She walked hurriedly in the opposite direction of Eli to her dorm, where she gathered as much of her clothing and belongings as she could. Lumi confirmed that she would arrive soon.

Lumi's cherry-red Mustang appeared after several moments, and Noelle could see it from the window. She hurried downstairs, and to her dismay, Eli appeared at her side. She inwardly groaned, despising him.

"Where is the bald man? And *who* is this?" Lumi asked as she eyed Eli.

To Noelle's surprise, Eli seemed to have put in colored contacts. His normally dark green eyes were a deep brown color.

Eli extended a hand. "I'm Eli, Noelle's friend. She told me everything about the necklace. I'm here to join the adventure," Eli said and shook Lumi's hand. "She also didn't want to be alone without me. She said I make her feel safe."

Lumi looked distressed. Confusion was written all over her face as she eyed the handsome stranger. "You told him about the necklace?"

Noelle tried to open her mouth to inform Lumi that she had not, in fact, informed him about the necklace. But her tongue remained glued to the roof of her mouth.

Noelle frantically looked at Eli, but an arrogant smirk rested on his lips. His Naturei pact did this, she realized. She couldn't go against the Naturei pact, and when she tried, her mouth remained closed.

Noelle tried to form the words *we aren't friends*, but when she opened her mouth, she said, "Yes, we are friends!" She sighed and racked her brain. How had *those* words escaped her lips? She was trying to say the opposite.

Eli slid a hand around Noelle's shoulder, and she glanced at him with disdain. She wrapped her arm around his back in a mock hug, where Lumi couldn't see her hand, and dug her fingernails into his skin. He winced. She hoped it was the *friendly* greeting he desired.

"He is a nature... nature..." The word *Naturei* would not emerge. It didn't matter how much Noelle willed the word to come forth, it simply would not.

Eli began to laugh. "I'm a naturally wonderful guy? That is what you meant to say, huh?" His arrogant smile deepened.

Noelle simply stared. She pinched his back, hard. He sucked in a breath and pushed her away, dropping his hand from her shoulder. He said she had to appear friendly in front of others, but he failed to say she had to *actually be* friendly where others couldn't see.

She knew she couldn't disagree, so she just nodded. She was thinking of how to pay him back. She would make him wish he'd never met her and especially that he had never fooled her.

"Elle and I actually have been hanging out a lot since we met. She has told me so much about you all," Eli said with a smirk.

Noelle snapped her head toward him after hearing the nickname. Nobody ever called her Elle before, and she would have liked the nickname if somebody—*anybody*—else had given it to her. Noelle began to laugh.

"Well, Lumi, the truth is..." But the words wouldn't come. He had said *if I tell a lie to protect myself, you will not negate it.*

Noelle wanted to punch him. She balled her fist at her side, but it wouldn't budge. Apparently punching was not friendly behavior and therefore forbidden. He had really protected himself with that Naturei vow.

"What is the truth, Elle? Don't be shy." Eli faced Noelle now and clasped both her hands in his. Noelle flinched at the use of the nickname paired with his intimate gesture. He was behaving as if they had been best friends for years. "You know, Lumi, we just met recently on the train. But she worked up the boldness to approach me and told me she had never seen a man so handsome in her life."

Noelle tried to scoff, but it turned into a choking sound.

"Are you all right?" Lumi's brow furrowed.

"Yes, Elle, you're okay, aren't you?" Eli held her hands gently.

"Never better," Noelle coughed. Her head spun with ways she could bring Eli to absolute ruin. She ought to focus on the report of a dead body in some other realm, with her name written beside it, or the fact that she had been tracked and stalked. But her rage and annoyance with Eli clouded everything else, and she wanted nothing more than to make him pay.

"Well, that is really bold of you. Welcome to the team, I suppose. I didn't know she had met you. She hadn't mentioned you," Lumi said, and Noelle could see she was visibly aggravated.

"It's new." Eli smiled and pulled Noelle toward him as if they were best friends. His warm hand rested on her shoulder.

An idea sparked in Noelle's mind. "Yes," Noelle said enthusiastically. "I can't wait to introduce him to Marko." A wide grin appeared on Noelle's lips as she peered up at Eli.

She could tell the enthusiasm in her voice had caught Eli off guard. Until that moment, he'd seemed to be enjoying this, but now a look of doubt clouded his features. Sheer confusion even flashed across his eyes.

"Let's go before that guy wakes up," Lumi said as she looked past them and in the direction of the scar-faced man.

CHAPTER 10
THE SNOW QUEEN LUMI
THE THAWED HEART

Lumi walked briskly toward her American car and opened the door for Noelle. She looked up through her lashes at the boy who walked close behind Noelle. Lumi knew she ought to play her role and practice some form of niceties toward him, but she *despised* him. If he meddled with their plan to find the necklace or took the girl off course, she'd lure him into an alleyway and take care of him.

She didn't like the way he carried himself. He didn't slouch his shoulders like other boys his age, but instead, he held his head up high in the air. His confidence seemed unnatural and rare. But she hated him not because of his cocky demeanor but because she resented the fact that yet another human might be able to get their grubby fingers on *her* locket.

Before they could reach Lumi's car, a man approached on their right side, and Lumi's ability to sense danger and deadly motives began to ring. Lumi gave the man her attention and froze as she realized he had a gun pointed at her chest.

Lumi couldn't help it; a sinister grin overtook her face. A human man with a gun was nothing to her. With a flick of her wrist, she could send him flying into the air with ice, or she could instantly craft thousands of ice arrows and plunge them into his body. She could touch him and give him frostbite that would wither his internal organs so that he died slowly and painfully. The options were endless.

"What do you want?" Lumi asked, nearly bored.

"Give me your phones, purses, and keys," he demanded and looked around nervously.

"Leave and I'll spare your life," Lumi said as she continued to think of ways to end his miserable life.

Noelle moved in front of Lumi, shielding her. She held her hands up, and the man pointed the gun at Noelle.

"I'll shoot!" he warned.

"What are you doing?" Lumi asked, clutching at her jacket as blazing fire erupted in her chest where her icy heart rested.

Humans were not supposed to be protective or anything less than full of selfish ambition. Lumi had been enslaved by humans and knew they were treacherous. So why wasn't this one?

The human girl's kindness seemed to melt the icy hardness around Lumi's frozen-over heart. Lumi closed her eyes and pressed both hands to her chest, and when she opened her eyes, she heard the click of the gun, and before she could think, she shot ice shards from her fingers and froze the bullet in midair.

It landed safely on the ground with a loud sound and Noelle's shriek.

Lumi looked over at Noelle's shocked expression and sighed as heat rippled through her insides. Why would this young girl be willing to give her life for a stranger? Lumi covered her face and then leaned over and panted with her hands on her knees. Her heart began to beat, faintly, and with it new emotions that had been suppressed for years emerged. Lumi focused and managed to conceal her heart with ice again, and the heat dwindled almost entirely.

Lumi held out her hand. She needed to move quickly if she wanted to recover from the situation. She considered abandoning Noelle and the annoying boy and retrieving the necklace alone. She was quite the nuisance—but something about her made

Lumi feel *alive*. Lumi knew she might regret it, but she was intrigued by Noelle since she was willing to sacrifice her life for Lumi's.

Lumi waved her hand toward Noelle and reached into her memories. She pulled on the threads of different ones until she found the most recent one and wiped it. She was careful to avoid watching any of the girl's other memories. It wasn't out of politeness that Lumi did this, as if she wanted to protect her privacy; it was because she was becoming increasingly afraid of being attached to the girl. Not that she cared for her, at least that was what she told herself.

Noelle began smiling, stupidly, as the euphoric feeling rushed over her.

Lumi then looked at the man with the gun and reached into his recent memory and destroyed it. She reached for the frozen man's gun and crushed it in her palm like it was mere clay. She threw the gun's remains into a nearby withered bush and let out a huff. She then made a stream of ice under the man's feet so that he was stuck.

Lumi eyed Eli, who surprisingly simply had a blank face. She also reached into his mind and cleared his most recent memory.

She crossed her arms and rolled her eyes as they giggled with glee. She waited until they settled. When Noelle and Eli came to their senses, they followed her. Except this time the man was frozen in place.

Lumi panted as she walked, feeling drained from using so much of her power. She blinked slowly as her eyelids became quite heavy.

"What in the world?" the man said aloud, trying to shift his feet from the frozen ice, but he remained stuck.

"Oh no! We should help him!" Noelle said and began to walk toward the man.

Lumi grabbed her hand and redirected her toward the car. "No time. He will be okay."

"Help!" the man called out to them. Noelle tried to move toward the man, but Lumi pulled her along.

"We need to get going. Somebody else will help him," Lumi said and ushered Noelle to the passenger side of her car.

Eli's eyes narrowed on Lumi after examining the man.

"Oh, Elle. I wanted to sit in the front," he said. His hands were in his pockets as he came to an abrupt halt at Noelle's side.

Lumi made her way to the driver's side and pushed the seat forward so he could crawl into the back. "Here, princess."

Noelle laughed loudly.

"It looks a bit small back there for somebody my size."

Lumi tilted her head. "You'll be all right."

With a sigh, Eli walked to Lumi's side and balked at her before crawling into the back seat, where his knees bunched up against his chest. Lumi pulled her seat forward and then sat in the driver's seat.

Eli leaned forward, and his head hit the ceiling. "It's really tight back here. Can you move up more, please?"

"No," Lumi said. "I have long legs." It was bad enough she had to spend so much time with humans, but this one seemed especially exasperating. She was already tired of his company.

Noelle laughed and glanced in his direction. Eli frowned and glared at the back of Lumi's head.

"How did you get away from Marko?"

"I just told him that you needed me." Lumi pulled out, and drove into traffic. Lumi sighed as she considered that Noelle had come into contact with a Leizei. "But enough about that. You need to tell me everything. Start from the beginning."

Noelle tapped her snowy boots together, ruining Lumi's clean floorboard. "Please don't tell Marko. I want to be the one to do it."

"Okay." Lumi nodded.

"I've had these letters for years. But I didn't really believe in the legendary necklace until the snow storms started in Chicago. The letters were from my grandma, and I've missed her so much." Noelle fiddled with her hoodie sleeves.

"What happened to your grandma?" Eli asked.

"She was sick and passed away a few years ago. I'll get to that part. Hold on."

"I'm really sorry. I didn't know," Eli said in a quiet tone.

Lumi swallowed. The young girl seemed to have had a cruel, unkind life in her short span of years already. The girl's spirit somehow seemed unbroken and resilient, and for that, Lumi admired her.

"Do you want to talk about it?" Lumi asked. If it were any other human, she wouldn't bother to ask such a question. But the girl struck a chord with her, and she just couldn't help but offer any form of comfort that she could.

"I don't mind," she said and looked out the window. "My grandma was a remarkable caretaker, and she did her absolute best, but she was ill most of the time. I never met my grandpa or knew any other family. She died four years ago. I got put into a foster home, and that is how I met Marko's family, because we lived on the same street." Noelle's face looked entirely drained recalling her short but unfortunate life story.

"Are you close with your foster family?" Eli asked.

Lumi's neck strained as she tried to get a glimpse of the girl. She told herself she only cared because Noelle held the remaining letters, but she felt a pang of worry stir in her heart as she looked at the girl. A lick of a warm spark emitted in Lumi's cold, dreary heart, and she pressed a hand to her chest. As quickly as it had occurred, it was gone.

"No, it's a long, messy story. But I essentially, for all intents and purposes, was rejected. I got a legal emancipation, and thankfully Marko's family took me in. Marko is literally like my older brother, and they're the best! They still invite me over for holidays and special occasions." Noelle's eyes drifted down.

Lumi pulled into her parking space by her apartment and rested her head against the headrest. She was so utterly tired. Lumi tried to keep her eyes off the downcast girl, but she struggled. She was intimately familiar with the pain of loss and the never-ending grief that accompanied it. She pitied the girl for understanding such pain at a young age.

"You and I are not so different," Lumi blurted out. "I haven't shared the details of my family because my story is messy too. And I *struggle* to trust people, to put it lightly." Lumi looked away and then back to Noelle. "But I understand you and your pain. I don't think I can share all the details with you, because, well, it's complicated. But I lost my family too. In a really tragic way, and I've never really gotten over it. I also had an amazing daughter, and I—" Lumi bit her lip. "I'm sorry." She held back tears. "I don't want to discuss it more."

"I'm so terribly sorry," Noelle said and looked up at Lumi with her rich, chocolate-brown eyes, two pools of empathetic concern.

Eli cleared his throat. "I'm sorry for you both."

Lumi imagined what it might feel like to have lost all family at such a young age, and as she looked at Noelle's large eyes, she felt a spark in her heart again. Heat ripped through Lumi's heart, and intense emotions overcame her. Pity for Noelle, concern for the girl's future, and the uncanny resemblance to her own daughter troubled her. Lumi wondered what might have happened to her daughter if she'd had to navigate the world alone, and in that moment, Lumi made certain that Noelle wouldn't face the world alone any longer—at least, not if she could help it. She would help her in whatever way she could, because life had been utterly cruel to Noelle, just like it had been to her.

And then, to Lumi's shock, the first tear she had shed in 150 years rolled down her cheek and turned into ice against her cool skin. But the tear wasn't for her; it was for Noelle and the pain that she had endured. Lumi was grateful for the dark car as she wiped the frozen tear off her cheek.

"Oh merca. Have I lost my ever-loving mind?" Lumi muttered under her breath and stared at the parking lot ahead of her, which became blurry with the tears that threatened to fall.

"Are you all right?" Noelle asked.

No, Lumi wasn't all right. Her icy, cold heart defrosted, and it was emitting warmth for the first time in a very, very long time. This wasn't what Lumi had planned. Lumi inhaled, breathed in and out. She felt *everything*, and she wished her heart would harden again, because she wanted to curl up in a ball and scream.

"I'm fine." Lumi gave a nod and opened her car door, then pulled her seat forward. "For our princess."

Well, at least she still hated the boy. The girl might have managed to thaw out her icy heart, but she'd maintained her dislike of the overly confident boy.

Lumi walked with uncertainty onto the icy sidewalk. It felt like only moments ago she'd seen the world in black and white, and now the new feelings that emerged seemed to color her world—and she was entirely overwhelmed by the warm heart that beat inside her chest, full of emotions that drained her.

"Careful, Elle! It's like ice-skating," Eli said and pointed at the ice.

"I won't fall."

"You might if I push you," Eli said and playfully placed his hands out toward her.

Lumi's boots clicked against the ice, and she turned on Eli. "If you ever hurt her, I'll find you and pin you against a wall upside down, where all the blood will painfully drain to your head. And then let you go, only to do it all over again every single day of your life. You'll try to outrun me, but you will never succeed."

Eli went rigid, and Noelle laughed.

"She is so funny! She's joking," Noelle said and clapped Lumi on the shoulder.

But Lumi just continued to stare at Eli. "Well, don't hurt her, and you'll never find out if I'm joking."

Noelle laughed and leaned over, but Eli didn't laugh. He simply stared.

"Your humor is a bit dark. Anyway, where is your apartment?"

"Follow me," Lumi said. Noelle and Eli followed behind her as she headed toward a luxury apartment building that was both pristine and modern.

Lumi led them into the entrance, where an employee greeted them. The upscale lobby hosted several pieces of white, overstuffed furniture. A large, uniquely shaped fish tank stood in the center of the room, with varying sorts of fish.

Similar to Lumi's car, the place looked immaculate and new. They walked toward the elevator, and Lumi pressed the button and watched the girl carefully.

Once inside the elevator, Lumi pressed again. "So what exactly happened?" She spoke softly, as she still nursed her own pain. "With the man," Lumi clarified. The elevator door closed, and Lumi pressed button fourteen.

"Well, the man started following me around the time the snow started. He appeared pretty scarcely, but his visits have increased. He keeps telling me to find the necklace, and I don't know—"

Lumi grimaced. "*How* does he know about the necklace?"

"Did you tell him?" Eli asked. Lumi side-eyed him.

"He knows about everything," Noelle said. "He even knows about you."

Lumi's naturally pale face grew even more pale. "You... you told him about me?" Lumi stammered. She suddenly regretted not looking more carefully at the Leizei. She had been distracted by the *stupid boy* and didn't get a close look at his crumpled body in the snow.

"No! I would never! I think he followed me around or something! Well, actually, I saw him in the window of the café the night we all met. And he said there was a dead body with my name written next to it."

"What did he look like?" Lumi asked, anxiety apparent in her voice. The elevator dinged, and the door opened. Lumi walked out of the elevator first, and Noelle and Eli followed her. The long hallway was white with pale yellow doors, each adorned with gold-plated numbers.

"He is tall—well, he is tall to me, at least! Which isn't saying too much." Noelle laughed. "He looks older and he has a distinct scar on his face. I think he's called Leizei," Noelle added.

Lumi stopped dead in her tracks and felt the blood drain from her face.

Noelle bumped into Lumi. "Lumi?" Noelle asked, horror creeping into her voice. "You look like you've seen a ghost. Have you seen him or something?"

Lumi remained silent, trying to keep her emotions in check. "Yes," she said finally. Lumi recalled with a sigh the last time she'd seen Lars. He'd told the humans about merca and then helped several other Leizei slaughter an entire village—and blamed it on Lumi. She knew him intimately.

"Where? At school?" Noelle inquired. "Let's call the police and report it."

"I have seen him many times, Noelle. And the police can't help us," Lumi said. She gestured toward her apartment. "How did you know that he is Leizei? We must find that necklace." She threw open her apartment door and rushed inside.

Eli looked around with eagerness. Noelle took in the luxury apartment filled with gold details and accents and overstuffed white furniture like the lobby.

"This is pretty nice!" Noelle said and walked into the living room, peering out the huge window where it overlooked the city.

Lumi looked around the upscale apartment. She'd had many homes, and this one was hardly anything in comparison to some of the others. But it would do for now.

"I heard about the Leizei from you initially, but mostly Eli told me about them."

Noelle smiled at Eli, who looked sheepish.

Lumi paused, then looked over Eli, who swallowed. "I've heard legends about a group called the Leizei. You know that there's a fire realm and people can manipulate fire and heat." Eli shrugged. "I figured he belongs to that because I saw him move really fast. He definitely isn't human."

Lumi wanted to interrogate the boy. She wanted to pry information from him—going to any length to do so—but because he was friends with the girl, she would play nice. For Noelle's sake.

"And how do *you* know about the Leizei?" Lumi asked. If the boy knew about the necklace *and* the Leizei, he could be a real problem.

"I've heard stories," he said and shrugged.

"So how do you know Scarface?" Noelle asked.

"Scarface?" Eli turned to Noelle.

"Yeah, I nicknamed the creep." Noelle set her navy bag on the kitchen table.

Lumi sighed. "Can you just trust me?"

"Lumi, I'm trusting you as a friend. You don't have to tell me about your family or even about where you've seen Scarface. But loyalty and honesty are really important to me," Noelle said. She eyed Lumi.

"I will never lie to you. I might have many failures, but lying is not one of them." Lumi's eyes shifted to the floor.

"Well, you're quite secretive," Noelle said.

"Who wants to go out?" Eli interrupted, looking back and forth between them.

"She probably needs to rest," Lumi said.

"Or let's go out," Eli suggested again. His face lit up in a childish way.

"I like the sound of that," Noelle admitted.

"And what about Scarface?" Lumi asked.

"He's out cold for the night," Eli said. "I made sure of it."

They walked together around Millenium Park and held cotton candy. Both Eli's and Noelle's teeth chattered, and once Lumi noticed it, she pretended to be freezing too.

Eli curiously ate his cotton candy, and his eyes widened. Lumi didn't drop her guard as they laughed and roamed the park together. Large crowds formed around them, and a street performer played impressive drums with plastic paint containers.

"Wait until you meet Marko's family! You'll love them. They're really sweet and super hospitable. But his mom won't stop asking if you want more food," Noelle said.

"That is pretty typical of Serbs."

Lumi looked at a stand with glowing lights that appeared like swords and crowns. Noelle followed her gaze, then gave a small laugh.

"Please buy three, Lumi!"

If it were anybody else, Lumi would say no and inform them of how stupid it was. But because it was Noelle, she rolled her eyes and obliged.

"I'll take three, please," Lumi said to the stand owner and handed him cash. He gave her three light-up crowns. Lumi wondered what sort of amusement this might bring to the girl, but her bright eyes glowed as she placed the crown on her head and the flashing light streamed across her brow.

Eli gladly wore his crown, but he held it wearily before he placed it.

Lumi eyed Cloudgate. She pointed at the silver bean-shaped statue. "I've seen so many famous photos of this."

Eli looked utterly disgusted. "What is that?"

Noelle shrugged. "A tourist thing. Come on, you can stand underneath it and even see the city in the reflection!"

They stood underneath the silver bean, and when Lumi looked up at it, she could see their reflection perfectly in the belly of the bean's reflection above their heads. She shook her head as she took in the childish glowing light-up crown on her brow. Only Noelle could manage to convince her to wear such a hideous, outlandish thing. The heat in her chest spread, and she grimaced as she realized she was becoming increasingly soft because of the girl.

But then Lumi audibly gasped.

"Lumi, what is it?" Noelle looked upward at the reflection, and Eli did too. And then they gasped.

In the reflection, a blue light glowed from Noelle's right pocket where the hint lay. They all stared at the reflection at the blue light that emitted from her pocket, speechless. Lumi snapped her head down, noticing that Noelle's pocket wasn't gleaming. Yet in the mirror of the bean above their heads, it shone.

"Look up," Eli whispered.

Lumi began to look around. Nobody seemed to notice the light in Noelle's pocket in the bean's reflection. In reality, coupled with their beaming light-up crowns, her glowing pocket didn't draw much attention. Had they not known any better, it could easily be dismissed as light from their crowns. Noelle's fingers retrieved the brown, crumpled paper, and she held it with the tips of her fingers.

"Hint three says to find the next clue, you'll need to look up. Your inspection will be in the reflection." Noelle looked down at the brown paper with blue ink.

Lumi tapped Noelle's shoulder and pointed up. When they each looked up, they saw a bright sapphire light glowing from her fingertips. She looked down again but gasped when all she saw was ordinary brown paper.

"The writing changed!" Lumi smiled, pointing at the bean's reflection. Lumi looked around, but still nobody seemed to notice. She squinted, trying to make out the letters as she looked up in the reflection. Noelle held the paper closer to the bean, and Lumi noticed the words could now be easily read in its reflection. Eli watched Noelle with fascination and placed a palm against the statue.

Dear Noelle,
Congratulations on finding the next hint! You're

getting close! Hint #4: I was married at this place, and the necklace is at the door.

Love,

Lolli (Rose Hudson)

"So we had to look up in a reflection this whole time?" Noelle asked, putting the hint back in her pocket.

"Where did your grandma get married?" Eli asked. "And why is she making you find it through hints?"

"At my childhood home, I think. But to be certain, I have photos stored at Marko's parents' house. We can look at them on Christmas Eve and find out. And my grandma *loved* to play games," Noelle said, and her demeanor sank.

Lumi wondered what could possibly ail the girl when they just discovered their treasure.

Eli walked with an amused look on his chiseled face. "Do you know what the necklace does?"

"Yes," Noelle said. "It can undo things once. I'm going to use it to bring back my grandma."

Lumi would've laughed if it weren't so tragically awful for the girl. She wouldn't be able to wield the necklace's power. "Only a Merklei can utilize the necklace. The Snow Queen means to bring her entire family back from their death and undo the betrayal," Lumi said.

"The humans didn't betray them," Noelle scoffed. "On the contrary, they turned on the humans."

"That's a funny version you've heard." Lumi grimaced. If she had to hear this false narrative one more time, she might lose her ever-loving mind.

"And what version have you heard exactly?" Eli asked.

"I think your version has a lot of loopholes and is extremely flawed. The Snow Queen was a part of a group of beings called Merklei. The Merklei possessed the ability to manipulate cold and snow, and they didn't intermingle with humans at first. The

Merklei lived side by side with the Leizei, a people with the ability to manipulate heat and fire, and the Naturei, a people with the ability to manipulate the earth."

Noelle's ears seemed to perk up when she mentioned Naturei.

"The Leizei king from the fire realm was brutal and considered himself and his kind superior to the humans. He also wanted to scare anybody against rebelling, and he would threaten a life of torture against anyone who opposed his rule. The Naturei king is no different." Lumi sighed.

"I don't know about this version." Noelle sounded skeptical.

"The winners write the history," Lumi reminded her.

"Lumi," Eli said. "I promised Elle that I'd take her to my favorite coffee place. They're open pretty late. She and I need to discuss something alone. Would you mind?"

Lumi turned to Noelle. "Is that what you want?" Lumi wondered why the boy had suddenly shifted the conversation.

Noelle opened her mouth, and after a long pause said, "Yes. I absolutely want that."

Lumi felt her answer was odd but honored it. "Okay, when you're done, you should come back to my apartment. Do you feel you can return safely? Do you know where to find my apartment?"

"Yes."

"Of course." Eli smiled.

"Good. Because you should remember what I said earlier. Have fun!" Lumi said and turned to walk away.

CHAPTER 11
NOELLE
THE NATUREI REALM

Noelle watched Lumi walk away, and dread fell over her. She turned to face Eli, who cocked his head to the side.

"Don't look so offended to spend some quality time with me," Eli said. He looked around at the falling snow, as if it were foreign, and stood in sheer awe.

"What do you want?" Noelle folded her arms. She hated that she was bound to him and couldn't get away from him.

"I told you before; you're the first human I've met, so I'd like to get to know you. I also have a few questions." Eli shrugged and gestured at a nearby coffee shop. "I've heard about coffee shops. Can I get you a coffee?" His smug smile returned.

"Can I say no?" Noelle rolled her eyes.

"Of course. You're not a hostage; you're only tied to the mission of letting me observe your *friend* Lumi. Everything else is completely up to you." His words were steeped in disappointment, as if he had truly hoped Noelle would spend time with him.

Noelle wanted to laugh at his pathetic tone. "You sound like you really want to spend time with me. Are you that desperate for attention?" Noelle grimly smiled at him.

Eli's eyes closed as he laughed. "Attention is not something I need or crave. I have far too much of that in my realm. But I'm interested in your human experience. I've read so many books on it and studied so many lessons. Yet I've always been forbidden to interact with your kind. I figure if I'm playing with fire, I might as well really step in." Eli stepped in closer to Noelle.

Noelle's heart raced slightly as he leaned in toward her. His dark hair danced against his forehead with the wind, and his eyes steadied on hers. Did they not value personal space where he came from? Noelle's eyes tightened on his as she realized his brown-colored eye contacts were gone, and his bright green eyes watched her.

"All right, I'll get coffee with you. But you need to give me some answers about Naturei. And I want to see your realm."

Eli bellowed out laughter and leaned forward, holding his stomach. "No human has ever seen my realm. They'd kill you." His dark hair swayed again in the wind, and the warmth of his smile reached his eyes.

"Then I'm not getting coffee with you. And I'm going to make your life miserable as long as you come around me." Noelle's fists balled up. The urge to strike Eli was intense, but plenty of people were around and she couldn't manage to raise her hand against him. *Lucky him.*

Eli's arrogant smirk remained. "Elle, you already make my life a jumbled mess. You have *no idea.*" He shook his head and looked at her, slowly, and traced his eyes from her feet up to her eyes. She pictured herself punching the smile off his face, which made her grin.

Noelle hated that he seemed to control everything. So in an effort to take back some control, she took a step toward him and hoped that she could portray confidence. "Well, Eli, I never asked you to be in my life, so it looks like that is on you. And if you want me to spend any time with you, outside of what I must suffer in the presence of others, then I demand answers and to be taken into your realm. Whatever that is." She stood so close to Eli that they almost touched each other.

He simply remained where he was and peered down at her.

"Fine, I'll answer any questions that you have. And I will give you five minutes in my realm. But you will do everything that I say while in the Naturei realm, otherwise I cannot protect you. And if you die, then that is on you, and I can't save you."

Die? Noelle thought he must surely be bluffing.

"Deal." She reached out a hand, which he took and shook.

Noelle rolled her eyes. "Jerk. Come on. Let's get that coffee, and I'll get my answers." Noelle proceeded down the pavement toward the coffee shop, and Eli followed her. "Wait! Make it a Naturei vow."

Eli took Noelle's hand in his, and he took her scarf off and wrapped it around their hands to conceal any onlooking eyes from seeing the flash of green light.

"I, Eli Goldner, give you my word that I'll answer any question you have about myself and my realm unless it might put me or my people in danger. And I vow to take you to the Naturei realm for five minutes, where you promise to do everything that I say while we are there." Despite the scarf covering their interlaced fingertips, she could see a flash of green light, and then it was gone. The busy Chicagoans didn't notice. Everybody was far too engrossed in their own affairs to pay attention to it.

"Your last name is Goldner?" Noelle asked.

"Yes, why?" Eli looked down at Noelle curiously.

"That might be the prettiest last name that I've ever heard." Noelle regretted the words as soon as they escaped her lips. Eli looked far too pleased. "Don't get a big head."

Eli's lips turned upward, and he leaned in even closer. "Are you trying to tell me that you would like to take my last name, Elle?"

And with that, Noelle shoved him, hard. "Let's go, you big oaf."

They entered the coffee shop and headed toward the register where a bored barista stood.

"What will it be?" the barista asked tiredly. Her eyes flicked between Noelle and Eli. Eli, bright-eyed and seemingly puzzled, looked over the menu.

"I'll take a latte and whatever he wants," Noelle said and pointed at Eli. But he stood, mouth agape, and scanned the words over and over again. Somebody behind them cleared their throat. "Would you like a suggestion?" She felt anxious by his long pause. Chicago moved fast, but clearly he didn't.

"Yes," Eli said finally.

"Make it two lattes," Noelle said.

The barista tapped on the register. "That'll be $10.47 please." The barista flipped the screen to face them and then disappeared.

Noelle looked at Eli, who didn't budge. "You're supposed to pay now," Noelle said through her teeth.

Eli looked surprised and patted his pockets. "I think I left the money in my realm," he said with amusement. "I guess you'll have to cover it."

Noelle glared at him and hastily pulled out her own wallet. She found two dollars inside of it. Her credit card and debit card were no good either. "Change of plans, Goldner." She grabbed him by his arm and dragged him to the counter; but she loosened her grip when she felt the strong, tense muscles under her fingers. He seemed strong, and she worried she might truly be in over her head. His face was blank, but he carefully watched her with his striking green eyes.

"You made this wrong. It doesn't look right," a customer said and refused to pick up the coffee on the counter. The barista rolled her eyes and went to the back room. Noelle eyed the incorrect drink and then swiped it off the counter. It had the name Tom scribbled on the side.

"What are you doing?" Eli asked with brows knit together.

"Shut up." Noelle grabbed his arm again, perhaps against her better judgment, and led him out of the store quickly into the snowy outdoors. They walked briskly for a few steps, and then she dropped her hand.

"Did you just *steal* that coffee?" Eli asked incredulously.

"Oh, so you have morals now? You can stalk, manipulate, and lie, but I'm the bad one for taking a coffee?" Noelle threw a haughty glance in his direction and then sipped Tom's drink, to discover he ordered a cappuccino. "Besides, it would have just gotten thrown away."

"I'm saving many people's lives by being here," Eli said with a serious tone. "So my deeds are excusable in the grander scheme of things. But yours? Stealing is *low*."

Noelle scoffed. "It is only low to people who have never known the feeling of going to bed hungry. And I *know* they would have tossed it out!"

Eli flinched. He hesitated, then met her eyes. And for the first time since she had met him, Noelle could see remorse on his typically pompous, confident face. But she didn't want his sympathy, so she turned away from him.

"There is a bench up there. Come on," she said. She walked to a cold, black bench and sat down. Eli joined her and sat stiffly.

"I'll take your questions now." Eli's eyes rested on Noelle. He watched her curiously, as he had all night. It was as if everything she said and did was foreign and fascinating to him, and his full attention was laid on her.

"What on earth is *Naturei*?"

"We live in our own realm, sort of like a different world. We have the ability to interact with nature. We work hard to bring up plants, crops, and use our abilities to live. But things have been out of alignment for a while. The Snow Queen's curse has prevented us from using our abilities whenever she is around. We rarely visit Earth, and interacting with humans is forbidden according to our realm's laws." Eli's eyes trailed across Noelle. She tried her best to not show any emotion, but she was intrigued. He pointed at the falling snow. "And she is here."

"But you can use your abilities in your own realm, away from the Snow Queen?"

"Correct." He studied her. "You're taking this well for a human."

Noelle considered that for a moment. A lot had happened over the course of a few weeks, and if she really stopped to consider it all, she felt she might go insane.

"What exactly can you do?" Noelle asked, eyeing him.

Eli leaned forward and placed gentle fingers over her wound. Before she could shove him away, she realized her wound from earlier had completely healed under his fingertips. She raised her own hands to her neck and gulped.

"A few things. I can heal injuries, for example. But all Naturei can move anything made of nature. We can grow any plant, and we can also make weapons out of the earth for protection. We can do many things with the earth, but our role is mostly to help protect our realm and society while providing for our realm. And we had discussed helping your world, but everything is out of order."

"So your realm isn't on this planet? And you said no humans know about you?"

"Correct," he said with a wry smile. "I've committed treason by finding you. But I'm desperate. A man that was like a father to me told me to find you. That advice cost him his life. And there are rumors that a dead body was found in the Leizei realm with your name written next to it." His face fell gravely serious as if he were lost in thought.

Noelle noticed the dark circles under his eyes. "I didn't have anything to do with that. Why did somebody do that?" Noelle tried to hide her fingers that now felt shaky at the mention of the dead body. Whether Noelle liked it or not, she was now at the center of a powerful necklace hunt, a murdered body, and several realms that tracked her. Noelle hated too much attention, and this seemed to be the worst sort of it.

Eli closed his eyes and sighed. He gripped the bridge of his nose between his thumb and index finger. "There has been an uprising, and the dead Leizei body belonged to the king's adviser, so that alone sent a message. But my realm doesn't understand it, and neither do I. I've tracked you for months, and it appears that you've had no connection to the Leizei realm, besides the recent Leizei who has harassed you about the necklace. The Leizei realm keeps to themselves, and we only recently interacted with them because they have remained very separate. *How* did your family end up with the necklace?" His eyes scanned hers.

Noelle felt her stomach tie into knots. She shrugged.

Eli's features softened; he must have believed her. "Could I try the coffee?"

"No." Noelle huffed. "It's stolen. Get your own," Noelle said and took another sip. When his cocky grin grew wider, she shook her head. "I'd punch you if I could."

"*You* fight?" Eli looked far too entertained for Noelle's liking.

"Lift the vow, Goldner. Find out. If you really tracked me, you should know I'm decent from my gym sessions." Noelle smiled her sweetest smile. "Can we go to your realm now?" She hadn't known what to expect, but she hoped for something brilliant. The idea of visiting some far-off realm sounded exciting and adventurous to her.

Eli sighed. "All right. Once we get there, we must change your clothes immediately, otherwise they'll know you're not Naturei. We also must find a cloak to cover your eyes. I'll say that you are one of my armor bearers, since you're quite short. Most of them are only thirteen or so, so you should look about the right size."

Noelle grimaced at his comment about her height, then shrugged and decided to let it go. All she truly cared about was seeing this foreign realm.

"And you will not speak to anybody in the realm. If you get caught, then you're on your own. Do you understand?" Eli's face looked intense again.

"Okay, when do we go?" Noelle asked excitedly.

"Now," he said and stood up. He walked toward a plant in the snow. Oddly, it was very similar to the one by her apartment; it was lively, bright green, and healthy. Eli leaned down and held the leaves in his hand.

"Give me your hand," he said and reached out toward Noelle.

She hesitantly gave it to him, and his warm fingers wrapped around hers. As he slid his fingers across her hand, the heat from his touch made Noelle's cheeks turn scarlet. And then all she could see was a flash of green light, and she couldn't see anything besides it.

They were on a dirt floor. Noelle sat up and gasped. Her disheveled dark hair was strewn around her face, and she pushed it back. She was inside the most exquisite bedroom she had ever seen. The tall ceilings were made of dark wood, and every inch of them were carved and decorated with flakes of gold and lapis lazuli stones.

Plants adorned the large window, and colorful butterflies floated among them. Noelle spun around, gaping at the many plants that surrounded the bedroom. She had never seen some of them before; the ones with the blue stems and dusty violet petals quite literally took her breath away. In the middle of the room, a bed made of one large pillow stood in the center, draped with gold sheets. Noelle inhaled, and the scent of the fresh saplings refreshed her.

She looked around, and it looked like the most lush, beautiful botanical garden and less like a bedroom with the numerous greenery surrounding them. One plant in particular caught Noelle's eyes because it was bright orange coated in dusty blue swirls, and it just so happened to be her grandma's favorite colors. She wished she could take it with her to her grandma's grave. But once she found the necklace and brought her grandma back—she would be able to tell her all about this orange plant with the long, pretty orange petals and the blue stem that protruded at the top.

"This is my room. I need to get us both some clothes," Eli said. He disappeared momentarily behind a curtain and then returned with an array of green garments in his hands. Except they weren't ordinary clothes. They weren't clothes at all.

"What is *that*?" Noelle pointed a finger at the leafy outfits. In Eli's hands were vines, leaves, and petals all sewn together. It took Noelle a moment to realize her mouth was open. She closed it. It was no longer a wonder why Eli found humans fascinating. She found his world fascinating too.

"We wear nature in my realm. Here, try this on. You can change over there," he said and pointed to a gold curtain made from some unknown material. "You'll need to put a cloak over it since it's for boys."

She gingerly took the leafy garment and concealed herself behind the curtain. She pulled off her clothes and tried to unravel the leaves. It was structured similarly to a pair of pants, with several leaves intricately stitched together with what appeared to be vines. She put it on, but it was unlike anything she had ever worn. How was she supposed to wear this? She managed to place the strap of leaves across one shoulder, and the vine belt went around her waist. It reminded her somewhat of overalls. Noelle looked over her shoulder at the mirror on the wall, and her eyebrows rose. The garments were stunning—they formed on her body like art. She ran her fingers over the leaves that seemed to fit so comfortably.

"I think it fits perfectly! Lucky guess on my size!" Noelle excitedly called out from behind the curtain.

"No, that is how our garments work. When you wear them, the leaves will wrap themselves around you."

Noelle peered down and eagerly ran her fingers over the material. "I've never seen any clothing so beautiful in my life."

She looked in the mirror and with satisfaction, threw the hooded cloak over her face. She was covered nearly entirely with only her hands exposed. The cloak had covered much of her body, and to her surprise, it didn't form to her like the other leaves.

She stepped out from the golden curtain and faced Eli, who gave an approving nod. "Well, as long as you manage not to yap, they won't know. Keep your eyes covered with the cloak, or they'll know that you're human."

Eli stood in a leafy ensemble which had a bare chest. He had one taupe vine strap across his chest, and it was attached to what resembled pants. Chestnut vines circled his arms and fingers. Armlets of vines gathered on his right arm, and a circlet wreath of leaves crowned his head. Noelle inhaled as she took in the sight of him. If he weren't so haughty, she might have given him a compliment—he was strikingly handsome, perhaps even painfully so. However, she wouldn't dare risk increasing the size of his head. She simply stared in awe at the odd outfit he wore.

"How do you like our clothing?" Eli asked.

"It's stunning," Noelle said quickly. She could afford that compliment at the very least. "I've never seen anything like it." Noelle whirled around Eli's room and took in the sight. She felt so lucky to have seen this, to simply be able to see this realm. At that moment, she felt like the luckiest girl in the world. "I really like that orange plant. What's it called?"

"It's my favorite. It is called the alanis." Eli walked over to it. "It is extremely rare, and it takes nine years to grow."

"It's the most beautiful plant that I've ever seen in my life," Noelle said as she admired it. It was tall, nearly as tall as her. It had an ombre orange with faded shades as it went up.

Eli, with his eyes fixated on Noelle, stretched out his hand toward the alanis plant. A brown vine came sprawling toward Noelle, and then an orange flower with long, flowing petals grew instantly from the vine. Eli plucked it and then tucked it behind Noelle's ear. His fingers brushed her ear.

"A pretty flower for a pretty girl," Eli said as he looped vines with his index finger through her hair. The flower wasn't going to go anywhere now that the vines had intertwined behind her ear.

Noelle's eyes widened as she ran her fingers along the vines. She had just watched Eli manipulate nature, forcing her mouth to fall open. She tried to recover quickly but couldn't.

Eli gave a half smile as he studied the flower in her hair and then her. "Come on, I'll give you one lap around the palace grounds, and then we're leaving." Eli motioned toward the wooden door that had art carvings in it. Noelle couldn't recognize the art; they were distinctly Naturei.

She would have been perfectly content to simply stay and stare at the plants in his bedroom. She pulled the cloak down on her face and walked toward the door.

Once they stepped into the hall, she realized it was also filled with exotic plants that lined the hallway. Plants with blue hues and purple spots stood against the walls, perfectly lined up. They each emitted mist that evaporated after a few moments but left a sparkly residue.

Eli walked and Noelle fell into step and walked behind him. But her face constantly looked to the left and the right as they walked past the plants. The dirt hallway felt strange to her though. She hadn't ever seen dirt floors inside before—but if they really relied on the earth for things, it made sense to her. The entire building seemed to be made of all natural materials.

Noelle nearly bumped into Eli when she realized he stopped. There were people ahead, and they walked toward them.

Eli craned his neck toward Noelle. "Do not say a word. I'll protect you as long as you don't speak."

The seriousness in his voice was enough to make Noelle understand the graveness of the situation. Not only was she in danger, but so was he. He had said it was treasonous to mingle with humans, and here she was in his realm and by his doing. She gave a nod to show she understood.

He clenched his jaw and turned to the approaching Naturei. They were dressed in similar outfits with green leaves sewn together beautifully and perfectly aligned to their bodies. Except they each wore body armor on top of their garments, and it covered much of their bodies. But this armor was made of some material that she couldn't fathom. They each held weapons in their hands, and although they looked similar to guns, they also hardly resembled them. It was obvious that the weapons were made of natural materials, yet they looked lethal. They each wore a green leafy beret-style hat on their heads too. Noelle then understood it—they were soldiers.

She sucked in a breath. Noelle wondered why Eli had a

bedroom on the castle grounds and assumed he must be a soldier too.

"Prince Eli! Where have you been?" one soldier called out to him and made a fist over his chest. The other soldiers also made the salute, and Eli did it back.

All eyes fell on Noelle, who quickly made a fist to her own chest, then returned her hand to her side.

Noelle's eyes snapped to the back of Eli's head. *Prince?*

She tugged on the cloak again, making sure that her face was concealed entirely. It was. Noelle's legs suddenly felt wobbly at the realization that Eli was the heir of this realm. She recalled his words on the train about if she had just known who he was and all the other arrogant words. It suddenly made sense. He had an inflated sense of worth because he was *royalty*.

"I've been in my bedroom," Eli said. "What might be the occasion that you're here on my grounds?" Eli's voice was stern and suspicious.

"The king sent us to check on you." The soldier spoke almost apologetically.

"I'm fine, thanks. I was just returning to my room." Eli turned on his heel, and Noelle stayed in step behind him. Her legs felt wobbly when she realized the soldiers' eyes were glued to her.

"Actually..." The soldier spoke up hesitantly. "The king demands that you see him now."

Eli stopped and begrudgingly turned to face the soldiers. "Right, then we'll go. My armor bearer will just return something to my room for me."

"Sir, one of your armor bearers always accompanies you during their allotted time; it is your duty. Why would you break the tradition?"

Eli sighed. "I guess he will be coming with me to the meeting with the king. We wouldn't want to spoil his apprenticeship training." Eli shot a look in Noelle's direction, which seemed to emphasize the danger she was in. Noelle felt her throat go dry and walked forward on her shaky legs.

She tried her best to keep her gaze on Eli's back. The soldiers walked in a line, effortlessly keeping in pace with one another. She hoped they couldn't see her legs trembling. They walked on the dirt path, and Noelle tried hard not to glance around too much; surely armor bearers were used to the sight of the palace. But she just couldn't manage to pry her eyes away too long.

There were hedges along the path that held glowing violet flowers inside them. A purple dust that fell from the flowers permeated the air. The fragrance smelled something like lavender but spicier. Noelle hated that she had to tear her eyes off the beautiful plants, but she had to keep pace with the soldiers and Eli. Her eyes roamed over the palace grounds, and then she saw it. The palace was grand with tall pillars at the front and a large citadel with walled fortresses.

On top of the castle were green flags, and Naturei soldiers lined the entrances and stood guard at the top with weapons in hand. Exotic plants adorned the grounds outside the castle, and many vines spread across the castle walls in elaborate designs.

Noelle suddenly regretted coming to the Naturei realm. She simply hadn't given it much thought, and it had sounded adventurous; but now it seemed dangerous. She hadn't expected to see the king. He was the last person she wished to see.

At the sight of Eli, the guards each saluted by putting a fist over their heart. Eli did the gesture back, and all whom he passed by stopped to look at him. Noelle felt self-conscious about so many eyes on them. She pulled on her hood, again, and hoped it hadn't risen up on their walk. It hadn't.

The guards allowed them to pass, and nobody seemed to notice Noelle was human. They passed through a long dirt hallway, and ahead were several Naturei guards that stood beside a man with a leafy wreath crown on his head, except his crown was gold, unlike Eli's. It dawned on Noelle that each of the Naturei had the same deep green eye color.

The king faced Eli, and a warm smile grew on his face. He was tall and regal, yet he didn't seem to resemble Eli at all. His long dark hair was swept back, and his handsome tawny complexion was radiant and smooth like a diamond surface. He stood with such authority that Noelle was certain it had to come from a lifetime of his position and stature.

"Eli." The king greeted him. They both reached out their right arm, gripping one another's wrists. "I've been worried about you."

Eli's entire body went taut for a very brief moment, and then he composed himself. "There isn't anything to be nervous about, father," Eli said with a blank face. Noelle noticed that they didn't look anything alike, except that they both had green eyes. Otherwise, none of their features matched. The king certainly wasn't his father.

"You've been absent lately. You've been secluded in your room ever since your traitor educator suggested you find the human girl. I'm concerned." The king's apple-green eyes looked over Noelle, and she could feel the sweat that built on her brow and behind her knees. Her heart hammered against her rib cage. Noelle panicked as realization set in; on the train, Eli had said destiny intertwined their fate. She now had so many new questions for Eli.

The king returned his focus to Eli. "You will not be interacting with the girl regardless of what your educator said or the rumors. Do you understand? You will not interact with humans; I forbid it as your High King." The king returned his gaze to Noelle. Her heart thumped even faster.

"Understood," Eli said with a nod.

The king intertwined his long fingers. Noelle studied him for a moment. The king looked like he was in his early thirties.

"Eli," the king's deep voice rang. He fixed his eyes on Noelle.

"Father," Eli said with a nod. *Father?*

"I'd like to say one last thing," the High King said and kept his eyes on Noelle. It seemed the message wasn't for Eli at all. "If you decide to interact with her, then I'll have to remove your access to all keiloki portals."

Eli's face fell, yet he remained silent.

"And unfortunately, I'll have to kill the girl myself. She will be a danger to our people if she knows about the Naturei." The king laughed without amusement.

Noelle's throat felt so incredibly dry. She tried to hold her hands steady, though they trembled.

"I suppose you have some things to take care of—that is, unless I should take care of them for you." The king said the words with malice and stared at Noelle, and then he turned and left. Everyone followed him except for Eli and Noelle. Noelle let out an exasperated breath once they were alone.

"You have to go." Eli took her hand in his as soon as the king exited, and he hurriedly rushed her outside where a keiloki portal plant was.

"This realm is incredible," she said.

Eli looked around and then reached for the keiloki plant. "I'd say you're welcome anytime, Elle. But that just isn't true. I hope you enjoyed it."

"Will I ever see you again?" Noelle placed a hand over his strong, muscled shoulder.

He stopped just before he made contact with the portal. "That depends on whether he kills me or not." Eli gave a half smile.

He took her hand into his and then touched the keiloki plant, and with a flash of vibrant green light, they were back in Chicago.

She looked down, but they still held hands. His warm skin against hers sent a fire along hers. She quickly let go. To her surprise, the Chicagoans didn't seem to notice their comings or goings. The portal must have a way of not drawing attention, or perhaps it even repels onlookers' attention.

Eli tore his eyes from their hands to Noelle's eyes. "I'm going to try to come back, because I do have orders to track and kill the Snow Queen. But I'm curious—what you said in the car—about your family being gone. Was that true?" Eli asked, dropping her hand.

Noelle stood in disbelief. His king was ready to pounce on

him, yet he was curious about her family. His eyes pooled with sympathy.

"Yes," Noelle said finally.

"I lost my parents too. The king adopted me because he lost his partner and child. You and I aren't so different in some ways," Eli said with a shrug. Noelle had noticed he had become much kinder since the car ride and wondered if empathy had seized him.

"My head is spinning. You're going to kill the Snow Queen? Wait, *you're a prince?*" Noelle asked and stood shakily.

She heard Eli sigh loudly. "Yes, I will and yes, I am. Well, I might be stripped of my titles if I don't hurry." He grinned at her and crossed his arms.

"Then what are you still doing here? Go!" Noelle pushed him toward the keiloki portal plant.

"Do you promise to get back safely?"

"I promise." Noelle nodded.

"Bye, Elle. I hope this isn't my last time seeing you." He looked back at Noelle and gave her a warm smile before touching the portal and disappearing.

CHAPTER 12
NOELLE
LUMI'S APARTMENT

Noelle knocked on Lumi's apartment door, and she quickly opened it. Lumi's tall figure ushered her into the room and gestured for her to sit on the couch.

"How was your coffee?" Lumi crossed her arms. Of course Lumi's pajamas were silk and matched. Noelle expected nothing less from Lumi; even her pajamas were fashionable. Noelle couldn't picture Lumi wearing pajamas like hers—oversized shirts with holes in them.

"It was fine."

"Really?" Lumi said and blinked. Her long blond hair draped her face. "You seemed pretty uptight around him tonight."

Noelle swallowed. "Yes, I was. Um, maybe it was nerves." She shrugged. It was true that only a few hours earlier, she was horribly annoyed with Eli. Noelle shook her head. Perhaps she should still hate Eli. Feelings of bitterness and intrigue mixed together and collided inside Noelle. Her fascination seemed to outweigh her frustration with him.

"You *really* like him?" Lumi cleared her throat.

"I do." There was much more that Noelle wanted to say, like how Eli got on her last nerve also. However, the Naturei vow wouldn't let her say that.

Lumi gave a simple nod. "Well, just be smart."

Noelle gave her a sideways glance. "Lumi, what is going on with you and Marko?" Noelle asked, eager to get the attention off her.

Lumi stirred in her seat slightly. "What do you mean?"

"You're guarded. I have never seen Marko fall for anybody with such intensity. In fact, I've never even seen him show any interest in somebody before. You literally have him wrapped around your finger," Noelle said. "I just hope you understand how involved he is." Noelle hadn't meant the words to sound like an accusation. But judging by the way Lumi flinched, that was exactly how it came off.

Lumi's mouth twitched. She looked entirely caught off guard. "I-I haven't been close to anybody in a very long time. I struggle with letting people in, and you're right—I am guarded. But Marko has been so kind and reminded me that there is still goodness in this depraved world. Sort of like you." Lumi's eyes trailed to the ground where she seemed to be lost in thought. "Marko is everything that is good about humanity." A ghost of a smile appeared.

Noelle gave a nod. She was pleased to hear that. She had worried that he moved too quickly and became too attached. "I'm really glad. If you two keep going at the pace you're at, you might have a ring by spring."

Lumi didn't laugh. She simply looked at Noelle with a blank face. Sometimes Noelle thought Lumi might be the oddest person she had ever met in her life.

"It's a joke," Noelle said.

"Why would I get a ring by the spring? I don't understand."

Noelle groaned. "It is a joke." She had reiterated the words, but they didn't seem to help. "It means you're both moving really fast. He might even propose to you by the spring."

Lumi sat and stared at her. "Your joke is stupid."

Noelle shook her head and laughed. She couldn't help it—Lumi was by far one of the most bizarre and interesting people that she had ever met. That was, besides Eli. Noelle eyed Lumi, and suspicion crept onto her as she did. Surely she couldn't be the woman behind the legend. Surely she wasn't *the* murderous Snow Queen.

A shudder went down Noelle's spine as suspicion manifested deeper and etched its way into her mind. What were the odds that Lumi was *the* Snow Queen? She didn't look like a monster, nor did she seem like a bloodthirsty maniac. She seemed more like an odd, out-of-place foreign exchange student. Lumi couldn't hurt a fly, let alone masses of humans.

Noelle pondered Lumi's words about the legend being wrong; her words about the Snow Queen being innocent and framed for crimes she didn't commit.

"Noelle." Lumi interrupted her thoughts.

"Sorry, I got lost in thought!" Noelle remarked quickly. How had she found herself at the center of all this? Noelle wondered if the hints to the necklace had somehow drawn the Leizei, the Naturei prince, *and* the Snow Queen to herself.

"Lumi, you know you can trust me, right?" Noelle said with a smile. But then her smile disappeared as she remembered she had a pact with Eli to spy on her, and he planned to kill the Snow Queen. Guilt suddenly weighed heavily on her shoulders. Perhaps it was best if she didn't get official news that Lumi was the Snow Queen.

Lumi said nothing but watched Noelle intently with a slight trace of something in her eyes. Her light-colored eyes hardened, and they looked downright icy.

"I promise that you can trust me. No matter what and no matter what your past looks like. You've gained a friend for life." Noelle wanted to reassure her. And she meant every word of it. She wished she could exchange a Naturei vow with Lumi to show her how certain she was about it. She wished Lumi would open up to her, but instead, she sat there—with uncertainty that clouded her features.

"Thanks," Lumi said in a quiet tone and gazed out the window.

"And I'd like you to dress me for Christmas. Your style is impeccable, and I'd love to borrow something."

That was enough to make Lumi jump off the couch with glee and delight. She grabbed Noelle's hand and led her to her bedroom where the large closet was filled with multitudes of dresses in seemingly every style and color. Lumi pulled dresses and held them up to Noelle's shoulders.

"We'll find the perfect outfit for you!" Lumi beamed.

CHAPTER 13
NOELLE
CHRISTMAS EVE

Noelle hadn't seen Eli for days, but her mind often drifted to him.

Noelle wore Lumi's sparkling dark green high-low gown with flowing fabric at the bottom. The long sleeves, which likely fit Lumi perfectly, felt slightly too big—as did the hem. But it felt very comfortable, and Lumi's face illuminated when Noelle came back into the living room.

"Oh, Noelle," Lumi said and clasped her hands. "It looks absolutely brilliant on you." Lumi placed her hands on her shoulders and guided her toward the mirror.

Noelle stood in front of Lumi's elaborate black bedroom mirror. She first looked at Lumi in the mirror, who stood a whole head taller than her. Then she looked at herself and admired the dress in the mirror. The deep green contrasted nicely against her bronze skin, and she could hardly recognize herself since she always wore hoodies, jeans, and sweats. The elaborate details of the dress were quite intricate with emerald gemstones at the waist, which reminded her of Eli's eyes. He hadn't said when he might be back, but she hoped it would be soon.

"Wow. I look a lot more sophisticated," Noelle said incredulously.

"We could style your hair in an updo, and I have heels you can borrow since it is a bit long." Lumi pointed at the dress, which pooled around Noelle's ankles.

"Yeah, I'd like that. And tonight we could look at the pictures from my grandma's wedding." Noelle changed the subject, eager to take the focus off herself.

"Sounds like a perfect plan," Lumi said, and she grinned in the mirror. She looked quite pleased that Noelle wore her dress. Noelle imagined if she allowed her, she would dress her up every day.

Lumi parked in front of Marko's family home, where slush abounded. She stepped out in a sparkling gold sequined gown. Her hair had been curled and pinned back, and she wore matching dangling earrings. Noelle also exited Lumi's bright car, holding up the borrowed green dress.

"Merry Christmas Eve!" Marko leaned against his porch and gazed at Lumi and looked her up and down before he offered his arm. She took it and gracefully walked in her big heels. Marko's parents and sister emerged from the doorway.

Noelle hobbled and Lumi offered her free arm to her.

"Wow, you both look great," Marko said as they walked toward the home. Marko's black suit and black tie seemed to be drowned in cologne.

"Thank you!" Noelle smiled at Lumi.

"Noelle!" Danica embraced Noelle on the sidewalk just outside the home. Her dark lipstick framed a magnificent smile.

"This is Lumi," Marko said, facing his family. Danica let go of Noelle and hugged Lumi. "Lumi, this is my sister Danica and my mom and dad—Nikola and Katarina."

"We have heard so many amazing things about you. We're so excited that you're in Chicago and spending Christmas with us! Welcome to the states!" Danica squealed.

Their mother, Katarina, greeted them both. Her dark hair looked as if it had been blown out, and her dark eyes appeared warm. "Oh, Noelle! We are so happy that you're here. And Lumi, thanks for joining us." Katarina hugged them both, and then their father, Nikola, hugged them too. Nikola and Marko looked strikingly more similar now compared to just a few years ago. As they stood side by side, there was no question that they were father and son. Yet Nikola still maintained about an inch on Marko.

"Are you doing okay?" Marko asked Noelle.

"Um, yeah. What do you mean?"

"Well, Lumi had to dash the other day. Something about some emergency you had. Is everything okay?"

Noelle put a hand over her neck, where the healed wound had been. "Oh, right. Yeah, I'm fine— I just—"

"It's so cold! Let's get inside," Katarina said. "We just came back from the church service. It was so lovely!"

They walked toward the tall, white home, where Christmas lights were strewn across the trees, plants, and lined the home. As they stepped inside, Noelle quickly flung off her shoes in relief. The warm, cozy living room was decorated in Christmas decor. A well-decorated tree was in the corner of the living room, next to the fireplace, which had large flames emerging from it. Assorted foods of ham, chicken, Serbian beef dishes, vegetables, and a plethora of desserts were sprawled out on the dinner table. In the center of the table was a chocolate birthday cake with the words HAPPY BIRTHDAY, JESUS sprawled across it in cursive.

"Please, let me take your jackets." Marko took Lumi's first and helped her out of it. Noelle had already taken hers off and handed it to him. Lumi and Noelle made their way to the kitchen. Several framed photos were on the walls, many of which featured Noelle.

Once everyone had arrived, they all sat together and Nikola prayed, giving thanks to God, and then began their Christmas Eve meal.

"To family." Nikola raised his glass. Katarina, Marko, and Danica raised their glasses, then turned to Lumi and Noelle.

Noelle shakily picked up her glass, filled with sparkling grape juice. Noelle lit up. The Jokovics were the closest thing she had to a family. And now they were adding a new member, which Noelle was grateful for. She wasn't the only newcomer any longer, and she also had quickly grown to love Lumi. After spending several days at her apartment, she couldn't blame Marko for loving her. She was quirky, funny, and irresistibly sweet like confectioners' sugar, albeit she seemed quite reserved and cold to strangers.

All eyes rested on Lumi now. Her dangling earrings shone in the light.

"Oh! *Me?*" Lumi quickly picked up her glass, and she toasted. Marko wrapped his arm around her.

"You're family now too." Katarina warmly smiled and took a sip of her drink. A lipstick mark remained on the rim of her glass. They all drank from their cups, but Lumi remained frozen. She seemed to snap out of it after a moment, then also savored her drink. Her chest seemed to rise, then fall at a rapid pace. Her hand went over heart.

Just when Noelle started to become concerned, a wide smile appeared on Lumi's face.

Lumi straightened in her chair. "That means a lot. Thank you." Marko reached for her hand underneath the table.

They ate far too much. Noelle pressed the napkin to her mouth when she finished.

Nikola pulled a small wrapped present from his pocket. "This is for you, Katarina." He handed her the red wrapped box with a silver decorative ribbon on the top. Katarina took the box, and she pulled the wrapping paper off, and inside was a black jewelry box with the name Key & Co. written on it. Katarina opened the black box, and inside was a pair of ruby earrings.

"These are beautiful! Thank you, darling." She kissed his

cheek and sat back down. She then pulled five envelopes out from her black purse, which hung on the back of her chair. "This is for all of you."

Danica took it and gently opened the envelope with her name on it. Marko also took his envelope.

"Yes! Thank you so much!" Danica clasped her hands together. She held a cruise ticket to the Bahamas in her hand.

"Really?" Noelle said aloud and held her own ticket to the cruise. "I have *always* wanted to go on a cruise!" Noelle jumped out of her seat. "This is the best gift *ever*! Thank you, thank you, thank you!" Noelle hugged each of them, then stared at her ticket.

Lumi held a ticket in her own hand, turned it over, and then back again. "You—you are inviting me on your family vacation?"

"Yes, we are inviting you on our family vacation," Marko said with a smile.

Lumi's lips twitched into a smile, but her eyes betrayed her. She was getting emotional.

"This... this is far too kind. Thank you so much for including me in your family trip." Lumi hugged Marko and buried her face into his shoulder.

Eventually, after long conversations and laughter, everyone retired to bed except for Lumi and Marko. Who now sat together by the fireplace, intertwined. Noelle peeked over her shoulder before going to the guest bedroom, which had always been designated "her room." Marko had his arm wrapped around Lumi, and she leaned into him. His other hand twirled in her hair, and she spoke to him in a tone so low that even Noelle, only a mere few feet away, couldn't hear. Noelle averted her eyes and went into the guest bedroom. It was small but clean. The nightstand featured a black-and-white family photo with Noelle. She got into bed, pulled the fresh sheets back and puffed her pillow up, before lying down on the twin-sized bed. She stared at the white plain walls and tossed relentlessly. She ran her tongue over her teeth and realized she had forgotten to brush her teeth. She picked up her toothbrush from her bag and headed toward the bathroom.

Christmas music flooded the living room, and the fireplace was slowly dying down by now. Noelle made it across the hallway, when she looked up, surprised to find Lumi and Marko slow dancing in the living room. It took great willpower to keep from laughing. Marko, who had never had any time for a girlfriend, who hated rom-coms, stood in his own living room, dancing with Lumi on Christmas Eve.

Lumi's fingertips lay on his shoulder, and they held hands while they rocked back and forth. Marko placed his hand on the small of Lumi's back and led her into a spin. He lifted his hand and spun her again. She gave a slight smile, and then Marko closed the gap between them. With their faces inches apart, Marko dipped Lumi, then pulled her back up. She wrapped her arms around his neck, and he leaned down so that their noses touched. Marko moved in, and just before his lips planted onto Lumi's, he locked eyes with Noelle.

Noelle smirked and tried not to laugh at this Romeo version of Marko and walked to her room and gently shut the door. She looked down at her toothpaste and toothbrush, sighed, and placed them back into her bag.

Noelle played a game on her phone for what felt like hours. She lay in the dark room, her phone glowing. The music suddenly died down, and she heard footsteps outside the door. She heard indistinguishable whispers. The door began to open, so Noelle quickly locked her phone, closed her eyes, and pretended to be fast asleep.

"There is an extra twin bed in this guest room that you could sleep in. Noelle usually sleeps in here," Marko's deep voice said. "Thanks for spending Christmas Eve with my family; it means a lot."

"Thanks for everything. I haven't felt this close to a family in a *really* long time." Lumi spoke as if she were surprised by her own words.

"Lumi?"

"Yes?" she whispered.

"I hope this isn't too forward, but I think I'm falling in love with you," Marko said. Noelle's eyes shot open, and her eyebrows rose high. She stayed perfectly still, face to the wall.

A long pause occurred, and Noelle felt horrified for Marko.

"It's mutual," Lumi said in a whisper. Noelle felt some relief for Marko, who might have otherwise had a bruised ego had she not said anything. Marko and Lumi seemed to have some sort of obsession that progressed more quickly than Chicago's fast-paced culture. Noelle closed her eyes again as she listened to Lumi crawl into the other bed. A wide smile spread across Noelle's face as she thought of how she might tease Marko tomorrow.

Noelle tried desperately to sleep, but she just lay in bed in that dark room. She heard a rustle in the backyard but ignored it. Lumi, however, left the room. Noelle didn't think much of it at first, until Lumi never returned. But after a long time, she sat up. She walked into the hallway, then she looked at the bathroom, and everywhere else in the open, but Lumi was nowhere to be found. Noelle peered out of the window into the backyard and saw the silhouette of a person. Noelle opened the back door.

"Hey, what are you doing out here so late?" Noelle whispered. She stepped out onto the patio, her socks dampened with the freezing snow. Noelle neared closer, and the outline seemed larger than Lumi. The Christmas lights shone dimly in the dark and revealed the outline of a man. Noelle froze as the man approached.

"Merry Christmas Eve." Scarface's image materialized as he neared the Christmas light decor. Noelle's heart began to pound, and she stepped backward and fell onto the patio with a loud thud. "So any updates on the next hint? Found the necklace? I'm just checking in," he said. His dark eyes were now visible in the

Christmas lights and they seemed hungry, searching for something from Noelle.

She stood up, but he was close now. He shoved her down.

Another person rounded the corner of the house. A slimmer figure but one that walked very boldly toward Scarface.

"Back up!" Lumi's voice sounded authoritative. She held her hands out, yet Noelle noticed she had no weapon.

Scarface turned toward Lumi and cackled. "Long time no see," he snarled and held his hands out in a similar manner as if he held an imaginary ball. But he also didn't have any weapon in his hands.

"Noelle, go inside. Now." Lumi spoke with an authority in her voice that Noelle hadn't known her to have before.

"No, I'm not leaving you with this creep!" She grabbed a nearby shovel and held it out toward Scarface.

"What will you do with that, darlin'?" Scarface laughed.

Lumi closed in on him, palms still facing each other. "Get out of here!" Lumi's voice was thick with desperation and perhaps a hint of a warning.

Noelle shook her head. "He won't hurt me. He needs me to get the necklace for some reason!" She became increasingly worried as Lumi and Scarface closed the space between them in the snowy backyard.

"According to who?" Scarface turned his face to Noelle, and to Noelle's horror a ball of fire emerged in his hands. It spun in intricate flames. To Noelle's dismay, he launched it toward her, and the loud whoosh that accompanied it was terrifying.

"The Leizei do exist," Noelle gasped and held up her shovel and squinted her eyes in a poor attempt to shield her face. A crackling noise followed the rapid fireball, and Noelle opened her eyes to find a large wall of very thick ice was in front of her. The middle seemed nearly melted where the fireball had hit. Noelle's mouth fell open. She reached out and felt the thick, cold ice with her fingers. Water dripped from the middle where the ice and fire had collided.

THE SNOW QUEEN'S HEIR

Lumi held out her hands, and two large icicles appeared, shaped as sharp daggers. Noelle gasped as she noticed the fine details on them; even the handles were intricately woven.

"Go inside!" Lumi called out and lunged at Scarface. She swung her right dagger in his direction, but he dodged it. He held out his palm, and a flame flowed from it and melted down her left dagger. Lumi lunged forward again and drove her icy dagger into his right thigh. He yelled in anguish. He swung at her with his fist and caught her left temple. She pulled away and stood up.

Noelle remained frozen, unable to move. Lumi spread her hands out as if she were playing an imaginary accordion, and as she did, many tiny, sharp icicles formed in the air above her, all pointed in Scarface's direction. He moved quickly and held his hand out, and a shooting flame like a blowtorch emitted from it. He managed to burn up most of the icicles, but a few landed into his right arm. He gritted his teeth and angrily heaved. He held his hands out together and pushed forward, and a large beam of fire moved toward Lumi.

"No!" Noelle cried out. But Lumi intertwined her own fingers, and a blue light surrounded with icy particles met Scarface's fire. At first the ice and fire met in the middle, but Lumi's icy flow began to overtake his fiery one, and she pushed and pushed until his flame was closing in on him and nearly snuffed.

Just then, a light turned on inside the house. Scarface snapped his face in the direction of the home and then began to sprint away. Lumi chased him for a few steps and threw blocks of ice at his back with both hands. But then she, too, stopped as the door opened.

Marko, wearing red flannel pajamas, stepped onto the patio. He groggily looked around at the snowy backyard and Noelle, who remained on the ground with a shield of thick ice in front of her. Lumi stood surrounded by icicle shards strewn across the snow.

Marko scratched his head, then rubbed his eyes. "What am I looking at?" Marko asked.

Noelle turned to the backyard where Scarface had just jumped the fence. It was an absolute mess. She brushed past Marko and went inside, unsure of what to say to him.

Noelle took off her wet socks and sat by the embers left in the fireplace. She folded her arms around herself. After a moment, Marko entered, followed by Lumi.

"What is going on?" Marko demanded, the sleepiness seemingly gone. He looked wide-awake now.

But neither of the girls spoke. They just looked at each other. Noelle then looked around the familiar living room, which only moments ago held a promising romantic future for Lumi and Marko. Now she wondered what might happen next.

"You should sit down," Noelle said. Marko took a seat by the couch, and Lumi sat next to him.

"Well?" Marko asked and looked at them both.

"I think we've been wrong about the Snow Queen," Noelle said. Noelle wanted to test the waters with Marko. He frowned. "We were always told one version of the legend. How she was a monster, killed many humans, and now she cursed the earth with wintery snow until she got the golden necklace."

"That is the correct version," he said dryly.

Lumi shared her side of the story and watched Marko's face as he seemed to carefully consider it.

"But she killed all of the humans in that kingdom that she turned against," Marko said.

"No, that is not true. She only killed the king and the soldiers who killed the Merklei," Lumi said, looking down.

Marko thought for a moment. "Rubbish," he said.

Noelle winced and figured it might be harder to explain to Marko after all.

Lumi's eyes looked like icy daggers as she looked at Marko.

His hard exterior softened. "What?" He managed an uncomfortable laugh. "I'm not sure about this version. So who wants to explain the backyard?" Marko wrapped an arm around Lumi, but she didn't respond; instead, she sat rigidly. His eyebrows pulled downward, seemingly confused. He reached for her hand that rested on her lap, but she withdrew it.

"I think you should know what I am," Lumi said.

CHAPTER 14
NOELLE
THE REVEAL

Lumi stood to her feet. She held her palms up toward the ceiling, and sadness engulfed her strong features. Lumi looked to Noelle, who nodded in encouragement. Lumi breathed in deeply, then turned to face Marko.

"I know I should have told you both sooner. I just didn't know how to or if I could trust you." Lumi closed her eyes, as if it were a struggle to get the words out. "Look, I've been horribly betrayed by humans, and you're the first people in a really long time that I've become close to. I think you both showed me that I've made a mistake. And honestly, it has been really healing for me and sort of redemptive in a way." Lumi sighed, and Marko sat perfectly still. Lumi's face looked confused and mixed with some sort of internal battle that seemed to struggle within her. "I'm sorry for not telling you both sooner. I owe you both an apology because when I found out that you were going to look for the golden necklace, I was going to take the hints from you and take the necklace. But that was before I—"

"You *what*?" Noelle frowned.

"But that has changed! I didn't know that y-you were... kind," she stammered. "You were *kind* to me, reminding me of why I believed in humans in the first place. You invited me in, made me a friend." She looked sheepish. She didn't look anything like a powerful, treacherous Snow Queen at that moment.

"Lumi, are you delusional? You need sleep," Marko said dismissively.

"You're the first humans that I've been close to since I was betrayed," Lumi said quietly, ignoring Marko's dismissiveness. "You've made me think that I've possibly made a huge mistake by pronouncing a curse."

Lumi extended her fingertips, and a small cloud of falling fluffy snow appeared in front of her. The snowflakes appeared inches above her hands, then disappeared when they touched her skin.

Marko's gaze wandered toward Noelle's, and his eyes widened as he watched Lumi's proof. He swallowed. "So you are Merklei?" Marko asked, his face stoic.

Lumi nodded and then dropped her hands. The snow cloud disappeared with the movement.

"You're *the* Snow Queen?" Marko asked after a beat.

She again nodded. "Oh merca. But your legends are all wrong. I never killed an entire kingdom! I only went after the soldiers and the king who killed my family," Lumi said, her voice raised.

"This is a lot to take in, Lumi." Marko didn't betray any emotions.

Lumi nodded in agreement, then faced Noelle.

Marko seemed to have taken the information much better than Noelle figured he would.

"Then why does the legend say *you* killed the entire kingdom in revenge?" Marko remained unmoved, serious.

"I'm telling you it was the Leizei behind it. How else did the humans miraculously know that the merca drink would make my people weak? They used it to weaken them, then killed them all! Including the children. The Leizei convinced them that we would turn on them, despite remaining faithful and loyally fighting at their side for many years! I did manage to not drink the entire merca they gave me, due to a tip from a *friend*." Lumi said the last word like it was bitter in her mouth. "Well, he betrayed me too, really. But I only went after the soldiers and the king that did it," Lumi said defiantly.

Noelle looked at Lumi with fresh eyes and saw her as possibly ruthless and a cold-blooded killer or perhaps a pained victim in the entire scheme of things. She thought the latter was more likely, but nonetheless, Lumi seemed very dangerous now.

"I understand if this changes things," Lumi said.

Marko now looked at Noelle, perhaps to try to read her thoughts.

"I believe you," Noelle said. Noelle did, in fact, believe her, but she wasn't sure why her grandma had written several warnings about not allowing Lumi to get the necklace. Lumi was not anything like the legends had said she would be.

Lumi put a hand over her heart and clutched at her chest.

"Are you okay?" Noelle asked.

Lumi looked astonished. "Yes."

Marko folded his hands together. His face still remained emotionless. His features looked so different now than a few hours earlier when he and Lumi had danced. All traces of Romeo Marko seemed to have disappeared.

"Why didn't you tell me sooner?" Marko frowned.

"I'm sorry. I would have liked to, but I didn't know if I could trust you."

Nobody moved until Noelle stood up and hugged Lumi. "I'm so sorry about your family, Lumi. I'm sorry you were betrayed. I'm sorry you've become a monster in our legends, and I just have to know one thing." Noelle looked up at her friend. "What will you *really* do with the golden necklace if you get it?"

"I'll be honest. I don't know how your family got ahold of the golden necklace. But it has always been mine. I gave it to my daughter—"

"*You had a daughter?*" Marko asked, surprise riddled on his face. It was as if he finally connected the dots between the Snow Queen's story and Lumi's.

"Yes."

Marko's eyes hardened. "What else have you not told me? Hold on a minute. My grandparents have really suffered because of this weather, Lumi! They've been holed up for months. Has Chicago really gotten such bad weather because of some supposed curse that *you* created?"

"Yes." Lumi bit her bottom lip.

Marko stared at her; then he shook his head. His lips pressed into a straight line.

Lumi swallowed hard. And then there was silence.

"I can lift the curse as soon as the golden necklace is used," Lumi said.

"What will you do with the necklace?" Noelle repeated her question.

"I will bring back my family as if they were never killed. The necklace holds a blue gem inside it that gives the ability to make one change," Lumi said.

Noelle looked to the floor. "I intend to use it to get more time with my grandma," she blurted out.

Lumi locked eyes with Noelle; a flash of frustration danced there. "The only reason I have stayed alive all these years is the hope of finding that necklace," Lumi said. "It belongs to me. Besides, I can save my *entire* family."

Noelle clenched her teeth and looked down again. She wanted the necklace for herself so she could see her grandma again. That was always her plan.

"This is so much to take in all at once. How old are you actually?" Marko asked.

"Well, I stopped aging at twenty-seven," Lumi said. "The Merklei, Leizei, and Naturei stop physically aging when they take on the rites of their people. Everybody chooses to do this at different ages."

"When was that?"

"Around 207 years ago."

"Are you immortal?" Noelle asked, intrigue taking over. She wondered how old Eli might be.

"No, I have a soul just like you. We live much longer than humans. Sometimes for hundreds of years," Lumi said and sat on the couch opposite Marko. Marko and Lumi seemed so close and warm only hours ago, yet now every glance they shared looked defensive.

Marko's gaze rested on Lumi for a moment, but something was wrong. He normally watched her with fascination and perhaps even an unhealthy level of infatuation.

"I'm going to bed," Marko announced and rubbed his eyes. "This is just too much to take in at this time. Don't misunderstand me. I'm not mad, per se. It's just that this is a lot." He started toward his room but stopped and walked to Lumi, who sat rigid on the couch. He leaned down, slowly, and indecision controlled him for a brief moment. But then he made up his mind because he kissed her forehead—let his lips linger on her skin for a long pause and then whispered something into her ear.

She nodded. And then he left.

"What did he say?" Noelle asked. The Christmas decor train set moved in a circle, making faint noise, filling in the silence.

"He said he still stands by something he said to me earlier," Lumi said. "I don't understand either of you. Aren't you scared of me?"

"Yes," Noelle admitted. "But I believe you."

"Why?" A single tear fell onto Lumi's pale cheek as she blinked.

"Because that is what friends do."

"Friends." Lumi repeated the word like it was foreign. It was clear that Lumi had expected them both to reject her and to utterly dismiss her.

Lumi's hands covered her face, and ice began to form around her fingertips as she cried. Noelle hugged Lumi tightly. Lumi's tears hardened into ice, and she brushed them away. The ice tears fell to the floor and made a small noise as they did, like glasses that clink together.

And then together, they walked to the guest bedroom.

Marko suddenly appeared in the guest room and shut the door.

"One last thing. I remembered the snow looking pristinely perfect on the grass. Were you two out here in front of the window?" Marko asked and stared at massive footprints in the snow.

"Scarface," Noelle said and grimaced.

"What?"

"Scarface was the one who fought Lumi in the backyard."

"I'm sorry, *what* happened in my parent's backyard?" Marko's tone dropped.

"I should have told you. This man has been following me. And he has been demanding the necklace," Noelle said. "And he is a Leizei that Lumi knows, but Lumi saved me."

A muscle in Marko's jaw twitched. That was one of the reasons that Noelle never told Marko about Scarface. The muscle twitch was enough of an indication; she knew he was going to blow up.

"Lumi, what have you brought to my parent's house?" Marko glared at her.

"She didn't bring him! Didn't you hear me? He has been harassing *me* for weeks! Even before we met Lumi!" Noelle said. Panic had risen in her voice.

"Why wouldn't you tell me this? My family could be in danger! At least I could have found a way to protect them if you had just told me what is going on!" Marko said and shook his head.

Lumi blanched. Marko's features softened after that. It was enough to redirect his frustration.

"I just feel like so much has changed in a short amount of time." Marko's intense face softened even more. His tall, brooding presence faltered as he watched Lumi. His voice became lower and softer. "I promise I'm going to keep both of you safe."

Noelle was surprised. He seemed to take this better than she had realized. Lumi seemed to bring out a soft side to Marko that she had never seen before. Noelle was impressed that Lumi was the one person who might be able to make Marko gentle and more thoughtful. A smile spread on Noelle's lips as she realized it took *the* Snow Queen, rumored to be a villain of all sorts, to make Marko temper out. Of all the people to manage to bring a soft side to Marko, it was the *least* likely person.

Lumi sat on her bed and placed her face into her hands. Marko's hand reached for her but then fell to his side as if he had thought better of the gesture.

"I'm sorry for getting upset. This is a lot of news, and I'm bothered that some man has been following you both around," Marko said and rubbed his jaw. His eyes were on the footprints—it was clear he was calculating his next moves. "I found this." He handed Noelle a picture of her grandma, dressed in a beautiful white wedding gown. She and Noelle's grandfather were holding hands in the backyard of her childhood home, smiling.

"Just as I thought. Looks like we're going to my childhood home."

CHAPTER 15
THE SNOW QUEEN LUMI
NOELLE'S BELIEF

The next morning, after breakfast, Marko, Noelle, and Lumi stood in the entrance of Marko's family home with their bags.

"Merry Christmas, Lumi! It was so nice to meet you. I can't wait for the vacation!" Katarina embraced Lumi and kissed her cheek.

Lumi's heart felt like a steady flame, and she clutched at it, again, as she felt the dormant emotions come alive and swirl inside her warm heart. Noelle and Marko had single-handedly managed to thaw out her icy heart, a feat no person had been able to manage for a very long time. And she wished desperately that the feelings would go numb and that her heart might freeze again —because the new intense emotions were too much. Everything made her want to cry, and the soft, warmth that beat in her chest was the culprit.

"Merry Christmas," Lumi said. She smiled as she watched Marko's mom cradle Marko in her arms. She had forgotten what the beauty of family looked like.

"All right, Mom. We need to get going. We'll come back and get Lumi's car later."

Once they exchanged hugs with each of them, Danica, Katarina, and Nikola stood on the snowy porch and waved as they pulled away in Marko's car.

"Before we head back to the city, we want to stop at a local gas station because they have the best coffee! It is a tradition that we stop there every time we visit," Noelle said eagerly and peered at Lumi from the back of the car.

Lumi turned and faced Noelle—whose bright eyes seemed to glow with eagerness. Lumi wished she didn't look at her the way that she did; she seemed to have complete and total trust in Lumi—as if she were somehow good and seated on a pedestal. Lumi was anything but good—she had so much blood on her hands from many wars where human kings used her as a pawn against her own will. She had sworn a Merklei vow to one king that she and her people would protect their people until the end of time, but his line grew more and more wicked with each generation. She had no choice but to honor her vow, and they used her abilities like she was a mere slave.

Lumi wished she would encourage them to run from her for their own benefit if it weren't for the fact that she was so incredibly selfish.

"Okay," Lumi agreed. "But I don't know how to feel about gas station coffee."

"You'd be surprised," Marko said with a shrug.

When they arrived at the gas station, Lumi opened the car door and looked over the little shop where she could see a stocked coffee bar.

"You coming?" Marko asked, but Noelle didn't move from the back seat.

"Nah, I'll wait here. Can you get me a latte?"

"Sure," Marko said and closed the car door. He met Lumi on the snowy sidewalk and offered his arm. She took it, and they strolled toward the door. They passed two men dressed in bulky coats, who leaned against the building.

It was cozy inside and looked unlike any gas station shop that Lumi had ever seen. It resembled a quaint coffee shop instead.

But Lumi's ability to sense danger gripped her entire being. She froze and waited for confirmation. Noelle's face emerged in her mind, and the two sordid men she had passed had their hands on her.

"I'll be right back!" Lumi said and hurried toward the door. When she saw that Noelle wasn't inside the car any longer and the men weren't by the door—she sprinted. She scanned the small parking lot until she saw Noelle hovering over a bright green keiloki portal plant in the snow. Lumi gasped—how had the Naturei managed to put a portal *here*? She needed to get Noelle away from the portal before the Naturei saw them.

And then the two men were at Noelle's sides. The burly man on her right put a hand on her shoulder. Lumi tensed but let out a sigh when she realized they were only human—destroying humans was like ripping up paper for Lumi—incredibly easy.

Lumi's hands were up before she could think. Nobody would harm the girl, not with her around. She had failed Lorelei, but she wouldn't fail Noelle.

Streams of ice came from Lumi's hands and moved rapidly toward the two men. It pelted their bodies and knocked them to the snowy ground. They turned to face Lumi, and the whites of their eyes shone. Lumi imagined she probably looked like the summation of their nightmares—because she was a figure of torment for anybody who dared to become her enemy. She curled her fingers into fists, and the whites of her knuckles shone. Thankful for her ability to sense danger and malicious intentions, she could spare Noelle's life.

She slammed her fists together, and dangerously sharp ice shards flew in the direction of the two men, which sent them running. Each ice shard hit their intended target, and they screamed in horror. Lumi stalked forward and put her hand up, prepared to finish them.

Noelle shook her head frantically. "Don't hurt them!"

"Why?" Lumi watched as the men ran down the road. Lumi was at Noelle's side now and sighed. The girl believed in her *far* too much.

"Because that isn't who you are."

"I should warn you that I'm a terrible person. All I've done for years is sit around and relive all the terrible things I've done," Lumi said through her teeth as she watched the men run farther away. Lumi exhaled. "I couldn't resist the orders of the human kings because of my Merklei vow. I was a weapon and killed so many people."

Lumi stiffened as Noelle placed her hands on top of hers. "I believe you. But it wasn't your fault if it wasn't your choice. And I'm not going anywhere. Now don't hurt them."

"Do you have any idea what they were going to do to you?" Lumi asked.

Noelle gave a small shrug. "Do you?"

"Yes, it's one of my abilities. I know when people have malicious intentions toward others before they act on it." Lumi watched as the men disappeared in the distance. She desperately wanted to end them but held off for the sake of the girl. For some reason, the girl's belief in her delighted her, and she would hate to spoil it.

Lumi turned on the bright green plant and held out her hand toward it. She needed to kill this monstrosity before it became a problem. She had managed to escape the Naturei and Leizei for such a long time, and she wasn't about to face them now that she was so close to the necklace. Noelle spun Lumi toward her, away from the keiloki plant.

CHAPTER 16
NOELLE
THE RETURN

"Lumi! Wait!" Noelle's head throbbed. From the corner of Noelle's eye, she could see a bright green light. But she didn't dare look when Lumi was so close. A figure appeared and swiftly moved toward them. She knew who it was and so did her heart, which began to beat quickly.

"Noelle?" Eli closed the distance between them.

She faltered at the thought that he shouldn't be here. It would surely cost him. She pulled back to see the emerald eyes that she had pictured for so many days, but then balked at the brown color contacts. He was incognito, she realized.

"I'm fine," Noelle said. With Eli's back to the keiloki plant, Lumi shot out her hand toward the plant and froze it. She blasted it with such a cold temperature that it turned black and wilted. Apparently it was not entirely immune to the cold.

Noelle's thudding heart slowed as she realized that Eli's portal had been destroyed. Now he would be stuck with her; while she was grateful to see him, she knew that his absence from his realm might be troublesome.

Noelle's breath caught as she looked at Eli, and a cocky grin unfolded on his face.

"Who is this?" Marko stepped out of the gas station with three coffees in hand.

"This is Noelle's friend," Lumi said.

Noelle spun around to see what remained of the men, but apparently they managed to get away.

"She approached me on the train and said I was so *handsome*," Eli said, and the corners of his mouth hiked upward even more.

Noelle had forgotten about her plan for revenge for Eli. She might not be able to do much, but she certainly could make things uncomfortable for him, compliments of Marko.

Before Noelle could lose her nerve, she slid her fingers into Eli's. Confusion appeared in his eyes as they tightened on Noelle. But she gave him a shy smile.

"Yes, I did. Eli is my boyfriend. I met him on the train when you sat with your friends. I just couldn't help myself. He truly was *so handsome*." Noelle emphasized the last words to really emphasize the absurdity of it all. Noelle didn't dare look at Eli. She could feel his gaze on her, with wide eyes. However, she ignored him and watched as Marko scowled.

"Boyfriend?" Marko said the word like it was unpleasant on his tongue.

Her plan worked; she had never dated anybody, and this would come as a shock. She couldn't help the grin that now appeared on her own face.

"You're dating somebody, and I've never even met him?" Marko's heated gaze went from Noelle to Eli. "Who are *you*?"

"Hi, I'm Eli." He offered his hand, and Marko begrudgingly took it. The coldness that came from Marko's stare was hard to miss. "It is so nice to meet you. Who are you?" Eli, without missing a beat, unlocked fingers with Noelle and slid his arm across Noelle's shoulder. He seemed far too comfortable. Noelle had hoped this would make him uncomfortable—but he seemed to enjoy it.

"I'm Marko. I'm Noelle's older brother," he said.

"It's great to meet Noelle's brother. Maybe if she plays her cards right, you'll be my brother-in-law." Eli gave a nonchalant shrug.

Her cheeks went hot, and she felt flustered. How had this backfired? This was supposed to make *him* miserable, not her. She bit her bottom lip.

Marko began his interrogation. "How old are you?"

"I'm nineteen," Eli said. "And you all?" Eli pulled Noelle closer. Her heart thudded, and she hoped Eli couldn't feel it. He smelled like some fragrance that belonged to the Naturei realm. She could faintly recall it but not quite. She scanned Lumi's face to see if she had smelled it—yet she didn't seem suspicious. Lumi just watched with a blank face. Noelle eyed the keiloki plant and winced as she recalled that Eli wouldn't be able to get home. Hopefully the Chicago keiloki plant was still there, or Eli might be in serious trouble.

Marko didn't even try to hide his annoyance now. "You don't know how old she is?"

"Noelle is eighteen—and she turns nineteen in a few days. Of course her *boyfriend* would know that." Noelle was surprised that he really had kept tabs on her. The longer his arm was on her, the more anxious she felt. This wasn't supposed to happen; he was supposed to be the nervous one. Eli rubbed his cold fingers against Noelle's shoulder, and it made her scarlet cheeks deepen to a darker red shade. Eli seemed pleased by this because his smile widened.

Noelle, annoyed by his arrogance, tore away from him. She meant it to be much more forceful; however, the Naturei vow must have made it natural and sweet because neither Lumi nor Marko seemed to notice anything.

"I'm twenty-seven and Marko is twenty-three," Lumi answered, but she failed to mention how long she had been twenty-seven. "Noelle introduced me to Eli. He came over, but I didn't know they were dating."

Marko simply scowled at Eli. It was evident that he wasn't

impressed. "Well, anybody who dates Noelle should meet my entire family. You should get our approval."

Eli laughed, but Marko didn't join him. "My apologies," Eli said, thick with sarcasm.

Marko looked Eli up and down.

"Well, I'm going to take Noelle now. We wanted to spend time together," Eli said and grabbed Noelle's elbow.

"Where do you think you're going?" Marko said. "Noelle is hanging out with us. If you want to join, then you can. But it is Christmas and we are going to the city." He turned toward his car, with Lumi in tow.

Eli tugged on Noelle's elbow, and it was clear what he wanted. He wanted to get away. Noelle looked at the keiloki plant, now withered, and winced.

"Let's get to Chicago," Eli whispered against Noelle's ear. His lips brushed her ear.

"We're coming too!" Noelle called after Marko and Lumi. Eli didn't bother to hide his frustration. Perhaps he was uncomfortable with Marko after all.

"You shouldn't be here," she whispered.

He sighed. "I got alerted about those two men, and I just don't think I could sit with myself if I allowed them to beat you to a pulp and I just watched."

"Well, we had it handled. You weren't needed."

Noelle snapped her head in her friends' direction. Lumi and Marko were already in the car, waiting.

Eli caught her by the wrist. "Things have gotten worse, Elle."

"How could things be worse?"

Eli eyed the car, and once he seemed convinced they couldn't hear, he nodded. "We found out your friend Lumi has an heir. We haven't located the heir yet, but the Leizei king plans to call forth a duel between the heirs. In your world, you fight wars against opposing countries. In ours, they've made a pact that the heirs would fight to the death to settle disputes. I'm going to have to fight against Lumi's heir."

"They say her daughter died in the Merklei Massacre. It's probably a misunderstanding," Noelle said aloud. Possibly too loud.

"Right, but apparently she has another heir. I don't know who though. We only found out because the Leizei king has sent word that he will declare the duel. All the kingdoms watch it like a competition, and it won't end until somebody dies." Eli frowned. "I don't even know who the Leizei heir is either."

Noelle felt her insides twist at the news of such a dreadful setup. "I'm so sorry, Eli. That is *really* awful, and I can't imagine how you're feeling. But I don't understand what this means. Did Lumi have another child?" Noelle locked eyes with Lumi, whose patience seemed to wane.

"I guess. Her heir is apparently old enough for the duel." Eli's face fell, and he seemed lost in thought. Noelle wondered if he was worried about being killed or, even worse, about having to kill another. Her eyes trailed to Lumi's again, and she bit her lip. She felt guilty for betraying Lumi's trust. If she knew that she was "dating" the Naturei prince, she might feel rather let down. And Lumi just let all her walls down, too, and cited Noelle as one of her inspirations for doing so—which made Noelle feel dreadful.

"Come on." Noelle grabbed Eli's arm and led him toward the car. Noelle's gaze lingered on Eli's colored contacts. It was odd to see him without his green eyes. Eli smirked as he caught her eye. She rolled her eyes and looked away.

CHAPTER 17
NOELLE
THE NECKLACE

The weather outside was chilly, but it seemed colder inside the vehicle due to Marko and Eli's exchange.

"So how long have you been dating Noelle?" Marko looked at Eli in the back seat through his mirror.

"A while," Eli answered lazily. This didn't seem to please Marko, who frowned. "Elle started the entire thing actually." Eli smirked.

"Elle?"

Eli leaned over to Noelle and wrapped his arm around her. His strong, muscled arm nearly swallowed Noelle. Eli's lips twitched as Marko's frown deepened. "Yeah, she instigated the entire thing."

Technically that wasn't a lie. Noelle inhaled as Eli's hand wrapped around her shoulder. Marko shot Eli a look—the intention of it was clear, but Eli smiled deeper. He brushed his fingers against Noelle's shoulder and traced circles. Noelle's heartbeat quickened with his touch. She wished he didn't have this effect on her; she wished she wasn't keenly aware of the gentle brush of his fingertips. Noelle tilted her chin toward Eli, who looked down at her. She hated that she ever had the idea to call him her boyfriend. What a stupid idea. He was supposed to be uncomfortable by Marko's interrogation, but he seemed to not care one bit, and this idea backfired.

He pulled her tighter toward him until she was against his chest.

That caught Marko's attention. "You two look a little too comfortable."

"Agreed," Noelle said and pulled away. Part of her wanted to lean into his embrace, but she couldn't. How could she forget what he was doing to Lumi? And how *she* helped him do it.

"I think it is great that Noelle met somebody," Lumi said and turned to face them. Her heart-shaped face and long, flowing hair was only inches from Noelle's.

Noelle grimaced as she contemplated how Lumi would surely be livid when Noelle used the necklace for her grandma and not Lumi's family—and she would probably be quite upset when she found out Eli's true identity. Noelle also wondered why Lumi's ability to sense danger didn't pick up on Eli's true intentions.

"What?" Lumi asked, a mix of perplexity and humor on her face.

"Oh, nothing," Noelle said with a small laugh to stifle her embarrassment.

Eli watched Lumi with something like malice in his eyes. Marko noticed, and by the way Lumi recoiled, it appeared she did too.

"I don't like you," Marko said.

Eli didn't say anything. He just laughed. "That is a shame. We might be brothers one day."

Marko's eyebrow rose, and he turned to say something, but Lumi interrupted. "You know, I think we should all focus. Why don't we get to Chicago and find the necklace?" Lumi crossed her arms.

Marko turned to Lumi and gave her an incredulous look.

"Oh merca. Noelle already told him about the necklace, and he is helping us find it," Lumi said with a bitter tone.

Marko's face grew slightly red. "Noelle, you did *what?*" The vein in his neck appeared, and Noelle understood that he was probably only moments away from shouting.

Truthfully, Noelle hadn't disclosed anything to him. He already knew about the necklace, but she couldn't break the Naturei vow even if she wanted to. "Yes, I couldn't help it."

The look of sheer disappointment on Marko's face was hard to miss. He shook his head and mumbled something under his breath. Lumi placed a pacifying hand on his shoulder. They drove almost the rest of the way in silence.

That was, until Eli broke the silence. "You know, I think this could be the beginning of a beautiful friendship, *bro*."

"Don't call me that," Marko said and clenched his teeth hard enough to where his jawline looked more pronounced. His annoyance seemed to grow by the second. "And let me make something clear to you—if you tell anybody about this necklace—"

"I won't tell anybody," Eli said, suddenly serious. "So the last hint said that the necklace is at the door where Noelle's grandma got married. Do we have any idea where to go?"

"She always told me the story. We confirmed it with a photo. I know exactly where the necklace is," Noelle said. She felt three pairs of eyes hungrily stare at her.

"Well?" Eli asked.

"Here, I'll type in the address in the GPS. It was the house that I grew up in. She always mentioned the door to me, and she always described it to me. I didn't know why she always talked about the door, but now it makes sense," Noelle said and typed the address into the keypad. Then she leaned back in the car's seat and sighed.

Marko followed the directions. The screen said they would be there soon. Noelle swallowed. They were only a few minutes away from finding the necklace, in the presence of the Snow Queen, which is precisely what her grandma warned her not to do. What if Lumi were truly a monster? What if she were a liar? What if her sweet demeanor was a facade and letting her near this necklace was a mistake? Noelle worried that if she found it, Lumi might pry it from her hands. This was Noelle's necklace—and she would use it to bring her grandma back. Noelle tried to shake the thought away. But the idea of seeing her grandma again, the only family that she ever truly had, seemed so alluring.

"Only a Merklei can use the necklace," Lumi said aloud, as if she could read Noelle's thoughts.

Noelle's hope was suddenly dashed. Lumi had said she only remained alive all this time to bring back her family. Yet she had her own plan for the necklace.

Marko pulled in front of a shabby, worn pale yellow home. The neighborhood seemed quiet, but Noelle remembered it fondly. She had so many pleasant memories in this small house; it had been filled with love, snickerdoodle cookies, and old movies.

Noelle sighed and closed her eyes. She hadn't visited the home since her grandma died and the bank foreclosed on the property. Returning felt like a knife had wedged itself between her ribs. Noelle looked at the faded yellow color, which once was so bright and full of memories. The grass had become unmanageable. Noelle wasn't even sure if somebody inhabited the home by the looks of it. The idea of it being vacant bothered her tremendously.

Marko seemed to notice. "Lumi and I will go knock if you need a moment."

Noelle could feel the cold air as they opened the car doors. Noelle looked down at her feet, and Eli watched her.

"What's the matter?" Eli asked, hesitation in his voice. He placed a gentle hand on her shoulder.

She shook it off. "I grew up in this home. It holds a lot of memories, and I haven't been here in a long time. It is painful, honestly."

Eli's face looked glum. "I'm really sorry." He pulled out a twisted vine bracelet and handed it to her. "I made this for you."

Noelle took the thinly twisted vine bracelet into her hand. A thread of gold ran through the bracelet, and she smiled. As she brought it to her hand, it opened around her fingers, and it shrank on her wrist until it fit perfectly.

"Thank you, Goldner." Noelle peered down at the bracelet in amazement. Maybe he was capable of being somewhat decent.

"A pretty bracelet for a pretty girl," Eli said and watched her intently. He covered the bracelet with her jacket.

"Well, we should start looking," Noelle blurted out.

He sighed. Noelle froze, uncertain what might have suddenly bothered him.

"I hate what I'm about to do. Mostly because I think you're going to hate me for it, but the reality is I'm protecting you. The entire Naturei realm knows you came to the realm, and they've been calling for your death. But I protected you. I made a plan where you're safe," Eli said.

Noelle cocked her head to the side and watched Eli smile broadly, as if she should be thanking him. She stared down at the bracelet and tried to rip it off. It wouldn't budge.

"What have you done?" Terror shot through her.

"Elle, you have no idea what I've been through the past few days trying to spare your life. They've been tracking your every move, and they've made dozens of plans on how to assassinate you." Eli's voice strained. He ran a hand through his long dark hair and composed himself. "They agreed not to kill you as long as you come back to the Naturei realm with me."

"*What?* That doesn't make sense!" Noelle's voice hitched. "What is the catch then?"

"You will never be able to return," Eli said.

Her eyes narrowed. "I won't do that."

"Then you can stay here, but the Naturei soldiers will come for you and that bracelet is a tracking device. If you stay here, then there's nothing I can do to help you."

"Let me get this straight. The Naturei realm hates humans and—"

"That isn't true," Eli said.

"Okay, but they refuse to intermingle, and I'm supposed to just go live there, and they will treat me like one of them?" The idea of going back to the Naturei realm sounded extremely inviting to Noelle; however, going as a human sounded terrible.

Eli didn't say anything, and after a moment, Noelle understood what he meant.

"Oh, if I go, then I'll be a prisoner." Noelle said the words aloud. Noelle's head began to pound. "And what is prison like in the Naturei realm?"

"You won't be a traditional prisoner. You'd lawfully be my prisoner, which means you'd roam free."

"That sounds terrible."

"You have no idea what I've negotiated, trying to spare your life," Eli said, clearly offended.

"Thanks for negotiating a stellar deal for my crime of being human and setting foot in the Naturei realm." She reached for the car door.

"The choice is yours," Eli said in a whisper. "Stay and it is certain death, or come with me."

"I think I've had enough time with you. Death might be a better choice."

Eli laughed softly. "I don't think I could just let you die. I'd rather not drag you back to the Naturei realm if you'd come willingly."

"Would you drag me back there?"

"Yes," he said, matter of fact. "I'd absolutely drag you if it meant you lived."

Noelle turned to Marko and Lumi, who eagerly beckoned her to come.

"And what about my friends?" Noelle eyed them on the porch.

"You'll have to come up with something good."

Noelle would not go willingly with Eli. She couldn't say goodbye to Marko and his family. They had treated her like a sister and daughter, and she couldn't simply disappear. She could only imagine how much pain that would inflict on them. And although Lumi was a new friend, she had been kind to Noelle. She opened up to Noelle and even cited Noelle as part of her journey of trusting people again. Yet Noelle had a nasty secret—that she betrayed Lumi's trust and engaged in spying on her with Eli. The guilt of it all washed heavy on Noelle's shoulders.

Noelle reached for the car door again and headed toward the pale yellow home. Dread seemed to weigh down her steps; she moved very slowly and dragged her feet against the overgrown grass.

Eli followed behind her.

"It doesn't seem like anybody is home, or perhaps nobody even lives here," Lumi said. Her eyes lingered over the shabby house and then returned to Noelle. "You said she got married here, so where should we start?"

Noelle already knew the answer; her grandma had gotten married in the backyard, and she always told Noelle about the intricate back door when she recalled the story.

"How about two search the front door and two search the back door?" Noelle suggested and then walked toward the back door.

"I'll join you!" Lumi said eagerly and rushed to her side.

Eli frowned and Marko eyed him. "Well, come on, brother. I'll bet I find it before you," Eli chimed.

"Don't ever call me brother again."

Noelle and Lumi headed to the back door, and heaviness seemed to settle on Noelle as they did. It had been years since she had been there; the memories of her grandma flooded her mind. She glanced at the pavement where they blew bubbles, and then she glanced at the backyard where she used to show off her gymnastics skills.

Noelle wiped away a tear quickly and allowed her hair to fall over her face. She looked over the red, intricately carved door. Lapis lazuli stones were etched into it, with flecks of gold, which looked eerily similar to Eli's room.

"I've never seen something so beautiful," Lumi said. She

seemed to pretend not to notice that Noelle had become emotional, and Noelle was grateful for it.

"We always loved this door," Noelle said and walked forward. She took out the hint from her pocket and found it had started glowing a pale blue color.

Hope engulfed Noelle, and she smiled. Lumi smiled too.

Noelle felt the piece of paper move on its own, as if it were a magnet and it was being attracted to the door.

"What in the world?" Noelle gasped. The crinkly brown paper zinged toward it, and Noelle had to hold on tightly. Once it made contact, a rectangle carving in the door opened and protruded out. It looked like a jewelry box, and Noelle's lips parted.

Inside the rectangle drawer protruding from the door was the golden necklace. It was a dark, boisterous gold color, and there was a shiny oval at the base. The entire rectangle glowed.

Lumi's hand twitched, but before anything else could happen, the necklace began to slither toward Noelle's hand, as if it were a snake.

Noelle withdrew her hand and dropped the hint. But the necklace, cold to the touch, now slithered up her arm toward her neck.

"Lumi!" Noelle said with hands that trembled and tried to pry the necklace off her skin, but she couldn't.

Lumi didn't move, and her face turned ghostly white. Lumi's own face mirrored the shock on Noelle's.

And then the necklace reached Noelle's throat and clasped around it. But it didn't choke her, as Noelle had worried it might; it simply lay against her skin.

Lumi covered her mouth, and a tear spilled over and turned to ice. She looked jarred and took a step back, yet veneration appeared in her eyes. Her eyes looked over Noelle, as if she had never seen her before, and perplexity took over her features. "Only Merklei can wear that necklace. *How* is this possible?"

Noelle reached up for the necklace and tried to pull it off. Then she tried to unclasp it. But it wouldn't budge. "*What?* I can't get it off!" Noelle tried to slow her breath. But the panic from seeing an inanimate object slithering like a snake had made her pulse race.

"You're Merklei and you weren't even going to tell me? I thought I was alone all this time. Why didn't you tell me? Oh merca. How much of your memories did I wipe?" Lumi sounded hurt, and her voice was coated in offense, and yet something lingered on her face like hope. Her eyebrows were pulled down tight, and steady tears fell down her face and froze. "How did you survive the massacre? Why have you been hiding?" Lumi's words gushed out.

"What? You took my memories away from me?"

Lumi brought a finger to her lips and then pulled Noelle away from the side of the pale yellow home. "We met once. For maybe a minute, and I took that memory away from you. Oh, and another time too. But you really didn't know? The necklace only responds to Merklei, and since you were the first to touch it, it clasped around your neck. It wouldn't have done that if you were just human."

Noelle shook her head in disbelief. She had met Lumi once?

Lumi gave her a deliberate look. "That must be how your family obtained the necklace," Lumi said, breathless. A warm, slight smile appeared on Lumi's pale face. She even gave a tiny laugh, but then all traces of humor were gone. "You cannot tell a soul about this, do you understand me? Not Eli, not Marko. *Nobody.* I intentionally never had another child all this time because the other realms need a Merklei heir to declare something called a Heirling Duel. You being Merklei means you're automatically the heir since we are the only two known Merklei alive. If the other realms find out about you, they'll call for the duel. And it is the most nasty, vile thing to ever exist."

Noelle's mind wandered to Eli and the Naturei realm. "Other realms?" Noelle asked, and she hoped she conveyed innocence. Her guilt for betraying Lumi's trust now weighed heavier. "And heir?" Noelle's stomach dropped.

"The Merklei, Naturei, and Leizei all made a pact that instead of going to war with each other, should we ever come to disagreements, we would send our heirs to fight in a competition until one fell—to avoid bloodshed of thousands. The losing party had to make amends for the disagreement—but the biggest cost would be their heir." Lumi's eyes looked haunted. Her eyes lowered to Noelle's neck where the necklace lay.

Noelle frantically tugged the necklace, but it simply wouldn't budge.

"You won't get it off until it has been used," Lumi whispered. "And you cannot use it until you've been initiated. So don't get any ideas." Lumi definitely knew her intention was to use it for her grandma, but that was the least of Noelle's problems now.

Noelle stopped tugging and swallowed. Lumi tucked the necklace under Noelle's shirt and gave a firm nod. "Don't let anybody see it." She hugged her. "I thought I was all alone," Lumi whispered. And from the gentle rise and fall of Lumi's shoulders, Noelle wondered if she were crying. Noelle placed her cold, icy fingers on Lumi's back in a comforting embrace.

And then she heard Marko yell.

Lumi pulled away and wiped her wet face.

They sprinted toward the front of the house, and to their dismay, Scarface and a red-haired Leizei stood side by side. Scarface smiled when Noelle rounded the corner of the home.

Marko and Eli stood in front of them, fists balled.

The red-haired Leizei looked Marko and Eli up and down. "Hey," she breathed. She twirled a strand of her bright red hair in her fingers and coyly smiled.

The woman's hand began to glow a fiery red, matching her hair. It became difficult to tell where her hair started and where her hand was placed as the color morphed.

Lumi shot a blast of icy shards toward the woman, who dodged it with a scowl.

"Oh, *so angry*. What's wrong, Snow Queen? Trying to get your family back?" The woman's hands both glowed red now.

"Don't let her touch you," Lumi said sternly and pointed at her fire-scorched hands.

"I'd like to touch the one in the back." The woman looked up through her eyelashes at Marko and bit her lip and gave a coy smile again.

Eli took advantage of her distraction and stepped to her side and planted his fist across her jaw. "That's too bad. I really hoped I'd get the attention." The blow sent her to the snow.

Scarface lunged for Lumi. Lumi reached out her own hand, which glowed a pale blue, and made contact with Scarface's face. Instantaneously his face withered to a coal-black color, and he screamed. Lumi had implemented frostbite right to his face and allowed him to have a new scar to remember her by. Lumi shot ice at him, which pinned him to the pale yellow home.

Marko and Eli closed in on the red-haired woman. "You'd hit a lady?" She threw a swirling fireball at both Marko and Eli, which forced them to part and jump to the side.

"You're not a lady. You're a Leizei," Eli said and charged at her.

Lumi made an ice spear and lunged it at the woman, who turned her attention toward Lumi and the now crumpled Scarface on the ground.

"Lars!" she screamed. She tried to run toward Scarface, who lay in the snow and made ragged breathing sounds, but Eli had caught up to her. He picked her up and slammed her into the snow, but she wrapped her arm around him and burned him, which forced him to let go. Then he punched her in the back of the head and she, too, fell. She tried to pull herself up, her palms on the snow, but all four of them encircled her now.

Lumi crafted an ice sword and held the sharpest part at the Leizei's neck. It seemed to melt slightly at the touch of her neck.

"Why did the Leizei king send you?" Lumi demanded.

"He wants the girl," the red-haired Leizei said with a cruel grin. She made eye contact with Noelle, who shuddered. "The dead body of our adviser to the king was found in our realm with her name written next to it. It seems she has made quite the stir in the fire realm."

Lumi silenced her. "Say anything else, and I'll cut out your tongue."

The Scarface man's breath grew shallow. It seemed Lumi had given him far more than just a new scar.

The red-haired Leizei looked down at him. "For the Leizei kingdom!" she said and blasted a stream of fire toward Lumi. Then she threw a purple powder at Noelle. Eli and Marko restrained her, but it was too late.

Noelle coughed and coughed as she inhaled the purple powder. It covered her clothing, her eyelashes, and she tried to shake it off, but it seemed to be a cloud around her. She began to gasp for air, and her legs gave out. She fell onto the snow, and suddenly her eyesight dimmed. She had lost control of most of her body, but her hearing was perfectly intact.

"Noelle!" Marko shouted, and she could feel strong hands that scooped her up as if she were a small child. Somebody hoisted her into the air, but by the feeling of the rough calluses on the hands, it felt like it might be Eli. He leaned her against his chest and ran a hand over her hair.

Noelle could hear a gut-wrenching noise of something slice, and then she heard a loud thud against the snow. The red-haired woman went quiet.

"What do we do?" Marko asked urgently.

Noelle couldn't see anything, but she could feel the warmth of Eli's chest. She still couldn't move, and it was possibly the worst feeling ever to feel so out of control.

"How did Leizei get ahold of Naturei poison?" Lumi asked, sounding horrified. "That means they have an alliance."

And then Noelle felt goose bumps cover her entire body. If Eli worked with the Leizei realm, it meant they were indefinite enemies. Noelle felt so silly to have allowed this to happen.

"It is simple to fix this. There is a Naturei herb for this," Eli said, very calm.

"And how do *you* know that?" Lumi demanded.

But Eli didn't answer. He simply ran. Noelle was jostled against him as he did. She could hear Marko and Lumi run behind him as they called for him to stop. But surely there must have been a keiloki plant nearby because Noelle could feel them crash into the snow, and then instantly it was warm dirt.

CHAPTER 18
NOELLE
THE NATUREI PRISONER

Eli's callused hands gently laid Noelle onto something soft. Sweat formed on Noelle's forehead as the temperature was instantly warmer.

Then he began to laugh. "Well, our first day of being in a relationship was pretty eventful. I'm afraid you're going to hate me for bringing you here. But it was the only way to save you. I'm sorry you didn't get to say goodbye to your friends—but I've got to move quickly to get the herb antidote before this becomes permanent."

She listened to his steps grow faint.

It felt like an eternity before he returned. She could feel his weight shift whatever she lay on as he sat next to her. She could hear something like a lid being unscrewed, and then Eli rubbed ointment across her face, particularly heavy under her nose.

"Just breathe it in, and you'll regain movement and sight in a moment." Without being able to see him, Noelle focused on his deep voice. It was raspier than she had remembered.

She wondered how indeed the Leizei had gotten hold of what seemed to be some sort of Naturei poison. If Eli worked with Scarface, she'd never forgive him. However, by the way they opposed each other, it didn't seem like it.

Slowly, Noelle's fingers began to twitch. Her fingers were first to regain movement, and she bent them repeatedly. Then her arms and legs, and finally she could open her eyes.

Her lips felt numb, and she felt dizzy, but she could see. Eli leaned over, his dark hair like thick curtains against his face, and he smiled. His contacts were no longer browning his eyes, but green looked back at her. He reached out for her face and brushed away sweaty hair, now mixed with ointment, from her forehead.

"Welcome back," he said, a little too cheerful. Noelle looked around the room to find she was back in Eli's bedroom. She was on a large pillow that seemed to serve as a couch, and she looked around until she could find the orange plant she liked so much.

While she was glad to have her sight and movement back, she frowned. "I'm here forever?" She thought of Luis, Marko, and Lumi. She didn't even get to properly say goodbye. She didn't want to live in the Naturei realm *forever*.

"I'm sorry, but I had to move quickly, and your friends wouldn't let me take you without an explanation. If I told them who I was, they'd die for it."

She closed her eyes due to dizziness. "What is going to happen to me?" Now that she could move, panic and fear began to set in. Would she live behind bars? Eli had made it clear it was death or imprisonment, but imprisonment sounded severe.

"I convinced my father that you would be under my care. But that is a good thing because it means that I can set the standard for everything. You'll live free among the people and do as you please. You just can't leave, unfortunately. I'm so sorry, Elle."

Noelle grimaced at the news. She wished she hadn't met the handsome stranger on the train. He had ruined what little remained of her humble life.

"Do they hate humans?" Noelle opened her eyes and saw piercing green eyes that watched her with curiosity.

"No, not everyone. We hide ourselves from humans to protect ourselves. But I'm not sure how they'll handle being around a human. To manage your expectations properly, I think some will hate you."

Noelle let out a breath. Her face felt numb, and her lips tingled as she recovered from the poison.

"But," Eli continued, "I think there will be some who will befriend you with an open mind. And probably there will be some who will oddly be obsessed with you." His lips turned upward.

"Like you," Noelle said and scowled at him.

"Yes, like me," Eli said, and a ghost of a smile appeared.

Noelle wanted to hit him. She wanted to say cruel, colorful things to him. He had ruined her life. But she had operated in survival mode before, and now she would really need him as an ally. He might be her *only* ally in the entire realm. She also had the necklace now; and she was so close to seeing her grandma again. She just needed to survive this. Eli had acted, so she would act too.

"You're an idiot, Goldner."

Eli didn't hesitate. "I was afraid you'd hate me for this. But like I said, it is *better* than your death."

"I don't know about that."

He sighed. "I hope you'll like your life here. This is all my fault."

"Yes, you did ruin my life. So the least you could do is tell me what your educator said, which clearly intrigued you enough to come find me." Noelle tried to sit up again, but her head spun.

Eli softly pushed her back toward the pillow. "I don't know if that is a good idea. You should rest."

Noelle ignored him and sat up. "I want to know what made you come find me. It had better be something great."

Eli broke eye contact and looked around his room, as if he suddenly found it interesting. "I can't tell you everything, but I'll give you some of it."

"Well, my entire life is wrapped up in this now, so I think you owe it to me." Noelle reached for his chin and forced his strong jaw to face her.

His intense green eyes looked her over, and he raised an eyebrow. She hadn't meant to pull him so close, but their faces were inches apart from one another. She let go, as she realized that he was now granted so much authority over her life; more than she could possibly imagine. By the way he raised his eyebrow at her, she guessed that not many in his realm dared to talk to him, or touch him, the way that she did.

Noelle leaned away.

"So now I'm your boyfriend *and* you're demanding a kiss?" Eli's eyebrow rose even higher.

Noelle leaned even farther back. "I just wanted the information, Goldner."

"Oh, well if you wanted anything else, all you had to do was let me know." And then he also pulled away.

Eli studied Noelle's face for a moment. "My educator was like a father to me. He was entrusted with the highest seat of knowledge in our realm. He told me about you. I was informed that there was a human girl that I needed to find, who would find the necklace. According to my educator, you and Lumi were going to become quite close, which I admit I don't know how he knew that. And he advised me to also become close to you."

Noelle waited, but Eli didn't say more.

"That's it?" she demanded, voice shrill. "You ruined my entire life because your educator said we should be close? You truly are an idiot."

Noelle regretted the words. He was *a prince* and had charge over her life.

But to her relief, he laughed quite loudly. She made a mental note to be more careful in the way she spoke to Eli moving forward. He would be the one person to not cross, given the situation.

A knock at the door interrupted them.

Noelle looked down to see if the necklace was visible, but to her relief it wasn't. It was still hidden under her shirt. She tried to lean up, but Eli pushed her back onto the pillow.

"Rest," he ordered.

A young teen was at the door, dressed in green leaves and vines. He was bare chested and looked quite young. His green eyes, the same color as Eli's, locked onto Noelle's eyes.

"You really did it?" He pushed past Eli into the room and walked toward Noelle. "Hi, I'm Cedar. I'm one of Prince Eli's armor bearers, and I can't believe he actually managed to bring you back!" He excitedly rushed forward. "I thought he'd just kill you and call it a day."

Noelle lazily eyed Eli, who stifled a laugh.

"You're the first human I've ever seen before. She looks just like a Naturei, except for her eyes. Her eyes are a dead giveaway that she's human, but otherwise you wouldn't know! You did an excellent job capturing the human prisoner."

Noelle rolled her eyes. "You seem like a suck-up."

"Wow, humans are really sassy."

"No, just this one," Eli said, amused. "Elle, Cedar is one of my apprentices. I'm always surrounded by at least one. In our realm, we value hands-on training, and this is one that my father has assigned to me."

"I'm going to be a soldier when I get older," Cedar said with too much excitement for Noelle's pounding headache. "Anyway, the king is expecting the prisoner! I'm so glad the plan unfolded as we planned it."

Noelle used what little strength she had left and launched herself off the pillow. "What did you do?" She pointed an accusing finger at Eli. Had he planned the entire thing?

"I saved your life, Elle. And don't worry—"

"I can't stand you," Noelle said. She couldn't keep it in. She was sick of the half-truths, sick of the spying, and sick of the secrets.

"I'm well aware." Eli's dark hair fell over his face as he smiled at her.

Cedar looked perplexed as he looked between the two. "You

shouldn't speak to the Crown Prince this way. It won't be tolerated."

Noelle looked at Cedar. "What will you do to me, Cedar? Am I breaking a law?"

"Actually, yes."

Noelle shook her head and laughed. Of course they would make up a law that Eli couldn't be disrespected. He was horribly arrogant. Noelle sucked a breath in and then out. She needed to keep Eli as an ally—she needed to calm down.

"The king demands your presence and the girl's." Cedar pointed at her.

"Come on, prisoner! Time to meet the kingdom!" Eli said with far too much enthusiasm. He reached for her hand and tugged at it.

Her lips pulled down as she realized she would have to face the king again. It sent a shudder down her skin.

"The king said you both needed to look presentable before the nobles." Cedar pointed at Noelle. She looked down and realized the purple powder was still all over her clothing. Noelle quickly brushed her hair backward and tried to smooth it out. "Some Naturei are outside your room, waiting to be let in. They'll assist her."

"Bring them in." Eli gave a nod, and Cedar opened his bedroom door. A beautiful Naturei with long, dark hair and pretty mocha skin was the first to step in. She wore what appeared almost like a corset at the top, and then it flared out with several leaves to form a skirt that went to her knees. She curtsied at Eli and placed a fist over her heart. Eli placed a fist over his own heart and saluted. Two more Naturei girls with dark, straight cascading hair, who looked strikingly similar, entered and they, too, saluted and curtsied.

"Prince Eli, if it pleases you, we will help the girl get ready," she said and politely bowed her head.

Noelle scoffed at her words. The Naturei girl snapped her head in the direction of Noelle, and Noelle shrank back. The girl's eyes looked genuinely confused, and Noelle realized she made a mistake.

"Excuse her, she's new. She'll learn our ways. And yes, please help her find something more suitable," Eli said and looked at Noelle. "Elle, you'll find that everyone who works on palace grounds has mastered their abilities and their skills make room for them here. These are some of our best, most talented Naturei."

Noelle needed to make friends and to make allies. And with that thought in mind, she turned to the Naturei girls. "I'm so excited to meet you! I'm Noelle—I'd love your expertise and help on picking an outfit."

The Naturei girls looked pleased. "Nice to meet you. I am Eden, and these two sisters are Aurora and Blossom," she said and extended a hand toward the other two. They each made a fist over their heart and bowed to Noelle.

Perplexed, Noelle made a fist over her own heart and bowed her head toward them. She hoped she had done the greeting right, but she wasn't certain. She didn't want to offend them.

The two sisters had vines entwined in their hair, and vines ran down their arms and legs. One had a giant leaf on each shoulder, which draped over her like sleeves. The other wore green leafy pants and a jacket made of dried brown leaves. A wreath of sage flowers hung around her neck.

Noelle couldn't help but feel excited as she looked them over. She had loved the armor bearer outfit she wore, but this looked entirely more exciting.

"What do you want to wear? I'll create it for you. This is my service to the kingdom," Eden said.

"Wait, you can just create clothes?"

Eden nodded with great enthusiasm. "Of course. Would you like a dress? What color? What style? If you can imagine it, I can create it. Or if you leave it up to me, then I'll make something for you," Eden said.

"Well, I don't know your customs. Whatever you feel would be appropriate for meeting the king." Noelle glanced in Eli's direction. He crossed his muscular arms and leaned against his desk and watched her with his deep green eyes.

They all had the same deep green eyes, despite the different skin, hair colors, and features. It was eerie to Noelle.

"All right then, how about you step behind the curtain?" Eden pointed to the gold curtain in the room, and Noelle eagerly stepped behind it. She removed the stained clothing and dropped them on the floor.

Eden placed a hand over the gold necklace. Would Eden know what this was? Eden stood in front of Noelle, and Noelle kept her hand over the necklace so it was hidden. Eden raised a finger toward Noelle's body, and suddenly leaves flew from around the room from Eli's various plants. If Eden had noticed that Noelle was hiding something with her hand, she didn't mention it.

Eden had fashioned a leafy, poofy long skirt with long petals protruding from the waist. And she formed a heart-shaped corset with green leaves over Noelle's chest and stomach. Then she waved a finger toward her stomach, where vines wrapped around it and created a belt-like structure. Finally, she crafted a cape-like structure of bright green leaves and placed it over her shoulders. The cape draped nearly to the floor, which was perfect, because it covered the necklace entirely.

Eden stepped back and seemed to admire her work. She clasped her hands together and smiled.

"Blossom and Aurora, can you please assist her?" Eden called to them, and the other Naturei girls quickly made their way to Noelle. Aurora began combing her fingers through Noelle's hair, and then she began twisting certain strands, braided others, and smoothed out the rest. Blossom applied a damp leaf to Noelle's skin and removed the remaining excess powder.

After a few moments, all three Naturei girls stepped back and bowed their heads in a shallow manner. Noelle, uncertain and uncomfortable, bowed back.

"Prince Eli, she is ready to meet the king and the nobles," Eden announced.

Noelle stepped out from behind the gold curtain and eyed a gold mirror by the door. She hardly recognized herself as she peered into it. Her hair was intricately and beautifully woven together with various braids and resembled a flower in the back. The leafy dress that Eden had designed looked like a majestic ballgown. Noelle hadn't worn anything so regal in her lifetime.

"This is beautiful," Noelle said, eager to hand the Naturei girls a compliment. She hoped to win them over by whatever means necessary. Noelle pressed a hand over her neck where the necklace was, but thankfully it remained concealed. Then an idea struck Noelle; Lumi had said only an initiated Merklei could use the necklace. Perhaps she could figure out how to become initiated.

"You look beautiful, Elle," Eli said and walked beside her in the mirror. He had dressed in a green leafy uniform with a matching green wreath perched on his head. He, too, like all Naturei men was bare chested, and several leaves were knitted together to form his uniform. He looked less like the Eli she knew and more like a soldier.

He turned to face her, and she turned toward him too. He looked her up and down, but she refused to do the same. She could see from the corner of her eye that his chest was muscled and exposed, and she wouldn't give him the satisfaction of looking at anything except his eyes.

Eli leaned in close so that only Noelle could hear him. He took Noelle's hand into his own. "I'm giving you my vow that I'll protect you and keep you safe. I'll do everything in my power to ensure you have a good life here in the Naturei realm." A green ribbon of light flashed and tied their hands together and then disappeared as suddenly as it had emerged.

Noelle raised her eyebrows in surprise. He had just made a Naturei vow, which meant he couldn't break it. Noelle looked up and gave a firm nod.

"Thank you," she said, but her voice was weaker than she intended. His reassurance meant more than she could possibly say, because she was terrified at this moment. She tightened her hand around Eli's and squeezed it. She hoped this communicated her gratitude because she was afraid if she spoke more, she might get emotional.

"You'll get questioned. But your fate has already been determined by my father, and we agreed on the conditions. There is just the matter of service, and I'm going to let you pick what your role is. Naturei are different; we all have a collective role, and then we serve in various ways. I'm going to let you form whatever that looks like for you. I really am committed to helping you find happiness here in my realm," Eli said and squeezed her hand back. And then he slid his fingers away, and Noelle wished he hadn't. Because despite being angry with him, he was her only friend here, and she felt so utterly alone. His touch felt comfortable and reassured her; she wished he left his hand joined with hers.

"Oh, and Noelle?"

"Yes?"

"My adoptive father hates humans. But don't take it personally; humans betrayed the trust of the mother and killed his daughter," Eli said and stroked his chin as if lost in thought. "But you already know about that story."

Noelle's mouth made a round shape. Noelle struggled to picture it; she couldn't imagine a more poorly matched pair—Lumi and the Naturei king.

CHAPTER 19
NOELLE
THE NATUREI KING

Noelle stepped into a grand room where the floor was made of gold dust, and it felt like sand under her feet. Several gold plants grew out of the gold dust and surrounded them. The king sat on a throne, made of intricately curved vines, and glared at her. His handsome dark skin shone under the light, and his green eyes pierced her gaze. He watched her as she strode into the room with Eli and Cedar.

Many finely dressed Naturei sat on wooden tree-stump chairs in several rows. Many Naturei women had fascinating hairstyles woven into their hair, and some had colored paints that adorned their faces. They watched her eagerly and whispered as she passed by. Others gawked as if she were a strange sight.

"Look at her eyes," she heard one woman say.

"Take my arm, Elle," Eli whispered and offered his arm. "I'd like to make a show that you're with me and therefore under my protection to everyone here."

Without missing a beat, Noelle took Eli's arm. She looked at the king, whose eyes bore into hers. Her breathing quickened, and she tried to hide her nervousness. She made sure that her face appeared neutral. She even considered smiling; however, that felt foolish. Why would she smile at her own trial?

Eli and Noelle reached the center of the aisle, and Eli made a fist with his free hand over his heart and bowed low. He then turned to Noelle and nodded his head. Noelle followed and copied Eli's salute. She tried to imitate what she saw Eden do and hoped she seemed respectful. She just needed to survive, and she needed allies in order to do that.

"We are gathered here today because my heir, Prince Eli, made some grand errors." The king looked away from Noelle, and his eyes landed on Eli. But then the king fixed his eyes back on Noelle, and his sneer grew. "After receiving a deceitful tip about a human girl from the traitorous educator, he decided to go find her. And unfortunately for the Naturei realm, he was successful."

The audience of nobles murmured. Eli kept his head forward and watched the king.

"It is against Naturei law to interact with humans. You have seen what happens when we interact with humans. They're treacherous, treasonous, and wicked in every way, and putting our faith and trust in them was a poor choice, to say the very least." He held his nose high in the air and said the words, as if he spoke only to Noelle. Despite a crowded room with rows of nobles, he kept his eyes on her and only her.

Noelle gripped Eli's arm tighter. She looked at him, but he didn't take his eyes off the king. Noelle swallowed. She could feel the eyes of everyone in the room on her.

"I ordered my son to execute her, but he begged for me to spare her life. Instead, he proposed that we bring her here as a prisoner. He argued that it wasn't her fault and that he was to blame. He argued that we should spare her life since she did us no wrong except she knew too much. We cannot leave her to expose us with such knowledge."

Noelle worked hard to keep the surprise off her face. She concentrated on keeping her face neutral, void of emotion. But she was surprised to hear how fearful the king was that she would expose the Naturei realm. It also appeared that Eli had, in fact, saved her life.

The crowd murmured again. Noelle held her head up high; it was true that she hadn't done anything wrong. She refused to wear any guilt for being human and having knowledge of the Naturei realm. This trial was unfair at best and ludicrous at worst.

"So to conceal her knowledge, she will permanently be a prisoner here in the Naturei realm," the king announced and faced the nobles. Some laughed, others audibly gasped, and the noise increased as they talked among themselves. No human had ever entered the Naturei realm, let alone lived in it; it was scandalous.

"She will be Eli's responsibility since this is his doing—and he will train her in our ways. Humans live short lifetimes, yet for whatever time she has, she will be banished here. Do you accept our conditions?" The king's eyes rested on Eli now.

"I accept," Eli said and placed a fist over his heart. Then the king looked at Noelle.

"What if I don't accept?" Noelle asked. She willed her voice to be strong and not waver, but it was smaller than she had liked.

"Then you die," the king answered her in a condescending tone.

Noelle quickly placed a fist over her own heart. "Then I accept my fate."

"I see Eli put the tracking bracelet on you as he was instructed. We will always know where you are, and if you ever try to leave, it will stop you. You will always remain within eyesight with this too. You'll never be able to take it off," the king said. "Eli will also be punished for his foolish actions. But he will stand trial another day. As for the girl, she needs a service." The king stood up from his vine throne and walked toward her as if she was under inspection. "What can you do to contribute to the Naturei society? What skills do you possess?" He walked in a circle around her as if he might suddenly realize what she could do.

Noelle simply shook her head.

The king stopped in front of her. "Surely you have some

skills," the king said. "Can she cook? What if she became a cupbearer?" He directed the question to Eli, who shrugged.

"Can you cook?" Eli asked her, as if he were her interpreter. She didn't mind it though. She preferred to speak to Eli over the king.

"Not exceptionally well," Noelle admitted.

"She can't use Naturei power to help grow food or farm, she can't cook, and she looks slightly small for a soldier." The king clicked his tongue to the roof of his mouth in disapproval.

Noelle wanted to say something to him about his comment on her size, but he was the king and she was a prisoner. She had to survive; so she kept her lips sealed.

"Almost every role of service requires using Naturei power," Eli pointed out.

"Yes, indeed. Where is the adviser?" The king snapped his fingers in the air, and a Naturei man with large glasses walked to his side.

"Yes, m-my king?" the adviser said and rubbed his hands together nervously. His eyes flicked from one part of the room to the next very quickly.

"What do we do with her? She must find some purpose in our realm and contribute." The king looked at his odd adviser.

The adviser clasped his hands and fiddled with a button on his shirt and twitched. "Yes, h-humans can do m-many things. Can s-she help with children?"

Noelle had babysat before. She didn't mind it; but she frowned at the memory of the one time when she lost a child during hide-and-seek. "I'm decent with kids!" Noelle said with a slight feeling of triumph.

However, the adviser frowned. "No, we n-need excellence. Not just d-decent skills."

"Oh." Noelle looked around and then looked over the adviser, who still twitched every few moments.

"There are a few r-roles we can c-create for her in our realm. However, I t-think a good role for her could be to become Prince

Eli's concubine, g-given the educator's advice to h-him." The adviser tapped his fingers together and twitched.

Noelle couldn't wear the mask on her face any longer. Her emotions slid through as aggravation rose on her face, and her cheeks reddened from the sudden warmth that coursed through her.

Murmurs erupted behind them.

"Although our r-realm has never had c-concubines, only queens—this term c-comes from her world. And this w-would ensure that the educator's advice d-doesn't transpire." The adviser looked to the king, who seemed smug and pleased.

"I do like this idea," the king said and turned to Noelle. "You will never sit on my throne in this realm."

Why would he say such a thing? Noelle didn't want anything to do with this realm or that throne. But then it finally clicked; Eli had mentioned that the educator told him that he ought to get close to her. Exactly how close? Noelle squeezed Eli's arm, as if it were a plea for help. She hated the adviser and the king for even suggesting such a terrible idea.

Noelle, her face red, turned to Eli. A muscle in his jaw twitched, but he kept his eyes on the king. A ghost of a smile turned up on Eli's lips, as if he might burst into laughter at any moment.

"No, I won't take Noelle as a concubine. She has many talents to use in serving Naturei, and that would be a waste of her service," Eli said, and relief flooded Noelle. She was so grateful for Eli and his forward thinking in the midst of absolute insanity.

"Then what are they?" the king pondered aloud.

"She is pretty good at taking things," Eli said, and for the first time since they entered the grand room, he looked at Noelle. He flashed her a quick grin and then set his eyes back on the king.

She wished she could hit him.

Whispers overflowed behind Noelle's back as the nobles shifted and spoke.

"I know how I can contribute!" Noelle announced boldly,

because she no longer wanted to hear any more stupid ideas from the adviser. She had to take control of this situation quickly. "I was going to be a journalist where I came from. In this realm, I could tell stories. I could interview people here and share news and tell stories that are entertaining, thought-provoking, and heartwarming. I can add morale to your people and contribute my skills this way!" Noelle spoke with enthusiasm, not making the same mistake that made her sound like her skill set was *only* decent.

"We've never h-had a journalist b-before. Would s-storytelling please the king?" The adviser peered up at him. The entire room seemed to go quiet as they waited for the king to give his answer.

"I'd like to try a trial period where we see what she can do. Humans are liars, and we'll see if she is a good storyteller. Every time a royal dance is called, she will share a story; and she will be judged for her storytelling skills. Do you agree with this?" The king eyed Noelle.

She placed a fist over her heart and nodded eagerly. "Yes, absolutely!" she said with a grin. She smiled with relief, because she felt she could actually manage well here with this role. Perhaps, and it was a strong *perhaps*, the Naturei realm wouldn't be so bad after all.

"Good, you are dismissed." The king turned and sat on his throne, and the nobles began to file out.

"Come this way or else they'll all want to talk your ear off." Eli guided Noelle by her hand, and they exited through a side door. Guards greeted him on the other side, and they both stiffened at the sight of Noelle. They placed a fist over their hearts, and both Eli and Noelle did too.

Eli walked her to the side of a balcony, where she could view the vast hills of the Naturei realm. The sun was setting, and the sky had ribbons and hues of violet and magenta that kissed it. Noelle could see Naturei gardening and farming many crops on the horizon, and she sighed at the beauty of it all. The Naturei seemed to live simple lives; but it looked peaceful. But then Noelle realized that while she had looked at the scene that unfolded before her, Eli had looked at her.

Noelle removed her hand from Eli's arm. She smiled at him.

"Why the smile?"

"Thanks for not making me a concubine," she said with thick sarcasm in her voice.

Eli laughed loudly. "Don't mention it."

And then Noelle shoved him hard against his chest. The vow she took said she had to be friendly in front of others but nothing about how she behaved privately.

"And what was that for?" he demanded and placed an elbow against the citadel wall.

"For saying that my skill set is taking things," she huffed. She watched a Naturei woman and man exchange crops below.

"You are good at taking things. My attention, for instance," Eli said, and he leaned in close. "I find you fascinating. Everyone here is annoyingly polite and says whatever they think will please me, even if it's a lie. But not you. You're not fake and you say what you mean. You don't worry about saying the right thing. I wish more Naturei were like you, but everyone is so scared." Eli's long dark hair swayed in the wind and with it carried a scent of strong spices.

Noelle swallowed as a cocky grin appeared on Eli's face. That was a backhanded compliment, and she wasn't certain if he expected her to say thank you or to act insulted.

"I couldn't care less about saying the right thing to you," Noelle said and looked up at him.

"I'm well aware," Eli said. "But you should consider being kind. I'm sort of in control of the rest of your fate." He grinned.

"You don't control my fate. I do," Noelle said.

"Oh really? Would you like to test that theory?" He leaned his weight against the wall and leaned even closer.

Noelle grimaced. She needed Eli as an ally, but she couldn't help but feel resentful toward him. It was his fault that she was here.

"I control my life." She looked out over the citadel and exhaled slowly. She reminded herself to be kind, to get Eli's favor—but she hated that she even had to. She shouldn't even be here in the Naturei realm.

A smug smile spread across his lips. "I have zero interest in controlling others. But just so you do know, I can do this." Eli flicked his fingers up, and Noelle's hand shot straight into the air.

Her eyes widened, and she gave him a threatening glare.

He raised his hand, and with it, the bracelet led Noelle up until she was several feet off the ground. Eli apparently had full control of the bracelet and used his ability to operate it.

The strain of the twine bracelet pulled against her skin and pinched it. She cringed as all her weight was held by the bracelet suspended into the air.

Noelle looked down and refused to whimper.

When he pulled his fingers apart, the bracelet grew into shackles of vines and cuffed both her wrists.

Her wrists turned raw and red, and she winced as it continued to pinch her skin. But she wouldn't cry; she wouldn't give him the satisfaction of an admission that he was in control.

"Just ask me to let you down, and you'll be good to go," Eli called to her, as if this were a game.

"No!" Noelle called back, stubborn. She would rather let her skin become bruised.

Eli seemed to give up and waved his hand. With it, the cuffs disappeared, and the bracelet reappeared. A blue, thick flower grew from her bracelet, and Eli lowered Noelle until her feet touched the ground.

He gently picked off the stem of the blue flower and handed it to Noelle.

Noelle took the flower and threw it to the ground. She crushed it under her foot and then rubbed her aching wrists.

Eli eyed her wrists and recoiled. "Oh, Elle, I'm so sorry. I didn't think that it would do that. Here, I can help with that!" Eli reached a hand out, but Noelle retracted her hands away from his.

She had to be diplomatic. She wanted to bring both her fists to his face for being so stupid, but she also needed to maintain her good standing, and it took every ounce of self-control that she had. But that didn't mean she couldn't try to reason with him.

"Why would you do that?" Noelle asked bitterly. Her voice sounded prickly and accusatory rather than curious.

"I'm sorry—I meant it as a fun joke. I didn't realize it would actually hurt you. I feel terrible. But let me fix it. I can—"

"That is just it, isn't it? You do things, and I get hurt and pay the consequences." Noelle said the words gently, but she hoped they might resonate. Eli made the choice to come visit her over silly advice from his educator, and now she was a prisoner in his realm. Eli wanted to play a stupid game, and now her wrists were on the verge of bleeding. He seemed destructive and chaotic even in his best intentions.

"Let me fix it," he said and held out his hand.

He was pure chaos. And it seemed that if she gave him an ounce of trust, then she would be a fool. But what else could she do in such a place? So she extended her hands out to him, and her eyebrows rose high as her skin instantly healed as he brushed his fingers across her wrists.

Noelle took a step backward and brushed her own fingers over her wrists.

"How did you do that?" she asked. Her eyes studied him, and she looked him up and down. His tanned skin looked as if he had spent a large amount of time in the sun. Her eyes trailed until it landed on his bare chest, where one strap of leaves went across his body. All the Naturei men wore bare-chested outfits, which made little sense to her. But what did she know? She wasn't a Naturei.

"Are you checking me out, Elle?" Eli's lips tightened.

Noelle rolled her eyes. "Why would I want to do that? You

think so highly of yourself." A rouge color of embarrassment appeared on her cheeks.

Eli walked around her to the other side of where she was standing. "I think you pretend to hate me. I like when your cheeks turn pink."

Regrettably she felt more heat rise to her cheeks.

"How did you do that?" Noelle redirected him back to the important conversation.

He lifted his eyes to hers. "In the Naturei realm, all can use the nature ability to grow plants of all kinds. We can use it to provide food, or we can use it to create weapons. We can mold the earth in any way we desire. But we *also* each have special abilities. In your world you might call them superpowers or something like that."

"I'm sorry, did you just say *superpowers*, Goldner?" Noelle shook her head and laughed.

He shrugged. "Laugh if you want. I'm trying to put it in terms that you would understand. We refer to it as somebody's ability."

"So you can heal injuries?" Noelle inquired.

"Yes, I can heal injuries. I have another too."

"Show me," Noelle said in barely a whisper. Her fascination seemed to possess her, because she couldn't hide her emotions any longer.

Eli walked toward a round boulder perched on the citadel. He picked up the large boulder effortlessly and then slid it into one hand. Noelle imagined the boulder weighed much more than a car and perhaps even as much as an elephant.

"Are all Naturei able to heal people and have strength like you?" Noelle asked, amazed.

Eli placed the boulder down gently. "No, everybody has different abilities. And some are born with none."

Eli took a step toward Noelle, and she held her breath. He was not only reckless but *very* dangerous. Perhaps even more dangerous than Lumi. Noelle realized in that moment how little she knew about either of them or their realms. How had her fate become so intertwined in these realms? How had she been

Merklei? And although Lumi warned her not to tell anyone, could she tell Eli? She wasn't certain if he was safe or not to entrust with this knowledge. She couldn't tell anyone; it was her secret. She just wanted to figure out how to utilize the Merklei necklace and get her grandma back.

She closed her eyes, and as she leaned forward, she suddenly became aware of the necklace around her neck. She worried Marko and Lumi would search for her without any way to reach her.

"So what becomes of me now?" Noelle asked with a weak smile. She wanted to think positive, but she doubted her new reality would be pleasant. The king hated humans, she lived a much shorter lifespan than them, and now they had abilities. She would likely be inferior in their eyes in every possible way.

"Come eat lunch with me," Eli said.

"Is that a command? Or do I have a choice?" Noelle asked.

Eli's brow furrowed. "You always have a choice with me."

"All right but only because I don't know anybody else. Because trust me, I'd rather have anybody else's company," she said.

"Oh, you don't mean that." He walked right past her, and she turned to face him.

"Where are you going?" she called out. But he said nothing. He just kept walking alongside the citadel wall.

CHAPTER 20
NOELLE
A NEW LIFE

Noelle hurried after Eli. She refused to be found by some other Naturei when she knew some hated her kind. She simply did not know this realm at all, and she needed to stay close to Eli for protection. She looked down where the necklace lay on her neck, under the cloak. She wouldn't be without family much longer—as soon as she could find alone time to figure this out.

"Goldner," Noelle called after him. "Where are you going?" They approached a bustling bazaar full of people under tents that traded many goods. She saw foods of all kinds being traded between the Naturei. But as they approached, nearly everyone seemed to have come to a standstill and watched Eli and Noelle.

They reverently put a fist over their hearts toward Eli, but they just glanced at Noelle. Some Naturei had eyes on her as if she were a vile monster that perhaps at any given moment might reach out and strike them. Others watched her with curious eyes, and yet others seemed timid and uncertain. One thing was for certain—nobody seemed to look at her without some sort of strong emotion. But one Naturei girl in particular stood out as her eyes fluttered while she saluted Eli, but then her green eyes locked on Noelle. The freckles sprinkled on her face moved as she scrunched her nose.

After a few steps, many returned to their normal business. Still many kept their attention on Noelle and Eli. Noelle was particularly intrigued by the Naturei who sat on a stool and made clay pots as others watched.

Eli put a hand on the small of Noelle's back. She turned to face him.

"I'd like to send a message to all of them—that we're friends," Eli said.

Friends didn't hold each other the way Eli held Noelle. But she played along, grateful for the display—perhaps they'd accept her if they thought Eli did. She slid her own hand around his back and leaned against him. Her heart hammered wildly as his hand left her back and he swept his hand up and down her arm. His hand felt like fire ignited against her skin, and she was keenly aware of every gentle motion of his fingertips.

"Should I tell them that we're dating too?" Eli leaned down and whispered in Noelle's ear. His lips turned upward as he poked fun at Noelle's claims earlier in Chicago.

She had only told Marko that they were dating because she thought Marko might go ballistic on him and make Eli uncomfortable. She wanted revenge for all that he had done to her. Unfortunately, he only seemed to enjoy the tension.

The Naturei girl with freckles had her eyes on Noelle's and Eli's hands and then trailed her eyes back to Eli with a pained look. It dawned on Noelle what had bothered the Naturei girl.

"I think your friend might not like that."

Eli scanned faces until he found who she mentioned. The girl turned away, but Eli let out a small laugh.

"Oh, you mean Jasmine?" Eli asked.

"Yes, she was gawking at your hand."

"Good."

Eli led Noelle into a violet tent inside the bazaar, surrounded by Naturei guards. They saluted Eli and then eyed Noelle.

"She's eating with me," Eli said with ease. The soldiers stood aside, and they entered the tent.

Inside, there were rows of plants; each displayed several ripe vegetables and fruits. Noelle's mouth began watering when she saw the rows of peppers, tomatoes, and many fruits she simply didn't recognize.

She watched as Naturei went through, buffet-style, and plucked fruit and veggies from the plants, only for them to immediately reproduce and regrow. Noelle's mouth parted as she realized that they had a never-ending food supply; nobody in this realm would have need of anything, it seemed. She imagined nobody suffered from hunger here because of their abundance.

A Naturei woman stood to the side, her hands raised, and she was clearly the one who regrew the plucked food. The others gingerly took what they wanted and placed it on their plates.

"Hello, everyone!" Eli said.

Everyone inside the violet tent stopped and turned to face Eli. Many greetings and shouts emerged.

"You made it back in one piece! And you managed to defy all laws and still get the girl!" a Naturei soldier said playfully.

"Oh merca! You brought her back? Only you would find a way to fulfill the educator's advice." A soldier already seated shook his head.

Eli left Noelle's side, and he greeted the Naturei in the tent. It was evident to Noelle that they were close by the way they greeted and teased each other.

"Well, introduce us to the future queen! Don't be rude!"

"Everyone, this is Noelle! She doesn't know the advice of the educator, and we're going to keep it that way."

Eli slid a hand around her waist, and the soldiers in the tent laughed, as if it were a game. Noelle felt like the center of some joke or, rather, the center of some foolish educator's tips that she only had bits of. She wanted to jab Eli in the ribs for the embarrassment and because he openly mocked her. But she had to make nice among her new peers, so she simply laughed along too.

"You're so funny!" Noelle said through her teeth.

"Wait until you *really* get to know me," Eli said.

They each greeted her with warm enthusiasm. One soldier even mockingly bowed before her and called her his queen. She played along and laughed as if she were delighted. But she found none of it amusing.

"Prince Eli, weren't you going to introduce me to this beautiful human? I've never seen one in person before. I didn't imagine they could be so lovely," a Naturei with a muscular build and defined jaw said as he walked toward them. He placed a fist over his heart, and Noelle did too.

Eli's lips pressed into a straight line. He seemed to reluctantly place a fist over his own heart.

"Adam, this Noelle. Noelle, meet Captain Adam—one of our royal soldiers who leads the Naturei army," Eli said and saluted him.

Curiously, Eli placed a hand, again, on the small of Noelle's back. The soldiers in the tent all seemed to note it too.

"It's really nice to meet you, Captain Adam. And thank you for the compliment," she said with a bashful grin.

Eli watched Noelle, and trepidation seemed to pool in his eyes as he did. He tightened his grip around her waist and pulled her toward him.

Adam smiled politely at Noelle, then nodded at Eli. He went back to his seat.

Noelle turned to face Eli. "What was that about?"

"Adam is loyal to me."

"And I don't belong to you."

Eli's lips curled upward. "I didn't say you were loyal to me—I said Adam was. But what is this? I thought *you* told people we were dating?"

Noelle had told her friends that, but it was with an ulterior motive. Her motive was to annoy Eli, something she was not successful at.

"Are you going to tell people that we're dating too?" Noelle asked coyly.

"Only if you agreed to it," Eli said and leaned in close, as if the tent weren't full of onlooking soldiers. He was chaotic—and he seemed to hardly care what people thought. Shouldn't a prince of an entire realm give some care to how people viewed him?

But she couldn't deny that she felt a spark between them. Despite how annoying she found him, she did think he was interesting and *very* attractive. Every time that he placed a hand on her skin, it made her heart sputter, and his smile was enough to make her feel dizzy at times. Still, romance couldn't happen; it was strictly forbidden. The king himself had warned her and even tried to derail whatever that educator said to Eli.

The way Eli looked at her with intense curiosity and the way his eyes searched hers made her feel slightly unsettled. She probably shouldn't trust him—yet he had made a promise to treat her well, and so she did.

She wanted to reach out and pull Eli closer to her. But that couldn't happen; they could never happen. And besides, he was the reason she was a prisoner in the first place. Remembering that, she pulled away and broke eye contact.

"I'm hungry." She eyed the food.

"Right," Eli said and withdrew his own hand from the small of her back. Noelle knew it was the right thing to do, but she wished he hadn't removed his hand. It was a comfort in the midst of this foreign realm.

"I had some of our best food chefs bring in some veggies and fruits that you're familiar with. I had them bring some that you don't know either so you could try something new. But I suggest sticking to what you know mostly so you don't get sick from adjusting your diet too much."

"Wait, you brought in these plants for *me*?" Noelle asked, surprised.

"I wanted you to feel like you were home." Eli shrugged. "I really am sorry for getting you in this mess. I'll try to make the best of it for you."

Eli and Noelle joined the buffet line, behind some soldiers. Eli handed Noelle a plate, and then they plucked whichever vegetables or fruits their hearts desired. The chefs stood on either end, and with a wave of their hands—the food was instantly finished.

Noelle's eyebrows rose as she watched them with fascination.

Eli seemed to notice and leaned over. "Their ability is cooking. They're pretty amazing."

Noelle was suddenly grateful that she hadn't gotten assigned to cooking duty. How could she keep up with these Naturei who simply waved their fingers and managed to cook an entire meal on a plate in the blink of an eye?

She was distracted as she watched the chefs. She instantly plucked some vegetables that she recognized, like corn, tomatoes, spinach, and carrots. She also plucked some strawberries, an apple, and blueberries. She eyed one plant with a foreign-looking fruit. It was violet and round. She reached her hand out and gently pulled. It was squishy to the touch, and she wondered how it might taste.

"Good choice!" Eli held his plate out, and a chef waved their fingers over it, and it was instantly cooked and organized on the plate in a beautiful manner. It hadn't dawned on Noelle that they could control the vegetables and fruits. It looked like it was seasoned and spiced to perfection too. "That is a vivi fruit."

She nodded, eager to bring the vivi fruit to her lips. She wondered what sort of flavors it might have. She eyed several other mysterious fruits, but she didn't want to overdo it. She took heed of Eli's warning about her stomach.

She held the plate out to the chef, and the Naturei woman grinned.

"I've been eager to meet you ever since I heard about the educator's words," she said and waved her hand over her plate. She cooked the food instantly, and Noelle could smell a delicious glaze over it. Her mouth watered.

"Maybe you could tell me about that?" Noelle smiled.

The chef laughed. "I would if it weren't for Prince Eli forbidding me to do it. I'm going to be one of your chefs. My name is Sage."

"One of my chefs?" In Chicago, she didn't always know where her next meal would come from, and now she would have a personal chef? If this was being a prisoner, she didn't mind being a Naturei prisoner at all. Sadly, in Noelle's opinion, this was pathetically an upgrade for her.

Sage warmly smiled. "Yes, I work for Prince Eli and the Goldner family. He has assigned me to work for you too. I'm very pleased to meet you! You're the first human I've ever encountered, but we read about you in school."

Sage was tall with beautiful dark skin and a hearty demeanor. Noelle instantly liked her. She seemed warm and welcoming, but Noelle was perplexed by Sage's fascination with her. Adam and several others also seemed quite interested in her simply for the fact that she was human. Above all, Eli seemed eerily fascinated with her humanness. She turned to find him, but he sat down with his eyes on her.

Sage seemed to notice. "So maybe there is something to the educator's words after all."

"Sage, you can't talk about the educator's words unless you plan to tell me what he said."

"Very well, enjoy your food!"

Noelle joined Eli, and they sat among several soldiers. Noelle watched as everybody quickly ate their fill. Her plate was a swirl of flavor and spices that she didn't recognize but *loved*.

Noelle listened as soldiers and Eli told stories and laughed. It was evident that Eli had been among them and one of them. But it seemed like he had moved on, perhaps toward his royal duties.

Noelle picked up the soft vivi fruit and bit into it. The inside was a pale green color, and juices emerged with every bite. It reminded her of the texture of a kiwi, but the flavor was much sweeter and richer, and yet it was gooey, sort of like honey.

"I'll get you more of those if you like it that much," Eli said.

Noelle wiped her mouth, and her fingers were now sticky. "This fruit is amazing!"

"I'll make a vivi plant in your room then," Eli said with amusement.

"My *room*?" Noelle asked, surprised.

"Yes, your room. What?"

"Well, I just didn't think I'd have my own room. I suppose I figured I'd stay in a cell or something with guards."

Eli's lips glided into a soft smile. He seemed so easily amused. "I told you, I am going to try to make this as good as possible for you. I know it isn't your home, and I know it will take adjusting, but I really do mean it when I say I hope you'll grow to like it here. It is the least I can do after forcing you to come all this way, by my father's decree."

Noelle swallowed. Eli had been really kind to her. She was grateful, and she felt guilty for speaking unkindly to him earlier. He still deserved it, though, somewhat.

"Eli, do you think we could go for a walk? Maybe have a chat?"

"Of course."

Noelle gave a gentle nod. She planned to apologize for her treatment toward Eli and her unkind words. She made an inner vow in that moment that she would be kinder to him; he had gone to great lengths to try to help her, and yet she repaid him with anger. He had treated her much kinder than she had treated him, and guilt weighed on her. She also hadn't been honest with him about everything. He didn't know that the necklace that they sought hung on her neck or that she was Merklei.

Eli stood from the table and waved his hand over his plate, and all the rubbish disappeared. He then waved his hand over Noelle's plate, and her rubbish also disappeared.

Eli chuckled at the surprised look on Noelle's face. Together, they walked out of the violet tent, with many eyes that watched, curiously glued to them.

As they walked past the bazaar, many stopped to pay respect to the prince. Others whispered as they passed; news surely had spread by now about the scandalous fact that a human had joined the Naturei realm by decree of the king.

"There was a dead body with her name written by it in the fire realm! I heard she is a murderer," a Naturei said loud enough for Noelle to hear.

With each step, and with every turn of the Naturei people's heads, Noelle increasingly began to understand just how big of a deal Eli was to this realm. The quilt-makers froze as they passed and saluted Eli with enthusiasm, but they eyed Noelle with disdain. It seemed that the king's antihuman sentiment ran deep in different circles here within the realm. They seemed to revere Eli as he walked past, and she rolled her eyes. He didn't need any help with his puffed-up pride.

When they finally retreated past the busy bazaar, Noelle let out a sigh. She didn't particularly enjoy being the center of attention.

Eli turned his focus to Noelle and took her chin gently into his hand and tilted it up toward him. "Is everything okay?" A worried line appeared between his brows.

Noelle leaned into his touch because she found it comforting. But then she seemed to come to her senses and pulled away.

Eli dropped his hand, and he looked her over for a moment. "Did you have something in particular you wanted to talk about?"

"Yes, let's go somewhere. Anywhere you like," Noelle said and looked over her shoulder. She didn't want to stick around the bazaar where somebody might come by.

"I know the perfect place—follow me." Eli began to walk toward a nearby keiloki plant, and then he grasped the plant with his thumb and index finger. And then he extended his left hand out to Noelle, who confidently took it.

A flash of green light emitted from the plant, and after a few blinks, they were in a field of flowers. A splash of colorful flowers washed over the grassy meadow, and Noelle sighed as she took in the sight.

She spotted several orange alanis plants scattered throughout the meadow, and a cool breeze comforted her. She felt she could finally relax. She turned to Eli, who looked her over patiently. He outstretched his hand to the closest alanis plant, and a flimsy, leafy flower blossomed under his palm. He plucked it from the alanis plant and tucked it behind Noelle's ear but not before he ran his fingers through her dark strands.

"Orange suits you really well," Eli said.

"Eli, I needed to talk to you." Noelle crossed her arms and sighed. She wasn't particularly skilled at apologizing. "I think we've gotten off on the wrong foot. You've been tremendously kind to me, given the circumstances, and I don't think I've been very nice to you. I just wanted to apologize."

Eli took a step toward her. "It's all right. I did ruin your life in Chicago—I'd like to ask for your forgiveness. I will do anything I can to make it up to you."

"Let's call it even then."

"So you'll stop calling me names?" Eli inquired with a half smile.

"I didn't say that."

"In my realm, you can't insult the prince." He tilted his head to the side.

"Oh no, what could happen? Would I become imprisoned?" Noelle held her hands up in mock surrender. She eyed one of the giant alanis plants and couldn't help but let astonishment wash over her.

Eli followed her gaze to see what held her interest. "I created it so anybody can use it. Here, put your hand on the base, and then it will emit an orange liquid that heals," he said, and he took Noelle's hand into his own. His gentle fingertips felt electric and smooth against hers.

Eli placed her hand on the base of the orange plant, and as soon as he did, a small amount of liquid protruded out of the flower. Eli swiped the liquid and dabbed it on a random bruise that Noelle had on her arm. Noelle watched as it instantly healed.

"Why did you create this plant? You mentioned it takes nine years. I mean, it is the most stunning plant that I've ever seen—but you have a healing ability. Wouldn't you just heal people?"

"I created it so that future generations will be able to heal after I'm gone. Also, I can heal others but not myself. But the alanis plant's ointment works on my injuries."

Noelle hadn't expected that answer. In that moment, he looked less like the annoying boy from the train and more like a future-oriented ruler who cared deeply about this realm. Maybe he would make a good king someday.

"Goldner?"

"Elle?"

"Please don't be offended. But you mentioned your father adopted you. How did you get adopted by the king?"

Eli's green eyes seemed unfazed. Noelle sighed in relief.

"You met Adam—he is sort of like a military general in our realm. My father was the king's captain, the leader of the Naturei military, and supposedly he died in a battle when I was young. The king made a Naturei vow to take care of me, and he has fulfilled it. I'm the heir to the throne, but that is also because the king lost his only child." Eli's eyes seemed lost in thought. "But the educator has made me doubt that story. He said my parents died in a rebellion."

Noelle watched him and fought the urge to wrap her hands around his. She knew what it was like to lose your loved ones; she wouldn't wish it on her worst enemies.

Noelle knew she shouldn't reach for him in the way she desired. She ought to keep him as a friendly ally and work to maintain a good relationship with him. But in that moment, his handsome features with the backdrop of the flowery field did not do her desire to be just friends any favors.

"Want to play a game?" He interrupted her train of thought.

She eyed her wrist where the twine lay. "I don't know if I like your games."

He shook his head. "No, a real Naturei game. Here, I'll show you!" And then he waved his hand across the field, and three wooden loops appeared in the air and floated. One loop was small, and the others were medium and large. He then waved his hand, and a large ball made of some sort of earthy material appeared in his hand. "This is called Splatta. Because if you don't make it, your ball goes splat! You have to get the ball in each loop, largest to smallest. The first person to do it wins."

"Sounds easy enough," Noelle said, confident.

"Oh, and the loops move." He tossed the brown ball in his hand, and then the loops began to move in erratic directions.

"Okay, maybe not so easy."

"Ladies first." He handed her the large brown ball. It felt somewhat heavy, yet she managed to throw it easily. It missed the large loop and landed in the dirt and cracked into several pieces.

Eli laughed and waved a hand over the ball. It vanished and appeared in his hand, completely restored. He held it by his side and swung it backward and then launched it into the air, and it went through the large hoop.

"Cheater," Noelle groaned. "You've clearly done this before."

Eli waved a hand over Noelle's outstretched hand, and the brown ball appeared. She eyed the large hoop, and it zigzagged about. She tried to mimic Eli's form, but she did it all wrong and the ball landed far below the loop.

Eli let out a whistle. "You're not holding it right. May I show you the right form?"

She nodded.

He neared her, and his chest was against her back. He paused, as if he seemed to ask her permission to continue.

She nodded again. "Go on."

He waved his hand over hers, and the big brown ball appeared. "You need to guide the direction with your wrist and follow through with your throw." Eli placed gentle fingertips over her right arm and guided her arm in the correct position. Then he placed a hand on her left hip. "You also need to be careful where you place your hips. If you keep leaning sideways, then your ball will go sideways." He rotated her hip forward but then rested his hand on her waist.

"Maybe we should do the next one together." Noelle shrugged. She didn't want him to let go.

He placed a gentle hand under her chin and tilted her face up toward him. The sun hit just behind his head, and his handsome features seemed even more irresistible this close.

"Together? You're trying to cheat," he said.

She was playing a dangerous game. The alarm bells in her mind rang. Everything was telling her to stop. She knew this could mean trouble, but she ignored it.

Eli seemed to have thrown all caution to the wind also, but that seemed to be common for him.

Noelle's heart shuddered, and she could feel Eli's heart beat quickly too. He drew her impossibly closer to him and spun her around to face him.

She dropped the ball, and it broke into pieces on the dirt ground. Noelle knew this was a mistake, but she ignored everything that told her to stop.

"Please tell me what the educator told you. I think I have the right to know about it."

"I'll tell you but only if you understand that the educator was the most revered in our whole realm for his wisdom and knowledge. So I respected everything he said. But they've dubbed him a traitor now." Eli's green eyes searched hers.

She nodded.

He gave a resigned sigh. "He said he found out where the necklace was. He said that a human girl in Chicago would find the necklace and that she'd be close with the Snow Queen. He advised that I marry the girl, and it would lead to a Merklei on the throne as queen in our realm. He called you the rightful queen of Naturei. We also think he may have lost his mind"

Noelle's eyes widened. She now understood why he hadn't wanted her to find out. She was grateful he seemed to hold it with at least some reservation.

Noelle felt exposed. She was human, yet she was also Merklei, and the educator's advice seemed more believable now.

"Oh," she managed.

"My father is under the impression that the girl, um, *you* would turn over the throne to the Snow Queen—which he doesn't want to happen because they have a history," Eli said and sighed.

Noelle also sighed in relief. So he hadn't known she was Merklei, since they seemed to think that Noelle would give the power to Lumi.

"So Lumi and the Naturei king were together?"

"I'm sorry I didn't tell you before, but Lumi and the Naturei king were engaged. They had a child together, Lorelei, who died when all of Lumi's people died. They both blamed each other for it and had a major falling out. She called off the wedding and hasn't been seen since—he has sent guards and spies to find her for years. He believes she is to blame for the death of their child. It is part of the reason he wants to enact the Heirling Duel."

Noelle had thought Eli was sent on some sort of mission with sinister motives, and yet she now realized that he had been sent by a heartbroken, bitter king. Noelle wanted to laugh at the absurdity of it.

"So you spied because he was trying to keep tabs on his ex? And he really thinks that she is the reason for her daughter dying? She was betrayed!" She looked up at him.

"No, we think she is extremely dangerous. She mixed with the humans, and it cost her entire family their life. She is still willing to mix with humans, and look where it has gotten you. She is even dating a human!" Eli's lips turned upward, and his eyes roamed over Noelle. "Well, I guess I can't blame her for that one."

"I'm not here because of Lumi. I'm here because of you," Noelle said.

"You're right. They had tabs on you, and the Naturei soldiers had orders to eliminate you after news spread about the dead body. But I intervened by meeting you myself and spared your life. I guess I couldn't stand the thought of not following the educator's wisdom and allowing you to die for no real reason. So you're welcome."

Noelle hadn't known that they planned to take her life even before she met Eli. Her legs trembled.

Eli caught Noelle and held her up.

"You're okay," he said and reassured her. "Nothing will happen to you here. I won't let it happen." He wrapped a strong arm around her.

"What about my friends? Marko and Luis?" Noelle said, and worry lines appeared on her forehead.

"I didn't report them. I only wrote reports on you because you were the Naturei target. For all I understand, they might not know about your friends."

Noelle nodded, and she wished that erased her fear—but it didn't. She worried about their safety and for Marko's family too.

"Will I ever see my friends again?" Noelle bit down on her lip.

Eli steadied her and shrugged. "It is possible. I still have my trial, and I'm almost certain the king is going to sentence me to participating in the Heirling Duel since apparently Lumi has an heir. I don't know if she had a child with a human or what. But it is the first time in a long time that a Heirling Duel is even possible. They need at least two out of three rulers to vote in favor of it. The Leizeis have declared it as of yesterday," he said and closed his eyes. When he opened them, his green eyes were oozing concern.

Did he think he might die? Was he worried about killing somebody? She imagined her life in this realm without Eli.

"No, you can't die," Noelle said. "The king won't do it. He's your father."

"He is my father, but he would do it."

Noelle considered that—and considered what her role might be as the Merklei heir. And with that thought, she threw all of her own caution to the wind too. If the days ahead were deadly, who cared what they did today? Noelle wrapped herself under his arm, and they watched the sunset with dark violets and magentas that illuminated the sky. Eli welcomed her embrace and intertwined his fingers into hers and stroked her hair with his free hand. It was two young people, seeking solace in each other's arms when they both had battles to face soon.

He waved a hand and crafted a twine hammock right in the middle of the field. He lay on it and looked at Noelle, who joined him. She admired his ability to craft anything with nature and examined the twine hammock as she cautiously sank her weight onto it.

She lay next to him, and he wrapped his warm arm around her. He stroked her hair gently.

Maybe this was why he was so carefree. Maybe he thought he only had a few more weeks or even days to watch sunsets. Maybe he didn't care what the Naturei people thought because he didn't have time to care. As Noelle considered that, she felt that she understood Eli much more significantly.

He wasn't as chaotic or careless as he had seemed only hours ago; he was exactly like her. He was trying to survive. And sometimes you do seemingly crazy things in survival mode. But here they both were, just trying to get by and survive.

CHAPTER 21
NOELLE
THE CONFRONTATION

Eli's hand found Noelle's, and he traced his finger over the palm of her hand. She was so aware of every stroke of his finger on her hand and every gentle movement of his chest that rose and fell against her head. She rested her cheek against his chest and nuzzled in closer.

"Do you miss your parents?" Noelle wondered aloud. "Has the king been kind to you? And what about this educator? He seemed like he meant something to you."

Eli stirred. "I miss my parents every day. The king has tried his best and loved me in his own way. He can be very tough and extremely hard on me though. He says it is for my own good, though, since I'm the heir of the throne. Truthfully, the educator was the closest thing that I had to a father. We spent so much time together." He cleared his throat.

Noelle lifted her head. His green eyes drifted from the sky and then toward her, and they rested just below her collarbone.

In a panic, she reached for the necklace. But then exhaled when she realized it was still concealed under her Naturei cloak. She worried that she drew attention to the necklace by doing that and tried to relax her hand.

"I really love this cloak and the Naturei clothing." She tried to conceal her real anxiety. She wanted to appear as if she had meant to touch the base of the cloak that covered her collarbone. She stroked it absentmindedly.

"You look beautiful in that dress," Eli said, and he grabbed her hand and brought it to his shoulder, then dropped it there.

"Don't you think this is a bad idea? The king kind of said this can't be a thing." She propped herself up on her elbow and faced Eli. Not to mention that she might be dueling against him in a matter of days. She should stop this right here, right now.

He ran a hand through his long dark hair and mirrored her with a propped-up elbow. "I sort of like irritating the king." Eli smiled a large, toothy smile, and the dark lashes that lined his green eyes fluttered.

Noelle's face twisted with concern. "Don't you think we shouldn't be out here like this? Your father might send you to some duel, and he might kill me."

"Kill you?" Eli frowned. "For what crime?"

"I don't know how things work here. But I suppose disobeying him? Isn't he in charge around here?"

Eli laughed a slow, meticulous laugh. "He only said you couldn't take the throne. He fears that you'll give it to Lumi somehow because of the educator's words. He abhors her, and they're entirely at odds despite the fact that she once would have inherited the Naturei throne." Eli scoffed. "But he never said I couldn't get to know you or enjoy your presence. Besides, he is just afraid of the educator. His wisdom is unmatched."

"Is that what we are doing?" Noelle demanded in disbelief. "Getting to know each other and enjoying each other's presence?" Noelle plopped down on the twine hammock, and it swayed gently. She eyed the colorful sunset and sighed.

Eli was silent for a moment with his eyes also on the sky. He faced Noelle, and his eyes were suddenly soft. "Our first meeting didn't go so well. But now that our destinies are intertwined, I look forward to getting to know you more." Eli began to trace his finger on the back of her hand but then suddenly stopped.

"That is, if you want to."

She knew if she were smart, she would tell him friendship was all she desired. If she were thinking of her survival and maintaining a good relationship with the king, she would tell him they wouldn't be more than friends. But Noelle didn't care about anything at that moment, except the way his green eyes seemed to always find their way to hers and made her cheeks turn scarlet. She liked the way his fingers felt against hers, and she liked the sweetness of his deep voice. There couldn't be anything between them, but that didn't stop her from wishing that there could be.

Against Noelle's better judgment, she said, "I'd like to get to know you better. But I don't know where this could ever go. We are natural enemies, despite your educator's supposed knowledge." Noelle wanted to tell him that she wasn't just human, but she was Merklei. If only he knew. Then he would rightfully understand her warning about being enemies. They might be dropped into an arena in a few short days. The thought sent a shudder down her spine.

Eli's lips curled upward. "And I might be dead in a matter of days because of this Heirling Duel that is being declared. So it sounds like we have an agreement. What if we just enjoy each other's company? Would that be so bad? Or wrong?" Eli lifted an eyebrow and lay still as he awaited her answer.

"Fine. But you won't die in the Heirling Duel—you'll win. And then we'll get to know each other some more." She watched as the tension in his eyes eased, and he pulled her onto his chest and wrapped his arms around her.

Noelle bit her cheek. She knew that she was the only other Merklei and Lumi's heir by default. The necklace around her neck was evidence of that. If the Naturei king declared the Heirling Duel, she'd have to fight Eli. She sucked in a breath and winced as she realized she had bitten her cheek so hard that it drew blood.

Eli, perplexed, traced his finger over her bottom lip.

The pain suddenly wasn't remembered as his finger brought healing to her cut.

But then a twig snapped behind them, and Noelle immediately sat up and flipped off the hammock. The king and several Naturei soldiers had found their way to the flowery field and were several yards away, where they stood.

Noelle's heart shuddered. How long had they been there? Eli had just embraced her and had his finger on her lip. It looked bad. *Really* bad.

Eli sat up, too, and helped Noelle up to her feet. He placed a protective arm around her as if he hadn't a care in the world.

Although the sunlight was dimming and dusk was gathering, Noelle could clearly see the fire that burned in the king's eyes from beside the hammock. His eyes weren't on Eli but only her.

"You'll both be coming to the throne room," the king called out, his voice agitated.

"This was my idea," Eli called back.

The king turned to leave, and the soldiers remained. Eli sighed, then turned his head toward Noelle. He gave her an apologetic look, and they both followed.

Noelle followed the king through the keiloki plant portal, and she stood before the king in his throne room. The twine bracelet must have given the ability to use the keiloki portals. She hadn't been able to do it before. He sat on his throne as if he were exhausted, and his eyes rested with fury on her. She guessed he likely saw much more than she had anticipated by his expression.

He frowned at her as Eli and the others joined them with a flash of green light. Eli stood at Noelle's side, and she could have sworn he looked indifferent. Was he used to being in trouble? Likely.

"It seems I'll need to relieve you of your duties." The king gestured at Noelle.

Eli looked forward. "No, that won't be necessary. I can do my duties with excellence."

"I don't think you can. Can you administer discipline with impartiality when you're lying in a flower field with the human prisoner?" The king's voice was eerily calm and soft. "One day here, and you've already managed to bend Eli to your will and take the upper hand. I'd say you were talented if you weren't so manipulative."

"Actually, that was my plan, and I'd like credit where it is due," Eli said with a hint of satisfaction.

The king didn't share his humor. He glared at Eli with disdain heavy in his eyes. The king's eyes went back and forth between Noelle and Eli, and then he sighed.

"Adviser?" the king called with a deep voice.

The twitchy adviser appeared from the back of the room and tapped his fingers together nervously. He looked around the room and then looked at the king.

"Eli and Noelle seem very cozy and quite on track for the educator's advice already. But his words will not come true—how can you advise me to ensure that it never comes true?" The king looked over Noelle with fury and fire in his eyes that seemed to build with every moment that passed.

The adviser twitched as if it were a nervous tic. "W-well," he stuttered. "You could cast the girl out of the Naturei r-realm. You could forbid Prince Eli to ever s-see her again." He looked over the two, as if he evaluated their fates.

"No," the king said. "The girl knows too much, and she is our prisoner in this realm forever. And besides, I already made laws to forbid Eli from going to her world again. That was little use for his curiosity." The king shot an annoyed look at Eli and then folded his hands together. "He was supposed to kill the Snow Queen and leave, but he failed."

The adviser nodded frantically. "Yes, if it pleases the k-king that she is a p-prisoner, then it should be so. Another suggestion w-would be you could k-kill her, then she will never m-marry Prince Eli and become queen."

Noelle glared at the adviser.

"I'm not a murderer, Adviser. The girl is a liability with her knowledge but not a criminal. At least not yet." The king raised an eyebrow at Noelle.

Noelle didn't dare make any facial expression at the king's words. Not when her fate was in his hands. She wanted to sneer at the words *not yet,* but she kept her face neutral.

The king sighed, clearly out of patience. "What else, Adviser?" he growled.

All eyes were on the adviser. "Then y-you must forbid them to be a-alone and ensure it doesn't happen by assigning g-guards to her. Don't take away his r-responsibility of being in charge of her b-because the realm will suspect something, and the rumors w-will begin. She might even gain some s-supporters, and w-we don't want that. So instead, let him k-keep his role over her. After all, t-this is his mess!" The adviser twitched violently and then regained his composure. He pushed his round glasses up the bridge of his nose and continued. "But they m-must never be a-alone. She must have g-guards at all times to watch her. And they m-must remain c-cordial and nothing more. If they v-violate this, then she must be k-killed."

The king looked as if the adviser's words were an irritant in a wound. "Or I could banish her to prison walls. I doubt any romance could blossom there," the king mused.

"You think the realm won't notice? She has already been out and free all day. They'll know something is wrong if she suddenly disappears," Eli said.

That was the straw that broke the camel's back. The king went into a rage and threw his hands into the air. "You have put this entire realm in danger because of her! I have worked tirelessly to train you, raise you, and prepare you to take this realm with wisdom and authority! Yet you receive this traitorous advice from your educator and you've undone all my work because you cannot control yourself. I can't have a Merklei on my throne, not after all the destruction and ruin that the Merklei brought me and this entire realm! She'll deliver the throne right to the delicate snowflake herself." The vein in the king's neck emerged and pulsed. He composed himself with a hand that he rubbed over his face. Noelle noticed a gold signet ring on his index finger. Eli wore a similar one.

"No, I won't," Noelle said. She refused to cower at this moment.

The king was in Noelle's face instantly. "Do you know that our educator has vast knowledge that far surpasses anybody else in this realm? When he has uttered wisdom and decrees, they've always been accurate. He isn't a liar but a traitor. So spare me your lies," the king said with wild eyes.

Noelle flinched backward. His eyes were crazed and looked almost feral. "I-I would make a Naturei vow that I'd never pass the throne on to Lumi." The king's eyes made her voice tremble.

Eli didn't respond. He kept his eyes on the king.

The king scoffed. "You humans are manipulative. You'd find a loophole in the Naturei vow. No, you will be cordial with one another and nothing more. You will always have guards with you, and if you cross any lines with Eli again, then you'll be behind prison walls for the remainder of your life. You wouldn't want to do that to her, would you, Eli?"

Eli shook his head.

"Then it is settled! I'll pick her guards myself," the king said cheerily, as if he hadn't just yelled. "And the budding romance will die, and she will never have the ability to bring Merklei into this realm. Having a human here is bad enough."

Noelle realized the king disliked humans, but he *despised* the Merklei. How could he have been engaged to Lumi, had a child with her, only to turn to this level of bitterness? If he only knew that Noelle was both human and Merklei, what would happen to her?

She eyed Eli, whose handsome features were disgruntled by the king's anger.

No, she would not be queen. She would be in a prison cell, and this was the end of any romantic feelings that might have gotten stirred up. She was human and Merklei, and he was Naturei. This was never meant to be. Besides, she might be fighting against Eli if the Heirling Duel truly did happen. He surely would hate her then.

"Eli, you can show Noelle to her room, and the two Naturei guards behind her will accompany her and stay with her for the night," the king instructed.

Noelle was surprised to hear the king call her by her name instead of being called *human girl*.

It was clear that they were all dismissed. The guards saluted, and then Eli led the way out.

Once outside the throne room, one of the guards sighed loudly. Clearly they weren't excited about this either.

CHAPTER 22
NOELLE
THE FORBIDDEN TOUCH

Eli led the way through several hallways, each lined with exotic plants that sprawled along the dirt floor. Noelle still couldn't get used to indoor flooring being dirt. She supposed it made sense in a place like the Naturei realm, where the people were one with nature, but it didn't sit right with her.

Eli walked past many doors and stopped abruptly at one door in particular.

"This is your room," he said. It was the first thing he had said since leaving the throne room. Noelle tried to read him, but he remained expressionless. He looked entirely blank, and she wished she could ask what he was thinking, but she felt the guards were listening to everything, so she didn't bother. With them here, it wasn't safe to share intimate thoughts.

Eli opened the door, and a grand room stood behind it. Of course the floor was dirt, but inside there was a bright orange alanis plant by her bedside and a vivi plant on the other side. Eli had said he would put it in her room, yet it surprised her nonetheless. Several interesting plants were sprawled out across the dirt floor in an intricate fashion. One plant in particular took her interest because it was hot pink with flowers that seemed to melt off the stem every few seconds, and when it did—it simply evaporated into mist. A sweet fragrance permeated the air every time it happened.

There was gold furniture, a gold mirror, and an oversized gold bed in the center of the room. She had a huge window with gold curtains draped over them. It was a beautiful room, albeit quite different from her world's standard of beauty.

"You brought an alanis plant! This is perfect. Thank you, Eli." She spun to look at him.

But there was a touch of sadness in his eyes as he looked back. Noelle felt distant, unsure of what to say. She ignored the nagging feeling to reach for him.

"I hope you'll be happy here. These guards are Ash and Aster—you're in good hands with them."

Noelle turned and faced them. "Hello, I'm Noelle."

The taller one nodded. "I'm Ash. Welcome to the Naturei realm."

"And that means I am Aster. Pleased to meet you," the bald, shorter one said and saluted. Noelle hadn't considered it until now, but all the Naturei seemed quite young.

"How old are you?" Noelle asked.

"I was initiated at age twenty. So I appear to be twenty, but I am eighty-four," Ash said. "And that old man was initiated at twenty-seven, but he is 309." He poked Aster, and he grunted.

"And I'm technically nineteen, but I was initiated at eighteen," Eli said.

"So you'll forever look eighteen?" Noelle's lips turned up. "I wouldn't have chosen eighteen to be frozen in time."

"Oh? If you were Naturei, what age would you be initiated?" Eli crossed his arms.

"Initiated?"

"Yes, it is the age where you take the vows of your people and receive your full abilities. When you do, you stop physically aging," Eli said. Noelle recalled Lumi had mentioned she needed to become initiated.

"Oh, well then I'd pick twenty-five or something. But I'd make sure I wasn't a teenager," Noelle said. "Too many breakouts."

Noelle saluted the soldiers. They seemed friendly enough. She despised their presence, though, as if they were her babysitters. She wished she regretted her time with Eli, but she didn't. She'd do it all over again if she could. She could still feel the buzz of his finger against her lip. She looked at Eli, at his lips, and he seemed to catch her stare because his familiar gratified smile appeared.

"Well, you'll have to go to school tomorrow, so I'll let you get some rest." Eli turned to leave.

"School?" Noelle said in disbelief.

"Yes, in our realm we all go to school each week. It's called the Naturei School of Education, and we never stop attending. We really value education and believe it is an honor to continue our education. Even the king goes to school regularly," Aster said.

"Once a Naturei has mastered a skill, we teach that skill to other Naturei, and we continue to learn from others and grow," Ash added. "In our realm, you are always a student, and once you've mastered a skill, you're always a teacher of that skill. We believe in community and helping one another."

Noelle looked around her room, and the quaint, cozy feeling it gave her made her suddenly sleepy. But she was too fascinated to dismiss the conversation.

"What will I learn about?" Noelle asked.

"Well, since you've been assigned to me, you'll attend my classes with me. Sorry about that—you may not find my subjects interesting. Maybe in the future, I'll pick subjects you might be more interested in. Tomorrow the classes are Governing a Kingdom with Diplomatic Relations, and Warfare."

Noelle's eyebrows shot up when she heard warfare was a school subject. She supposed she shouldn't be surprised since Eli learned how to govern an entire kingdom.

"Those sound like appropriate subjects for a future king." Noelle shrugged. "And appropriate subjects for a future queen too, if I don't say so myself." She thought they might laugh at her joke. But nobody in the room laughed. The tension was palpable in the room, and Noelle shifted uncomfortably. She was on thin ice, and she seemed to skate carelessly into dangerous territory.

"I wouldn't joke that way." Ash frowned. "I'll let that one slide since I understand you meant it as humor. But we are loyal to the king, and we will report your activity to him daily."

Noelle didn't move. Realization struck, and she had, in fact, made a terrible decision. She was human and Merklei, and now she had guards who reported daily to the king. What if they found her secret? What would they do to her? Noelle's thoughts drifted to her friends Lumi, Marko, and Luis. And suddenly the concealed necklace felt mightily heavy around her neck; the necklace felt burdensome because of the secret it contained.

"Why do you learn warfare if there is no war in your realms?"

Ash shifted his feet. "Our soldiers train to protect the king and his ruling."

Sweat formed on Noelle's brow with the realization that they trained to turn on their own people, for the king. They may not have war with other realms, but it seemed obvious that there was a war brewing within it. Noelle glanced at Eli, who had admitted that the educator said his own parents were killed by the king. Perhaps the Naturei realm wasn't as quaint as it appeared.

Eli cleared his throat. "We should probably get some rest."

"I'm pretty tired." Noelle didn't wait for them to leave the room. She crawled into her massive gold bed and lay under the sheets.

"We'll be outside your room, and in the morning you'll have a different set of guards," Ash said and walked outside the room.

"I'm sorry about everything, Elle. I see your point that I do tend to make selfish decisions and that you're the one who pays for them," Eli said. His green eyes looked heavy, weighted down with some sort of distress.

"Goldner, don't be sorry. I'm definitely not sorry about today." A grin tugged on her lips.

Eli raised an eyebrow, and then he, too, smiled. But then his smile quickly faded, and the sober expression from earlier returned as he watched her. "We should get going."

Aster and Eli walked out the room but not before Eli looked over his shoulder to look at Noelle once last time. "You have plenty of clothing in your dressers, Elle. You don't have to wear that to sleep. The Naturei girls who helped you dress will wake you up in the morning," Eli said and then he was gone.

Noelle wanted to search every inch of the room. She wanted to inspect the plants, go through her clothing and figure everything out. But she was simply far too tired. She felt her eyelids get heavier and heavier.

When the door closed, she ripped her cloak off. She held her gold oval necklace in her palm. She tried everything. She made a wish, muttered, tried every last thing that she could think of. Yet the necklace didn't respond to anything, nor would it open.

"Bring back my grandma, *you stupid necklace!*" she whispered to it. She had been at it for nearly an hour. What if the necklace didn't actually work? No, she hadn't been initiated. Lumi hadn't lied when she said it needed Merklei power to work. She would have to figure out how to be initiated.

Eventually she just fell asleep.

Noelle opened her eyes to Eden, Blossom, and Aurora standing at the foot of her bed. Eden called out instructions to the other girls in a loud voice. Aurora took the golden curtains and flung them backward and let the light in.

"You didn't even take off your evening outfit?" Eden asked with her forehead crinkled. She waved her hand, and suddenly all of Noelle's Naturei clothing was gone. She was grateful for the sheet that covered her, and she pulled it up to her chin.

"Hey!" Noelle called, voice groggy. She was careful to cover up the necklace, and her heart fluttered. She didn't want them to see the necklace; in fact, she couldn't let them see the necklace. Her life depended on it.

The door to Noelle's bedroom opened, and it was Sage, her personal chef. She carried a plate and mug with her, and she'd draped a napkin over her arm. She walked to the side of Noelle's bed. "Girl, it is already late! You should be up. What do you want for breakfast? I'll make it for you." She wore a brown vine dress that went down to her knees and flared out.

Noelle shrugged under the blanket. "I guess toast and coffee."

Sage waved her hand over a plate, and suddenly there was toast, topped off with avocado and spices. She then waved her fingers over the mug, and brown liquid poured into it. Noelle could smell the rich scent of freshly roasted coffee beans.

Sage held it out and offered it to Noelle. "Prince Eli told me about coffee beans in your realm. I learned how to make coffee for you."

Noelle wanted to take it, but that would mean she'd have to sit up and expose her necklace. She gave a grateful smile, feeling entirely unworthy of the best Naturei in the realm using their abilities to help her.

"Sorry, I'm shy. Could you set it on the counter? I'll eat it in just a moment. Thank you so much, Sage!" Noelle said.

"We aren't shy about our bodies in the Naturei realm," Eden said.

Noelle took her in for the first time that morning. She wore a green leaf hat, styled as if it were a cocktail hat. And she wore a very tight green bodice that resembled something like a corset. Bright pink roses were at her waist and trailed down to her mid-thigh. What Eden had said was quite true and already noted by Noelle. The men wore bare-chested outfits, and the women wore outfits made of natural elements.

Aurora and Blossom wore identical dresses; they obviously played up their sister bond. They both had leaves for sleeves, and the leafy fabric bunched at their waist and sprawled out in several directions.

The truth was Noelle needed to keep wearing a cloak or at least cover her collarbone to hide the necklace.

"I understand. But I'm shy about my body. So do you think you could put me in another cloak? Or maybe something where it covers my chest and neck?" Noelle asked, sheepish.

Eden shrugged her shoulders and shook her head. "Humans," was all she said.

Eden waved her hand over Noelle's body, and Noelle could feel material against her skin. She lifted the covers and witnessed a bright orange material, identical to the alanis plant, covered her. It certainly smelled similar to the alanis plant. Little alanis flowers protruded down the side of her dress. An orange cloak covered Noelle's shoulders and concealed the necklace. Noelle threw off the covers and admired the gown that Eden had crafted so beautifully.

"I can make edits if you wish," Eden said.

"No! This is beautiful! And it is absolutely comfortable." Noelle jumped from the bed and grabbed the toast.

Aurora and Blossom waved their hands over Noelle's hair, and it was immediately braided across her head like a crown. Aurora then plucked a little orange flower and tucked it behind Noelle's ear, which made Noelle gasp.

"Eli said you liked the alanis plant best, and he specifically asked me to put one flower in your hair for him," Aurora explained and withdrew her hand.

Noelle felt a pang of hope that he had thought of her. Then it was gone as she realized he'd likely never be able to put a flower behind her ear again. He'd likely never be able to touch her ever again, not with the guards watching.

"What is the matter?" Aurora asked.

Noelle hadn't realized her face fell. She quickly removed all traces of emotion off her face and shook her head. "Not a thing."

"The guards are waiting for you outside. They are Hazel and Clay," Eden said and gestured at the door.

"And Eli?" Noelle asked hesitantly.

"You'll see him at school," Eden said.

Noelle went for the door, and the rest followed her. She stiffened when she saw the guards.

"I'm Noelle, nice to meet you," she said and bowed her head. She put a fist over her heart as the other Naturei had done.

They repeated the gesture with a shallow bow. A man with pale blond hair said, "I'm Clay, nice to meet you."

Noelle turned to the female guard, who she assumed was Hazel.

Hazel had short buzzed black hair, and she bowed her own head. "I'm Hazel, and I look forward to serving the king and keeping tabs on you."

Noelle hadn't liked Hazel's comment. It was clear her politeness was out of duty and nothing more and her loyalty lay firmly with the king. Noelle wished Ash and Aster were there instead.

"Well, I guess we'd better get to school," Noelle said. She wanted to find Eli.

The guard turned toward the keiloki plant outside Noelle's room and took hold of it. With a flash of green light, they were suddenly in a massive forest.

Noelle gawked as she looked up and saw beautiful tree house structures, except that they weren't like children's tree houses, but rather they looked as if they had taken keen architectural skills and crafted them through many years. She had seen Eli craft a hammock in a second and wondered how long something this extravagant might take.

There were several round, brown buildings attached to the trees and ladders and ropes leading up to them in every direction. Each round building appeared to be a different classroom, and Naturei men and women were going to and fro. Some climbed ladders to get into the tree house classrooms, while others used the vines and ropes to hoist themselves up.

"This is the school?" Noelle asked her guards in disbelief.

"Pretty neat, huh?" Hazel said and walked toward the ladder. It looked like a jungle gym that master architects had crafted themselves. "We are to begin with Governing a Kingdom with Diplomatic Relations, which is in the fourth building up," Hazel said.

Noelle felt a knot form in her stomach as she craned her neck to look up the massive tree. The only way to get to the fourth classroom, it appeared, was to climb.

"Hope you're not afraid of heights," Clay called and took hold of a ladder that swayed. He began to climb. Hazel, likewise, took another ladder and climbed.

Noelle sighed and then held on to the same ladder that Hazel had begun to climb and lifted her legs onto it. She grasped the wood handles and gripped hard.

She refused to look down. After a while, her arms started to ache. She looked up and saw they had passed through two classrooms. When they passed the third, she craned her neck around to see several Naturei with eyes on her. Murmurs occurred as she did this. She was a human prisoner after all. It didn't look much different than her classrooms, except that they were suspended in a tree.

Noelle continued to climb, and to her relief, she saw Eli in the next classroom, and he waited at the edge. He saw her, and entertainment danced in his eyes at the sight of her wobbly arms.

She wanted to pretend it was from exhaustion, but she was afraid; she hated heights. Eli clearly seemed to pick up on this and was far too amused. She gave him a menacing look.

"Welcome to our school!" Eli called down.

Noelle reached the final classroom building, where a little oval opening allowed students to enter.

Eli held out his hand to Noelle, and she eyed him. They weren't supposed to be too friendly. But she supposed this was cordial enough and nothing guards would balk at.

She took his hand, and he brushed his fingertips gently against her hand, intentional. He seemed to take his time. He gingerly wove his fingers through hers and then pulled her up the rest of the way into the classroom.

The guards were already inside, and they settled in the back.

But Eli didn't let go of her hand immediately. Eli's fingers brushed the back of her hand, and she withdrew it, afraid the guards might see. She figured that for any eyes that roamed, it probably looked like nothing more than a simple "friendly" help.

She glanced at the guards and then Eli. "I like my room, thank you." She said the words as a code. She hoped he understood her intention; that she didn't want to end up in prison walls because they couldn't manage to avoid romantic gestures.

A ghost of a smile appeared on Eli's face. "And I really like the alanis flower in your hair. Orange is your color," Eli said as his gaze trailed slowly up and down her hair.

Noelle shook her head. Eli was entirely a swarm of chaos, uncaring about anything but the present. Did he really think he was a dead man in a matter of days? He seemed to act like it.

A familiar face entered the classroom and stepped in close. It was the freckled Naturei girl. She flashed a smirk at Eli and then looked at Noelle.

"Morning, Eli, you haven't introduced me to our newest friend," she said coldly. She blinked through her lashes at Eli.

"I'm Noelle." She did the Naturei salute.

"Jasmine," she said and didn't bother to salute back, that was, until Eli frowned at her. She then immediately returned the salute. "Sorry." She forced a smile. "I'm still waking up."

"No matter," Noelle said and looked around the classroom. "What sort of Naturei take this class?"

"The ones who go into leadership," Jasmine said and scrunched her nose. "Why, exactly, are you here?"

"She is with me."

A flash of frustration could be seen in Jasmine's eyes. "Oh, I'm so sorry, Eli. How frustrating to have to babysit a human."

"Actually, she has become a friend," Eli said. Jasmine's sharp green eyes lowered to Noelle.

Eli turned to find an empty desk and motioned at Noelle to join him.

Noelle took her place and found Jasmine had kept her eyes on her from the back of the room. She didn't like her, but she needed allies—and she had already ruffled too many feathers. She couldn't afford to ruffle more.

Noelle sat through the lesson and listened as the teacher instructed them on the importance of remaining calm and poised during negotiations with enemies. It struck Noelle that the enemies were their own people. He spoke of recent rebellions that they had snuffed out, which turned violent. She tried listening, but Noelle's mind drifted away to Lumi, Luis, and Marko. Noelle couldn't help but wonder what had happened to them. She knew Marko would stop at nothing to ensure that she was safe; she imagined he probably had colorfully made up many new threats against Eli.

By the time the lesson ceased, Jasmine was already at Eli's side. She was clearly infatuated with him and eager for his attention. She twirled her long golden-brown hair in her fingers. Noelle wondered what sort of leadership role Jasmine might already fill. She looked deceptively young, but that meant nothing in this world. She could be seventy with a long career.

Jasmine placed a hand on Eli's shoulder, then turned to face Noelle. "The king invited me over to dinner tonight," Jasmine said. "Will *she* be there?"

Eli looked over at Noelle. "I hope so."

Jasmine inhaled sharply and dropped her hand. "Can't you leave her with the guards?"

"I could, but I think the king would like to keep her under his surveillance. She is a sneaky one—so I'll be keeping her close. Did you know she steals?"

Noelle snapped her head in his direction and glared at him. He only grinned in return.

"I'm not surprised to hear that humans steal. What else should I have expected?" Jasmine laughed.

"Yeah, I'll have to keep a close eye on her. I don't trust her alone much," Eli said loudly. Was he trying to ensure everybody heard him?

Noelle knew he had to play down their interest in one another, but he was slightly too good at it. She rolled her eyes and faced forward and crossed her arms. She squirmed in her seat after she considered that she would dine with the king. She anticipated he might grill her when Jasmine wasn't, and she sighed.

They made their way down the wooden tree ladders that swayed in the wind. Noelle wished they had made more stable fixtures, and she noticed several people slid down the vines. The vines obviously allowed the Naturei to get down more quickly than the ladders, and she grasped a nearby vine. She crossed her feet around it and put her body weight on it and began to slide but moved much quicker than she originally thought possible.

Noelle zoomed past all the other Naturei and screamed as she tried to tighten her grip on the vines, but it didn't seem to slow her.

A net made entirely of vines formed below her, and she landed with a thud on it. She peered up and looked for who might have crafted the net, but nobody took credit. She shakily slid her fingers through her hair. She needed to get out of there; she needed to get initiated so she could use the necklace to bring back her grandma.

If she were Merklei, would her grandma also be Merklei? Surely, since she had the necklace! Does that mean Noelle could bring back both Lumi's family line and hers? She hoped that both were possible, because if her grandma were truly Merklei, then perhaps this could be done. Noelle felt her hand instinctively go to her neck where the necklace lay. It was still hidden under her orange alanis cloak, and she sighed in relief.

"Having too much fun?" Hazel pulled Noelle from the net.

"I'd hardly call this fun."

They walked down the forest, and sunshine peeked through the trees.

"The next lesson is on fighting tactics," Hazel said.

Noelle might not have any abilities, and she might not live as long as them, but she could fight. This much would work in her favor, at least she hoped.

Naturei everywhere seemed to be moving at glacial speed to their next classrooms. Noelle had noticed that the Naturei were a relaxed realm, and they didn't seem to ever be in a hurry, but this speed was maddening for a Chicagoan. They seemed to slowly dawdle toward a ring in the center of the forest where everybody came to a stop.

A bare-chested Captain Adam stood in the center. "Noelle, I hadn't expected you to join our lesson. Today is a fighting day—you think you're up for that?"

Jasmine snickered behind Noelle.

Noelle turned to face her. "Absolutely."

Captain Adam stepped into the center of the ring. "We have a newcomer with us today. We switch partners every two minutes. You need to throw your partner out of the ring to make it to the next round. If neither you nor your partner can't manage to throw the other out of the ring, then you're both out. Noelle, you can start with Jasmine. I've tracked you in Chicago, so I know what you're capable of. Be careful, Jasmine."

Jasmine stepped into the ring and paced around the circle, as if she were a predator ready to pounce upon her prey. She stalked Noelle's movements and aggressively moved toward her.

"I haven't whistled yet, Jasmine," Adam yelled, and she stilled.

"Sorry! Just so eager to fight my new friend." Jasmine wrinkled her nose.

Noelle rolled her eyes.

"You have just under two minutes! One of you must get pushed out, or you're both out!" Adam yelled over the noise of the Naturei who cheered. Adam whistled, and Jasmine crafted a gun-shaped weapon into her hand instantly with some natural nearby materials that whizzed toward her and formed in her hand.

"Wait, you can do that?" Noelle asked.

"I can do that," Jasmine said and shot the gun's pellets at Noelle.

Noelle was quite literally dodging bullets.

"Get the weapon away from her, Noelle!" Adam instructed.

Noelle froze in an effort to tempt Jasmine to fire again. She took the bait, and Noelle grabbed Jasmine's wrist and shoved the weapon to her side. Noelle struck Jasmine with her fist and then withdrew it and struck Jasmine in her stomach. Jasmine dropped the weapon and bellowed over—then disappeared and became invisible.

Noelle frantically moved around as she felt something whizz past her ear.

"How is this fair?" Noelle muttered and then a fist met her temple. Noelle grabbed a fistful of dirt and threw it around in the air, which clung to Jasmine and revealed her invisible silhouette was right in front of her. The dirt covered her, and Noelle could see that she had her hand cocked back, ready to strike. Noelle ducked just in time to avoid the punch.

The dirt-covered silhouette of Jasmine's leg kicked out, but Noelle caught it in the air. She then held on to it and pulled as hard as she could toward the edge of the circle's line. Noelle turned and flipped Jasmine over her, and she fell to the ground. Noelle could feel Jasmine's hands clutched to her clothing. Noelle had to act fast—she couldn't let her cloak rip off.

Noelle, with a renewed intensity for her secret, shoved Jasmine's face into the dirt and then pushed her toward the edge. Jasmine's other hand, which didn't have dirt on it and remained invisible, found Noelle's hair, and she tugged it menacingly. Noelle's head thrust back as she felt hair rip. Noelle cried out and struck the area that she believed was Jasmine's face.

Jasmine tugged on her cloak again, and Noelle punched, anywhere and everywhere, desperate for her to stop the tug on her cloak. She shoved hard and inched Jasmine toward the circle's edge. Jasmine's upper torso was already pushed out.

Noelle gritted her teeth together and picked up a fistful of dirt, intending to throw it on Jasmine's invisible frame to get more visibility. But then Jasmine reemerged entirely.

She leaned up to Noelle's ear and said, "I used my invisibility ability to watch you in the meadow last night. If you ever go near Eli again, I'll ruin you. That is *my* throne."

Noelle threw the dirt into Jasmine's face and eyes and then proceeded to shove her outside the circle. Jasmine clutched her face.

Noelle took a step back and spun around to a cheering Naturei crowd.

"Next fighter!" Adam called.

"What? Where is my break?" Noelle panted and leaned over with her hands on her knees. A bead of sweat formed on her brow, and she wiped it away.

"I'll heal you," Eli said and stepped into the ring. He waved a hand over Noelle's body, and all injuries, bruises, and pain instantly left her. She felt entirely refreshed. She stood up and sucked in a breath.

"And what about me?" Jasmine cried and rubbed her eyes as tears streamed down them from the dirt.

Eli waved a hand over her, and she calmed as the pain seemed to ease.

"I'll take you down, Goldner."

Eli shrugged, and his dark hair swayed with the wind, and it carried rich spices with it. "I'll heal you after you lose."

The Naturei gathered around the outer edge of the circle. It was evident that they loved their prince, and he was the crowd favorite. Even Captain Adam, who had seemed genuinely warm toward Noelle, smiled at Eli with a pleasant, proud look on his face.

Eli's proud face scanned the small crowd that cheered for him, and he nodded with their cheers. He soaked it in; relished it even.

"I'll knock that cocky grin off your face," Noelle said as they neared one another.

"I'd like to see you try."

Adam whistled to start.

Noelle definitely wasn't stronger than Eli, so she'd have to be quicker. She brought her knee up and launched a kick into Eli's stomach. He did a backward roll, and Noelle grabbed his right leg and intended to pin him and limit his movement, but Eli flipped her over when he lifted his leg.

Noelle landed on her back in the dirt, and Eli leaned over her. They both scurried to their feet, and Noelle kicked out her left leg toward Eli's shoulder, but he blocked it with his arm, then he brought down his right elbow to block her fist, and Noelle withdrew her hand entirely. She tried to strike his face with her right fist, but he blocked that with his left hand.

Eli grabbed Noelle's wrist and then turned so that his back was to her. Before she could understand his intentions, he flipped her over his back, and she landed onto the soft dirt. He pinned her wrists to the ground.

He leaned over her and smiled. His strength ability was in full use as she actively sank into the ground. She tried to press against his hands, but it was futile.

Eli leaned in close so that his mouth was against her ear. "After you perform your journalism duties tonight, I'd love to dance with you."

"What?" Noelle glowered, as he seemed to press harder against her wrists. She had sunken so deep into the ground now that only her face and the tippy top of her body was still visible; everything else was submerged into the dirt by his strength ability.

"You said you wanted to contribute to the Naturei realm with your journalism abilities, and there is a dance tonight," he said in a whisper so quiet that Noelle could barely hear it amid the cheering Naturei.

Noelle tried again to free her hands, but they remained pinned. "And you didn't think to tell me that I had to be a journalist tonight?" Noelle was a planner, and this wasn't in the plan. Her throat went dry, and the feeling of his skin against hers was a distraction. She tried to ignore the dizzy feeling he gave her when he was this close in proximity.

Eli laughed against her ear. "I'm telling you right now so you can prepare. But then afterward, save me a dance?"

"Maybe, it depends on how much you use your strength ability," Noelle said through her teeth.

"You want me to hold back?" Eli asked and eased up. "I'll let you win."

"No," Noelle said, and then she slid her knee out from underneath him and kneed him right in the groin.

He groaned, and Noelle earned a loud hiss from the crowd in disapproval. It was a cheap shot, but he was too strong to rely on anything else.

"Okay," Eli said and hoisted himself up with a look of agony on his face. "But only if you're sure."

She nodded. "I'll dance with you tonight if you stop holding back."

Eli cringed. "But I don't want to hurt you."

Noelle shook her head. "You couldn't even if you tried."

Eli gave a nod and then sprinted toward Noelle. She had a plan—she might have to actually fight Eli in a few days during the Heirling Duel if it came to that. She needed to see how strong he truly was. Right now she couldn't imagine him trying to hurt her, but if he knew she were Merklei, would he remain friendly? She shuddered at the thought and worried that he would truly become her real enemy. Would Eli try to kill her?

Eli pulled a punch, and Noelle let out a disapproving hiss. He punched again, but he was intentionally missing or not allowing his blows to land.

Eli struck again, and this time Noelle leaned into the punch. His fist landed square in Noelle's jaw. She had never been hit so hard by anyone ever. She had fought many opponents in her martial arts training, but nobody was ever this strong. It sent her off her feet into the air, and she landed with a loud thud onto the dirt. The breath was immediately knocked out of her, and she writhed in pain on the ground.

He had definitely, in every way, held back until now. He had a beast of an ability.

She lifted her head and gasped for air. Her jaw ached, and it was likely broken. He wasn't even trying to hurt her—and yet this was the worst blow she had ever received. But no matter, because he could heal her afterward. She needed to see more. Her body begged her to stop, but she willed herself to stand up. She staggered.

"Is that all you got?" Noelle baited him.

"I'm sorry—that punch wasn't supposed to make contact. You don't want more," Eli said and looked concerned. His tall, muscular frame now seemed warmed up, as the crowd cheered him on.

It was true, Noelle did not, in fact, want more. But she needed to see what he could do. In a few days, they might become *actual* enemies depending on how he took the news that she was the Merklei heir. Noelle wouldn't lay a finger on Eli in the duel; she would do anything to keep him alive. But she didn't know what he might do, so she needed to know what he was capable of.

"My grandma could hit harder than that," Noelle said. She felt woozy but kept her head up. It hurt to speak; she winced in an attempt to stop the tears from coming.

"I'll fix the damage afterward," Eli said with a curt nod. "But I don't like messing up your pretty face," he whispered so quietly that only Noelle could hear.

Noelle wondered why he hadn't used his Naturei ability to make any weapons, but then she realized it was his hands that were the true weapons. They had outstanding potential for harm with the strength that he possessed. His blow to her jaw was enough to make her want to end the fight.

"You should be worried about your pretty face," Noelle said and ran toward Eli. She weakly launched a punch in his direction, but her exhaustion got the best of her. Eli grabbed her by her cloak and then lifted her as if she were nothing more than a small animal. Eli gathered her to his chest and looked at her with concern.

"No!" Noelle cried and tried to sit up and strained against Eli. She grasped at his wrist that held her and dug her nails into his skin.

He groaned but moved forward. They were nearly at the line, and Noelle leaned all the way up and bit his arm. She dug her teeth deep into his skin, and he dropped her. She wasn't proud of much in this fight; but her pride wouldn't let him win.

Her jaw ached with the reverb after she landed on the ground. She groaned and lay on her side.

She looked up and saw Eli had moved toward her. She flinched as he picked her up like it was easy. He held her to his chest and carried her back toward the edge of the circle. Noelle's limbs flailed as she tried to stop him, but the pain in her jaw and her body made every movement feel so incredibly weak.

"I look forward to our dance, Elle," Eli said, and she could feel his healing ability pulsing through her body. The wounds throughout her body, and especially her jaw, slowly ebbed away. She looked up at him, and his deep green eyes watched her as she regained her strength.

"Well, that was a mistake," Noelle said and smirked. Before Eli could react, she kicked her legs down and tripped Eli. They both fell to the dirt, where their torsos were halfway outside the circle. With a laugh, Eli reached for Noelle and began to drag her. She shoved against him and pulled him along with her. They struggled against one another, and then they both landed outside the circle with a loud thud.

Noelle felt her jaw and all traces of her injuries were gone. She searched the rest of her body, but there were no bruises, no breaks, and not even a single scratch. She looked up at Eli, whose muscular frame was being patted and congratulated on all sides by the gathered crowd. The Naturei people saw Eli as their future leader, and they wanted to see him strong. And he was *quite* strong.

"Well done, class. And well done, Noelle! You did fairly well for your first fight. Eli beats almost all his opponents. The only person that beats him is me," Captain Adam said.

Eli stopped smiling and looked over at Adam.

"Don't ever pull your punches with me again," Noelle said to Eli with a frown. "Captain Adam, what is your ability?"

Captain Adam turned to face Noelle, and then in a blink, he stood right next to her. He towered over her, and she realized his ability was speed. It made sense that his speed could outmaneuver Eli's strength. All the strength in the world didn't matter if you couldn't catch somebody. She wondered if he was faster than Scarface—who had moved so quickly to disarm Noelle of her knife.

"Impressive," Noelle said. And she swore, from the corner of her eye, she saw Eli's jaw tighten with her compliment to Captain Adam.

"Let's all meet up at lunch," Eli said and turned to leave.

The crowd dispersed, and Noelle saw Hazel and Clay approach.

"Good try," Hazel said and pointed in the direction of the others, who were now far away.

"Thanks, say, you wouldn't happen to know if anybody else has ever beaten Eli, would you?" Noelle asked and watched as they each used the keiloki plant to transport to lunch.

"No, the only person we can recall ever winning in a fight against Prince Eli is Captain Adam. And you ought to call him Prince Eli, that is his proper title," Hazel said.

"Sure." But Noelle would not be calling him that.

It was eerily quiet now. All the Naturei had left for lunch, and the woods teemed with buzzing noises from insects.

Noelle turned toward the keiloki transport plant. She could hear branches that crunched under the guards' feet behind her when suddenly she heard a strangulation sound.

Both the guards were being choked by vines that came from the trees. They smothered their airflow, and they both grunted and gasped for air.

Noelle ran toward them, but the vines flung them hundreds of feet backward. Their bodies flew so far that Noelle lost sight of them as they went deeper and deeper into the woods.

Noelle gasped, and then the vines turned on her. She sprinted toward the keiloki plant; but the vines caught up to her. She held her hand out as the vines encircled around her wrists and pulled her into the air.

Noelle wiggled her arms in an attempt to free herself. But the vines simply twisted harder.

Jasmine stepped out from behind a tree.

"If you ever throw dirt in my eyes again, we're going to have a real problem."

Noelle sighed and pulled against the restraints of the vines. She managed to get one to snap, but Jasmine simply recrafted another vine to take its place.

Jasmine waved her hand so that a vine snaked its way toward Noelle. It lashed against her back and Noelle cried out. And then it struck her, again and again.

Noelle screamed and pulled at her wrists, but the vines wouldn't budge.

Her back felt raw and screamed for relief. And then the vine coiled itself around her body as if it were a snake, and Noelle felt her breath become labored.

Jasmine brought Noelle to her so that they were face-to-face. The vines coiled even tighter around Noelle's body, and her breaths became shorter.

"I want you to leave Eli alone. And if you don't, I'll tell the king that I caught you alone with him today. He and I are very close, and he will believe everything I say. You'll be thrown into prison, and I'll get what I wanted all along."

Noelle laughed in between what little breath she could manage to inhale.

"Eli... will... tell... the truth," she breathed out.

The vines coiled even tighter around Noelle.

"I didn't work this hard to get where I am only for some insignificant human to ruin it for me. I am the king's pick for Eli, and you will not get in my way."

And then Noelle's eyesight dimmed. She couldn't quite feel control over her body anymore, but she blinked rapidly. Her head tilted forward, and her eyes closed.

Everything went dark, and then she had lost consciousness.

Noelle awoke to Eli's callused hands on her shoulders. He ripped away the vines, and Noelle inhaled and gasped for air.

He yelled, but Noelle didn't make out the words.

She tried to sit up, but she felt dizzy. Eli picked her up and held her to his chest. He ran and looked around the woods, as if he might spot the person who had done this. He reached for the keiloki plant, and with a flash of bright green light, they were inside Eli's room.

"Who did this to you?" he demanded. Eli placed Noelle on a plush pillow, and she realized they were completely and totally alone, against the king's orders, in his room no less. This was the perfect setup for Jasmine's lie.

Eli noticed Noelle's ragged breath and reached for her ribs.

"Somebody broke your ribs," he said, and then he mended them with a wave of his hand.

"No! Leave it!" Noelle cried aloud.

Eli stared at her in disbelief. "You're in so much pain that you're delusional. Here let me—" Eli reached out again, but Noelle swatted his hand away.

"No, leave it! We will need proof for the king. We are being set up at this very moment." Noelle winced.

"Noelle, what are you talking about? Where is Clay and Hazel? Who did this to you?"

"Jasmine is irate. She sent them flying, and she struck me with vines and wrapped them around me like a python," Noelle gasped. "She intends to tell the king that we've been alone so that I'll be in prison."

"That doesn't make any sense. Clay and Hazel would easily defend the truth."

"Not if they were in on it," Noelle said and turned on her side in pain. She writhed on the overstuffed pillow.

"Impossible." He scooped her up in his arms and frowned. "Let's go to my father now." He reached for the keiloki plant.

With a flash of green light, they were in the throne room, where Jasmine stood before the king. She bowed her head and then turned to face them. A cruel grin rested on her lips, and Hazel and Clay stood next to her.

"Told you," Noelle said.

"See, sir? I told you they managed to escape their guards, and they've been together this entire time," Jasmine said with a soft shake of her head.

"Jasmine, what do you think you're doing? I've been at lunch, and I have multiple witnesses to confirm that. I also can attest that Noelle was attacked and has several broken ribs, because *you* attacked her. I only went looking for her when she never came to lunch with the others. And oddly, you have been missing too." Eli held Noelle close to his chest, and she felt his heartbeat increase.

"Is this true, Clay and Hazel? Where were you?" the king asked.

"My king, the girl snuck away from us," Hazel said.

Noelle sneered. "If I could so easily get away from you, then you're terrible at your jobs and you should be fired."

"Eli?" The king's fury seemed to surface as if he teetered on the edge of a full-blown fit.

"It isn't true, Father. Ask anybody at lunch—I have multiple witnesses."

"Yes, witnesses who are his friends and would defend him loyally in anything," Jasmine said.

"What do you think you're doing? You're a liar," Eli said.

"Me? *I'm protecting us.* What do you think you've been doing ever since this girl arrived?" Jasmine asked.

"Then explain why Noelle has multiple broken ribs," Eli said through his teeth.

She shrugged. "Maybe you did that to hide your intimate moments with her." She wasn't just doing this to get rid of Noelle; it was evident she wanted revenge on Eli.

The king glanced around the room.

"Somebody is lying here," the king said, and he didn't bother to hide his annoyance. "And I punish liars with what they deserve."

"I'm willing to make a Naturei vow to always speak the truth," Noelle said in desperation.

"Elle," Eli said, and it sounded like a warning.

"You would do that? Humans are liars," the king said, as if he were in disbelief.

"Humans can be but not always. I want to show you that not all humans are scum." Noelle said and gasped in pain. She figured if she were already going to go to prison, might as well take all the risks.

The king sharply inhaled. "I'll accept your vow. But I want you to make it to both Eli and myself, since you're under his responsibility."

"Can I please heal you now? My father has seen your condition," Eli said and gently shifted her closer to him.

Noelle nodded and then felt all her pain diminish. He set her down, and she shot a look at Jasmine, who now looked terrified. She hadn't seemed to plan on this.

"Are you sure about this? You do understand the implications of this, right? You'll never be able to lie to me or the king," Eli said and looked down at her.

Noelle nodded. "Yes, I am fully aware of what I am doing."

Eli held out his hand, and Noelle took it. His skin felt warm against hers.

"Do you promise to always tell me the truth and never lie to me or the Naturei king?" Eli asked.

"Yes," Noelle said. And then a flash of green light emerged and circled around their hands. An emerald-green ribbon tied around their hands and sealed the promise.

Eli gave Noelle a pained look, as if she had just made a horrible mistake. But she had saved herself from prison. How could this be so terrible?

"Now question her," the king ordered from his enormous throne.

"Noelle, what happened to you? Why didn't you come to lunch, and who broke your ribs?"

"I was walking with Hazel and Clay toward the keiloki plant, when they both got picked up by vines and chucked far away. Then Jasmine came out, and she whipped me with vines repeatedly, and then she sent vines around me like a python snake, and it broke my ribs." Noelle felt compelled to share the details to Eli's questions.

"Ask her why Jasmine did this," the king ordered.

"Why did she do it?" Eli asked with a sigh. Noelle understood now. Eli hadn't wanted her to do this because now the king could access anything he wanted from Noelle, anytime, and there was nothing she could do to prevent it.

"Jasmine was angry that you've given me attention that she feels should be reserved for only her. She said she saw us in the field, and she warned me to stay away from you or else she would tell the king that we had spent time alone so I'd get thrown into prison."

The king now faced Jasmine, who cowered away.

"My king, I am so sorry! It was just that—"

"Clay and Hazel, you're demoted and relieved of guard duties for the remainder of the year. You can try again next year, but you won't finish this year in your duties. And as for you, Jasmine, this is vile behavior. You're dismissed from castle grounds for the remainder of the year. You're all lucky that I know how loyal you are to me, Otherwise, you three would be in prison."

"What? Then that means I can't come to the dance! Or dinner!" Jasmine squeaked.

"So be it, you three are dismissed."

They each left the throne room, guided by several soldiers.

"Noelle?" The king tapped his fingers on his throne.

"Yes?"

"I think I've been overly harsh in my judgments and prejudices against humans, given my past with them. I tend to view all humans in the same light, but even tonight I realize some Naturei have great character and others do not. I haven't given you the opportunity to show your character. And I recognize I'm wrong for that," the king said.

Noelle couldn't believe what she heard. She looked at Eli, who also seemed surprised.

"Thank you, sir," Noelle said.

"I was going to arrange for Jasmine to be on the throne with Eli, and until tonight, I was absolutely certain I knew what was best. I thought she was best, but now I question myself," the king admitted.

"So what does this mean?" Eli asked.

"Ash and Aster will be with her at night. You *still* won't be allowed to be alone together for many reasons. But during the day, she is free so long as you aren't alone together. That is, unless she gives me a reason to take that away. I realize I must give her the opportunity to show what sort of character she has, and I've failed to do that."

Noelle excitedly nodded. "Thank you, sir!"

"Dismissed," he said.

Ash and Aster walked beside Noelle, and they all left the throne room and immediately used the keiloki plant to go to Eli's bedroom.

The large bedroom felt slightly crowded with the two guards

in it. Noelle wanted to jump into Eli's arms. The plan went even better than she hoped or imagined. But she restrained herself.

"Why would you do that? You know he is going to force me to question you all the time now, right?" Eli asked and sighed.

Noelle considered that and nodded. "Right, well, it is unfortunate. But better than me being behind bars!"

"You do realize we'll never be able to have fun now, right?"

"We weren't supposed to be having any kind of fun together anyway." She pointed at the guards.

"Them? Oh, I had plenty of plans to lose them. But now that won't happen. I wouldn't be surprised if the king brought you in every night for questioning," he said. He plucked an alanis flower and raised it to her hair.

"He'll probably extract all the information about anything that I say or do toward you," Eli said, and then before he placed the flower behind her ear, he shook his head. A vine wrapped its way around her hair to keep the flower in place.

"So you can't lie now. You think I'm handsome, Elle?" Eli said and his lips turned upward.

Noelle rolled her eyes. She couldn't lie, but that didn't mean she had to stroke his ego and pour out her soul. She needed to learn to manage this. She said, "I don't want to puff up your already too big ego."

There. She insulted him, but she also didn't lie at the same time. She could do this.

Eli laughed. "So you do think I'm handsome. I knew it."

Of course he already knew that. But her cheeks burned anyway.

"This could be fun actually. I look forward to torturing you with your vow."

CHAPTER 23
ELI
THE JOURNALIST AND THE DANCE

Eli's palms sweated profusely as he stood before his father and the entire court. The High King had just announced that Prince Eli would enter the Heirling Duel as punishment for finding the human girl despite the risks it brought to the Naturei realm but also for advancement of his character, according to the High King Pierce Goldner. His father dismissed the entire court after he rendered his judgments but called on Eli to stay.

Eli's heart thumped, yet he held his head high. His father was known to be cruel by many—but surely he had his reasons. Eli was grateful for the adoption by the king, who had promised Eli's father to watch out for him... supposedly. He trained Eli to be a warrior, a leader, and strong—and he was strong—arguably the strongest in Naturei history. Yet the educator's words about his real parents dying by the king's hand bothered him far more than Eli would like to admit.

"You likely don't understand why I instruct you in the way that I do. You likely despise me at times even." His father folded his hands together with each finger adorned with precious stones and gold rings. His prized possession, his signet ring, sat on his index finger.

Eli sighed through his nostrils. "I don't hate you, but I don't think this is your wisest decision. I understand you're angry about the girl—but sending me to the Heirling Duel? Did you forget about the Merklei curse? I could *die* in that arena! I won't be able to use any Naturei ability with the Snow Queen present due to the curse she crafted in revenge against our realm after Lorelei died."

It was true that Lumi had crafted a curse against humanity that wherever her foot stepped, there would be blizzard and ice. And because she had believed the Naturei betrayed their vow to her, she crafted the curse so that no Naturei could use their ability around her or the curse. She is perhaps the most powerful Merklei leader to have ever lived.

"You aren't reliant on your Naturei ability; your advantage lies in your strength ability. Your strength, which will work despite her curse, is what will bring you victory."

Eli closed his eyes for a brief moment. "And what if I don't win? You've sent me to my death."

"Everything I do is for your betterment and for the betterment of the kingdom. You will survive this Heirling Duel, I'm certain of it. And it will force you to finally grow up. Your weakness is that all you want to do is have fun, and you never think of any future consequences for others."

Eli wanted to believe his father. He knew, in his father's own mind, that he believed he would return home and that somehow, in some way, he was doing the right thing. But Eli swallowed at the thought of being forced to kill another heir—it seemed entirely wrong to him. All this to teach him a lesson? He would force him to kill another, to be spared of his own life, and that repulsed him.

"Can I take my leave then?"

"No, we need to discuss your future," the king said, and his eyes narrowed. "I think you should do the traditional pageant to find a partner. That is what I did."

Eli's head fell. "And look how that turned out for you."

Eli's thoughts trailed to the human girl. He saw her bright

eyes in his mind, and he sighed. He knew he shouldn't, but he longed for her touch and recalled the gentleness of her lip against his finger. A profound fascination had sprung up inside him since he listened to the educator, and he knew he needed to find this girl. Only now he wished he hadn't. He wished he had never met her, because he was forbidden to have her, and yet his mind couldn't stop drifting to her.

"You'll take my throne someday. You need an heir."

Eli, not one to miss an opportunity to irritate his father, instigated. "If you want an heir so badly, I could simply marry the human girl and bring up about four heirs in a short number of years."

"She's highly manipulative. You can't even see what she has done to you. She's weak, Eli. She will live a short life, and she offers nothing to you except pain."

"You're wrong. She just might be one of the strongest people I've ever met. She basically had to raise herself in some ways, with her family's deaths. She is extremely resourceful and clever. She had to learn how to get by, and she beat Jasmine with no abilities. She fought me too."

The king scoffed. "Oh, so you've found your life partner because she would roll around in the dirt with you?"

Eli shook his head. He didn't understand. Noelle possessed a different kind of strength; not one that relied on abilities, but rather it was a mentality of grit where she refused to be a victim and likened herself to be an opponent in any and every situation.

"You're a fool for not seeing the stronghold that she has you in. She is wise like a serpent, and she has ensnared you."

"I'm taking my leave then."

The king opened his mouth to say something, but Eli left.

E li sat on his throne in the ballroom. He swirled his glass in his hand, and the deep red contents spun around and around. He watched as Naturei danced all around, merry and joyful.

Women had approached him repeatedly. If his father hadn't been seated next to him, he would have rejected their requests for dances. But he would be scolded later for that, so he politely smiled and groaned inwardly as he took each of them to the dance floor and politely danced. He returned to his seat after each dance, quickly, and hoped they might read his body language. Yet they never seemed to.

He scanned the faces of the intricately dressed Naturei but didn't spot Jasmine. He was grateful, he supposed, that she had gotten caught.

And then he spotted her. He sat up on his golden twine throne to get a better look.

Noelle entered, wearing an extravagant gown. The burnt orange that looked so good against her dark skin seemed to turn nearly everyone's heads. Crystals lined a sweetheart shape around her chest and then scattered throughout the center of her stomach. The fabric cinched at her waist and then spiraled down.

With each step she took, the luxurious-looking gown sparkled under the light. Her dark hair was swept up in a simple bun at the nape of her neck, and a cloak rested on her neck—but unlike her other cloaks, it only covered her neck at the clasp, and the trailing cloak behind her was sheer and sparkly, as if it were a part of her gown. She was always pretty, but tonight she looked radiant and incredibly beautiful, and Eli couldn't tear his eyes away.

Eli's face must have expressed his thoughts, because the king gave a disapproving huff.

Eli stood, but to his dismay, a Naturei girl was at his side.

"Prince Eli, a dance?" It was Jasmine's older sister. Eli looked over her shoulder at Noelle. She walked and seemed to scan faces. He hoped she looked for him.

"Sure." Eli didn't bother to hide his frustration. He took her by the hand, and together they walked to the dance floor, and hand-in-hand they twirled to the song.

In the corner, royal court Naturei musicians played on various Naturei musical instruments. The lylop, a stringed instrument, was Eli's favorite because it was soft yet vibrant in sound.

Jasmine's older sister looked at him longingly. He spun her and took the opportunity to scan the crowd. He caught a flash of burnt orange from the corner of his eye and craned his neck to see who had pulled Noelle onto the dance floor.

Of course it was Adam. She smiled at him as he whispered something into her ear. Eli glanced away. He shouldn't have felt jealous that she was dancing with Adam, but he wished it had been anybody except Adam.

She looked in his direction, and Eli looked away before she could lock eyes with him. He didn't want her to know he had stared. But how could he not?

"Naturei! Welcome to the ball!" Roman, one of the announcers of the court, called out in a loud voice. "Feast, dance, and be merry! As you all know, we have Noelle among us, our very first journalist! Please welcome our storyteller." The crowd clapped their hands, and the musicians stilled. Drinks continued to clink.

Noelle walked to the front of the room where Roman stood. She picked at her nail bed. For a girl with such a big mouth, she seemed so timid in group settings.

He ought to feel bad for her, perhaps have some sort of sympathy. But instead, Eli found her discomfort comical. The girl who would challenge anybody to a fight and often had sharp words for all seemed nervous to speak in front of a group. This was, after all, her idea to be a storyteller. Could she not tell stories after all?

She locked eyes with Eli. Jasmine's older sister seemed to understand he was done with her presence, and she left.

Noelle smiled and held the mic. "Tonight I will conduct an interview with the Naturei king. Will you please join me on the stage, sir?" The audience clapped enthusiastically, and the king made his way to Noelle's side.

"Sir," Noelle started. "What were you like as a kid?" She smiled sweetly.

Eli wanted to laugh. He knew if it weren't for the large gathered crowd, his father would have sneered at such a question. But instead, he answered, "I was stubborn and loved a good time. Sort of like my boy, Prince Eli."

The crowd loved that. Cheers erupted and laughter ensued. Everyone knew Eli to be a bit of a rascal and a lover of a good time. Eli couldn't picture his father as somebody that ever cared about pleasure.

"And what advice would you give to your son since he will be entering the Heirling Duel?" Noelle asked him with a stiff expression.

Eli wanted to be the one to tell her the official news. Who had told Noelle? Had rumors really swirled in the realm that quickly?

The king faced Eli now, and much of the crowd spotted him in the back. "I'd tell Prince Eli that I have full confidence that he will return after a job well done. I wouldn't have declared this Heirling Duel otherwise. My encouragement to him is to really focus on his strengths, and he will bring honor to the Naturei realm."

The crowd erupted in applause, and soldiers gathered around Eli and patted his back.

"Thank you for the brief interview. We will allow you to enjoy your evening! I hope to be able to do more interviews about different roles in the kingdom soon," Noelle said and handed the mic to Roman. The applause continued. They loved interviews, or so it seemed. Eli was glad that Noelle seemed to have found her place in the realm—it went well enough.

The crowd scattered, and the musicians and dancing resumed. Noelle was alone, and Eli made a beeline for her before another could reach her.

She turned to face him.

"Elle, you look absolutely beautiful tonight," Eli said with an impish grin.

"You clean up pretty well, Goldner," she said, and her eyes rested on his.

Eli extended his hand.

"May I have a dance? I think you owe me one." He didn't want a dance. He wished he hadn't said that. He wanted her entire night—he wanted every dance for as long as she would allow it.

Noelle blinked, then took his hand. Eli wove his fingertips into hers and gently tugged, leading her to the dance floor. Her skin felt so soft, smooth, and deliciously delicate against his rough hands. When they reached the dance floor, it was as if nobody else existed.

She placed her hand on his shoulder, and he placed his hand on the small of her back. He pulled her in close.

Her dress sparkled with each movement, and he sucked in a breath as he watched her. He would begin the Heirling Duel soon, and this dance felt like a reminder of why he wanted to return. He wanted more time with the girl, and he wanted to learn about her past and her desires for the future. He wanted to put more alanis flowers behind her ear and watch her laugh with her sweet smile.

But more than his wants, he needed to come back for her. What would happen to her if he didn't make it through the Heirling Duel? His father would throw her in the pit, he was certain of it. The only reason he hadn't was because he begged and pleaded. And when his father protested because somebody would need to watch her and oversee her, Eli volunteered to do it. What had felt like it might be a chore in the beginning had become a delight.

"What's the matter?"

"Nothing." He spun her. She seemed to come alive as she danced. Her voice became jubilant, and her face shone.

Eli held her impossibly closer. He could feel the eyes that darted in their direction. He knew their cordial dance morphed and had become oddly intimate; he knew the courtesy was to switch dance partners every so often, yet they continued into many more songs together.

She traced figures on his shoulder as she peered up at him. Her fingertips on his shoulder were enough to send a shiver down his spine. *Her touch was forbidden.* But here, under the guise of cordial dancing, it was accepted.

The air was quite warm and thick from all the dancing bodies.

"Do you want some air?" Eli asked.

Noelle nodded.

Eli led her, by her hand, through a door to a nearby vineyard. The music was distant, and nobody seemed to be too close.

She looked around at the vineyard and sighed. "I'm so relieved they liked the interview."

"You were excellent," Eli said, and perhaps before he realized what he was doing, he wrapped his arms around her stomach. She still had her back to him, and he pulled her to his chest.

He shouldn't embrace her. But they were close enough to the music that perhaps if an onlooker spotted them, he could say it was a dance.

He swayed them both, with Noelle pressed to his chest, and wrapped his hands around her waist. Noelle laughed and wrapped her own arms around his neck.

"Is our cover that we're dancing?"

She was clever.

"We *are* dancing," he pointed out.

Noelle spun with her hands still on his neck. "I need to speak to you," Noelle said with urgency in her voice.

Eli's hands gently stroked her hair.

"Good, I need to talk to you too," Eli said. "But you go first."

She seemed quite nervous and fidgeted with her cloak. She sweated more than usual; perhaps her gown material was too thick—it certainly looked very heavy and thick.

"I just wanted to say that you're going to do great at the Heirling Duel," she said quietly.

"Are you sure that is all that you wanted to say?"

She looked as if she were lost in thought for a moment. Then nodded quickly. Perhaps she lost the nerve to say whatever it was that she truly had wanted to discuss.

But before he could begin speaking, she pulled him closer.

The moonlight glowed against her skin, and she traced shapes on the back of his neck. Her touch was enough to melt him into a puddle; any conversation now seemed lost on him.

"I know we aren't supposed to be together. But maybe here, away from prying eyes?" she asked with a shyness in her voice he wasn't accustomed to.

He gently slid his hands up her arms until they rested on her bare shoulders. He leaned toward her but stopped just before his lips could graze hers. The king could ask if they had kissed, and he couldn't let her be thrown into the pit for it, despite the fact that he desired nothing more than to kiss her. Noelle remained completely and totally frozen, and it pained him not to let his lips crash into hers.

"Tell me, you're the strongest in the entire Naturei realm. What is your weakness? In case I ever get the chance to beat you," Noelle asked and stroked his hair gently. They began to sway again.

"You probably won't ever get the chance. But if you must know, the alanis plant actually emits a scent that slows me down. You probably *still* won't beat me, but now you know."

While it was true that the plant did slow him down, he still wasn't entirely sure that she could beat him with the exposure. It wouldn't take his strength away, but it would give her the upper hand on speed.

"How ironic that the thing that heals you also poisons you." She laughed.

Eli's restraint had waned. He slid his fingers toward her neck and brought his mouth closer to hers. She closed her eyes. Despite her warm skin, she shivered at his touch. He could feel her heartbeat increase against his skin.

But then he noticed a gold necklace just under her cloak. His brows lowered, and he pulled back. He picked up the gold oval necklace and brushed his thumb over it.

Noelle's eyes shot open.

"Elle, no." It was all Eli could manage to whisper against her mouth.

Fear emerged in her eyes as the whites shone, even in the dim moonlight. "Wait! I can explain everything!" She tried to pull back, but Eli caught both her wrists.

"Elle, *why* do you have the Merklei necklace? And more importantly, why is it hanging around *your* neck?" He took a deep breath and closed his eyes. How was this even possible? He had researched her. He found her. Had she played him a fool this entire time? Did Lumi put her up to this?

He winced as the truth set in. Noelle was the Merklei heir—and his heart felt like a knife had sliced it into two. But her eyes weren't Merklei eyes; they were human eyes.

"No, please! Eli, listen to me. I can explain everything. It isn't what it seems! Remember, I can't lie to you."

Eli's eyes tightened. As if she knew his skepticism had settled in, she began to pull and tug against his hands on her wrists.

She wasn't who she pretended to be. His father's words were accurate; she was as wise as a serpent, and he felt utterly daft that he'd fallen into her snare.

"Lumi and I found the necklace in the door! But it snaked up on me. Lumi didn't know!" Noelle said.

Eli, tempted to call her a liar, looked her over. But she had taken a vow, and it was impossible to lie. So he eased against her slightly.

Her eyes brimmed with disappointment. "I would have told you, but I didn't think it would go well for me! It was bad enough that I was human."

Eli softened his grip on her wrists as horror became reality.

"You're the heir to the Merklei throne, aren't you?"

Her eyes seemed to glimmer. She nodded. She was *the* enemy of his realm. She was his enemy.

He let go of her wrists entirely and turned away from her. He walked several paces and placed his hands over his head. He wondered if any of it were real or if she played his emotions like a musical instrument. He believed she had. She had just asked him what his weaknesses were, knowing full well they'd fight to the death soon. His father had been right all along. *Stupid, ridiculous educator.*

When he turned back to look at her, pain surged inside him. Not because she was human or Merklei. But because she deceived him. He regretted telling her about the alanis plant; she would likely find a way to use it against him now.

He nodded slowly. "My father was right."

"No, you're not understanding!" She reached for him.

Something inside Eli called for him to comfort her. He ignored it and withdrew from her.

"No, I understand entirely. I suppose I deserve it," Eli said and waved his hand. The twine tracking device on her wrist disappeared entirely. "I'll be seeing you in the Heirling Duel soon."

Noelle grimaced and shook her head. "It isn't like that! I cannot lie to you. Just listen to me! I will explain everything."

"Save it. You should get out of here. Because my realm will treat you horribly when they find out what you are. You can get a head start without the tracking device. And this is the final time I'm showing any fragment of kindness to you, to be clear. Because when the duel starts, I will not show any mercy."

Noelle flinched. "Eli—"

"No," he said and looked up as several tiny snowflakes emerged and fell. This could only mean one thing; Lumi was here. "You should go now—before the others find you. I cannot protect you any longer," Eli said. While he was furious with her deceit, he was mostly upset that he might have to truly fight her in the duel. He didn't think he could actually hurt her because of the feelings he had developed—and she seemed to become his true weakness in this duel. For that, he despised her. Besides, he truly hated Merklei—they caused havoc on his realm. They were troublesome, and he would never be close to one.

She didn't budge. "I'm not going anywhere until your cocky, idiotic self listens to me." But then she watched as tiny snowflakes fell. "Lumi is here," she said and pulled at his hand.

He withdrew his hand and laughed bitterly. "Only thing worse than a human is a Merklei."

Eli left her and walked toward the ballroom. She called after him, but he ignored her. She yelled, but he continued forward.

But he couldn't help but turn and face the beautiful girl, who stood where he had left her in her burnt-orange dress. Her brows lifted as if she might have gotten through to him.

He spit on the ground. "Merklei," he said under his breath.

"Don't be stupid! We will make an alliance against the fire realm! And we will both make it out alive!" she called out in what seemed to be her last-ditch effort.

Eli laughed to himself. She just needed to stay out of his way, and then he'd never see her again. He planned to target the Leizei heir, whom he had never met because they remained hidden until recently, because he simply couldn't imagine hurting Noelle, even though she had absolutely crushed him. Besides, if Lumi were here, then he needed to find his father.

CHAPTER 24
THE SNOW QUEEN LUMI
THE FIRE BOND

"I'm going to kill him." Marko slammed his hand against the table. He paced back and forth.

Lumi's heart sank. She sat on her living room couch with her head cradled into her hands and wondered how Noelle had been Merklei this entire time. Yes, she had the necklace passed down in her family line—but how did they get it? Did one of the Merklei find a human partner? Lumi had taken to Noelle since the moment she saw her because she reminded her of Lorelei. Noelle had really struck a chord with Lumi, but now? Now they were a true family. Lumi crumbled the note left behind from a Leizei. They had declared the Heirling Duel—and Lumi wanted to tear down their realms for it, and she just might.

As much as the ordeal gave her a headache, a fresh set of hope swelled inside Lumi's heart. She had family, *again*.

"You won't have the chance," Lumi said. "You can have his body when I'm done."

Luis sat opposite Lumi, his eyes wide. She tried to explain everything to him, but he asked too many questions. He eventually fell silent after she explained the Heirling Duel. He probably was terrified, Lumi judged from the empty stare he gave.

"Are you certain they both voted in favor of it?" Marko asked and paced.

"Yes," Lumi seethed. She had told them everything. She wouldn't have dared tell a soul about Noelle being Merklei, but now that she faced the Heirling Duel, they deserved to know. She faced certain death, unless she could reach her and initiate her.

"She hasn't even been initiated yet," Lumi said, grim. It wasn't a fair fight when the girl had no access to her powers—and she was lost in the Naturei realm. Lumi winced, worried about what the Naturei might be doing to Noelle. "I've managed to avoid them all for so long, yet now that they have Noelle—I have no choice but to turn myself in."

Marko was suddenly at her side. He rubbed her back and he tucked a few strands of her hair behind her ear. She didn't think it would ever be possible to even be close to humans; not after what they did to her—and what they did to Lorelei, not to mention the others. She hadn't liked him much when she first met him; she simply wanted to use their knowledge of the necklace to find it. However, Marko had grown on her. His warm love for his family and his fierce protection for his friends was so beautiful. He drew warm emotions from Lumi's beating heart.

He pressed his forehead to hers, his warm skin against her icy skin. She hoped it didn't repulse him—and she reached for his hand. Their fingers intertwined, and she felt his hand guide her hand to his heart.

She calmed her breathing as she felt his heartbeat move steadily under her palm.

"Lumi," he whispered.

She looked at him.

"I need you to know that meeting you is the best thing that ever happened to me. I'll do anything to help you. But right now I need you to know that everything is going to be all right. Noelle is going to be all right."

Lumi pulled little strength from his words, but she appreciated his steadiness in the midst of it all. Noelle was in dire trouble, and Lumi felt that somehow it was her fault. How had she not known the girl was Merklei? How could she miss that detail? And then there was the matter of the boy, Eli. She hadn't realized a Naturei was right under her nose—she knew something was off about Eli, but she hadn't known what it was.

"I'm worried he has poisoned her with lies, Marko. Posing as a boyfriend is horribly low. What if she falls for it? What if she thinks he is in love with her, and he lured her there to ensure their heir wins?"

"She is pretty clever. I don't think she will fall for any of his nonsense, but if he hurts her—I'll kill him." Marko shook his head.

Luis's eyes remained wide and serious. "Poor Noelle."

"I have a plan," Lumi said.

The hair on Lumi's neck stood straight up as she faced a dozen Naturei soldiers. She felt insulted—only twelve measly Naturei soldiers to handle the Snow Queen?

"If you hurt us, we will hurt the girl. We know about the other two humans. Bring them out, and we will all arrive safely to the Naturei realm," one stringy-haired Naturei soldier said and stepped forward. His gun, made entirely of natural materials, pointed in Lumi's direction.

Lumi also stepped forward and grinned. "No, I don't think I will bring them out. But I will appreciate your accompaniment to the Naturei realm." This was entirely polite language; she couldn't get into the Naturei realm without them. Still, she was a queen, and they spoke the stiff, protocol language that she had once recited when she lived in the Naturei realm as the future queen of the Naturei people and the Merklei people. Lorelei had been the beloved heir of both realms, and she was particularly darling among the Naturei. When Lumi was engaged to King Pierce Goldner of the Naturei realm, they had loved Lumi too.

"We—we are supposed to take you as prisoner," the stringy-haired Naturei said, and his voice nearly shook.

Lumi took another step. "I'm most willing to come, so there won't be any need for my imprisonment."

The smile on her lips was pleasant, but the stormy snow swirled around them in connection to her temper. Pierce, the Naturei king, had the audacity to call for her imprisonment long ago, and he still kept it up. She'd more likely freeze him alive before going as his prisoner willingly.

The Naturei soldiers, obviously aware of her temperament, shivered and looked around. They weren't buying her politeness, because the falling angry snow revealed her true condition. She was angry that for many years, she had to be on the run from the Naturei when they broke their alliance with *her*. *They* didn't come to her side to help against the humans. *They* let Lorelei die. She scanned their faces and dropped her polite smile as the snow swirled around them. She could kill all twelve of them; she could make them pay for their failures to help her people—at the very least, they could have helped *Lorelei*.

A small funnel cloud of snow swirled around the soldiers and danced around them. They each gasped and looked around. But when Lumi's mind drifted to Noelle, she ceased the swirling snow. She wouldn't kill them, not when they had Noelle.

"Bring me to the girl, and nobody gets hurt," she called out and dropped the pleasant charade.

The stringy-haired Naturei nodded, and the other soldiers looked his way warily. She imagined they'd rather arrive with Lumi than with nothing but dead bodies.

The stringy-haired soldier leaned down to the keiloki plant, and each soldier had their natural elemental guns on Lumi. Lumi outstretched her hand to the soldier, and then the familiar green light that she hadn't seen in so long engulfed each of them, until she couldn't see anything except the light.

They were in the throne room where Lumi had once entertained the court and given her own advice on the floor. She had been respected as the future queen of the Naturei realm, but all that had changed now.

She turned as guns pointed at her in every direction. She laughed in response. She could destroy each gun with a swipe of her finger, and she was tempted to do it—just to demonstrate how weak they were in comparison. Had time made them forget what she was and what she was capable of?

All the Naturei in the throne room who weren't in soldier uniforms wore elegant attire made of the finest natural materials such as flower petals, long luxurious and rare leaves, and even quite a few burnt-orange petals that Lumi couldn't recognize. Surely somebody, probably somebody younger, had a new ability and crafted this orange petal—she hadn't seen it before.

And then she heard the voice that she had never wanted to hear again. "Eira," he said. Her old name sounded soft, even delicate on his lips. As if at any moment, she might run away. She had eluded him for years, but now she came willingly to his throne because he had Noelle.

She swept her eyes up to the vine-twisted throne that once held so many fond memories, to see Pierce sitting on top of it, with his emerald eyes full of surprise. His skin flushed when they made eye contact.

"If it isn't the one who allowed all my people to perish. Including *our* daughter," Lumi said. "And it is Lumi now."

Pierce didn't flinch. He simply rested his hand under his chin. Gold rings graced each finger, and he stared.

The soldiers kept their guns fixated on her. She took a step toward the king, and the entire room also moved toward her. She paused.

"You think I've come all this way to hurt him? If I wanted revenge, I'd have done it long ago," Lumi said and scanned the room. She recognized many of the faces—yet many were entirely unfamiliar. "Where is my heir?" Lumi looked around the room for Noelle, yet she hadn't found her. "If you've done anything to her, you'll regret it."

Something formed on the king's face, like confusion. But he quickly neutralized his features to cover it. Audible gasps could be heard across the massive throne room, and Lumi swallowed as she realized her mistake. They hadn't known after all.

The king leaned forward, fascination heavy in his eyes. He gripped the armrests of his throne tightly. "Thank you for that valuable information. We weren't aware that our prisoner was more than human—but we see now that we have had a clever traitor living among us."

The crowd hissed and shouted in agreement with their king. The Naturei were always a rowdy bunch, and it seemed not much had changed.

"Touch her and I'll ensure you're all sorry," Lumi called out loudly. "I'm here for my heir!" Power pulsed through Lumi as her rage brewed, and the entire room shook with her outburst. The crowd quieted and looked to their king—perhaps for protection or guidance. He raised a hand to calm them, and they followed his instruction and quieted.

"Clever of you, sending your heir after Eli. He'll be so disappointed when he finds out that she is a scam artist," Pierce drawled.

Lumi stiffened. "Who is he to you?" She already knew something was amiss; she just needed to know how deeply wrong things had gone.

"Prince Eli is such an unruly young man sometimes," Pierce said and sighed.

Lumi's fists balled at the news that Eli was her daughter's replacement. After evading the Naturei for so many years, they finally succeeded in drawing Lumi back, compliments of Eli.

Lumi frowned. Pierce erupted in laughter, as if this were some sick joke.

The large, lofty double doors to the right suddenly swung open, and Prince Eli strode through, red-faced.

"Oh, look what got dragged in," Eli said and looked over Lumi. "Your curse is causing havoc on our crops outside. The sooner you can leave, the better." He turned his gaze to Pierce. "You'll never believe what I found out, Father!"

"Let me guess." Pierce sighed. "Is it about the girl?"

Eli nodded, solemn. "Yes, I just discovered she is Merklei—and the heir to the Merklei throne." Revulsion appeared in his eyes as he looked at Lumi.

"Lovely, glad we're all acquainted with the news," Pierce said and tapped his fingers on his throne.

Lumi squared up on Eli. "Nice to see you again, Eli. I'm so impressed with your acting skills and the boyfriend act with Noelle. Now I suggest you bring her to me unharmed. And if I find out that you hurt her, you won't need to worry about the duel." The room boomed with her rage and rumbled like an earthquake.

Eli's chest heaved. "The only actor around here is Noelle. How long had you planned this?" He stepped toward Lumi, as if he were ready to pounce.

She met his step and also moved forward. "Oh merca! We didn't plan anything. This is all *your* doing!"

But several soldiers moved between them, and the king, Pierce, stood now. "That is enough! I will have order in my throne room. Lumi, you must stand trial for the injustice that you caused all those years ago, which led to the death of our daughter, Lorelei, the entire Merklei race, and the whole village that you slaughtered."

Lumi reared her head. Any trace of self-control had escaped her entirely now. "You hold *me* accountable for Lorelei's death? And for my people?" Lumi laughed bitterly. "You should hold yourself accountable! You didn't come to my aid like you vowed—or my people's! You allowed the humans to betray us. You were, and still are, the most weak, cowardly king that ever sat on the Naturei throne!" Lumi said the words, like venom, that had remained with her since the night she saw Lorelei's lifeless body. The entire room shook, and heavy snow piled up outside.

"You dare speak to me like that in front of my court, in my realm? When you're at my mercy? You slaughtered the entire human village in your wrath. You must pay for the blood you've spilled!" Pierce's voice carried throughout the room.

"I'm not facing any trial. And I didn't kill the entire village. Try to kill me tonight if you like, but I will spill a lot more blood if you do," Lumi said and looked around the room, as if she extended an invitation. Nobody accepted the invitation, however, because her reputation had preceded her.

"I'm not going to enact any trial right now, because my hands are tied," Pierce announced, as if this were news to the entire slew of Naturei people present. He moved and acted as if this were a rehearsed speech. And then Lumi had realized why as hooded Leizei poured into the throne room.

They had formed some sort of alliance, and this wasn't good news for the Heirling Duel, or Noelle. Lumi sucked in a breath as multitudes of Leizei, dressed in all black, moved in perfect unison to Pierce's side. A black hood protruded over each Leizei's face, which obscured their faces. Only the most elite Leizei soldiers wore this uniform, and each had a circular tattoo on their wrist—indicating their status. Lumi hadn't seen this many Leizei hoods since the last time she encountered their wicked king.

"Oh, you've made a deal with the devil."

"The Leizei have enough wits to understand the deception and wickedness that happens when we entangle ourselves with humans, something you seem to lack an understanding of. It would seem you still haven't learned your lesson, dear snowflake."

Lumi lifted her chin—when she caught a glimpse of Luis in his golden crown's reflection. She turned around to see a Naturei soldier and hooded Leizei held his hands behind his back.

"Lumi! Help!" Luis cried out, and they drove him to his knees.

"Put your hands farther behind your back!" The soldier swatted at Luis.

"That is as far as my arms go! Do I look like a ballerina to you? I'm not flexible!"

"Luis," Lumi said with agony. Their plan had entirely failed.

"Let the boy go," Lumi growled. She took in the sight of the Naturei and Leizei soldiers that worked together and shook her head. "Do you know that it was the Leizei soldiers who killed the entire human village? I only killed the soldiers who murdered my people and *our daughter*!"

"Save your lies," Pierce ordered and adjusted his crown atop his head. Eli joined his side.

"Lumi, *this* is the father of your child? Oh, you have got to make better choices." Luis shook his head. The Naturei soldier struck Luis in the back of his head. Luis grunted.

Worry encircled Lumi, and her blood began to pump quickly in her veins.

Lumi eyed Luis, and he peered up at her. As if he knew where her thoughts might be, and he shook his head to confirm. *Marko was safe.* Lumi inhaled deeply; she wouldn't forgive herself if she ruined Marko's life too. She had already managed to get both Noelle and Luis captured.

"You called for the Heirling Duel, so remember the vows you took. You cannot harm any kings or queens of other realms and must remain at peace with them during the duel. So I'll take my leave," Lumi announced. If it weren't for Noelle and Luis, she would kill them all—every last one of them. And she wouldn't lose an ounce of sleep over it—she'd sleep like a baby. They were all monstrous, arrogant fools. They had believed they were far superior to humans and that they shouldn't interact. They were wrong. Humans were beautiful creatures, as Lumi had discovered. Sure, they're messy and lie, steal, and cheat—but they also create, love, and sacrifice even to the point of their own lives for the ones they care about. The Naturei and Leizei realms were wrong in their conduct with the humans, and it was the humans who suffered the most because of it.

"I know the vows," Pierce said. "And I intend to keep them all. You're free to do as you please and so will your heir. But you will stand trial after the duel, if Eli wins." And then Pierce nodded to a soldier next to her, but before Lumi understood the gesture, it was too late.

She had put up her arms defensively. He didn't strike—he placed a twine tracking tool that was used for prisoners on both her wrist and Luis's. It wouldn't come off unless he removed it.

"What do you think you're doing?" Lumi's eyes were intense, cold, and calculated. She crafted two swords made of thick ice, and each hand held one.

Several Naturei soldiers close to her cowered at the sight.

If he wanted a fight, she would gladly give it to him. "Remember," she called out with a triumphant smile. "You can't use your Naturei abilities around me while the curse is still active. And that curse is active until I get to use the necklace and bring my people back."

Luis's attention was elsewhere. "Aren't you Eli? Noelle's boyfriend?" he asked, incredulous.

"No," Lumi said. "He is a liar, and poor Noelle was tricked. Prince Eli is the heir of the Naturei realm."

"Wait, so does that mean he is your son too?" Luis asked.

Lumi shot him a look, and he shrugged.

"Where is Noelle, *Prince* Eli?" she asked through her teeth.

Eli pulled out a broken twine tracking bracelet. "She managed to get out of this. She's somewhere around here."

The boy was a liar. Only a Naturei who placed that prisoner tracking bracelet on her would be able to remove it. Lumi tightened her eyes on him.

"We found her." A hooded Leizei, an elite soldier, appeared from the back of the throne room with Noelle in his grasp. She squirmed against him.

"Noelle?" Lumi turned, but several Naturei soldiers blocked her path.

"Lumi! Luis! I'm fine!" Noelle called back.

Noelle writhed against the hooded soldier, who stood in stark contrast to her.

To Lumi's surprise, she wore an elegant, burnt-orange gown,

and it sparkled as the soldier forced her toward the throne. That meant she was a guest. The gold necklace stood against her neck, bold and proud.

Lumi looked, full of perplexity and confusion, at Eli, whose eyes were on Noelle. She spotted a tiny orange flower protruding from his pocket, and she shook her head in disbelief. It seemed he hadn't known at all.

"Arrest them all, until the Leizei king arrives," Pierce instructed the nearby soldiers. To Lumi's dismay, both Naturei and Leizei obeyed him, which meant there was certainly a pact between them.

They dragged Luis and Noelle, but Lumi gave them a warning look, and none of them dared to touch her. She followed their instructions and walked down a spiral dirt staircase in the back, which led to a small room below the throne room.

A hooded Leizei burned Noelle with their fiery hands, and she whimpered. Lumi caught sight of the burn mark on her forearm.

"Better cool off your hands, or I will," Lumi warned. And by cool off, she meant she'd turn their hands into shriveling frost-bitten ash.

Lumi felt quite uncomfortable, because the Leizeis' temperatures were polar opposite of hers and their very presence was smoldering hot. The hooded Leizeis held fire in their hands, as if they were torches that lit up the way.

"There is enough light without your stupid fires," Lumi spat out.

"Oh? Is the Snow Queen uncomfortable?" a hooded Leizei asked. He then increased the size and heat of the dancing flame in his palm.

Lumi sighed.

Once they reached the end of the small room, the hooded Leizeis raised their hands and crafted a fiery jail with bars made of roaring flames of fire. A Leizei waved his hand, and the fiery door opened.

Another Leizei placed shackles on Lumi's hands—which she

had expected. It forced her fists closed, which would not allow her to manipulate her snow ability. But as long as they had declared the Heirling Duel, they couldn't do much to her.

Comically, they placed cuffs on Noelle and Luis too, despite the fact that they hadn't had any ability at all. Noelle wasn't even initiated yet.

They shoved Luis and Noelle inside, and Lumi sighed, then stepped in. They closed the fiery jail door.

Lumi sat on the hot dirt floor and folded her legs toward herself. She rested her chin on her knee and looked around. The fiery jail bar flames generated more heat than was comfortable for her.

There were twelve guards, and each had donned black outfits with black hoods. She couldn't see their faces. She could only see their lips and chins.

The flames grew more and more uncomfortable against Lumi's skin. But this was the very least of her concerns. She glanced at Noelle, who would be fighting in the Heirling Duel very soon, and Luis, who knew about both the Leizeis and Natureis, which meant they would surely imprison him or kill him.

Noelle, to Lumi's surprise, looked to be well. Even more than well, she looked glamorous and well groomed.

"Now that she is cuffed, she can't do any damage. We'll be stationed upstairs, but don't get any ideas," a hooded Leizei said.

Lumi watched as they all, except one hooded Leizei, left. She looked at his tattoo on his wrist to confirm what she already suspected—he was an elite soldier. Even if they managed to escape this little fiery jail, more soldiers would be stationed upstairs.

"Let us out," Luis said, more like a demand than a request.

To Lumi's shock, the Leizei soldier walked over, took off his gloves, and pulled a fiery key out of his pocket. He opened the fiery door with it, and Lumi eyed him and wondered why he wouldn't just manipulate the fiery door open like the others.

Lumi sat up, prepared to coil her links around the Leizei's neck, when she heard a very familiar voice.

"Looks like you got into some trouble," Marko said and pulled off the hood.

Lumi nearly fell backward at the sight of Marko in an elite Leizei soldier's hooded uniform. Yet there stood Marko in front of them, even with the Leizei tattoo.

"Marko!" Lumi said in a horrified whisper. "If they catch you with this outfit on, they will kill you. The hoods are their sacred clothing. Only specific Leizei can wear it!" Lumi threw her arms around Marko, and he wrapped his arms around her, tight.

"Sacred hood clothing? Yeah, that sounds like a cult," Luis said as he walked out of the fire bars. "We should probably move fast. Before they come back." Luis looked ahead at the spiral dirt staircase.

"I've been so worried! I am so happy to see you!" Noelle hugged Marko.

"What is the plan?" Luis asked as he looked at the stairs. It seemed like the only exit.

Marko stopped and closed his eyes. "Lumi?" He said her name with gentle care. It was enough to stop Lumi in her tracks.

"What is it?" Lumi asked.

Marko took out another fire key from his pocket and undid her shackles. The metal cuffs clanged to the ground. She stretched out her fingers and held on to her wrists. "I need to know one thing. Do you want to be with me *forever*?"

Lumi looked flustered. "Of course I want to be with you, let's go! Let's talk about this another time. We need to hurry!" Lumi started to walk forward, but Marko grabbed her forearm and stopped her. Perplexed, she looked up at him.

"No, Lumi. This is *very* important, more important than anything else right now. I need to know right now. I need you to think carefully about your choice. *Do you want to be with me?*" Marko's eyes were intense and focused. It was as if nobody else was in the room.

Lumi gave a slow nod. "Yes, I'm falling in love with you." Lumi looked at Marko for a moment, as if she were uncertain what he was doing.

"I love you too, Lumi. I promise that I'll do anything in my power to protect you. But I need to know—do you want to be with me *forever*?" Marko asked, with hungry eyes that burned.

Noelle shoved Marko. "We don't have time for this, lover boy! Let's get moving! Share your romantic moment later on." But Marko didn't budge.

"Yes, I'd like that," Lumi said.

"All right, then I know what I need to do. What I'm going to do won't make sense. But I need you to trust me," Marko said and took out a large vial from his pocket.

"What are you doing?" Lumi asked and leaned away from Marko.

"Get back, Noelle!" Marko called out and poured the vial on Lumi. Lumi writhed in pain as the scent of merca filled her nostrils and lungs. It burned her insides, and she felt her power dim. Lumi collapsed into Marko's arms, her strength waned. Lumi's throat closed slightly with the scent.

Noelle took several steps backward until she was back in the fire cell.

"Marko! What are you doing? She is our ticket out of here!" Luis also backed away from Marko.

Lumi seemed hardly conscious. She was limp in Marko's arms. She could hear everything, but her body felt slow and unfocused.

"I need all of you to trust me," Marko said and then he took his index finger and wrapped it around Lumi's ring finger.

Lumi could feel the burn instantly—he had bonded her to him. The fire on her ring finger put her in anguish, but all she could manage to do was moan and lift her head. The stench of her own burned skin smelled vile.

Marko's index finger went red with heat, and then Marko and Lumi had identical burn marks on their ring fingers.

"I promise to protect you," Marko said as he held her hand. A crimson light encircled their wrists and then disappeared. He let her go, and she slumped to the floor with eyes closed.

Noelle was hysterical. Marko put the shackles back on Lumi and put the key in his black pants pocket. He dragged her back into the cell.

"What have you done?" Luis demanded. He gathered beside Lumi and Noelle in the cell.

Lumi watched Marko. He now had a perfect circle on his finger, and had she not known any better, she would think it was a wedding band if she didn't look close enough.

"I asked if she wanted to be with me forever. None of you understand what is at stake, but that was the *only* way I could protect her. They were going to kill her right after the duel," Marko said and he slipped his black gloves back on.

But then footsteps emerged from the staircase. Marko quickly shut the fire jail and faced the guards.

"What happened?" they asked and looked at Lumi on the ground.

"Her mouth got the best of me. I poured merca on her," Marko lied. Several more guards hurried downstairs.

"Prince of Flames, I'm sorry you were left alone. Why was the prince left alone? Do you all want the King of Flames to ruin your career?" a hooded Leizei yelled, and the hooded figures shifted uncomfortably.

Lumi looked for a prince but then let her head slump against the dirt when she realized who it was. Marko had tricked her, and tears began to trickle as she realized that the entire thing had been an act. She wondered why her ability hadn't picked up on Marko's deception and ill will toward her. In fact, why hadn't she picked up on Eli's either?

"Prince?" Noelle asked aloud, belligerent.

A hooded Leizei gave a slight bow to Marko, whose dark features glowed in the firelit room. And then it dawned on Lumi as she squinted at him. Marko's amber brown eyes matched all the other Leizeis' eyes. Marko's eyes were always a deep chestnut brown, but now they looked different—because they were Leizei eyes.

Marko gave Lumi a forlorn look. She could barely move, but her mind worked well enough, despite the hazy effect of merca. He had played her like a fool, and she fell for it. Thanks to Eli and Marko, they had finally succeeded in bringing her in.

A single tear fell down Lumi's cheek as she lay on the dirt floor.

CHAPTER 25
NOELLE
COMMENCEMENT OF THE HEIRLING DUEL

Noelle tapped her feet idly on the dirt floor. The dark circles under Luis's eyes revealed he hadn't slept well. Neither of them spoke but sat with their own thoughts.

Lumi still lay in a crumpled heap on the floor. Noelle slid her hand under Lumi's head and held it in her lap. Lumi looked up at her, but her lips didn't move. She writhed every few moments, and her body spazzed.

Noelle reached for the merca liquid that lay on Lumi's arm.

"Don't," Lumi hoarsely whispered—but it was too late.

Noelle shrieked and withdrew her finger as the merca stung her. She was most definitely a Merklei.

Soldiers appeared and forced them to their feet and back into the throne room. Leizei soldiers, dressed in black uniforms, lined the walls. Each soldier had their own hood lifted over their face, which concealed their identities. They stood erect with good posture, their hands at their sides. Noelle noticed the Naturei king, Pierce Goldner, sat upon his large, lofty vine throne. A new gold throne sat beside him—with a large man in a gold hood that sat upon it.

Noelle and the others walked up, and the guards forced them to kneel once they got close to the gold throne.

Lumi started to regain her strength, albeit very slight. She seemed to struggle to manage to keep her head up. It looked as if she were drunk.

Marko emerged, hood down, and a gold crown perched on his head. He folded his gloved hands in front of him and stood to the right side of the gold throne. The entire room gently bowed.

Before them stood the Naturei king and his heir, Eli Goldner, along with the Leizei king, and his heir, Marko Jokovic.

Eli looked straight ahead, hard to read.

Noelle bit the inside of her cheek.

"We have guests," the Leizei king said, and his gold hood swiveled in their direction. "The Queen of Merklei." He pointed a long, shaky finger at her. The Leizei in the crowd hissed in response. "It is so good to see you again." He stood, holding a cane. Noelle could swear that she recognized his voice. It sounded so eerily familiar. "I hear you go by Lumi these days," the Leizei king said, and he pulled his hood down.

"Dr. Locke!" Noelle's mouth dropped.

Luis blinked several times.

Marko remained unmoved.

Luis froze.

Dr. Locke's wild hair stuck up as usual, and his thick glasses stood on the end of his nose. Noelle felt her insides twist in her stomach. She had told Dr. Locke nearly everything about the necklace. He'd known everything *all along.*

"You know the King of Flames?" Lumi asked, dejected. She looked sideways at Noelle.

"He was my professor," Noelle said. She didn't dare tell Lumi more. She was the reason for the betrayal. She'd led Dr. Locke straight to Lumi and the necklace.

"Noelle," the Leizei king's voice boomed. Her heartbeat multiplied. "It is a shame to see you here. You had so much potential in the human world. I tried so hard to steer you clear of that necklace. The truth is I really liked you and wanted to see you succeed. But you just wouldn't listen. And now look where we are." He lifted his hands and gestured to the throne room. "I tried to deter your grandma too. But I think you get your stubbornness from her."

Noelle's heart scurried even faster now. "You knew my grandma?"

"Oh yes. I knew she was Merklei. After so many years, I had to poison her myself with small doses of merca. I figured if she were more bedridden, then she would stop the nonsense about the necklace. I was unfortunately wrong." The Leizei king sniffed and wiped his nose.

Noelle pictured the last several years of her grandma's life. She'd visited the doctor often, but they never knew what was wrong. She'd tried to be present, but she often missed many of Noelle's school plays, school trips, and they'd often had to leave events early so that she could rest. Many memories passed through Noelle's mind, and fury bubbled in her stomach.

"*You* were the reason she was sick all those years?" She stood to her feet now.

"Regrettably, yes. But I was protecting you and all the humans. From her." The Leizei king pointed at Lumi again. "She's the monster. I convinced your grandma to write in the hints that you shouldn't give the necklace to the Snow Queen, in exchange for a vow that I wouldn't hurt you. But it looks like you ignored your own grandmother's wishes."

"She isn't a monster! *You're a monster!* She didn't kill that kingdom of humans. You did! You've been lying to your people for years!" Noelle screamed and kicked against the guard and the chains that held her. Hot tears streamed down her face. "You killed my grandma!" She sounded like a wounded animal, less human and more feral. She bucked against the guards.

"I did everything for the good of all, Noelle. I had to keep my realm a secret from the humans."

"We'll make a deal with you though, since you are wearing the necklace," the Naturei king said and pointed at her neck. "We would like you to use it for our gain. We will call off the

Heirling Duel, which I'm certain you're now aware is imminent."

Noelle watched Eli and Marko, who suddenly made eye contact. A plea.

"What do you want with the necklace?" Luis spoke and shifted away from his guard. The guard grabbed him by his dark curly hair, and Luis cringed.

"We want you to bring back all the rest of the Merklei in exchange for killing Lumi. One life for many lives. The Merklei can live on, but without her," the Leizei king sneered. "You see, Lumi just wouldn't fall in line. She was insistent that humans be our equals. While we can all agree that we ought to respect one another, she was adamant that we must all work together and coexist. That sounds lovely in theory, but do you know what the problem with that is? The humans kept causing problems for us in the Merklei, Naturei, and Leizei realms with their lies, deceit, and treacherous ways. So we decided that we would separate from the humans and do our work in secret. But Lumi just couldn't agree." The Leizei king's eyes scanned Lumi's crumpled body. "How did that turn out for you, Lumi? Where is your Lorelei?"

Lumi looked crestfallen. She looked down at her knees. She didn't flail against her guards. She looked defeated.

"Say, where is Lorelei? King Pierce?" The Leizei king looked smug now. The Naturei king looked away. "Was it worth it? You sacrificed so much for them. Yet look how they've repaid you."

"Why are you doing this, Dr. Locke?" Luis cried.

"It is such a shame that you got caught up in this mess too. I am so terribly sorry to see you're here, Luis. You also had such a bright future and I know you really studied hard. You would have been a great doctor, like you planned. Lumi just knows how to ruin so many good things," the Leizei king said with a shrug. "But I must protect the lives of the fire realm, and I also have a duty to protect the humans too."

"Protect? You *murder* them! You murdered my grandma!"

Noelle swung out and struck the guard who held her hair at the nape of her neck. He struggled to contain her.

A petite Leizei entered. The beautiful woman made her way to Marko's side and then ogled Noelle.

"Don't speak another treacherous word against our king," she warned. Her long black hair was braided into several braids, and she carried a mischievous look on her features, as if she dared Noelle to say something else.

"Your king is a *murderer*!" Noelle screamed as loudly as she could, and the beautiful Leizei hurled a large blast of fire at her.

Dr. Locke, the Leizei king, raised his hand and extinguished the flame just before it reached her. "That is enough! You cannot harm any heirs during the Heirling Duel! Noelle, I didn't *murder* your grandma. I *protected* you. Just like when I put you and Marko together, it was *I* who protected you. Where are you getting this murderous nonsense from?" The Leizei king cocked his head to the side, as if he tried to understand her.

Noelle wanted to scoff—he truly believed he had done a good thing. He believed his tyranny was rooted in righteousness.

"Wait, what do you mean by putting her and Marko together?" Luis asked, his voice thick with offense.

"Don't be foolish. I knew her grandma wouldn't make it much longer with the amount of merca that was going into her system. My son and daughter-in-law are easy to predict, and I knew they'd gladly take Noelle in with their big hearts. I gave Marko the assignment of a protective older brother and encouraged the process along. Her grandma thought I was a friend, and I made a vow to protect Noelle if she followed my instructions about the hint. She didn't know who I truly was."

Noelle snapped her eyes shut. Her face twisted in agony. She looked down at the dirt floor. She looked at Marko. He simply looked ahead, above all their heads. Her grandma never talked about a friend like him; she didn't know if he was lying or telling the truth.

"Marko?" Noelle bellowed. A sob emerged in her throat, and

she tried to choke it back. "Is that true? I don't understand." Noelle looked around the room. "Where are your parents?" Noelle's lip quivered.

"My son refused the throne along with Marko's immediate family," the Leizei king said with disgust in his voice. "We had to wipe his memory, along with Marko's mother and sister, so they believe they're simply human. *Such a shame.*" The Leizei king hobbled forward. "Good thing Marko made a better choice." He spoke with pride and looked approvingly at Marko. But Marko's face didn't change at all. He simply looked forward.

Noelle was glad to know that at least his family wasn't a part of the betrayal; at least some part of her life wasn't complete and utter deception.

"I don't believe Marko would do this," Noelle said. "He isn't like you! He isn't like *any* of you!" Noelle looked defiantly at them all.

"What do you not understand? Come on, let's reason together. You're a bright girl. I sent Marko to be a spy for our realm. He gladly took the assignment, as he is next in line for the throne. He *always* knew you were Merklei. We knew you were vulnerable and lonely, so we hatched a plan for him to play a big brother role," the Leizei king said. This man was nothing like the caring professor that Noelle had come to know and appreciate.

"Marko? Is that true?" Noelle asked, cynicism in her voice. She let her arms go limp.

Marko didn't respond. His face remained unemotive.

It felt as if Marko had driven her own knife into her back. "Well, despite it all, you couldn't beat fate! Fate brought Lumi and I together," Noelle said and stuck her chin in the air.

The Leizei king gave a loud laugh. "My dear, Marko brought you and Lumi together. We had been tracking Lumi for a long time, and we knew who she was before she ever landed in Chicago. Do you really think you just happened to find the Snow Queen? We organized *everything*." He spoke slowly, and his voice irritated Noelle. "The only thing that wasn't organized was the romantic connection that you formed." The Leizei king looked at Marko now, who stayed in soldier mode. "Your fiancée would probably like to know about that."

Marko's jaw tightened.

"You have a fiancée?" Lumi snapped out of her dejected state with a ferocity in her voice. She stood to her feet now. Several guards moved toward her, obviously not prepared since she was so low on energy only moments ago. They struggled against her. Despite the merca, she was still *quite* strong. Noelle could hear wintry wind howling outside with Lumi's outburst of anger.

The Leizei king smiled ear to ear. "Allow me to introduce you! Yuri, meet Lumi. Marko has been running around Chicago with her."

Yuri, the beautiful Leizei with braids, took several steps forward, and her black braids swung as she walked.

"Oh." That was all Yuri said. But the massive fireball in her hands made her intentions clear. Although Noelle couldn't decipher if it was aimed at Lumi or Marko.

"I did what my role required of me. She wouldn't budge otherwise," Marko said. He betrayed no emotion. He reported the information as if it were his job or a duty.

"Lumi, you should have chosen me instead. I wouldn't have betrayed you! Also, I'm not engaged. Which, I didn't realize was much of a flex, but here we are," Luis said.

"Lumi, listen to me! Marko is *not* with him. He is with us! Sure, maybe he has some explaining to do. But I've known him for years. I *know* my connection with him and his family was authentic. And I think yours was too," Noelle said, trying to calm Lumi.

Lumi looked at Noelle with a tear-stricken face. "No, *you're* getting this all wrong. He is an actor. Think about it! What is the one thing that both you and I craved? What was the one thing we had in common? We were both miserably lonely and without a family. And then here comes Marko to be my doting love interest and your protective older brother. They *planned* it! We've been played by the man who will inherit the throne of the fire realm.

We are utter fools. They've been ten steps ahead of us this entire time." Lumi knocked two guards down with her cuffed hands, and more came and replaced them.

"Noelle," the Leizei king said. He folded his hands together. "Your greatest strength is your greatest weakness; you trust people so easily. You and Lumi are quite alike in this regard." He raised an eyebrow and pushed his glasses up his nose.

Lumi stiffened and then composed herself entirely. "Well, unfortunately for you all—you cannot imprison another ruler of a realm during the Heirling Duel. So you will let go of all of us or there won't be an Heirling Duel," Lumi said and knocked over a Naturei soldier. Noelle was astonished by her strength even with the merca.

Noelle caught Eli's eyes, but he looked away.

"Hold on. Noelle, do we have a deal? You can have Lorelei, the Merklei clan, and your grandma back! Just use the necklace. We'd take it from you, but we can't get it off your body," the Leizei king said with a delicate smirk.

Noelle glared at him. "No deal," she said defiantly. She would get her grandma back, Lorelei, and the entire Merklei clan—along with Lumi. She had hoped her grandma was Merklei, now that she knew it officially—both Lumi and Noelle could get their family back.

"Well then." The Naturei king stood. "We formally declare our votes for the Heirling Duel. The occasion for the duel is to decide the fate of the Snow Queen, Lumi Eira Hiver. She has caused havoc for the Leizei, Merklei, and Naturei realm by exposure, and she has much blood on her hands."

"No, she doesn't," Noelle said.

"She has my child's blood on her hands!" he yelled.

"Her blood is on *your* hands! You promised to help her people, and *you* let them die! Let us use the necklace and bring Lorelei back!"

"I agreed not to spy on them because of Lumi's vow. And look what her pact with humans brought me!" the Naturei king yelled, and Eli placed a hand on his shoulder. He exhaled.

"We will bring justice to your daughter. Both the Leizei and Naturei realms have cast their vote to begin the Heirling Duel. It has officially commenced!" the Leizei king said, and all the people in the crowd cheered in response.

"This is an absolute perversion of the Heirling Duel and everything that it stands for!" Lumi said. "It was created so we would avoid war with our realms—so that we would only call for it should we *really* need to settle a dispute. The lives of heirs *should* be precious. Do either of you care about your heir?"

Pierce scoffed. "To all my noble court visitors gathered here today, we announce the fourth Heirling Duel!" the Naturei king said.

Several Leizei shot flames into the air, and several Naturei saluted over their hearts. Cheers erupted all over the throne room.

"Nobody may harm the three heirs or the sitting rulers during the three days, per the vow we all took. Since we rulers took a vow, it is impossible to break the vow. But for anybody who may get any ideas, you will face life in prison should you decide to hurt a ruler or heir," the Naturei king announced.

"You should have just given them their way. You could have brought back our people and your grandma," Lumi said, sorrow filled her eyes.

"No, don't be stupid," Noelle shot back. "You're Merklei, and so am I. That means we're family. We've spent so much time looking for ways to get our families back, not realizing this entire time that we have each other."

Lumi held her gaze a moment, then nodded.

"Besides, I'm going to survive this, and we will get back *all* the Merklei," Noelle said.

Lumi sighed.

"One last matter to settle. Bring in the prisoners," the Leizei king said. Hooded Leizei dragged in two men, beaten and bloodied. One man's face was entirely swollen from a terrible beating. They dragged them beside Noelle, and the two men gaped at her.

"Stand," the Leizei king ordered. The two men could barely stand. They looked so thin, and their garments were filthy.

"We found the two leaders of the rebellion who worked together to murder my adviser. They wrote Noelle's name by the body because they believe she will be a threat to my throne. The Leizei educator, Cliff Blazen, and the Naturei educator, Tiberius Oak."

"Queen Noelle," the man closest to her said in a whisper. Noelle snapped her head in the direction of the starved, beaten man who smiled at her. "You will do great things, and you will bring down the wicked thrones." And then he began to laugh, which turned into a cough.

"Kill them," the Leizei king said. And then fires engulfed both the two men instantly.

Eli looked away, closing his eyes briefly. When he reopened them, Noelle could see his eyes become watery and his fists were clenched. Eli wiped his face and looked to the ground.

The two men dropped to their knees, and their lives wilted in front of everyone. Noelle covered her eyes and began shaking.

"We must act cordially during these three days and live peacefully," the Naturei king announced. "Show our guests to their rooms." Guards filed next to Luis, Lumi, and Noelle. He spoke as if two men hadn't just died in front of all of them. A few guards removed the shackles from Lumi's, Luis's, and Noelle's hands. Noelle grasped her wrists.

"Can I at the *very* least keep my room?" Noelle asked. But her voice shook nonetheless. She couldn't stop the trembling after witnessing two men burned to death because they wanted her to take the throne.

"Certainly," the Naturei king responded. "One last matter. Lock her necklace." A Naturei woman walked forward and waved her hand over Noelle's necklace and locked the necklace with her ability. "You won't be able to use this for the foreseeable future."

The soldiers guided them to Noelle's room, and Lumi and Luis filed into her room. To Noelle's surprise, the soldiers left them alone.

"What happens now?" Noelle asked, horrified. They each sat on her large, oversized bed.

"We need to get you initiated so you have Merklei power. You'll have an advantage over the Naturei realm due to my curse. Eli won't be able to use his Naturei abilities in my presence," Lumi said. "Unfortunately, that Naturei with the lock ability locked the necklace, so you won't be able to get the necklace open until we can figure that out. They can't use their Naturei ability, but they can use their personal abilities with the curse."

"But Eli is very strong, and he has a healing ability too," Noelle thought aloud.

Lumi nodded. "Do you know what his weaknesses are?"

Noelle didn't want to reveal his weakness. Not unless she had to. Part of her still wanted to protect him, despite everything.

"No," Noelle lied. She knew the alanis plant slowed him down. "Can't we run away?"

"No." Lumi shook her head. "I made a vow to follow the rules of the Heirling Duel. I couldn't run if I tried."

And then, besides Eli's weakness, she told them everything that she knew and caught them up on every single detail and didn't leave out anything.

CHAPTER 26
NOELLE
THE INITIATION

Lumi had fallen fast asleep on her bed, and Luis slept on the dirt floor with a spare blanket. Noelle plucked an alanis flower and tucked it behind her own ear and then tiptoed toward the front door.

She walked down the hall and looked over her shoulder. They said nobody could hurt them for a few days—at least until the duel was over—so she thought maybe she might look for answers.

That was until a hand roughly grabbed her forearm and pulled her into a different room. A callused hand covered her mouth, which muffled her scream. She stilled as she realized who it was.

Marko pressed a finger to his own lips, and Noelle quieted.

They stared at each other for a moment, and Marko closed his own bedroom door.

"I have a lot of explaining to do, but I—"

Noelle slapped Marko hard across his face. Her hand stung with the slap. A bright red mark with the outline of fingers appeared on his cheek.

"That was deserved. Are you done now?"

"You're Leizei? And a *spy*?" Noelle raised her hand to strike him again, but he didn't move to stop her. She lowered her hand.

"Yes, and yes. But I don't have time to explain. Lumi is not safe," Marko said. "Where is she?"

"I'm not telling you," Noelle said. "And yes, she is safe during the duel."

Marko sighed and rubbed his temples.

"The reason I poured merca on her was because I intercepted a plan to weaken her with that merca right after the duel. It was the only vial my realm had, and I had to have an excuse to use it up."

"And you burned that fire bond mark on her finger. *Why?*" Noelle asked earnestly.

Marko ran a hand through his hair and shuffled his feet. "Because now if Lumi dies, then I die too. My realm won't go through with their plan to kill her once they find out."

Noelle tensed. "I'll warn her. But just one thing—how much was real and how much was fake?" Noelle lifted her chin to meet his tall figure that towered over her.

"In the beginning, *everything* was fake," he admitted. "But over time, very little was fake. And the romance with Lumi was *very* real. Although I highly doubt there is any future with that now. I wish I could explain everything to you, but you need to go. If you get caught in here, they'll know that I tipped you off. I won't appear friendly moving forward."

"Fine, just tell me one last thing."

"What could possibly be so important to know after I just told you that Lumi's life is in danger?" Marko looked tired.

"How old are you *really*?"

"I've been alive for 147 years, now get out!" Marko said and shoved her toward the door. Noelle knew it. She knew he was an old man; he even wore those ugly itchy sweaters.

She silently walked back to her bedroom and hurried to Lumi's side and repeated the warning. They succumbed to sleep.

In the morning, Sage entered Noelle's bedroom, but her normal cheerful mood was now distant and cool.

"What do you want, Merklei?"

Noelle frowned. "You used to be so nice," she complained.

"That was when I thought you were a poor human girl and maybe the future queen! Now I just think you're rotten," Sage said. "If you hurt Prince Eli, I might poison you myself."

Noelle's frown deepened. "I could never hurt Eli."

And something in Sage seemed to believe Noelle, because she perked up after that and almost returned to her normal self. Almost.

"I'll take avocado toast and coffee," Noelle said.

Sage waved her hand, and a perfectly delicious avocado toast and coffee emerged before Noelle. She really did love the Naturei realm and Naturei abilities.

"Thanks. Could you pass a message onto Eli?" Noelle asked, her voice lowered.

"I don't know," Sage said and eyed a shocked Luis. "What is wrong with this one?"

Luis's mouth hung open. "You have a superpower to make food? This is the coolest thing I have ever seen in my life! Can you make me a breakfast burrito?"

Sage grinned. She waved her hand, and a breakfast burrito appeared before Luis, who gasped.

"He is easily entertained. I am too." Noelle laughed.

Sage refocused on Noelle. "What do you want me to say?"

"Tell him that I want to speak to him, please."

Sage nodded. "And what about you, Merklei?" She focused on Lumi.

"Coffee and toast sound great."

With a wave of her hand, she produced her order and then briskly left.

When Sage returned, she had a tiny slip of paper in her hand, which she handed to Noelle. It was sealed with Eli's signet ring marking.

> *I'll meet with you for 5 minutes. Meet in my courtyard outside my room. —Eli*

Noelle hurried to her feet.

"And where are you going? We need to start your initiation and Merklei vows." Lumi frowned as she took another bite of her toast.

"I have to speak quickly with Eli!"

Neither Luis nor Lumi seemed thrilled, but they didn't say anything to stop her either.

"I'll be quick!" Noelle called over her shoulder. She sped down the hallway, into the double doors toward Eli's bedroom. She looked out the huge window and saw him, where he paced. Noelle smoothed out her dress. She hadn't changed since last night.

She opened the doors. She hoped she could smooth things over and explain everything.

"Hey," she said.

Eli looked up at her and grimaced. "You look rough."

Noelle shrugged. "It was a very eventful evening."

He seemed unamused. "What do you want?"

"To talk."

"So talk."

Noelle bristled. She wasn't sure where to start. "Well, you know I can't lie because of my vow. So I just wanted to clear some things up. I'm sorry for not telling you everything."

Eli stared at her blankly. "All right, *and?*"

Noelle's brows pulled down. "And I haven't told anybody what your weakness is, and I will not tell anybody."

It was Eli who now went rigid. "You have three minutes." Eli's mind seemed elsewhere.

Noelle sighed. "I just wanted to tell you that no matter what happens, I won't hurt you and I definitely won't kill you in the duel."

Eli stopped. "That is stupid of you, because if you think that I'm going to be kind to you in the duel, then you're wrong." He let out a laugh. "Besides, you couldn't kill me if you wanted to."

She rolled her eyes. He was so painfully arrogant. Noelle struggled to imagine how so much pride could possibly be contained in one person.

"I'm sorry I wasn't honest with you about everything," Noelle blurted out.

Eli turned on his heel and really studied her for the first time since the previous night, and he slowly shook his head. "It doesn't matter anymore. You're the heir to the Merklei throne whether you knew it or not."

"So?"

"So we're not playing on the same team, and don't expect me to go easy on you in the arena. Stay out of my way."

Noelle sighed. "That's it then? We are just Merklei and Naturei?"

He licked his lips and shivered. Thanks to Lumi's presence, the normally sunny Naturei realm looked entirely different since it was now covered in snow.

"Yes, that is it," he said, annoyed. "That is all it will ever be. We can't be friends, don't you understand?" But something in his eyes betrayed him. His eyes looked *almost* remorseful.

Noelle slowly nodded and then turned to leave. But before she did, she snapped back. "Did you know about Marko? You knew this whole time?"

Eli laughed. "No, I didn't know. I knew they had an heir, but they're secretive and we knew nothing about their heir."

"Well, at least we have that in common then. We both got deceived," Noelle said, and before he could say anything more, she went back inside. Apparently there would be no alliance between Eli and Noelle.

When Noelle returned, she found Luis and Lumi by the door.

"How did it go?" Luis inquired.

Noelle just shook her head. "Nothing good to report."

"Figured. Let's get somewhere deep in the woods for your initiation," Lumi said, and they walked out of the room. As they passed a few Naturei and Leizei, they leered at them. Noelle even heard one call her a fraud as she passed. She ignored them and continued forward.

Noelle knew she would no longer age, and she shuddered at the thought of being a teenager forever. Her teen years simply were not her best years. She had high hopes for her young adult years. She wondered if this meant she would always have pimple breakouts.

"It's sort of ironic that you get frozen in time on your nineteenth birthday! Happy birthday, Noelle!" Luis cheered. Noelle hadn't realized it, but it was her birthday.

It was perhaps the heaviest birthday Noelle ever had—and she felt there was little to celebrate with death potentially knocking on her door soon.

The friends moved deeper and deeper into the woods. Everything around them looked like a dizzy snow globe with snow coming from all angles. They marched forward in silence for a while, with the occasional teeth chatter noise from Luis breaking the silence.

"I think this is a good place," Lumi called out as she stood in a small clearing. Withered trees stood all around them.

Lumi stood across from Noelle. Her long blond waist-length hair swayed in the wind. Noelle swallowed. Lumi held out her hand, and a blue light shone vertically.

"Once I activate your ability to manipulate snow and ice, it cannot be undone."

Noelle nodded.

"Merklei were given the power to manipulate snow and ice so that we can help regulate the earth. We are also stewards of this power. Once upon a time, we used to work closely with the

Naturei realm to help balance things." Lumi balked. "But now that has become complicated. With these powers, you have large responsibilities."

Lumi walked toward Noelle and held her hand out. Noelle took it, and a bright vertical light shone through their hands, and Noelle could feel something hover over her entire being.

"I bestow upon you, as the Snow Queen, the power of the Merklei."

"What is this?" Noelle could feel an energy that pulsed over her.

"The ability to manipulate snow and ice," Lumi answered with a half smile. The blue light grew intense, and Luis closed his eyes and shielded the light with the palms of his hands.

But Noelle kept her eyes open. The light didn't seem to irritate her at all. Instead, it allured her. As the light grew, Noelle noticed the cold temperature no longer bothered her. She could still understand and distinguish that it was cold, but it no longer seemed unbearable. Instead, the cold actually seemed like a comfort to her skin. Noelle exhaled. Her chapped lips no longer felt dry and irritable. She suddenly felt alive and energetic. Something new and foreign pulsed through her veins. Noelle lifted her hands to her face and examined them.

"Don't," Lumi warned. But Noelle didn't listen. She pointed a finger at the sky, and a streak of ice launched in the direction of her fingertip.

"No way!" Luis yelled excitedly.

Lumi tackled Noelle to the ground and pinned her hands down.

"Do you want to hurt Luis? You have no idea what you're doing!"

"This is the coolest thing to ever happen to me!" Noelle yelled cheerfully. She giggled, and Lumi struggled to restrain her.

"Stop it! You could hurt somebody!" Lumi urged.

"I won't! I won't. I'm just having fun," Noelle said, and Lumi stood up.

"Your emotions are connected to your powers. You need to control yourself. If you lose control of your emotions, then you can easily lose control of yourself and your ability to manipulate the cold," Lumi said, and as she did, she crafted an ice shield in front of Luis.

"What is that for?" Noelle asked and frowned.

"You need to learn how to use your ability," Lumi said, and then she crafted a shield for herself.

Noelle looked in the reflection of Lumi's shield, and her mouth dropped when she realized her eye color had changed to a light gray, just like Lumi's.

CHAPTER 27

ELI

THE HEIRLING DUEL—DAY ONE

She was in the snow and practiced her new Merklei ability, and Eli watched from his bedroom window and leaned up against it with his palm on the edge. He ought to do something else, anything else, to prepare for the first duel. But he watched with intrigue because he wanted her to survive. The entirety of the situation was lopsided and unfair to her in every way. Declaring the Heirling Duel was already cruel, but this was something else entirely.

Despite the fact that they were opponents, he refused to acknowledge the truth that he wouldn't harm a hair on her head. He simply couldn't hurt Noelle—he knew he wouldn't. But he also couldn't protect her in the duel. He just hoped she stayed out of his way and survived.

He watched below, as her dark, wild hair blew in the snowy wind. He watched as it tangled, and he recalled only last night he had his own hands on her soft hair.

He pondered what might happen if Noelle got into trouble in the duel. He sighed as the truth dawned on him—he'd intervene on her behalf if she needed him. He shouldn't, and he even told her he wouldn't—but he just couldn't live with himself if she needed help and he didn't step in. What would his father and realm say? The entire crowd last night despised her—it was shocking to Eli how quickly the night had gone sour.

He reluctantly looked over at the alanis plant in his room and plucked a singular small orange flower. He twirled it between his thumb and index finger, then his eyes drifted back to the girl.

She threw ice daggers at Lumi's shield, and she did a poor job of it too. Eli laughed as he watched her. It might be quite a chore to keep both himself and her alive in the arena by the look of things.

He hadn't noticed Sage at his side.

"It's a shame she is Merklei. You two seemed very snug before that news." Sage held out a mug.

Eli begrudgingly took the cup. He brought the mug to his lips and enjoyed the comfort of the warm touch.

"It seems you like a few things from the human world," Sage said and looked from the coffee cup to the girl outside.

Eli glanced at Sage and then watched as Noelle crafted a sword that split apart and fell onto the snow. Eli shook his head.

"She is terrible," he said and sighed. Noelle crafted another sword and aimed it at Lumi. Eli studied Noelle. Her pretty face looked the same with her cute button nose, big round eyes, and full lips. But her eyes looked different now. She had gray eyes that mirrored Lumi's, and Eli hated to admit it, but she somehow looked even more striking with the Merklei eye color against her tanned skin and dark hair.

Noelle's thick hair swayed with the icy wind, and she threw her head back in laughter. Eli loved seeing her crooked smile, especially when it was him who earned a flash of it. Noelle struck at Lumi with her icy sword and almost made contact.

Eli might need to watch his back around her or else she might best him in the arena. Surely she wouldn't use his kindness and mercy toward her as weakness. *Surely.*

Sage looked over the scene, then made a haughty noise. "Better than you when you first initiated! I remember you could barely grow a flower in a pot!"

Eli's lips curled up. It was true. He could barely do much when he was first initiated.

"And besides," Sage pointed at Noelle. "Maybe she gained some ability that she can find useful in the arena besides manipulating snow and ice."

"I hope for her sake that she has." Eli watched her again. She crafted sharp icicles and then threw them. Lumi ducked behind her shield.

"If I may be so forward, I like the girl. If it came down to it, I hope you would pick her over the other heir."

"That is quite forward."

He wished there were different circumstances. He wished he could go to her and laugh with her in the snow. He wished he could help her and somehow protect her. But she was Merklei, and he was supposed to despise her for it. Yet still, he couldn't quench the desire that welled up inside him as he watched her—to go to her and *be with her.*

He wished there was another way—he would miss the laughter that so easily fell from his own lips around her. Her fingertips were curled around an icy sword, in practice below, but he longed for her fingertips to be wrapped around his. Why, out of everyone, did the heir have to be *her*?

Sage cleared her throat. "Well, as long as I am being forward, you should know that I agree with everything the educator said. Tiberius wasn't lying when he told you that the king murdered your parents for participating in the rebellion. I was there, I just escaped and—"

Several Naturei soldiers arrived at his door and stood outside in preparation for the commencement ceremony. Eden, Aurora, and Blossom scurried into his room and bowed graciously.

Without a word, Eden waved her hand over Eli's body, and a special uniform appeared, perfectly fitted. He wore a green beret, a forest-green leaf vest, styled with military medals, and protective armor made out of special bark that not even bullets could penetrate.

Eli's pulse raced as he stared at Sage, who lowered her face to the floor. If the king were lying, that changed everything. Could it be that Sage, his parents, and the educator were all aligned with the rebellion? Eli's eyes still felt puffy from the previous night; he hadn't cried in that way since he was nine. The educator was the closest thing that he had to a real father. Eli's throat grew dry. Thousands had been killed throughout the years. Usually it began with protests, and it ended with violence.

"Eden," Eli whispered. She turned, caught off guard. "Please dress Noelle since she is our guest."

Eden's mouth pinched tight. "But she is Merklei and your opponent. I won't dress her; it would be a dishonor to our realm."

"No, she is alone and has nothing suitable to wear for the commencement ceremony." Eli eyed the wilted orange alanis dress that she wore out below. "It would honor me if you fulfilled my request."

Eden's eyes surveyed Eli. Her confusion was evident on her face. "I'll take care of her and make sure she is presentable for the ceremony." She bowed her head low and then left.

It didn't take long for Eden to appear beside Noelle in the snow. Eli watched them speak, curious what they might have said. He would give anything to be there, but it wasn't appropriate as her opponent.

After a brief moment, Noelle locked eyes with Eli from his window, as did Lumi and Luis. Too late to look away, Eli gave a nod and then turned his back to the window.

"Are you ready for the ceremony?" Sage asked, and Naturei soldiers came to Eli's side. Sage was shaking. His buddies weren't supposed to speak to him while they were in uniform, but their faces communicated more than words could. They were excited and saw this as an opportunity for Eli to establish his rule. A winner of a Heirling Duel would be one of the most respected rulers because they were so rare.

"I'm as ready as I will be." Eli stole a quick glance through the window to see Noelle was returning to her room with Eden to get prepared for the ceremony.

The soldiers led him to the banquet hall, where many grand feasts were held. Eli stood at the helm of the draped curtain, just outside the stage's entrance. The massive dining hall held a grand feast, full of Naturei's finest dishes. Many tables were filled with Leizei nobles, the court ambassadors, and anyone the Leizei king had deemed important enough to witness the Heirling Duel. Eli eyed them from behind the curtain; they all dressed in dark shades in varying styles. Eli spotted several Leizei in the front, dancing with fire—spinning flames intricately as their bodies moved in unison. The crowd cheered as they watched the spinning Leizei, who spun flames around as they tumbled and twirled. The soldiers gave Eli a salute and departed, which left him alone with his anxious thoughts and pounding heart.

The entire Naturei realm seemed to be in attendance at this banquet lunch, and he had never seen the banquet hall so full. Naturei chefs and waitstaff flowed from table to table in an attempt to keep up with the large volume of people to serve.

Eli stiffened as his competitor approached. Marko, tall and muscular, stood by his side. He nodded to him. There was so much Eli wanted to say. He hadn't liked him in Chicago much, and he hadn't even known who he truly was. He absolutely could not trust Marko, and he had very little incentive to get to know him now. He was his competitor, and though they had an alliance between their realms, he doubted Marko planned to honor it in the arena.

So Eli said nothing to him. He just stood and waited in silence. And Marko seemed content to do the same.

The crowd hummed with excitement. Eli couldn't hide the scowl from his face as disgust rested on his features. One heir, possibly two, were going to die in the next three days—and yet the realms were *excited*.

One table, reserved for the Merklei, held Luis and Lumi. They took their seats as people lewdly called out insults to them.

Light footsteps emerged behind Marko and Eli. He didn't need to turn to know it was *her*. Noelle had entered the holding space for the heirs, who were about to be brought out to be presented.

Eli wanted nothing more than to turn around and embrace her and pull her into his arms. He longed to hold her, to comfort her, but he couldn't do it with Marko there and not with so many watchful eyes nearby. They were supposed to be opponents, and she was Merklei—there was no alliance between them.

Marko had broken the silence though. "Noelle, you look absolutely beautiful."

Eli, surprised that Marko would extend friendliness to her, turned and he could see why he complimented her.

Noelle stood in a pale blue shimmery petal high-low dress, with pants underneath. She also wore blue armor made of a Naturei plant that couldn't easily be penetrated with heat or blades. The large pale blue petals started at her hips and jutted outward and trailed in the back. She wore the Merklei ice crown, crafted to perfected points. The necklace that she once hid from sight now stood out against her neck—she was the proud owner.

"Wow, Elle," Eli breathed. He had said the words before he even realized they'd escaped.

A light dusting of pink emerged on her cheeks. "Thank you," she mumbled and averted her newly gray eyes to the crowd beyond the curtain.

But Eli's eyes remained on Noelle, as he realized that her outfit was the Merklei color. The flag had been pale blue and orange, and she just needed a touch of orange to complete the Merklei representation.

Eli couldn't help the smile that formed on his face. She wore the Merklei color and represented the Merklei throne; however, she wore Naturei materials. He hoped the message that he intended to give his realm, and especially his father, was clear. While he had been forbidden by his father to form an alliance with her, he would rebel in his own ways in this ridiculous duel.

The symbolism surely wouldn't go without notice, unless they were entirely daft.

Insults were still being hurled at Lumi every so often. No doubt, Noelle was going to be booed when she emerged for the ceremony. And it would likely be his own realm.

"Ladies and gentlemen! I'm Autumn, and as the Naturei ambassador, I'll be announcing the main events!" Autumn said and silenced the crowd. The crowd eagerly stilled, excited for the presentation of the heirs. "Welcome to the opening ceremony of the Heirling Duel."

Shouts, cheers, and whistles emerged across the massive banquet hall, and Eli swallowed. Marko didn't seem to budge, and Noelle fidgeted with her fingernails.

"As you know, duel implies two. But the name was picked deliberately because only two can emerge and possibly only one! Please welcome our first competitor, the heir to the Leizei throne, Crown Prince Marko Jokovic." Autumn clapped with enthusiasm.

Marko strode past the massive curtain, and the crowd cheered. The Leizei in the audience blasted fire toward the ceiling in celebration of their prince. Marko, wearing all black and heavy armor, took his place at the front of the banquet hall. He was, without a doubt, the most dangerous heir for Eli.

Lumi folded her hands and glared in his direction. How odd it was for Eli to see the Snow Queen, in his realm of all places. And his hatred doubled as he ground his teeth together at the sight of her—her presence, demanded by the duel, removed access to his Naturei ability.

"Crown Prince Marko, engaged to Yuri Kim, will represent the Leizei king, the Leizei realm, and he will use his Leizei ability along with his special ability, which is flight. He fights for his king, and if he wins the Heirling Duel, Lumi Hiver will go to trial for her prior crimes."

The crowd applauded, and Eli craned his neck to see that many Naturei remained neutral. But no one dared insult Marko, as they had an alliance. It would mean going against the king, and result in them being sentenced to the pit.

As Autumn continued to speak about Marko, Eli noted that he had a moment alone with Noelle and turned to her. "You'll take people's breath away looking like that."

"Well, I suppose I have you to thank for that—as Eden made it very clear that it was you who sent her." She looked up at him. "Thank you. The armor will come in handy. Perhaps I'll last two days now instead of one." She laughed without humor.

Before Eli could lose the nerve, he pulled out an alanis flower he had in his pocket. He tucked it behind Noelle's ear, and then he took in the sight of her. She was mesmerizingly beautiful, and he could get lost in her gray eyes—he would gladly do it too.

"The old flag for the Merklei was pale blue and orange. I figured you should complete the look." It wasn't an apology, but he hoped it redeemed some sort of cordiality between them. He ran his hand through a few strands of her hair, then let his hand fall to his side.

Noelle looked up at him with a mixture of confusion and reverence. "They called you."

Eli turned, embarrassed. How had he missed his own name?

He threw back the curtain and walked out to his place in the front of the room—the bright lights obscured his vision, and he could only see silhouettes at tables. He knew how to play the part well. He had been taught these rules from an early age, and crowds no longer scared him like they had when he was a mere boy. But this event was different—this wasn't a public social event, it was possibly one of his last events. One of these heirs would die within the next few days. Eli tried to hide the shudder as he contemplated his options. Noelle would be the easier option since she was newly initiated and hadn't mastered her ability, but he refused to touch her—which meant he would have to kill Marko. He hadn't liked him, but he didn't feel he was worthy of *death*.

"Crown Prince Eli Goldner, adopted by our High King, is the

heir to the Naturei throne. Due to the curse, he can't use his Naturei ability in the arena while the Snow Queen is present." This drew many boos from the crowd. "However, he will still have his strength and healing ability. He represents his king and realm, and if he wins the Heirling Duel, Lumi will go to trial for her prior crimes."

Drinks clinked around the massive banquet hall in celebration as Naturei voices rose in excitement.

Eli kept the fake grin on his face, but he managed to find his father—despite the lights that blinded him. His father raised his glass to Eli, with a smug look strewn across his features. To Eli's pleasure, it was Noelle's turn to come out.

His fake smile shifted into a warm, natural smile as he eyed the curtain.

"And finally, we have Crown Princess Noelle Hudson of the Merklei realm."

Noelle walked briskly to the front. She kept her eyes between the floor and the table where her friends sat. To Eli's surprise, not one person leered or booed at her. Perhaps they, too, had some sympathy for the girl. Although he doubted that was the sole reason; it was more likely that they noticed the outfit she wore and understood the message.

Luis and Lumi stood to their feet and clapped for her with extreme enthusiasm. It was a pathetic sight really. A silent crowd, a doomed heir, and only a couple of supporters.

But then to Eli's delight and surprise, Eden stood to her feet, too, and clapped. Eli tried to keep his face soft and neutral—but he wanted to show appreciation to Eden. Although he didn't think it was selflessness that Eden acted out of but rather she was likely proud of her work and everyone would have known who'd dressed Noelle. This was likely a show of her pride—that if she were going to be punished in some way for this, then at the very least she would applaud her own work.

Sage joined Eden and stood to her feet and clapped vigorously. Sage made a defiant face and raised her hands high as she clapped. Eden's team joined her and also stood.

Did they see Noelle as a poor victim, a pawn in this duel—destined to die at the hands of more powerful heirs? Or did they *actually* like her? He had meant Noelle's clothing to be a silent protest and a snub at his father. But it seemed he wasn't the only one who wanted to protest the pathetic duel.

And then a few other Naturei, although not many, joined them in applause. It looked like Noelle had managed to create a few allies during her time in the Naturei realm. When Adam joined on his feet and clapped for Noelle, Eli's throat became tight.

This was a revelation that Noelle had many more supporters than Eli realized. It seemed harmless until Adam stood up—because he was the captain of the Naturei army. And several soldiers joined him in applause—which made his father grip the edge of his chair. He scowled at Eli.

"Crown Princess Noelle was initiated today," Autumn said. "Her abilities are a mystery. If Noelle wins the Heirling Duel, she has chosen that Lumi Hiver will be pardoned for all prior crimes."

Eli shifted uncomfortably as he watched his father's eyes on Noelle. Eli had meant to annoy the king with Noelle's dress, but he hadn't realized how much secret support Noelle had mustered in such a short time. Eli worried that he had unwittingly just made Noelle a much more dangerous target for his father now.

"Please give it up for all three heirs! They each fight for their ruler and realm to settle the dispute, as a sacrifice for us to avoid war!"

And then everyone was on their feet.

The clapping seemed to never cease. Eli looked around but struggled to make out whose faces he was looking at. Noelle's hands trembled, and her frown mimicked Eli's. They looked at one another, and then the Naturei soldiers ushered Eli off stage. Not one of his buddies dared to speak to him while they led him to a back room.

Eli prepped in the private room surrounded by guards. He sat alone on the ground and tried to picture himself in the arena. It was enough to make him retch, and anxiety began to weigh heavy upon him like a thick blanket. His own hands began to shake, when he heard a knock. He wiped the vomit from his face.

"I told you I don't want visitors until I have to go to the arena," Eli said and shakily raised a hand to his face. His stomach was in knots.

"Sir, it is the Merklei royalty. She requested an audience with you," the guard said, nervous.

Eli wiped his face and ran his fingers through his hair. "Let her in, please."

Eli straightened, but when Lumi entered the room, his brow furrowed. He thought it would have been Noelle.

"Don't look too disappointed that it's me." Lumi walked toward him—even her walk was stealthy and calculated. The guards kept their hands on their Naturei guns, clenched and ready to fire at her. She gave Eli a smile that could make somebody quake. She rarely smiled; she only eased up around Noelle. She seemed like two different people entirely—one soft, lighthearted woman around Noelle, and then outside of her interactions with Noelle, she was like a dangerous, *wicked* queen capable of producing great evil.

"What do you want?" Eli was tired. He didn't have any more motivation for false niceties and pleasantries.

"I liked Noelle's ceremony outfit today; I thought it was very nice of you. It seems that maybe you did want to strike an alliance," Lumi said.

"I don't make alliances." His position didn't allow him to make them, only his father could. Surely she understood.

She nodded. "Well then I've come to plead. Noelle has just been initiated—please just leave her alone. Let her be in the arena and don't harm her."

Eli wanted to laugh. He couldn't harm a hair on Noelle's head.

But he had to keep up appearances with the guards within earshot, so he nodded as if he considered her words.

"I'll definitely keep your request in mind," he said and glanced at the guards. The guards were loyal to his father, and they would report any misbehavior.

Lumi followed his gaze to the guards, nodded, and turned to leave. But Eli's father entered the room, and the air stiffened thick with tension—so thick that a knife could slice right through it. The air itself seemed permeated with unsaid strife between the two.

His father clasped his hands together. "Justice is knocking on your door, Lumi. Your trial will begin promptly when this is over."

Lumi said nothing, and she didn't bother to look in his direction; she simply walked away with perfect posture.

His father folded his hands behind his back and walked toward Eli. "This is for you," he said and held out a vial. It was unmarked, but the pale blue color of the liquid didn't leave much to the imagination. He handed Eli merca. Merca took many years to produce only a few drops. A vial this large surely took a century.

He took it, not willing to fight him on the trivial matter. But he wouldn't use it.

"You're angry with me."

Eli said nothing. Of course he was furious with him—Eli knew he deserved some sort of punishment for meeting the girl, but this was extreme.

"You'll understand someday. You know that I love you—and I am only doing this for your good. You'll grow because of it and become a better ruler because of this duel. I know you had a fondness for the girl, but she wasn't right for you."

Eli fought to keep his face neutral, void of emotion. He spoke as if Noelle were already gone—as if she were a mere insect or pest and the matter had been resolved.

"I'm going to look past her ceremony outfit, given that I know you had an affection for her." He had done it again. He spoke as if

Noelle were as good as dead. "I just came to tell you that I'm proud of you, and you'll do great." Those were remarkable words. Eli had only heard the king say it once before.

The Naturei soldiers came, and Eli stood. His heart thumped, and the blood in his veins seemed to pulse—adrenaline moved through his entire body. It was time to begin the Heirling Duel.

His father walked in silence beside Eli, as he followed the Naturei soldiers to the arena. When they opened the door to the arena, Eli felt the queasiness in his stomach return. Thousands of people had gathered in the massive arena; each peered down at the area that stood before them. Upon his entry, the Naturei in the stands stood to their feet and cheered—which drew a deep frown on Eli's face. What sort of people cheer for a murder arena where at least one heir would be slaughtered like an animal? The immorality of the Heirling Duel was like a stench in Eli's nose, and it repulsed him. He scanned the hungry eyes in the stadium, and it displeased him to see excitement in their eyes. This shouldn't be celebrated, let alone tolerated.

The king clapped a hand onto Eli's back and gave him a nod. "You'll make us proud—I'm sorry it came to this. You'll become a legend after this Heirling Duel."

Eli turned to face him. He didn't say anything, but his father's eyes lowered to the vial of merca in Eli's pocket.

Leizei soldiers approached and inspected Eli. They patted down his entire body. They pulled the vial of merca from his pocket. "You only get to bring one item with you into the arena. Is this your choice?"

He'd rely on his strength ability, so it only seemed appropriate that he brought a weapon with him. Instead, his father had made it clear—that he wanted Noelle dead. He considered it and wanted to smash it. But nobody would know it was in his pocket, and it would please his father. If he let on that he didn't plan to use it, then his father might turn to more drastic measures.

"Yes."

The Leizei finished their search and gave the all clear sign.

Cheers erupted across the rows of Leizei, and Eli turned his head to see Prince Marko had entered from the opposite door. He stood on the edge of the arena, which as of now, just looked like dirt—but that would change soon.

Marko eyed Eli and looked him up and down. Marko, tall and muscular, looked fierce and moved in a way that suggested he was confident of his abilities. He wore all black, and Leizei armor decorated his entire body—he didn't look like he came for a competition but rather a war. He held a dagger in his hand, and Eli raised his brow at his item choice.

Naturei soldiers patted Marko down, but his eyes remained fixed on Eli.

Leizei across the arena cheered, and fires blasted from palms into the air in salute of their Crown Prince.

When it had finally quieted, a third door on Eli's left opened. Eli looked across the dirt arena and watched as a small figure emerged, clad in pale blue and orange.

A ghost of a smirk appeared on Eli's lips. Apparently Eden had doubled-down on the wardrobe since his father hadn't reprimanded her. She wore Naturei armor, and pale shimmery blue leaves fastened to her. Eden brilliantly chose the leaves—resistant to fire and weapons. She looked beautiful in her competition clothing that looked like it belonged to a regal queen.

Noelle stepped forward, radiant. The orange on her vest seemed to catch the light as she moved forward and shimmered against the pale blue. An even larger amount of Naturei cheered for Noelle, to Eli's surprise.

Eli watched as many Naturei, perhaps even half the entire realm, applauded politely for Noelle. Some even cheered—but many strong loyalists to the king watched in stark silence.

Eli turned to see his father red-faced, with eyes on Noelle. Eli had unknowingly started an open rebellion against his desires.

Noelle, too, seemed surprised as she peered around the arena.

Marko had his gaze on Noelle, and Eli studied him. If he had truly fallen in love with the Snow Queen, he doubted he would willingly kill her heir. Marko folded his gloved hands and then faced Eli.

Eli looked back at the Naturei king, who pointed at the vial in Eli's pocket. He wanted Noelle dead, especially after half of the realm cheered for her. Eli feared that if Noelle survived this Heirling Duel, then he had just made things inexplicably more difficult for her in the days ahead; possibly even *much* deadlier.

Not far behind Noelle, Lumi and Luis sat, also dressed in pale blue and orange. Luis drummed his fingers against his arm.

"Welcome! Today we begin the Heirling Duel." Autumn stood to the side, not far from Eli, with a mic in hand.

Cheers everywhere erupted. Fires shone in varying parts of the arena, and many stood to their feet.

"When our drummers play, the Heirling Duel will officially begin. But first, the rules!" Autumn said, and several Leizei and Naturei appeared behind massive drums. They took their places and held their sticks in front of the drums. "Each heir can bring in one item. Soldiers checked each heir, and they were all cleared with their one item."

Eli craned his neck to Noelle. Her one item wasn't visible.

"When the drums begin, a maze will appear in the arena. There will be various obstacles throughout the maze, and the heirs must overcome them and get out of the maze within one hour. After one hour, the drums will cease to play and acid rain will fall over the arena, which will destroy anything and everything within the arena."

Eli drew in a long, steady breath.

"A Leizei will provide the acid rain with his ability. He will take a vow that no matter what, after an hour, he will bring the rain over the arena—even if his own heir were within it. The Naturei realm has graciously provided the maze and built it before the Merklei queen arrived—since with her curse, no

Naturei can manipulate the natural realm in her presence. The theme for day one is Naturei. If one heir dies within the arena today, the Heirling Duel will conclude. Each heir is playing to represent their king or queen, and should they win the Heirling Duel, they will settle the dispute of the Merklei queen."

Then the dirt floor seemed to move, and Eli realized it had been a tarp with dirt on it, which covered the actual arena. A corn maze emerged beneath it, likely twenty feet tall or so. Eli tried to study as much of the maze as he could while he was above it, but then he and the other heirs were lowered.

Normally, the Naturei would just move the earth with their ability, but they manually moved them downward with a crane.

Eli was now level with the maze, and it had a small opening before him so he could enter. The arena was now above him, and he realized the audience would watch with a sky view as they fought for their lives. He could no longer see Noelle or Marko, only when he looked up could he see watchful audience eyes.

"Heirs may legally kill their opponents within the maze, however they cannot legally kill another heir outside the maze. If all three heirs survive the maze and make it out, then they will each compete in the second day of the Heirling Duel."

Eli's heart rammed against his rib cage. The Leizei with the acid rain ability made the vow in the mic, but Eli just stared at the tall corn maze entrance ahead of him. He would take an immediate left when he entered, that much he saw when they removed the tarp. But otherwise, he hadn't seen what other directions to take.

"The Leizei king will provide a shield barrier with his ability. This way, nobody can use their abilities to help their heirs inside the arena. The shield will not allow anybody to touch the heirs or intervene in any way. It will also protect everyone from the arena's dangers. No outside abilities will be able to penetrate the shield," Autumn said. The Leizei king waved his hand over the arena, and a faint red, nearly sheer light surrounded the arena.

"Heirs, you may begin!" Autumn called, and the drums blasted. It was a steady beat, almost like a heartbeat rhythm, all in unison. Eli hated the drum noise and grimaced as he realized he would listen to it for a whole hour. It seemed almost worse than anything he might face inside the maze.

He wasted no time on hesitation. With a dry throat, he ran toward the maze and immediately took a left. The corn maze stalks seemed glum, and he pressed forward as quickly as his legs would carry him. Eli ripped part of his green leafy sleeve off and shoved it into the corn stalks on his right. If he got lost, at least he would know he had been there.

Eli ripped off more leafy bits from his shirt, and as he ran, he placed them on the walls and corn stalks. He took a right, then a left, and guessed entirely on the directions. For a moment, he briefly considered climbing the corn stalks but noticed the jagged spikes they had crafted on each one. He'd be far too bloody to make it to the top, and he judged he was better off just going through the maze. He rammed his shoulder into the wall, testing how much give it might have, but even with his strength ability, he realized they were much too thick. He pulled away, shoulder bloody and throbbing. By the time he would manage to ram through one wall, he would have lost too much blood to continue pushing through another wall. He was resigned to go through the maze and find the end. He ran and turned another corner.

From behind him, he heard a ground-shaking zing followed by a slicing sound that indicated the intended target had been hit. By the sounds of it, it was the corn maze wall that had been hit. It sent a shiver down his spine, and he increased his speed. He knew exactly what the sound was because he was well acquainted with it—it was Naturei arrows, coated in poison. He had been hit with one once, and it caused him to be bedridden for days, but that was because the alanis plant hadn't reached maturity. For a moment, the drums were nearly inaudible with the audience's gasps and horrified shrieks.

Eli turned and saw nothing but cornstalk walls. Then Eli slammed both his feet in front of him and halted to a fast stop.

The audience cheered loudly.

Noelle had run in front of him, in an opening, and she froze. She looked terrified, with gray eyes full of fear. A pain that throbbed emerged as he realized she thought he might actually attempt to kill her. He had told her that he wouldn't show any mercy, so how could he blame her? The fear in her hollow eyes was because of him, and he hated that he was the cause of her terrified state.

Noelle shakily raised both hands up as if in surrender and shook her head. "Just let me go," she said quietly. "We'll just go separate ways. Leave fate to the maze."

Eli took a step forward and frowned. "Elle, I wouldn't—"

The audience roared and gasped with several screamed warnings. Noelle pointed behind Eli, but he couldn't hear her words over the drums and audience.

He spun around quickly and saw shiny black scales, and a large head with sharp teeth stalked toward him. For a brief moment, Eli forgot to move. It was as if instinct had forgotten to work, and he simply paused—disbelief in what his own eyes saw. Dragons were very rare in the Naturei realm, and he had never seen one up close. This dragon was quite small, perhaps a juvenile, yet he had heard many stories of how lethal they were.

Eli turned to run toward Noelle in her direction. She had fastened a long, icy spear in her hand.

"Run, Goldner!" She threw the spear, but her aim was terrible. It went directly toward Eli, who had to roll to the ground to avoid it.

The audience began to shout, and they likely thought she did it on purpose. Whatever favor she had gained with the Naturei just dissolved.

Eli tried to get to his feet, but the silver-eyed dragon was right behind him now.

"I'm sorry!" Noelle yelled, hardly audible above the drums.

Those dreadful drums were *the most terrible* noise that Eli had ever heard in his entire lifetime.

Sharp pain gnawed at Eli's right calf, and he turned to find that the small dragon had wrapped its claws around his leg and forcibly pulled it toward his mouth.

Eli turned and grabbed the large animal's head. The mouth was open, and it sank its teeth into Eli's hands. Blood fell freely, and Eli, with his strength ability, pried his hands into its mouth and pulled in opposite directions, and the mouth began to tear. The dragon whimpered and pulled away, roaring with sharp teeth bared.

The dragon turned toward Noelle and flapped its small wings and moved in her direction. Noelle turned to run, but the dragon was much faster. It stretched out its claws, aimed to strike, and Eli shoved her out of the way, and the dragon, instead, pierced his back. Noelle fell to the ground from his shove, and Eli cried out as more blood emerged. He reached up and pulled with all his strength against the claws and tore them off. The dragon shrieked and pulled away from them both, and it retreated far away, out of sight.

The crowd erupted with cheers, and Eli groaned as blood spattered his calf, back, hands and now the dragon's purple blood was strewn across him and the ground.

Noelle stood, frozen. The whites of her eyes showed, and she looked absolutely horrified. Eli tried to ignore the impulse to comfort her, to hold her, and he got to his feet. They needed to move because there wasn't much time. He hastily tore a piece of the corn maze wall and placed it between them and the dragon, blocking the path. This would buy some time but not much—although juvenile dragons weren't supposed to have fire-breathing abilities yet, it still was deadly and it could fly—should it decide to come back.

Noelle brought her hand over her mouth and angrily shouted at something above Eli's head. But it was too late. Eli felt the heavy thud on his head before he could understand what happened.

Marko had used his flight ability to soar up, and he brought the blunt side of the handle of his dagger to Eli's head. Eli fell to the ground, and his head throbbed. He reached up and felt a pool of blood in his palm. His vision started to black out, and the strong inclination to lie down seized him. He fought against it; he simply couldn't lose consciousness in there. It would mean the end of his life.

"Are you *crazy*?" Noelle screamed.

Eli was on his hands and knees now. It took great effort to simply lift his head. The floor seemed to spin, and he saw two or three of everything before him. Eli blinked several times and tried to clear his vision—but it was no use.

"You should be thanking me. I just went against an alliance and will have to pay for it. I did this for you and *especially* for Lumi. If you think you can beat him in the next two rounds, you're delusional. This is your one opportunity to survive the Heirling Duel. Get out while you still can!" And then Marko used his flight ability and soared far above the maze. It was unfair really. He simply would fly to the finish area.

"We have our first winner! Crown Prince Marko from the Leizei realm!" the announcer called only a brief moment later.

Leizeis in the audience roared in triumph.

"He is right; you should run," Eli said and faltered as he tried to stand. He had lost so much blood, and his vision blurred. Pain throbbed everywhere, but mostly his head hurt the worst.

Noelle ran to Eli's side and steadied him. She wrapped his arm around her shoulder and placed a firm hand on his waist. "Come on, you heavy jerk." Noelle heaved, and Eli tried to put as much pressure as he could on his own legs, but his calf screamed in agony. He leaned slightly on her. She groaned. "How can you be *so heavy*? It has to be that huge ego of yours! Your head alone is massive," Noelle said and strained as she ran.

"It must be my big brain," Eli mused. He gritted his teeth as they continued to run. He could hardly see where they were going. "Happy birthday, by the way. I'm sorry that you're spending it in the Heirling Duel."

"Thanks." Noelle pulled him and shoved as they moved. She shoved him right into corn stalks a few times.

"What is the matter?" Noelle asked, her voice an octave higher than normal.

"I can't see. Really, you should let me be. You need to get out of here." Eli's head lulled to the side as Noelle pulled him with her.

To Eli's dismay, he saw a tattered piece of his green leafy shirt on one of the walls. "No, wait! I've been here. I left a trail of my shirt, and we are at the beginning of where I started," Eli said and winced.

"I figured your shirt was ripped up because you wanted to impress the Naturei girls," Noelle said and spun around.

Eli couldn't help but groan. Every move made his head throb worse. His vision seemed to dim with it. The lights in the arena really bothered his eyes, and he closed them as much as he could. He was horribly and completely reliant on Noelle to get out alive.

Eli brought a bloody hand to his shirt and ripped off a large piece and shoved it into the corn stalk as they ran. As he limped along, he supposed he didn't need to leave a trail of his shirt any longer. He simply could just watch for his own blood that trailed behind him.

Noelle came to an abrupt halt. He opened his eyes, despite the light that so bothered his head, and peered ahead to see several Naturei knives that darted horizontally.

"We could find another way."

"No, this has to be the right way. They wouldn't make it easy," Noelle said. She was likely right. "There is a pattern. Three knives swipe horizontally, but then it pauses for about three seconds. And then the next set happens with the same pattern. It looks like there are three sets altogether. If you lean on me, I'll lead us through."

Eli didn't like that his ability was strength, yet he was the weak one in this situation. Without many other options, he nodded.

The blasted drums seemed to get louder.

The three knives swiped across the cornstalk from right to left, and Noelle wrapped her arm around his waist tighter.

"All right, one, two, three, go!" And they walked steadily forward and then paused.

They had cleared the first set. They were safe. Noelle let out a slow breath as the knives continued and sliced behind them.

"All right, again. Exactly like that!" She gripped his waist. Eli found his free hand and moved it to her waist, where it seemed to fit perfectly. For steadiness, of course.

"One, two, three!" Noelle yelled and then moved them both forward with a tug.

They repeated the motion again. And they faced the last three sets of knives. They swiped horizontally and then froze.

"Now!" Noelle called. And just as they had before, they moved forward confidently. But this time vines reached for them from the ground. Eli was able to roll out of the way and fell to the ground. But a knife, the final knife, caught Noelle's shoulder blade.

She cried out with a shriek as she fell to the ground. The blood began to pour from her wound.

Eli lifted his hand to her, and she groaned. "I got you, just hold still. I'll heal you, but I have to take it out first."

Eli gripped the handle, and through long blinks of his eyes, he pulled. It had dug so deep that he had to utilize his strength ability just to completely remove the knife. Blood seeped down Noelle's back, but Eli put his palm over it and healed her.

His energy drained even further, as it was costly to heal another when he had so many wounds of his own. But he wanted her to get out alive.

"Get up, hurry, Goldner!" Noelle said, and the drums banged

on. She pulled on him, and he scurried to his feet. He flailed now. The blood loss made his head dizzy.

Eli leaned heavier on her now.

"We are almost out! I can feel it!" She turned a corner and staggered under Eli's weight. "There it is, Eli! I see the finish line!"

Eli tried to open his eyes to see the finish line, but he simply couldn't bear it anymore. His calf, his bloody back, his weakened energy from healing Noelle, and his bloodied head were more than he could take any longer. He deduced he received a concussion from the dagger. He wanted to hate Marko for it, but he couldn't. One of them had to die, so how could he blame anybody for anything they did in this dreadful, unethical arena?

Noelle tugged Eli forward. "Please! Keep going! We are so close! *Please!*" She begged.

Eli felt like he held on to consciousness by a mere thread. He opened his eyes, but everything spun. His eyesight felt so dim, yet he wished his hearing would dim so he didn't have to listen to the dreadful drums.

If it weren't for the voice beside him, he might just slip into the sleep that so allured him at the moment.

"Please, Eli!"

Eli smirked, stupidly. "You said my first name."

Eli collapsed onto the ground. His body refused to continue on.

"One more minute!" Autumn called, and the audience shrieked, cheered, and yelled things that Eli couldn't quite make out.

Eli tried to crawl forward, but even that proved to be an impossible task. His own blood, slippery and warm, made him fall to the ground. He bled far more than he realized.

Noelle let him go entirely. Eli was grateful. He felt there was no sense in them both dying.

"Run, Elle!" Eli's voice was a hoarse whisper.

And then he heard it. He knew the acid rain would fall, but he hadn't known it would begin at the last minute. A heavy rain sound appeared at the entrance of the maze, and Eli managed a quick peek at Noelle's face. Her newly changed stormy-gray eyes were glued to the rain clouds that soared above the entrance of the maze, and her face went white. He heard the dragon shrieking and winced. Even the foul beast didn't deserve that sort of death.

"Let's go," she called and moved in front of him. She grabbed his wrists and tugged and moved ever so slowly toward the entrance. She dragged Eli on the dirt ground, and he wished he had his Naturei ability. He would simply make a vine escort them both out of there.

Eli pushed off the ground with his good leg and tried to move forward. He rolled over onto his back.

Noelle pulled underneath his armpits, and they moved faster. But not quickly enough as the rain clouds closed in on them.

Eli pushed with his good foot toward the finish line. Noelle heaved and pulled even harder. They were so close.

"I'm not leaving you!" Noelle groaned.

The rain clouds, gray with foreshadowing intent, rolled upon them. The acid rain fell, and between blinks Eli could see that the entire maze was reduced to nothing as the acid washed upon it.

Noelle pulled even harder and panted heavily.

But the rain licked at Eli's feet, and he cried out in pain as the acid rain fell onto his feet. His skin instantly became red and splotchy. Eli pulled his knees up, tucking them close to him, and Noelle pulled. Half of Eli was across the finish line, and she pulled as the acid rain pressed on.

She pulled and pulled. And just before the acid rain could reach him again, she pulled him across the finish line where the acid rain stopped. The entire maze fizzled down to nothing except dirt, and Noelle collapsed onto Eli.

She laughed in relief, and Eli reached out to wrap his own arms around her as she turned to lay at his side on the dirt. He blinked slowly and tried to see her face. He cupped her face, and her cheeks were wet. She had saved his life when it would have been easier to leave him behind. She could have finished the competition today, and she and Marko would live on. She could have ended the life of the man who ruined hers, tricked her, and imprisoned her.

Eli didn't care what his father thought or his entire realm. He appreciated the beautiful Merklei girl for her selflessness, her humor, and her wit, and if she would have him, he would do anything to be with her. He blinked his eyes open and glimpsed her gray eyes on his. He reached for her and pulled her closer to him; he wanted nothing more than to feel her lips on his, and he didn't care who saw. She gasped and looked around as the audience cheered wildly.

He didn't care what the punishment was; he just wanted to be with her. He put his hand under her chin, and then when he leaned up toward her face and when their lips brushed ever so slightly, he felt something in his pocket become loose with the movement, and the vial fell onto the dirt ground. He reached for it and hoped to grab it before Noelle noticed it. But she swiped it from the ground first.

He closed his eyes and dropped his head to the ground as Noelle pulled away from his embrace and stood to her feet.

"Merca?" she asked and sounded wounded.

"It isn't what you think. I wasn't going to use it," Eli said and tried to stand up too. But he staggered back to the ground.

"Goldner, you could have one weapon. And you chose *this*?"

"Wait, Elle. I can explain. It was to appease my father," he said.

"All three heirs have survived the Naturei themed maze!" Autumn called out, and the crowd cheered loudly. Eli sighed as he listened to Noelle walk away. Several Naturei replaced her presence with alanis ointment in hand. He had never been so grateful for the alanis plant, as it washed away his pain. He felt his strength slowly return and his eyesight corrected. He needed to find Noelle.

When he had healed enough, he sat up, and Naturei were

crowded around him. Even his father was there with a mysterious look on his own face.

Marko was ahead, surrounded by Leizei on the dirt arena. He seemed happy enough with the attention of his people.

But there was no sight of Noelle, Luis, or Lumi. Eli looked everywhere for a trace of pale blue, but he couldn't find any.

He sighed.

Well, at least the drums had stopped playing. Those cursed things.

CHAPTER 28
MARKO
PUNISHMENT

Marko watched Noelle embrace Lumi, and jealousy seized him. The fire bond illuminated every single feeling he had for Lumi; and it was pure torture to desire somebody so much yet have them despise you. Marko could feel all of Lumi's feelings since he'd made the bond, and the hatred that she had for him flowed freely. She surely thought he was a fraud and betrayed her, and he had every intention of doing so—that was, until he met her. She was unlike everything he had been taught about her, and her side of the story unraveled the carefully crafted version of events the Leizei had taught him.

Marko wished he could explain everything. He had no other choice but to create the fire bond and tie their souls together. He would rather Lumi be alive and hate him than to willingly watch her perish after the Heirling Duel. Lumi had no idea what awaited her, compliments of the two realms' kings.

Marko shifted as he watched Lumi, Noelle, and Luis leave the arena. Leizei all around shouted in victory, but when the hooded Leizei appeared in a circle around him, he knew it was trouble. He had gone directly against the alliance and attacked Eli in an effort to save Noelle. He had become a failed spy and a traitor to his own kind.

"Well done, Marko!" The Leizei king slowly walked toward him with his cane. "Come with us to celebrate." He gestured to the doors.

Marko had suffered much worse before. They couldn't do much to him since he would have to continue competing. Marko strode ahead and accepted his fate. Once the doors opened and several hooded Leizei entered with him, he closed his eyes in anticipation of the beating.

The door closed shut, and he fell to the ground with a moan as electricity flowed through his body and scrambled him. The Leizei, Blaze, had the ability to electrocute, and he was glad Blaze did it; the others would likely bring much more excruciating pain. Blaze, his longtime friend and confidant, wasn't using his full strength. That didn't stop Marko from seizing on the dirt ground and groaning.

"Our alliance gave us alanis ointment to heal you because we are in an alliance with them. It seems you have forgotten that." His grandfather hobbled forward and handed the ointment to a hooded Leizei. "Give Marko a friendly reminder for the next hour. Then heal him so he can be prepared for tomorrow. That will give him time to think."

Marko gnashed his teeth as the electricity continued. It wasn't worthwhile to fight back; he would just add more time to his torture. He was very familiar with his grandfather's ways.

"With pleasure," Ember, a loyal follower of the Leizei king, said. And then Ember outstretched his arms, and Marko audibly sighed. He wished that it were anybody other than Ember, because he hated Ember's ability. Ember could manipulate emotions and bring the heaviest, darkest feelings over anybody. He had the ability to trick minds into the most fearful, dreadful situations where hope feels completely abandoned. Marko would rather suffer physical pain than endure Ember's mental torment.

But then the shadowy figures of depression, anxiety, and heaviness materialized over Marko, and voices tormented his mind with foul, sickening thoughts that he felt might drive him mad if he had to sit with it for an hour. Marko inhaled and looked at Blaze as a plea. Blaze, in response, did Marko a favor. He electrocuted him so heavily that Marko cried out and he continued seizing.

"What are you doing? He will pass out!" Ember shouted. Blaze continued with hands over Marko.

"Blaze, might you be trying to help your friend?" The Leizei king stepped forward.

Yuri hurried into the room and shut the door. She fell on her knees in front of Marko and bowed her head.

"Please let me take his punishment," she said. "He needs to prepare mentally and physically for the duel."

"No," Marko grunted. He shook his head violently.

The Leizei king smiled. "You don't deserve her, Marko. After everything, look at her loyalty. You could learn from her. I will honor Yuri Kim's devotion and give her Marko's suffering. Give her an hour of torment in Marko's place. And knock him out for his foolishness."

"No!" Marko shouted, but the electricity increased and he blinked a few times, and then everything went black.

CHAPTER 29
MARKO
THE HEIRLING DUEL—DAY TWO

Marko awoke in the middle of the night from a nightmare. He stepped outside in the cool of the night where Lumi's curse had transformed the Naturei realm into a wintry mix. The cold air relieved his heat, and he folded his arms. He rested his head against the elaborate building and closed his eyes.

He thought of the girl, Noelle, whom he had played the role of big brother for over the past several years. He couldn't manage to turn it off; he worried about her in the arena—enough that he went against his own alliance. Marko's eyes shot open as he wondered about what happened to Yuri. He grimaced. All that and Noelle still dragged Eli across the finish line; she had no idea what the Leizei and Naturei had planned for them, otherwise she would have let him die. The Heirling Duel was a mere mockery—the real fight would come after the trial. They had planned ahead—far ahead—and even planned for different outcomes. If Noelle survived the duel, she would pardon Lumi. If it came to that, the Leizei and Naturei king had made an alliance over a plot to kill Lumi.

Marko rubbed his fire bond finger. He worried Lumi would not survive her upcoming trial if it came to that. They had strategized it for years, and they were eager for her downfall.

Marko frequently let his thoughts drift to Lumi, the queen that he was raised to hate. And he had despised her, that was, until he met her. She was nothing like what his teachers had said; she was kind, endearing, and even thoughtful. He had expected a shrewd hunchback with warts, not the cute blond girl in the café. It made him question everything that he had learned in the Leizei realm and all the things that he stood for. And then there was the matter of Noelle; she had truly become like a family member. How was any of this fair to her?

Marko sighed.

He pictured Lumi's gray eyes and the pink that kissed her nose when they spent time outside. He could hear her laughter, and the fire bond burn pulsed. Since he placed the bond on her, he couldn't stop thinking of her, and he could feel all her emotions which were raw and intense. Her thawed-out heart seemed unmanageable, and Marko struggled to differentiate between Lumi's feelings and his. The fire bond connected them, and he found his mind veered toward her even without his permission.

"Marko?" Yuri emerged into the snowy cold.

"Yuri! Why would you do that?" Marko reached for her and pulled her into his arms. She stayed in his embrace for a moment and then pulled away and sighed.

"You needed your strength." She shrugged.

"Don't ever do that again." Marko frowned. "I don't need your protection."

"Well, someday you'll protect all of us when you take the throne. You should rest. The next duel will be here very soon." She held open the door.

Marko stood to his feet.

"You're okay?" Marko asked, his voice laced with guilt.

"I am, thanks to the alanis ointment. Same as you," she said and pointed at Marko.

Marko hadn't noticed it until now, but he had no side effects and felt fine. Somebody must have lathered him in the healing ointment. Marko held up his thumb and smiled. It was a gesture they shared since childhood, and without missing a beat Yuri held her thumb to his, and it glowed with a small flame.

"I promise I'll undo every wrong that you've endured."

"I know you will." Yuri returned his smile. A red flash of light circled around their wrists, and Yuri dropped her thumb. "You love her, don't you?"

It was dangerous to answer Yuri's question. So instead, Marko said nothing.

Yuri's smile widened. "You should tell her the truth. I think if she knew that our whole engagement was a sham that you crafted to protect me, she'd understand. I'll help you when the time is right. Get some sleep." She hurried away into the falling snow, and Marko went to his bed, where he didn't get much sleep at all. His thoughts just returned to gray eyes, shapely lips, long blond hair, and a heart-shaped face that belonged to the woman who probably despised him by now and plotted to drive a knife into his heart. And he'd let her because his heart already belonged to her, and she could break it, burn it, or care for it.

In the morning, Marko felt the lack of sleep. He woke up next to a spread of jams, toast, vegetables, and coffee, but nobody was in his room. He shook his head at the vegetables and longed for bacon or some sort of meat—he despised the Naturei diet. He looked around the simple room and stood to his feet and hurriedly ate the toast and jam. The sun peeked through his window, and he knew by the sun's position that he didn't have much time before elite Leizei fetched him for the next round of the Heirling Duel.

He tousled his hair and found his armor and uniform draped over a chair. He put them on and rubbed his hands over his face. He paced his room and shook his head as he considered his options for the second day of the duel. He hadn't had much time to strategize, as Leizei barged into his room.

"Good morning, Prince Marko," Blaze said and turned his palm up where a small fire protruded as a greeting. Marko, likewise, lifted his hand and greeted him with his own flame.

"Morning."

"Ready?" Blaze asked with only his chin and mouth visible. Everything else remained behind his ceremonial hood.

Marko liked seeing Blaze again. He had become so accustomed to the human world that it felt strange to see his friends again.

"Yes," Marko said and gave a nod. Several Leizei waited for Marko in the hallway and walked beside him as he neared the entrance to the arena. Oddly shaped plants lined the hallway, and Marko turned every few paces to view them. Each plant was bright yellow with hues of a burnt-orange color that seemed to swirl over it.

Marko stood in his gear at the entrance to the arena, and he balled his hands into fists. He had barely slept; and he didn't feel ready, but this would have to do. His grandfather appeared from the corner and stood at his side. The other Leizei bowed low and departed.

"If you continue in your antics, I will pull your title from you." He whispered in his ear. "And to be clear, you are hereby relieved of all future spying duties since you cannot seem to separate your loyalty and reality."

Marko sighed. He had never been demoted before, and it stung his pride more than he would like to admit.

"You got lucky yesterday—you know every five hundred years, they craft new Heirling Duel competitions so that no realm can bend the competition to favor any one particular heir or their ability. Those who craft the competitions do so without any knowledge of what future heirs will be able to do. It was just a coincidence that you got to be in a maze and have the flight ability."

"Any leads on today's competition?" Marko knew he hadn't had any, or he would have told him. Those in charge of the Heirling Duel had to make vows to never share anything about it so that everyone, including the rulers and their heirs, would never have an unfair advantage.

"Not a thing, but don't say I haven't tried to get information."

Marko could hear the crowd even with the entrance door closed. The Leizei realm was full of brutes who enjoyed power displays, and the Heirling Duel was something most cherished as a sort of ideal glory.

"The girl is gaining momentum with the Naturei—I need her dead. But it can't be too obvious. If she doesn't die this round, it needs to be the next round." His grandfather turned to leave.

The gray slate door slid open, and Marko walked into the entrance. He was covered in his black uniform with thick armor, but he felt vulnerable. It was standard protocol, and he looked like much of the other elite soldiers. Fire blasts shot vertically in the air to greet him all over the arena.

He scanned the crowd in the arena, which surely held thousands. He caught a glimpse of slate-gray eyes that watched him and long, wavy blond hair. His lips parted at the sight. Lumi had sat not far from him, and she glared in his direction.

His fire bond pulsed underneath his black glove, and he could feel venomous hatred flow from her. He couldn't blame her—but she had to know his true feelings. It wasn't all an act—and the fire bond would communicate that. Besides, she had the ability to sense when people had dangerous motives toward others, so Marko hoped she at least knew his feelings for her were authentic.

He noticed she wore pale blue gloves that covered her fire bond marking.

He stopped after a few steps in front of his entrance. The arena looked entirely different today. There were white marble pillars across it with decorative tops of green leaves, ice in the shape of a diamond, and a single flame. A pale red force field around the arena hummed, which blocked outside abilities. There would be no interference from any outsiders. Inside the dirt arena, there were three poles with something tied to the top of it, and then there were red, white, and black snakes in a container beyond it. And finally, there were three tables. The entire thing was enclosed with thick glass walls, which separated each competitor's space, and since today was Leizei themed, the edges of each competitor's space was lined with a river of lava that flowed around the arena. For Marko, this was no problem—he could simply mold it as he pleased. But the other two would need to be careful not to fall in.

Noelle appeared, clad in light blue, and looked sheepishly at the crowd as many cheered for her. She had effectively gained a small following.

"Welcome to day two of the Heirling Duel! Today our heirs will compete in a timed competition. We honor the fire kingdom today, and there is lava around the competitor's tasks. First they must climb their designated pole and fetch the puzzle pieces at the top. Once they accomplish this, they must run through the snake tank and make it to their table across from them. There they must completely assemble their puzzle, which will open the door and allow them out of the arena. They have one hour to complete this task, and then a fire will be released to destroy everything inside the glass arena. When the drums sound, the heirs may begin!"

He heard the drums and ran into the arena's glassy entrance.

He felt the dirt shift under his feet and ran toward the pole. He saw that it was greasy, obviously oiled with something. He shook his head—thankful, again, for his flight ability.

He lifted off the ground and floated toward the top, where the puzzle was tied at the top in a bright crimson-red bag, with twine wrapped around it. He unraveled the twine and pulled the bag free, then floated back to the dirt ground and avoided the lava that encircled it.

Marko peered to his left to spy Noelle as she slid down the pole; she struggled with the slippery aspect. He looked over to Eli, who seemed to fare better than Noelle—he was almost to the top of the pole.

Marko hurried toward the container full of snakes. He slowed to a halt as he realized they crawled over the entire tank. Again, he was thankful for his ability. He'd simply go above it. Marko lifted off his feet and slowly moved over the snakes.

Pain seared in his heel, and he looked down. One snake had sprang upward and bitten his heel. Marko hurried to the other side and gripped the snake in his hand and ripped it off his heel. He threw it back into the tank, and it landed with a loud thud. The snake's venom already had taken effect; Marko knew what sort of snake it was—they were native to the Leizei kingdom and caused delusions and affected his vision.

He tucked the crimson bag under his arm and stood up. Noelle was suddenly in front of him. "Help me, Marko," she whispered and began to cry.

Marko squinted. "Noelle? How did you get into my section?" Marko turned and saw that Noelle had just reached the top of her pole and grabbed her own crimson bag. He realized then that it was an illusion.

"You're supposed to be my big brother, but you tricked me." The illusion of Noelle suddenly grew fangs, and her face contorted. Marko rushed through the illusion of Noelle, and she dispersed as if she were gas.

"It isn't real," he said aloud.

The illusion of Noelle appeared by his side, just as he reached the table and emptied the contents of his bag. She leaned down, propped an elbow onto the table, and blocked his view of the puzzle pieces. "You think you're going to weasel your way back into my life and Lumi's?"

Marko pushed forward and discovered thick pieces, each colored in various hues of red and orange. The pieces were jagged, and some were rounded. "Oh, I know what this is," Marko said aloud. He looked at the marble arches, which held the symbols of each realm. His puzzle was a 3D symbol of his realm's symbol—a singular fire flame.

Marko looked to his side, where Eli was ahead. He formed a leafy puzzle with several pieces already completed. Marko hurried his fingers and felt the edges and placed them. But his vision became blurry, and he felt feverish. Sweat formed, and he panted as he continued to put the 3D puzzle together.

"Marko?" Lumi was at his side, and he swore he even felt her cool touch on his arm. He turned and saw her gray eyes locked onto his. She leaned down and pressed her lips to his neck, and wrapped her arms around his chest.

Marko looked down at his gloved hand and felt for his soul-tie with Lumi. He still felt her anger. This was also an illusion.

"It isn't real," he said aloud again. Noelle now worked on her own puzzle. She looked bewildered, unsure of what she was doing.

Marko heard cheers from the crowd and realized that Eli had finished and he was already outside his glass tube.

Marko placed another piece of his 3D fire puzzle together, and now he was nearly halfway finished.

Noelle scrambled with her pieces and seemed clueless. Marko sighed as he eyed her. He contemplated what to do, but he didn't want to see her die in her glass container. She looked at Marko's puzzle and Eli's completed puzzle, but Marko could recognize her familiar look of bewilderment. He had seen it before, many times, but never this intense.

Marko caught her eye, then drifted his gaze to the symbols on top of the marble and hoped she could understand his clue without the audience being tipped off.

She seemed to understand as she suddenly shaped her puzzle pieces correctly. Marko went back to his puzzle and clicked another piece into the correct position. But then suddenly, snakes slithered up the puzzle and wrapped around Marko's arms. He fell backward and knocked over his puzzle.

He yelled and flailed his arms and shook the snakes off. But more snakes came. When he tried to stand and pick up the pieces, a snake coiled itself around one puzzle piece. He grabbed it anyway, and the snake bit down on his gloved hand. He winced and lifted the other pieces.

The venom made things slow down. Everything seemed to move in slow motion. Marko held out his hand in front of his face and then pulled it away. He rubbed his eyes. "Don't stop, it isn't real!" he told himself.

He assembled three of the puzzle pieces together, again, and then he heard the crowd buzz with excitement. Noelle had completed her puzzle, and she was safely across the finish line. His years with her had become mangled and mixed with sentimental feelings, and he was grateful she completed day two.

"Hurry up! There isn't anything there!" Noelle yelled. He was thankful, because it helped ground him against the hallucinations. Suddenly the snake at his foot no longer seemed like a threat. *It wasn't real.*

Sweat poured from Marko as he placed several puzzle pieces together and formed more than half of the fire flame again.

Noelle cheered, loudly, outside the glass. "That's it! The one on your right goes on the top! Keep going, Marko!" Her eyes seemed frantic.

Snakes slithered all over the table and bit him, but he ignored them. But the real snake bite venom slowed his hands. His sight grew more and more blurry, and he struggled to continue as his hands began to feel numb and his fingers tingled.

"One more minute!" the Naturei woman called, and Marko could hear the roar of large flames being released into the glass arena.

"Marko!" Noelle screamed. She ran back into her own glass space and then stood next to Marko. She brought her shirt over her nose as dark clouds of smoke billowed.

Marko had only two pieces left. He raised a piece to the top, but his fingers moved slowly.

He turned to Noelle. It was too late. Marko shook his head at her. He tried to lift his hands to the puzzle, but his fingers could no longer grasp the pieces as his hands became paralyzed. Realization set in; this was his end. He would never fix things with Lumi, nor would he ever have the pleasure of holding her in his arms again. Noelle would surely think he was a traitorous coward, and yet he would never ascend to the throne of his never-pleased grandfather. Yuri would suffer terribly. He had failed entirely.

Noelle began to bang on the glass, but it didn't budge. She used her ability and froze the glass, then banged her fist through it, which broke the glass to pieces.

"It isn't real," Marko said aloud, downcast.

She hurried to Marko's side with her nose still covered by her shirt. She pulled the piece from his hand and put it on the fire puzzle. She grabbed the final piece and placed it at the tip top and then laced her fingers through Marko's and pulled him. Strangely, he could hardly feel her fingers against his numb hands.

"Run!" she yelled and started to half cough, half choke. Marko coughed, too, as his lungs burned with smoke that smoldered the air. But his feet were clumsy, and his heel burned.

"It's not real," he said and reminded himself. He stopped.

"What are you talking about?" Noelle said, panicked. She pulled an arm around Marko. "Come on, you idiot! I'm not telling your parents that you *died*! Let's go!" But Marko didn't move. He turned to look back at his completed puzzle, still covered in snakes.

"Why would you help me? It's not real."

Noelle tugged and forced him to move. "Because I know deep down that you are the person I came to know! And I'm doing this for your parents and sister. Now run!"

And then Marko picked up his feet. The exit opened, and they crossed the finish line. Marko fell to the dirt ground, and Noelle stood by his side.

The crowd erupted in chaos. Many called Noelle a cheater.

Several Naturei came to Marko's side and spread the alanis ointment over his ankle. His fever subsided, and he watched as

Noelle stood and looked at the bickering crowd with violent outbursts that emerged all over the massive arena.

"There will be deliberation over today's competition," Autumn called out to the unsettled crowd.

Marko was raised from the dirt, but he was covered in it. The hallucinations were gone, and he no longer felt feverish. He made his way to Noelle, and she peered up at him.

"Thank you. You saved my life." He shouldn't be surprised; Noelle was loyal to a fault—yet he couldn't shake the audience's gaze on them. He needed to make people think they were enemies, or she would pay dearly for it and so would he.

"Well, I don't really feel like I'm in the mood to explain your death to your family even if you are a backstabbing old man." Noelle beamed and crossed her arms.

Marko smiled slightly. He wished he lived in a different world where their realms were all cordial. When he would assume the throne, he wanted to smooth everything out and restore peace between them all. Despite all the faults of the Merklei, he had grown to love the only two Merklei that roamed any of the realms—and he would do anything to see them thrive. He owed it to Noelle, especially now. He would right his wrong for spying on her and lying to her, and he would ensure the Merklei could restore everything that was lost.

"Even if you win and make it out alive tomorrow, you and Lumi are in danger. They're planning to kill her after the trial."

Noelle looked over at Marko, then swallowed. "I'd like to think that far ahead, but I struggle to even think beyond one day at a time." Her face fell, and darkness seemed to lurk in her eyes.

"I'm going to make sure you make it out tomorrow, so you should start planning your future." Marko turned to see where Eli stood.

Noelle followed his gaze. "But that means that you plan to—no, don't do that."

"He isn't who you think he is. He brought you to his realm to manipulate you, regardless of whatever he said. He is in on the tactic."

"I don't know who to trust anymore," she admitted, and her gray eyes stared at him, blank.

"Attention, everyone! The deliberation has decided that the Merklei heir hasn't broken any rules, and all three heirs have completed the second day of the duel. The final and most exciting day of the duel will be tomorrow!"

Noelle smiled at Marko, and the warmth reached her smoky-gray eyes.

CHAPTER 30
ELI
FLOWERS AND CAKE

Eli poured into his room, sweaty and tired. He sat on the edge of the bed and wiped the sweat from his forehead, relieved that he was alive and that Noelle was too.

A gentle knock on the door alerted him that Sage had answered his request.

"Come in," Eli yelled. His entire realm was buzzing with excitement from the second day of the duel. He declined many invitations to celebratory dinners in favor of an idea.

"I heard you've locked yourself up in here and you're avoiding all the fun. That isn't like you," Sage said and shut the door to his large bedroom.

"Sage, in Noelle's realm they celebrate birthdays as individuals, and I wanted your help. She just had a birthday, and I wanted to do something for her as a gift."

"They don't collectively celebrate their next age on New Year, like us?" Sage frowned. "Humans are so odd."

Eli shrugged. "I was curious if you could make something called a birthday cake. I have a recipe in this book." Eli gestured to a book on his grand wooden table that was open with detailed instructions.

Sage took the book from him and nodded enthusiastically. "Of course." Sage read over the page a few times and then waved her fingers over his table, and a round, tall cake appeared with the words Happy Birthday, Noelle written on it in frosting. It sat upright upon a round bamboo fixture.

"Perfect," Eli said. "Well, at least I think it looks right. Can you make it green? Her room was green—I think she likes that color." Sage waved her finger, and the white frosting turned forest green. Eli gingerly picked it up and headed for the door.

"Where do you think you're going?"

"To give Noelle her cake."

"You stink. That poor girl will run from you if you get anywhere near her, smelling like that. If you're going to miss all the parties and try to give her a cake instead—the least you could do is clean yourself up. You smell like that disgusting arena." Sage laughed and turned to leave.

Eli paused and set down the cake. He examined himself in the mirror and saw he was still drenched in sweat, and his hair clung to his sweaty neck and forehead. He headed for his washroom and turned a dial, where water flowed out onto level rocks. He quickly peeled off his clothes, scrubbed himself under the warm steamy water, and poured a plant's oil used for showering over himself. The hot water seemed to soothe him and brought a relaxation that he didn't know he needed. The stress of the past few days had really seemed to build up. Eli tried to wash away all thoughts of the arena as the physical residue also left him.

He turned off the steamy water and reached for a leafy towel and dried himself. He walked to his mirror and ran his fingers through his hair and grabbed a nearby peppermint plant and plucked a portion of it. He chewed on it and freshened his breath and then found a fresh set of clothing in his drawer. Once he was dried and ready, he picked up the cake again, certain he wouldn't repel Noelle with his sweat. He gathered a bundle of black roses inside his room and cut them at the stems.

He made his way toward Noelle's room and hoped she might

be inside. She was free to do as she pleased during the Heirling Duel, and he wasn't sure how she might be using her free time. He knocked on her door and stepped back; he could hear voices inside.

Noelle opened the door and leaned against it. It seemed that she, too, had washed up because her wet hair was pulled back and she smelled of sweet, flowery fragrances. Her large, round eyes met his, and when she saw the cake, she smiled.

"You haven't come to poison me, have you?" Noelle gave a crooked grin. Her dark, wet strands clung to her neck and back. She wore a strappy, army-green dress made of vibrant leaves.

"I wanted to say sorry. I wished you could have celebrated your birthday under different circumstances. May I come in?" Eli offered her the cake, and she took it.

Noelle stepped aside and let him in. He walked into her room, and Lumi and Luis immediately stood to their feet and balked at him.

"Hi, Lumi. Hi, Luis! Long time no see." Eli greeted them. They didn't respond. Eli spun to face Noelle who carried the cake to the little table in her room, where she placed it. Eli extended the roses to her, and she took them and accidentally brushed her fingers against his. Her hands were so soft, and even though it was an accident, Eli relished the touch. "I just wanted to say I'm sorry for everything. I wish you a very happy birthday, and I hope your nineteenth year is your best year yet."

Noelle brought the roses to her nose and inhaled with her eyes closed for a brief moment. "Thank you," she said. "This is perfect." And then she slid a finger across the top of the cake and brought it to her lips.

"Gross! Don't ruin it!" Luis said. "Did you bring a candle?"

Eli shook his head. "Oh, right. You make a wish and blow it out, don't you? Where are those lousy Leizei when you actually need them?"

Noelle laughed and Eli could have sworn that even the stone-faced Lumi almost smiled.

"No matter! I've made my wish already. Did you bring plates and forks?" Noelle looked around, but Eli hadn't thought of that.

"Sorry," Eli said. "I'm new to this cake thing. I suppose I didn't think it through."

Noelle took a fistful of cake and shrugged. "Oh well."

"Now you just totally ruined it," Luis said.

Eli copied Noelle and also took a fistful of cake and held it in his hand, crumbled.

"Oh, there you go. That is disgusting." Luis shook his head and folded his arms.

"Oh, I have seen this with cake before in your realm! You have to smash it in each other's faces, right?" Eli said and brought his cake to Noelle's face but paused as if to ask for permission.

Noelle grinned. "That isn't for birthdays. That is actually for weddings."

"Oh."

"But that does sound pretty fun!" And with that, Noelle smashed her handful of cake onto Eli's mouth and laughed loudly. It felt good to hear her laughter after seeing so much fear and uncertainty from her in the past few days.

Eli, not wanting to hurt her with his strength ability, simply placed a dollop of frosting on her nose. And then he threw the remainder of the cake at Lumi, and it splattered all over her gown and hair.

If Lumi had the ability to kill with a look, Eli would be a dead man. She gave a fierce glare, and Luis, Noelle, and Eli bellowed in laughter in response. Lumi wiped the icing off her hair, and it dropped to the ground.

"Live a little, snowflake," Eli said and grinned.

"Call me that again and I'll make you into a snowflake," Lumi growled. Luis grabbed a handful of the cake and threw it at Noelle, who then tossed a clump of cake at Eli. They threw scraps of cake all over the room, and Lumi was the only one who refused to participate and rolled her eyes. Frosting covered the bed, plants, and dirt floor. Even parts of the window had frosting and cake bits strewn across it.

Eli felt a genuine sense of joy flow through the room, but as quickly as it had come, it evaporated with the sound of a knock.

"Prince Eli, you should be in your room." Eli wasn't certain which soldier it was, but he wondered how they'd found him. After a moment, they opened the door, and two Naturei soldiers that Eli wasn't very familiar with came to his side. They scanned the room and paused as they noticed the cake smashed on Eli's face.

"Always ruining my fun. See you later, Elle. Happy belated birthday." Eli walked to the door and held on to the doorknob. But before he closed it, he caught a glimpse of a smiling, cake-covered Noelle.

CHAPTER 31
NOELLE
THE HEIRLING DUEL—DAY THREE

Noelle awoke to Lumi and Luis perched on the end of her overstuffed bed. Luis gave her a cheerful smile when she had finally sat up, and Lumi refused to look at her.

Noelle formed a perfectly circular snowball in her hand, then threw it at Lumi. That got her attention.

She turned and scowled. Lumi's stormy eyes were enough to draw laughter from both Luis and Noelle.

"Laugh it up," Lumi said and wiped the snow residue from her blond locks.

"I think if anybody gets the right to be grumpy, it is me," Noelle said with a mock voice of chastisement.

"You need to get up."

Sage entered with Aurora, Blossom, and Eden in tow. Eden made her way past the others and said, "It is the final day—which means we are going to make you look positively fierce and deadly. Anybody who dares to look in your direction will think twice about crossing you."

Noelle looked down at her feet. She didn't want to fight Marko or Eli. Eden's words were practically treasonous to the Naturei king—at the very least she flirted with treason. But Noelle knew it had come from Eli's orders.

"So you've come to make me look pretty?" Noelle asked.

"I've come to make you look lethal. You will be adorned today as a queen, and I give you my word that your outfit today will be sharp, deadly, and everyone will know that it was *my* creation." And then Eden bowed into a steep curtsy reserved only for royalty. Noelle watched as Sage, hesitant at first, stood by the window and then joined her in a royal bow. Sage looked uneasy, not with fear but with a forlorn sadness. Blossom and Aurora joined and curtsied as well. Noelle had only seen Naturei dip that low for the Naturei king and Eli.

Noelle opened her mouth to say something, but nothing came out. She didn't know what to say. Did they think this was her final day, as so many others did? Was it their kiss of goodbye and a way to honor her?

"Thank you," Noelle managed to get out, and then she bowed in response, uncertain of what else to do with herself. She turned to Lumi, who looked stunned—and Noelle could have sworn something else that lay dormant in Lumi's eyes had suddenly come alive. It looked like hope.

"Well, let me feed you properly before your big day," Sage said and pulled her cart out from the hallway, retrieving her usual mug and plate. "We have high hopes for you, Noelle. Thank you, from the bottom of my heart, for helping Eli that first day. We see a bright future ahead for you. And if I may be so bold, he won't have use of the Naturei ability with Lumi here and her curse. So please, *help him again*." Sage waved her hand over the plate where avocado toast suddenly appeared, perfectly seasoned. She waved her hand over the mug, and warm coffee filled the mug. She handed both to Noelle reverently and bowed low again.

Noelle felt certain that Eli could utilize his strength ability just fine, yet Sage had a point. How could strength be a match for flight ability *and* fire ability? Any wise Naturei should realize Marko was the real threat and the deadliest heir. Yet the Leizei and Naturei had an alliance. Supposedly.

She bit into the delicious toast.

Eden stepped toward her. "I'm crafting you with blue and orange leaves that are resistant to fire. It will be comfortable and durable, yet nobody's knives or swords will easily impact it. It will be your armor and protect you today." Eden waved her hands over Noelle's frame, and blue swirls engulfed her. The entire room fell silent, and Noelle made her way to the mirror where both eyebrows rose in appreciation. She wore a pale blue jumpsuit, entirely remarkable. Her shoulders came to points and were covered in tiny spikes. Her wrist guards, a darker shade of blue hues, staggered in spikes too. Her shins, shoulders, wrists, and waist were covered in tiny blue spikes also. She looked nothing like a weak feeble girl and everything like a fierce warrior that wasn't to be crossed.

Eden walked beside her in the mirror and eyed the spikes. "You can touch the spikes, and they will do nothing to you since you wear them. But if another heir touches them, they're poisonous."

Noelle whirled around to face Eden. "But what if the king sees and—"

"I'm following Eli's orders," Eden said with a shrug. "Besides, we've collectively decided as a realm that we want you and Eli to be the ones to survive. Well, all right, several of us at least. You still have many who oppose you in our realm."

Noelle wanted to hug Eden, but awareness that her spiky armor might send her to the floor kept her from it. "Thank you, Eden. This is beautiful and really helpful."

"You can thank Prince Eli. I'm here because of him and because you saved him."

"He won't stop talking about you, you know. He speaks incessantly about keeping you safe. You should see the way he barks orders at us!" Blossom said. She then took her turn and fashioned Noelle's hair into a crown braid with Aurora's assistance. The sisters seemed pleased with their work after they studied it, then stepped back.

"Lumi? Can you crown her head with an ice crown? It would go so well if it could be right against the braid crown."

Lumi stood to her feet and waved a finger, and then the large, pointy ice crown emerged on Noelle's head. Lumi fashioned one on her own head too.

"Thank you," Noelle breathed. "I-I can't explain how much this means to me. I hope that everyone can have better days ahead."

"Maybe," Aurora agreed. "If the educator's words come to pass." She said the words with a wink at Noelle, and then all the Naturei in the room gave Noelle a royal bow reserved for royalty, which made Noelle's face flush.

"Well, I think I need some fresh air," Noelle said.

As the Naturei gave a final royal bow as she made for the door, Noelle couldn't hide her grimace.

Sage grabbed Noelle's hand as she departed. "You must survive this, *Queen* Noelle."

Noelle gaped, uncertain what to say. Was Sage allied with the educators? Uncomfortable, she hurried to leave.

Luis and Lumi followed her into the hall, where the dirt shifted under Noelle's feet with her haste. She flung some dirt up at Luis and Lumi as her heavy steps moved forward.

Some Naturei passed by in the hall and stopped to stare. One even wished her well for her duel today. Noelle eyed him warily and gave a brief forced smile. She worried someone might report him to the Naturei king for such words.

Lumi had lagged far behind. She seemed lost in thought and entirely unenthused.

"Oh merca." Lumi eyed several Naturei that paused next to her. They each gave Noelle a Naturei salute. She saluted back, unsure of what to do. And then Noelle's heart leaped as the younger Naturei bowed in reverence to her. Her friend elbowed the young Naturei, and she stood up, but she gave a firm nod at Noelle before she left.

Lumi watched with suspicion, but then a look of concern

filled her stormy-gray eyes. "Noelle, you can't trust this realm. I did, and it cost me everything. I can't let them do it to you too."

"I assure you, nothing will happen." Noelle brushed a finger past her wrist, and the spikes turned away from her as she did. "Merca," she said as she repeated the motion. With each swipe, the spikes pulled away from her touch and refused to penetrate her skin.

"Just when you think you've seen it all," Luis said with a shake of his head.

A small, skinny girl with wiry red hair burst into the hallway and ran to Noelle. She threw herself to the dirt floor and bowed her head so that much of her auburn hair covered her face.

"Please, you've got to help us." The girl looked up, and her hollowed eyes looked wild and crazed, hungry for help.

Noelle's face went white. "What?"

"You've got to survive the Heirling Duel. We are counting on you," the girl said through thin, chapped lips. "It's why the educators risked their lives. Anybody who challenges their power gets sent to the pit." But just then, Leizei soldiers entered the hallway and grabbed the girl forcefully by the shoulders and began to drag her away.

"Please!" the girl cried and weakly threw fists at the guards.

"Where are you taking her?" Noelle asked and tried to follow. But several Leizei guards blocked Noelle's, Lumi's, and Luis's view and prevented them from following. Noelle could only see a glimpse of thick red hair being hauled over a Leizei soldier's shoulder. When the altercation had ceased, the Leizei soldiers left them alone in the hallway.

Noelle turned to face Lumi, horrified. "What just happened? Is what she said true?"

Lumi nodded. "Both the Leizei and Naturei kings control everyone and everything. The people cannot go against the crown's wishes, or they go to the pit. The crown and court decide everything, and even trivial matters like how much money can be made in markets is decided by the crown and determined by favor and loyalty. Anyone who challenges authority is brutally enslaved and fed very little—and they're the lucky ones. Why do you think I left my realm for Earth? The Leizei and Naturei realms aren't what they appear to be."

Noelle's stomach churned as she considered that and what her role might be in it. She felt helpless. Surely the girl was mistaken. But the look of desperation in the girl's eyes lingered, and rage bubbled up as Noelle considered the girl's mistreatment. But what could Noelle do to help her?

She turned to see the regal Naturei king and Eli down the hall. Eli wore an expression that looked worried. Dark bags were under his eyes, and Noelle wondered what kept him awake at night. He had plenty of options to choose from—that much was certain.

He locked eyes with Noelle, and a ghost of a smile appeared on his lips.

The leafy crown that adorned his head looked stunning against his dark, long locks, and he wore no jewelry except his gold signet ring.

The Naturei king glared at Lumi. Eli simply stood at his side. They redirected and went the other direction.

Noelle began to crumble. "What do I do? I can't hurt either Eli or Marko."

Lumi's stance softened, and she faced Noelle with a somber look. "My advice is to hide and get as far away from them both as you can. I don't know who is trustworthy and who isn't. I think your strategy should be to hide, and only if you are found and attacked, then you defend yourself."

Noelle shook her head, unsure if she could handle the sight of such a thing. Her hands shook violently.

"Now that you have the fire bond with Marko, if he dies, won't *you* also die?"

"Merca." Lumi avoided her eyes. "Yes, he likely did this to keep himself alive. But if he attacks you, don't let that stop you from defending yourself. And I need you to promise me that you'll use the necklace and bring back our people after this."

"We'll bring back all the Merklei together." Noelle's eyes brimmed with hot tears. Lumi had spoken as if she might not be there much longer, and the thought burned Noelle's throat. She had just gotten some semblance of family because of Lumi, and she couldn't bear to part with her.

Lumi stood rigid. "Please just promise me you'll bring back Lorelei and the others."

Noelle started to protest, but Lumi yelled, "Please! I remained alive for agonizing years to bring them back! We've finally found the necklace, and I discovered that I'm not the only Merklei. I've lived my life—but my people, *our people*, haven't."

Noelle wrapped her arms around Lumi. Lumi held Noelle tightly and wrapped a cold hand around her head. Noelle leaned in, because she felt a maternal comfort in Lumi's hug. She had found her family after all, even without using the necklace.

A Naturei soldier entered the hall and gave a salute. "The heirs must be taken to the arena."

Fear began to choke Noelle—she wasn't ready. Lumi walked with Noelle to the same arena doors that Noelle had entered twice already. She could hear the crowd beyond it.

"What if we ran away?" Noelle whispered.

Lumi held up her wrist with the tracking device.

"Is there nothing we can do?" Her hands trembled with anxiety.

"You think we'd be here if we didn't have to?" Lumi looked almost offended. "When I took my vows, I vowed to submit to the Heirling Duel rules. It was never supposed to be like this; it was supposed to be an avoidance of war. They have perverted the entire thing for their own gain."

Noelle scoffed, and then anxious butterflies entered her stomach. She couldn't do this. She could never kill her friends. The thought that either Marko or Eli might try to kill her in the arena made her feel ill. Noelle leaned forward, and green bile covered her shoes.

Lumi held Noelle by her shoulders. Noelle trembled. "You're

going to survive this, but you need to be smart. They're both stronger, and they have way more experience since you've just been initiated. They can wield their abilities with more skill and precision—so you need to hide. Do not attack them unless they attack you. And then you do whatever it takes to defend yourself. Let them go for each other—I have a firm conviction that they will do exactly that."

Noelle hated to admit it, but she believed Lumi was right.

"It's time to go!" A Naturei soldier grabbed Lumi's arm, but she turned on him.

"Unhand me or lose your hand. I heard you." Lumi yanked her arm free. "You've got this." The Naturei soldiers began to beckon her.

"Don't I get any weapons for this one?" Noelle asked and shivered. She wasn't even cold, yet her body shook without her consent. She tried to hide the tremors, but they were evident.

"You're the weapon."

"Remember your Heirling duties. You must be in the arena!" A soldier reached for Lumi, who struck the soldier.

"I know my duties. Touch me again and you'll never live to fulfill yours." The soldiers whisked Lumi away. Lumi's gray eyes looked haunted as she glanced at Noelle, and Noelle swore she saw Lumi's eyes become watery. "We will use the necklace, and we will see your grandma, my daughter, and all the Merklei! I believe in you!" Lumi called before the Naturei soldiers dragged her past the corner, and then she was out of sight.

Noelle felt cool tears on her cheeks that froze halfway down. She didn't want to die, and this felt like a cruel way to go. There was still so much in life that she hadn't experienced, and what would happen to the necklace if she did die? She didn't know what awaited her in the arena. Alone, she heard a small tap against the side door, and it made her shaky hands tremble more violently.

She looked to the arena door ahead of her, but it hadn't opened. So instead, she investigated.

She opened the side door to find a bleeding, gagged, and tied-up Sage inside a closet. Noelle quickly knelt and began to pull the bindings off her. She had seen her only what felt like moments ago. How did this happen?

"Sage!" Noelle cried, horrified. "Who did this to you?"

Tears spilled onto Sage's cheeks. Noelle pulled the gag from Sage's mouth, and she began to weep bitterly.

Noelle's eyes widened at the sight of incredible amounts of blood pooling around Sage. It was far too much blood to possibly survive. The wound was fresh, but Noelle quickly began working. She ripped off cloth and began to apply pressure, panting.

"No use," Sage said. "L-listen."

"Tell me who did this!" Noelle's shaky hands held the crimson cloth, though it did little to slow the bleeding.

"Th-the king d-did it." Sage sucked in a breath.

Noelle screamed, "Help! Somebody help!" Noelle's hands were covered in Sage's blood now, and her bottom lip quivered. "I'll get Eli. He will fix this!"

Sage shook her head. She opened her mouth to speak, but no words came. She tried again, swallowing hard.

"He l-left me alive to give a m-message," Sage groaned.

"Who? What monster did this?" Noelle demanded.

"N-naturei king," Sage hissed. "My punishment f-for helping y-you." Sage's head went backward, and her breathing became shallow.

Noelle screamed, "I'm going to get help!"

Sage gripped Noelle's hand. "D-don't l-leave me." She groaned. "Take his th-throne... for m-me."

Noelle looked down at her friend, whose breath was becoming fewer and fewer. She looked at the ceaseless blood oozing from her stomach and then at her tear-filled eyes. The Naturei king had put on a good show, because the realm seemed innocent and fun. More sinister behavior was lurking beneath the mask though. Innocent people, simply differing in opinions, were being imprisoned or killed because they threatened his power. As Noelle looked at Sage, her heart shattered.

"I will," Noelle said, and a green light circled around their wrists. Sage took one big, deep breath, and then her head rested against the floor as Noelle clung to her lifeless body.

In cruel timing, the arena door slid open.

She had nothing else to do but step out onto the arena as Naturei soldiers emerged and ushered her forward.

"You killed my friend!" Noelle screamed. They threw her into the opening.

A swarm of Naturei and Leizei people in the audience cheered for her. Apparently she had earned a few fans because of her antics with Marko and Eli in the earlier duel events.

"The princess of the Merklei realm!" Autumn yelled. Several Leizei shot up flames in salute to Noelle, and many Naturei gave their salute. The roar of the crowd stifled her tears, but her hands continued to shake. Her knees felt wobbly, and she wanted to vomit again as her stomach did somersaults.

Noelle tried to look at the crowd, but she couldn't make out any familiar faces. Her pale blue jumpsuit that clung to her body gleamed under the light. She tried to hold back her surprise, but she didn't realize so many people would cheer for her—especially since she was from the realm with no alliance.

When she spotted Eden, she noticed that she looked thoroughly pleased with herself, and then to Noelle's horror—many Naturei in the crowd gave a reverent bow. It wasn't a royal bow, but it was one that belonged only to fellow Naturei. Her face felt warm, and she turned to find the Naturei king, certain that there would be grave consequences. The educator's words seemed to be weightier now.

When she found the Naturei king, she felt she might fall over then and there. The fury in his face was evident. Noelle, even if she survived this, was *dead*. The Naturei king's face promised death and revenge. His smug smile returned, and it sent a shiver down Noelle's spine.

But then Noelle smiled, wide and broad. He killed her friend, and he would pay for it. Noelle began screaming at him, but Autumn's voice carried over hers.

"And now please give a warm welcome to Crown Prince Eli Goldner of the Naturei realm!" Autumn said and gave her own bow—but this bow was a proper royal bow. The Naturei audience did too.

Eli walked out of his slate-gray entrance, opposite of Noelle, and looked over at her. His eyes scanned her hands, and his brow furrowed. Noelle pointed at his father.

Eli took in the audience, and if he were afraid, he wore a mask well enough that nobody could tell. He looked confident in his leafy Naturei uniform. His broad shoulders were pulled back, and he raised two fists in the air. The audience cheered and raised their own fists. Then Eli eyed the drums and a look of disgust appeared on his face. Noelle couldn't blame him; the drums had felt like psychological torture.

Noelle eyed the gray slate door where Marko would enter. Noelle scanned the arena where a tarp lay out over the dirt ground.

"Please welcome Crown Prince Marko of the Leizei kingdom!" Autumn said with enthusiasm. Across the way, Marko, dressed in all black, emerged. Marko eyed the crowd with an unemotive face. The Leizei in the audience went wild with cheers and fire blasts in an acknowledgment of their prince. Noelle spied Yuri, his fiancée, who sat next to the Leizei king. Yuri looked on at Marko with a slight clap. The Leizei king sat in his gold hood, and Noelle watched as he chatted with Yuri. Wrath began to swirl inside Noelle as she watched the Leizei king, who had fooled her and plotted the entire thing. He was the real mastermind behind everything and the monumental figure behind her pain—it was as if he were the puppet master and his fingers toyed with the strings of her life's pain and she were the pathetic puppet. He was the cause of nearly all her suffering and her grandma's death.

Then fear paralyzed Noelle entirely. The Naturei announcer

explained the rules, but Noelle couldn't seem to concentrate. She simply stared at Marko as reality dawned on her. If Marko died today, Lumi would die too because of the fire bond.

Noelle eyed Eli, who looked up at the audience. His mask seemed to have slipped some, and his expressionless face now looked uncertain and concerned. Noelle didn't imagine she could kill Eli either. But the options were either Marko and Lumi die as a pair, or Eli would die. Noelle shuddered as her bleak options presented a sickening feeling that lined her stomach.

Noelle raised her hands to her face and covered it entirely. She couldn't do this. She wouldn't do this. This was inhumane, and it was more than sick; it was twisted and immoral.

"Merca!" Noelle whispered under her breath. She removed her hands and saw the tarp had been removed and they had been lowered, yet she hadn't even felt it. She looked up and saw the audience far above her, who all seemed to sit on the edge of their seats in anticipation. *What vile vultures.*

The image of Sage dying in the closet haunted her as the crowd madly cheered. She hurled and began hyperventilating. Sage was dead because she'd helped Noelle. It was all Noelle's fault. Did somebody see the royal bow and report Sage? What about the others? Nobody was safe.

She looked forward, and she could no longer see the other heirs, only ice, and then her mouth parted. Today was Merklei themed, and the arena looked like a wintry haven, except underneath the thick ice were three mermaids swimming. They each had long violet hair, and violet, scaly tails that fluttered at the sight of her. Their piercing lavender eyes watched her carefully, and as their tails swayed back and forth, they sparkled with shimmery scales. From the waist up, they looked eerily human, but ethereal and beautiful. Noelle was entirely stunned because she had never seen such beautiful creatures in her lifetime—not even the most gorgeous models on earth could compete with their beauty. She tore her eyes away from the beautiful mermaids. Beyond the ice, a small building ahead of her looked drab and dreary in a boring gray, yet what lay inside was likely anything but boring.

Noelle found Lumi and Luis in the crowd.

You can do this, Lumi mouthed the words to Noelle. Lumi looked calm and poised. Luis sat next to her cross-armed, and his frown deepened as they made eye contact. His fingers drummed against his arm.

"Remember heirs, you won't be released from this arena until one of you dies. It is also acceptable for two heirs to die. The ability barrier shield is also in effect. Good luck! Oh, and don't let the mermaids bite."

The audience cheered, and Noelle eyed Lumi, who didn't cheer. She swallowed, and the look of pain couldn't be hidden from her gray eyes. They were evidently so full of worry, and so was Luis's. They watched Noelle in horror, and Noelle had to look away.

She wouldn't die. She needed to get her grandma back. And Lorelei and the other Merklei.

The drums sounded. Noelle moved onto the thick ice but paused. What if she didn't enter the door? What if she stayed where she was?

Something caught her eye, and she saw a blur of violet that flashed by quickly. She flinched and moved aside.

The three mermaids circled her. Noelle's breath hitched, and she watched as they swam around her. She half expected them to try to drown her, but they moved gently and peered up at her with seemingly innocent dove eyes.

One mermaid slowly came to the ice, and Noelle backed away. She put her fingertips on the ice, and it cracked. She bobbed her head up and gave a disarming smile.

"Noelle, we won't hurt you. We can help you," she said, breathy. Her lavender eyes matched her sparkling hair, and Noelle gasped at her beauty. She flipped her tail up behind her and perched on top of the ice. The other mermaids joined her, one with a deep skin tone and the other with ivory skin.

She raised her palms at them. They didn't seem dangerous, but surely they wouldn't be here if they were as innocent as they seemed.

"How?" Noelle's voice sounded skeptical.

"We can help bring your grandma back."

Noelle froze. She was curious how they knew her name and about her grandma.

"Come here," the three mermaids said in unison. Noelle, uncertain why, obeyed. She began to slowly walk toward them, careful not to slip on the ice. She kept her palms out toward them. The three lavender mermaids simply watched her with charming, inviting smiles.

"Sit with us, and we'll bring her back." Their voices might have sounded eerie to anybody else, but to Noelle, their singsong voices paired with their beauty called to her. It somehow intoxicated her, and she felt they could tell her to do anything, and she would do it. Noelle slowly made her way to them and sat down on the ice. The mermaids came close, and two took her hands into theirs. All three now perched on the ice.

"Would you like to be beautiful like us? We can transform you," the mermaid on her right said.

Noelle started to nod, but something inside her mind felt like an alarm. Something inside was screaming to run away. She ignored it because she wanted to look into their eyes more.

"With a bite, you can be like us. You won't have to die or kill your friends. You could even give the necklace to your queen. We offer a good solution," the lavender mermaid said and stroked Noelle's arm. Noelle considered it. It was very tempting. No death seemed like a very good option. Perhaps transforming sounded like a much more humane way of ending the Heirling Duel.

Noelle heard the audience roar in applause and briefly looked around. The Leizei across the massive stadium above her cheered with excitement. Marko must have gotten past the mermaids on his side and managed to get inside.

It was enough to break Noelle's focus, and she turned toward the crowd, away from the hypnotizing lavender eyes.

Lumi waved her hands frantically above her head. "They're hypnotic! Run!" Noelle hardly made out Lumi's words before the mermaids gripped her hands very tightly and began to pull her toward the icy water.

Noelle's head snapped back toward the three bewitching mermaids and yanked her hands back. They held on and dug their nails into her skin and yanked until she was partly in the water. Unfortunately for these mermaids, Noelle was Merklei, and albeit her ability was weak, she still controlled ice. Noelle closed her fists, and thick ice wrapped around the two mermaids, and ice sprawled up from her fingertips to theirs, freezing them. Noelle pulled at their fingertips and broke off their frozen fingers as if they were mere icicles. They gasped and began to growl at her as their plum blood permeated the water. She opened her palms and formed a new ice shield between her and the two mermaids, who were effectively blocked off. She formed an icy cage around them, and they rammed against it—but the ice was too thick for an easy escape.

The third mermaid gripped Noelle's arm and pulled her down into the water. Noelle kicked her legs, and the icy water hardly affected her now that she was Merklei. Days ago, this temperature would have been miserable, but now? She was in her element. Noelle felt the mermaid's hand clasp around her wrist, and she was moving her mouth toward Noelle's wrist. Noelle formed an icy dagger and shoved it into the mermaid's side. Deep plum blood made a cloud in the water, and Noelle squirmed against the mermaid, who continuously tried to bite her—the image of it was a total paradox. Some part of Noelle wanted to let the mermaid bite her, hypnotized by her eyes, but another part of her knew she had to fight back.

She heard the audience cheer again. This time the Naturei were the ones to cheer. Noelle figured Eli must have gotten inside too. Her heart thumped as she thought about what might happen inside the gray door. She didn't know if she could truly trust him, or anybody. He had shown so much kindness toward her when she was a Naturei prisoner, and he even defied his father at times for her sake. She didn't think he would hurt her, but she just wasn't certain of much any longer.

Noelle heard a bang behind the gray door ahead of her. She turned and eyed the mermaid, whose hair was now in Noelle's fingers, as she held her back and prevented her from biting her. She suddenly stilled.

"Noelle, look at me." Something inside Noelle wanted to do exactly as she said. Her silky voice lured her and made her want to obey her. Noelle shook her head and looked away. The other mermaids were nearly out of the icy jail she had formed for them. Noelle had planned to stay outside in the ice, but these mermaids seemed to have some sort of mind-control ability, and she needed to get inside to avoid them. She didn't know what might happen if they bit her, but it couldn't be good.

Noelle pried her hand away and shoved the mermaid into the water. She lifted her palms, and she created an ice barrier between her and the bleeding mermaid. She also formed a thick layer of ice against the other mermaids so they couldn't easily reach her. It was thinner than she would have liked, as the mermaids began to dig at it and she saw glimpses of fingers protruding, and they slapped their tails against the ice, which appeared to have much more power than Noelle would have imagined. They clawed at the ice with furious vigor, and Noelle hurried toward the gray door. She crafted another ice barrier, taller and thicker than the last. It drained her energy. She hadn't practiced her ability enough for such a challenge.

She reached the gray door and flung it open, louder than she would have liked. She froze the door behind her shut. She was on land now, but just in case they could reach her—she shut herself in.

Inside, there were barriers all across the room, and the three symbols for the three realms were painted on the wall—a bright green leaf, a diamond made of ice, and a single amber flame.

Noelle hoped that her entrance hadn't attracted too much attention. To her horror, she heard several Leizei and Naturei that cheered for her. She could even make out some shouts that said her name.

"Thanks a lot," she groaned. If Marko and Eli hadn't heard her entrance, they would be well aware now that she had entered.

Noelle assessed the room quickly. She saw no movements, but she did see many little yellow walls around the room. Obviously, the walls were meant to be small protections so the heirs could hide behind the obstacles and defend themselves.

Noelle crouched behind the closest yellow obstacle—a thick yellow wall no more than four feet tall. Her heart seemed to beat faster than it ever had in her life. She closed her eyes. Somebody was going to die today.

Sweat poured off her brow, and she could feel the sweat pool inside her jumpsuit, against her armpits, and at the back of her knees.

The crowd cheered. Noelle craned her head upward and was surprised to see the building had no roof. Of course it didn't. The audience would want to watch the heirs as they fought to their deaths—gladiator-style. Noelle bit down on her bottom lip as she tried to stop the tears that formed. She wasn't ready to die.

She also didn't want to see Eli perish. He would eventually make a fantastic ruler for the Naturei realm, and he could bring many important changes to the realm. Noelle didn't want her brother, Marko, to die either. He had a family that adored him, and he loved and protected his loved ones with a ferocity. She wouldn't be able to live with herself if she hurt either of them. She needed both Marko and Eli to live. And that was when she made her decision.

Tears sprang onto her cheeks freely. She stood to her feet and no longer hid herself.

"I know you can hear me!" Noelle shouted. "I'll sacrifice

myself. Please, I don't want to live without either of you. I *can't* live without either of you." Noelle's eyes became blurry, and she stood tall and accepted her fate. If either of them would kill her quickly, she would be grateful for the favor. This wasn't how Noelle had pictured her end—especially not at such a young age. "You both have realms to rule. I don't. I can't lose either of you. I just ask that you do it quickly!"

Noelle emerged into the room now. The entire audience was quiet, and tears fell down Noelle's cheeks. She waited a moment, but nobody came.

"*Please!*" her voice cracked. Her hands trembled, and she could hear footsteps from the right side of the room. She closed her eyes. She didn't wish to see who would do it.

She held her breath and trembled as the footsteps grew louder. She hadn't imagined it would be like this. What a *cruel* way to die.

"Keep your voice down," a familiar voice called back from the right side.

CHAPTER 32
NOELLE
THE ARENA

It was the low, familiar voice that she had dreamed of, which brought both comfort and fear in that moment. It was the voice that belonged to Eli, who made her heart race for entirely different reasons.

When he appeared around the corner, he held his own palms upward as if in surrender. He made slow movements toward her, and the corners of his lips curled up. His intense emerald eyes looked her over and landed on her wounds. She hadn't realized it, but the mermaids drew quite a bit of blood from her arms with their nails.

"Let me help you," he said, and he continued to slowly move toward her. He was almost close enough to touch her.

Noelle sighed in relief. Except, she didn't want him to heal her. She wanted him to end her life, to spare his. She hadn't anticipated that he might try to heal her instead.

"No," she protested. "I need you to finish this."

Eli moved toward her. He could do it easily, she realized. She had barely any control of her snow ability, and his strength could snap her in half, as if she were cardboard. When he reached her, he wrapped his strong, muscled arms around her, and she went limp in his arms. She buried her head into his shoulder, and the brief moment of comfort provided her with momentary peace and relief. His arms found their way to her back, and his warm hands rested there, and she wrapped her own arms around his strong shoulders.

She felt him heal her, as the pain on her wrists melted away. She sighed in relief.

Noelle pulled away from his embrace. "I didn't call you in here to heal me."

Eli frowned. "You can trust me."

A subtle noise occurred from the other end of the room. Eli pulled Noelle toward a yellow wall barrier. The room was quite barren, except the yellow barriers scattered throughout it. Eli tucked Noelle behind him. She sat in the dirt, not willing to speak.

She scanned Eli's body and searched for any wounds, but there weren't any. He crouched behind the bright yellow wall, perfectly whole.

The audience suddenly made plenty of noise.

Noelle felt queasy, as she knew this meant Marko had drawn near. Noelle clenched her fists, and ice covered them entirely as she struggled to control her panic. Eli turned to face her and wrapped his warm hands around hers.

"Your father murdered Sage," she blurted out.

"What?"

"She gave me a royal bow, and he did it because she helped me. Half the Naturei realm is turning against him because of me."

He leaned close to her ear and whispered against it, "I won't let anything happen to you. You're safe. I promise, you can trust me, Elle." His breath tickled against her ear, and his mouth brushed against it.

It was then that Noelle knew he had meant it when he made Eden give her the protective clothing. Eli had become her ally, which meant she wasn't the target. Marko was.

"You can't kill Marko!" Her voice sounded wounded. "Please, he is like my brother. Please, *kill me*."

Confusion clouded his emerald eyes. "I could never hurt you

—" His voice broke off and sounded so hurt that she would even consider thinking he would fulfill such a request. "Don't worry, I'll take care of this."

Noelle could see the sheer dread that welled up in his deep green eyes. He didn't want to, but to spare both their lives—it seemed his mind was made up.

Noelle could hear footsteps that were heavy. She made an ice shield that fully enclosed the space around them both.

"What are you doing? You just gave away our location!" Eli said. He didn't bother to conceal his voice with a whisper.

"Noelle? Get away from him! You can't trust him!" Marko's familiar voice was outside the ice shield. Noelle raised a hand and thickened it with more ice, uncertain of what else to do. She felt her moments had run out.

"I'm sorry, Elle," Eli said.

Noelle turned to face Eli. He brought rough callused fingers under her chin and tilted her face up to him. Noelle's eyes went wide as she realized perhaps Marko was right. But she decided she wouldn't fight back; instead, she just closed her eyes tightly shut.

"I'm sorry, grandma, for not bringing you back." Noelle squeezed her eyes even tighter, and a single tear fell and froze against her cheek. Her entire body trembled as she took in what might have been her final breaths. She had never felt such intense fear ever seize her body. After a quiet moment, she opened her eyes.

Eli peered down at her, with his lips close to hers, frozen. A look of bewilderment, and then it shifted to confusion.

She blushed at her mistake.

"You're glowing," he managed to say. But it was all he said before he pulled away and rammed his shoulder into the ice, repeatedly. "Stay here in this shield and stay away from both of us, Elle. If Marko comes for you, run. No matter what, don't come out until the duel is over."

Noelle looked down at her body, and it glowed a pale Merklei blue. She didn't feel any different except for the intense fear that ran down her entire being. When she looked back up at Eli, she saw red numbers above his head. The numbers 241:38:27:10 floated directly above his hair. She tried to blink several times and watched as he rammed the ice with his shoulder and effectively broke pieces off each time.

She watched as the far right number started to dwindle and become lower. It went down from ten to zero, and when it reached zero, the twenty-seven turned into a twenty-six. It was a countdown of some sort.

"You have red numbers above your head," she said.

"What?"

"There is a time clock of some sort above your head. It says 241:38:26:58... and now it is 241:38:26:54... and it is decreasing by the second. I think it is a clock of some sort."

Eli's mouth dropped open. "Your intense emotions just unlocked your ability. It's really common after being initiated. You just discovered one of your abilities. Do you think it is a life-span clock?" He suddenly became excited. "Elle, if that is accurate, then that means you and I are going to win!" A wicked grin spread across his face, and he continued to ram his shoulder into the ice shield with more force than before.

"No!" she yelled. "Marko! Please kill me! I am all right with it! I need you and Lumi to keep going. And Eli too!"

"Is this some kind of cruel prank?" Marko's voice sounded almost bored. His voice echoed off the walls, and he seemed like he might be on the other end.

Eli managed to break through the ice, and he moved with speed to a yellow barrier, and when Noelle emerged, he motioned for her to get back.

"Marko, please. Eli should know that you created a fire bond with Lumi. Please kill me. Spare everyone else."

Eli went rigid. His sweaty face became red and splotchy. "You did *what?*"

Eli's anger melted away, and he looked at Noelle with a

mischievous grin. *Trust me, please*, he mouthed to her from behind the yellow barrier.

She hurried down the middle of the room where there weren't any barriers, toward Marko. She had to hurry before Eli could intervene.

To Noelle's surprise, Marko emerged from a yellow barrier with his hands lit on fire with flames that danced. He kept them outstretched toward her. She sucked in a breath.

She nodded. "Go on then."

But then Eli was behind her, and he wrapped a warm hand around her waist. And the other was around her neck. She could feel his muscled chest against her back, and she swallowed. He held her tightly to him.

"You think Lumi will forgive you if you let her die? I could snap her neck right now." Eli said, and his breath danced against Noelle's skin. Eli's fingers tightened around her neck.

Marko didn't move. He stayed perfectly still, with no emotion on his face.

"That is fine. Just kill me, or let Marko do it," Noelle said, and she felt braver about it all. She was tired of this already. The audience's cheers made her glum demeanor even more sullen.

Marko sighed. Noelle observed that he, too, had red numbers above his head. It read 113:37:05:07, and the seven began to tick downward.

"Wait, it can't be a lifespan time. You're both going to live for a long time." And then after a moment, she understood. "Oh." Noelle dropped her head. They were both going to live on and become rulers, which meant she was going to die. "Please just promise me a few things before I'm killed. Please protect Lumi and Luis. And ensure that the necklace gets back to Lumi so she can bring her people and my grandma back. If you both can promise that, I'm content with dying."

Marko's flame grew bigger and brighter. He eyed Noelle, and regret and sorrow were heavy in his eyes.

A lone female voice, strangled with worry, rang out. "Marko! No! Please don't hurt her!" It was Lumi's cry, and she was on her feet, with icy tears that streamed down her face and froze on her skin. The wind in the arena moved massively, and snow flurries violently fell across the arena. Heavy snow fell all around them, because Lumi's love for Noelle had summoned every last bit of Lumi's hope. Lumi needed Noelle as much as Noelle had needed Lumi.

"The curse," Noelle muttered. Several soldiers had moved toward Lumi. It was evident to Noelle that of all the rulers, Lumi was clearly the most powerful. It was no wonder she'd survived a complete sabotage, even with merca. Nobody was supposed to be able to wield their abilities in the arena, yet Lumi could defy the rules. As Noelle watched, her awe faded when she realized that even Lumi's strength couldn't breach the arena—the snow stopped against the arena's parameters, and not even Lumi could help Noelle now.

Marko examined his fire bond, and frowned as he looked at Noelle.

"Don't touch her," Eli growled. He moved Noelle behind him and held her there, shielding her from Marko's flame.

Marko's dark eyes watched Lumi for a brief moment, then he turned to Eli. "As you wish," Marko said, and then Noelle audibly gasped as the red letters above Eli's head turned to 05:04. It seemed that the numbers had changed with Marko's decision, and Marko had made up his mind.

"Marko! No!" Noelle screamed.

Marko sent a swirling flame that roared toward them both. Eli dropped to the dirt floor and pinned Noelle beneath him and protected her from the oncoming flame. He winced and bared his teeth as the flame went across his back. His dark hair fell over his face and mixed with his sweat. The hair clung to his face, drenched.

"Stop! Please!" Noelle begged with tears. The time above Eli's head now said 04:45.

The flame ceased, and Marko began to move forward. "Stay out of my way, Noelle."

"I'll never forgive you!" she yelled and pulled on Eli's arm. His entire back was angry and hardly resembled skin. Burned flesh, mixed with angry splotchy places covered his entire back. His armor had been burned to a crisp, and Noelle had to look away at the sight; the smell of burned flesh made her want to vomit. It had been the most repulsive smell she ever inhaled.

Noelle pulled desperately and tried to put him behind a yellow barrier. "You have to get up! You have to fight back. Please."

Eli's green eyes fixated on Noelle, but she watched the red numbers above his head.

As if he could understand what she meant, as he looked at her eye placement, he got to his feet and moved to a yellow barrier. Noelle didn't bother to hide herself. Marko wouldn't hurt her—she knew it. She knew he wasn't just an actor—there were parts of him that were true.

She held up her palms and stood between him and Marko.

Marko stopped his advancement. He held his two hands out, both lit on fire. "Let him and me work it out. Stay out of my way." He began to move forward again.

Noelle shot a gust of snow toward him. "No," she said defiantly. "Just kill me." She lowered her hands.

"I can't," Marko said.

Eli had emerged from behind Marko, which caught both Noelle and Marko by surprise. Eli tackled him from behind and wrapped his strong arms around his torso. It was evident that he squeezed as hard as he could as Marko began to wheeze what little air was left in his lungs.

"Stop!" Noelle put her hands over her face. The time above Eli's head said 4:01.

They wrestled against one another on the dirt ground, and Noelle waved her hand and placed an ice barrier between the two.

"Please!" she begged. But neither listened. Marko melted

down the ice barrier and stormed toward Eli. He leaped into the air and sent a swirl of fire toward Eli, which caught his leg. Eli groaned and continued to move toward Marko. He had managed to get close enough to strike him in the face, which sent Marko rolling backward. Marko lifted himself off the dirt ground with his flight ability, and he now hovered over Eli.

Noelle felt helpless. Without Eli's Naturei ability, how could he fight against Marko? It was completely unfair. It was up to her to protect him.

Noelle sent an ice spear in Marko's direction. He didn't even look at her and held out his left palm. As the spear neared his hand, it melted.

Noelle's mouth fell open. Marko had mastered his ability, and she was barely initiated. She watched as the many full years floated above Marko's head. He would grow much older and probably have a full life. That fact would comfort Noelle, except she couldn't ever forgive him if he killed Eli.

Noelle threw another icy spear, but he melted it again. It was of no use. She imagined she had the damage capacity of a toddler in comparison to Marko. But she wouldn't give up. She made a cloud emerge above his head, and heavy snow fell on him. She hoped it might slow him down or irritate his fire ability somehow. But he seemed completely unbothered by it and even sent two blasts of lava toward Eli, who managed to dodge it on the dirt ground.

"Stupid," she muttered. Of course snow didn't irritate him. He had lived in Chicago under Lumi's curse.

Marko remained suspended in the air, as if he had become wiser in his fight against Eli and realized Eli couldn't win if he couldn't reach him. Eli might win if he could get ahold of Marko. But it seemed Marko knew this.

Noelle began to run toward Eli, whose wounds had driven him to the ground. She placed herself between Marko and Eli and faced Marko. "I won't let you do this!"

Noelle swore she could see something sympathetic in Marko's

honey-brown eyes. "I'm sorry. I never wanted to hurt you, Noelle. But I'm afraid, this time, it is inevitable. I refuse to kill you. So it has to be him." And with his apology, he sent a swirling fire ball toward Eli. But Noelle managed to throw enough snow onto it that it lost almost all its power. Her energy now felt totally depleted, and she had little strength to wield her ability. She was so weak and so freshly new at this—she had very little endurance.

She fell to her knees. She looked apologetically at Eli. The red number above his head now read 02:32. Tears fell down her cheeks as she looked at his mangled, burned body once so full of life, now on the dirt.

Marko angled his hands for another pitch, and a massive fireball emerged. He was poised to strike Eli.

Noelle reached out both her palms and formed a thick icy wall between her and Eli, and Marko. She ran to Eli's side and lifted his head into her hand. She could feel the ice cool the entire room, but Marko worked to breach her thick ice wall that separated them.

"Eli." Her voice was a whisper. He lay on the ground and hardly moved. He was covered in burns, and much of his skin had blotchy marks. Noelle's stomach churned at the sight. Only his face, neck, and right arm remained unburned. Marko had nearly killed him.

Eli pulled his strong hands around her waist and pulled her close to him. He winced as her weight met him. She tried to pull away, but he pulled her back. "I don't mind," he said in a whisper.

Noelle looked around the ice wall and realized the audience couldn't see them since the it had blocked them off entirely with an ice roof attached to the thick ice. She could see Marko blasted fire at the side wall in his feeble attempt to melt the it. Noelle put up her hand and crafted more ice where he blasted the ice with fire.

Eli's fingers found their way to her chin. "I'm sorry, Elle. For everything. I promise I didn't intend to use that merca."

Noelle shook her head. "Don't be stupid. That doesn't matter.

Listen, we have to fulfill the educator's words, right? I can't marry you if you die! So I need you to stay with me, okay?" She tried her best to smile with her joke, but tears flowed.

Noelle looked above his head. It read 01:49. As if Eli might have known entirely what she was doing, he pulled her chin back to his face. "I don't regret meeting you. You've brought me so much joy, and you are quite literally the most beautiful girl I've ever seen."

Noelle scoffed.

"No, I mean it." He grinned the type of grin that made Noelle smile back at him. "You put the alanis flower to shame. You've made me happier than I've ever been in my entire life. I'd do anything to see your smile."

Noelle struggled to believe anybody could like her crooked smile. But she flashed it nonetheless.

"You're going to survive this and see your grandma soon."

The time said 01:29 above his head. "And you're going to survive this too," she said. "Because we have to get married according to your educator's advice, remember?"

Eli tried to laugh but winced in pain. His body was bloody and burned. He hardly moved now. Noelle's hands cupped his face.

"Please stay with me." She leaned down close to Eli. His warm hands wrapped tightly around her waist, and his lips met hers. The softness of his lips beckoned Noelle to get lost in their kiss. She had imagined their first kiss plenty of times but not like this. His fingers stroked her hair, and she leaned in. Their kiss tasted like salty tears and terminated dreams. His hand trailed through her hair, and she pulled away, breathless. The red letters above his head read :59. Eli lifted his head again and pulled Noelle back to his lips. His kiss morphed from soft and gentle to a kiss that belonged to a dying man's goodbye and final kiss—it was more desperate and hungrier as if it were his last. His lips parted hers, and she got so lost in the kiss that she didn't want it to ever end. It was pure bliss.

She suddenly felt warm heat on her left side. She pulled away and turned to see an amber color glowed just outside the ice. Marko was about to break through the ice.

She held up her hand and steadied the wall. But Marko's fire ability seemed stronger, and the ice began to melt and deteriorate quickly.

"It's okay," Eli whispered beside her. He still hadn't moved, and Noelle looked over his body. His bloodied, burned body was hardly recognizable as skin. She groaned, as she could only imagine how much pain he must surely be in.

The red letters above his head read :22.

And then Marko managed to open the ice wall. He sent a blast toward Noelle, but it didn't burn her—instead, it materialized into a human silhouette set on fire, and it moved toward Noelle. Horrified, she backed away.

"Stay out of my way, Noelle." Marko advanced toward Eli's motionless body.

"No!" Noelle went to build another ice wall, to block Marko, but the fire figure stalked toward her and threw fire at her. She ducked and dodged and tried to avoid being burned.

Marko blasted fire at Eli's chest, and Eli screamed in agony as the flames met him.

"Stop!" Noelle sent icy shards at Marko. But the fire figure pulled on her wrist, and bright red burn marks appeared in the form of fingers. Noelle pulled her wrist back and flinched. She gave her attention to the fire figure and sent icy shards toward it. The fire figure just seemed to swallow her ice and melt it. Then returned it with more fire. "Please, Marko! Don't kill him!"

When she looked over at Eli, the red clock above his head read :08.

Marko coiled back a flame in his right hand, and Noelle knew what it meant. This was the final death blow.

"Stop!" Noelle screamed and brought her hands to her face. She screamed, a high-pitched wail. She couldn't watch Eli die, and she didn't want it to be Marko who did it. When Noelle opened her eyes, her vision was blurry with tears. But to her horror, she found that with her scream, it appeared that she had lost control. Lumi had warned her that new initiates struggled to contain their abilities, and this often proved dangerous. And now she understood why.

The entire room was covered in sharp jagged icicles, with many stuck into the barriers and walls. Noelle looked at Eli, who had been struck with several of them in his abdomen and side. But the letters above his head now returned to their normal time and read 241:38:21:04. Relief flooded Noelle. He would live on for another 241 years. Her lips curled upward.

But her smile disappeared when she caught sight of Marko. Many sharp icicles protruded from Marko's body, and the number above his head now read :04.

Noelle ran to his side and grabbed his hand. Marko fell to his knees, and blood poured from his lips. Several icicles stuck out of his abdomen and one right through his heart.

"Marko, no!" she cried in horror. Marko fell backward with a loud thud.

Noelle wailed. "I killed him!" Her hands began to violently tremble.

"We have two candidates for the win!" Autumn called out, and the Naturei audience members cheered wildly.

But Noelle couldn't hear anything beyond her own guttural screams that ripped from her throat. She rocked back and forth on her own knees. "I'm so sorry," she said repeatedly. "I didn't mean to!" Noelle was not certain that she could live with herself or how she might bring herself to inform his family that he was dead. Her older brother, Marko, who had always protected her and always been a friend to her in her lonely world, was gone. His brown hair was disheveled on the dirty arena floor, and a look of pain still twisted his features.

Tears spilled down Noelle's face as she screamed for help. She pressed her hands to Marko's wounds, and his blood covered her hands. Noelle pleaded and begged for somebody to help. Nobody came to help. Nobody brought alanis ointment. It was too late.

Noelle's panic increased as Marko's blood coated her hands. She turned to face Lumi, who lay lifeless in Luis's arms. Her cocktail hat fell to the floor, and Luis shook her shoulders.

"What have I done?" Noelle whispered. "I killed them," she groaned. Noelle laid her head on Marko's bloody chest and whimpered. Marko had been unwilling to kill her, yet she killed him. It was her fault that he wasn't there, and neither was Lumi. Sage was also lost because of her.

Lumi had offered Noelle a brighter future, one where she had a good friend and family member. Nobody could replace her grandma, but Lumi and Marko were the closest resemblance to family that she had. She had destroyed the tiny remnant that remained. Noelle wailed and grasped Marko's body tightly.

"I'm so sorry," she sobbed. "I didn't mean to!"

Eli lay still, too wounded to move. But he was going to be all right. The red letters above his head indicated it.

Noelle eyed Lumi's lifeless body that Luis still shook in a futile attempt to awaken her. She glanced down at Marko's bloodied body and sighed as his body temperature was already cooling. Noelle couldn't bear the thought that she had killed both Marko and Lumi, and the searing pain that pulsed through her body as she eyed Marko and Lumi overcame her. Noelle covered her face with her hands and let out a shriek of horror at what she had done.

CHAPTER 33
NOELLE
POWER

Nobody came to collect Marko's body. Nobody came to check on him. Not even Eli dared to say a word to Noelle as she lay there and wept. Several in the audience were quiet while others roared in cheers.

An idea sprang upon Noelle as she looked at the pale red shield barrier. She recalled that no abilities could affect anything inside the arena, which meant perhaps the Leizei who locked her necklace couldn't reach it currently. Could it be?

She peered down at the oval gold necklace and gripped it. She might be wrong, but she was willing to try. Noelle had been so focused on her past with her grandma and the pain that permeated her life that she hadn't realized that she had built a new family. She made a choice at that moment, that it was time to let go of her past and cherish it but to also focus on the future and build it. Marko and Lumi needed to be a part of that future.

Noelle placed a hand over Marko's heart that did not beat. His body had already remarkably cooled to the touch. His lifeless body didn't stir, so she closed her eyes.

"I don't know how this works," she whispered. "But I choose to undo the death of Marko and Lumi. Please work." Her necklace glowed a pale blue color, and the gold oval shape opened. A deep blue gem appeared in her hand, cold to the touch. She wrapped her fingers around it, and then when she opened her hand again, it became blue dust.

She looked back to Marko and then to Lumi.

And then Marko's honey-brown eyes opened. His wounds began to close.

"Marko!" Noelle pulled him into her and hugged him so tightly that he groaned.

Marko sat up and stared at her. Noelle exhaled deeply as the red letters above his head returned to normal. He was alive.

She spun to see Luis grinning madly with joy as Lumi seemed to come to.

Marko eyed the blue dust in her hand and then shook his head. "I can't believe you killed me." That was all he had to say.

"I brought you back to life though," Noelle said, sheepish.

A ghost of a smile emerged on his mouth, and he caught her by the wrist. "Thank you. I appreciate it. And before you go wailing more, because I know how you are, I know it was an accident. Thank you for using your only chance at getting your grandma back to help Lumi and me. How can I repay you?"

Noelle considered it. "Please don't let any harm come to Lumi, Luis, me, or Eli." She eyed Eli from the corner of her eye, and he watched them in awe, still unable to move. Noelle fought the urge to go to his side and comfort him.

"Deal," he said, and a red ribbon formed around their conjoined wrists. Noelle hadn't realized that they had just made a vow. She still wasn't used to it and quickly withdrew her hand.

Many Naturei came into the arena now. They applied ointment to Eli, and he groaned at their touch. His skin rapidly healed, and Leizei approached Marko to assist with his wounds.

But what frightened Noelle was the way the Leizei and Naturei each reverently bowed to her. She looked up and saw the audience, who roared with applause and shouts of victory. All three heirs had managed to survive.

Some people shouted that Noelle was a cheater, while others

shouted her name with admiration. She scanned the crowd and saw Lumi sit up, and Noelle watched as one single tear fell onto her cold cheek.

Noelle knew the tear was for Lorelei. The daughter that Lumi believed she would never see again. She turned to face the Naturei king, who sat with a cherry-red face and glared in her direction as his people shouted her praises. At that moment, Noelle realized the danger had only just begun. The Heirling Duel would be a battle won, but now an entire war was on the horizon.

Eli sat up now, and Marko did too, both remarkably healed from only moments ago.

"The judges have collectively decided that Noelle Hudson, the heir of the Merklei realm, is the winner of the Heirling Duel! That means that Lumi is hereby officially pardoned of her alleged prior crimes and must be accepted by all realms as the ruler of the Merklei. This concludes the Heirling Duel, and this settles the disputes among the three realms." Autumn said the words with excitement, and many cheered.

CHAPTER 34
NOELLE
DANCING AGAIN

In typical crass fashion, paired swimmingly with the Heirling Duel, the realms had a tradition that there would be a party directly after the Heirling Duel, because what better way could they celebrate the death of a person than throwing a party?

But in this story, the party was a welcome celebration. Welcomed by most everyone, at least. Noelle had gone from the most hated heir to possibly the most celebrated. And best of all, the three heirs had cheated death, and there was much to celebrate. There might be problems tomorrow, but today they would simply celebrate and be merry.

After several Naturei tended to Noelle's wounds, she had been whisked away to her room, separated from everyone else, where Eden had greeted her with a royal bow and kissed her cheeks. Noelle was slightly disturbed to see red letters above Eden's head that read 07:21:45:04. She only had seven years left to live. Noelle suppressed her idea to tell her. Noelle wanted to worry about Eden's future, especially with her design symbolism in the arena, but she decided she would worry about both their futures after today. She didn't believe the Naturei king would ignore Eden's symbolism in the arena, and she believed they were both in danger.

"No more bows," Noelle warned. She told them everything about Sage.

In response, Eden's cheeks were wet, and she bowed even lower. "Let him come for me. My mother is in the pit because of him."

Eden crafted a gorgeous gold gown for Noelle in silence, adorned with sparkling crystals across the bodice for Noelle. A slit went up to Noelle's leg, and the bottom material sparkled under the lights. The dress had a sweetheart neckline with straps. And of course, she wore an icy crown on her head with tall points.

When Lumi had arrived, Lumi fell into Noelle's arms, and she had imagined Lumi would scold her or perhaps even yell. Instead, Lumi silently held her.

"I'm sorry," Noelle said. "I'm sorry about using the necklace and not getting Lorelei and your people back." It took every ounce of strength to not break down. She felt ashamed that she had killed Marko and used the necklace, unable to control her ability.

Lumi's teary eyes met Noelle's. "I can't imagine how you must be feeling about not seeing your grandma. She was your only family."

"When you and Marko died today in the arena, I realized that I had it all wrong. I used to think that I didn't have family outside of my grandma, and that was why I was so desperate to get her back." Noelle sighed. "And I'm going to miss her desperately, but I realize that I've been looking in the rearview mirror of my life for too long. I recognize that I have you, Luis, Eli, and Marko." Noelle looked at Eden. "And Eden and the others."

Lumi went rigid at the sound of Marko's name. But then she eased and wrapped her arm around Noelle, tightly. Noelle hugged her back. "You're Merklei—which means *you are my family*. But I don't know what to do with myself now that the necklace is gone."

"Well, don't take this offensively. But with your age, you're kind of like my grandma. But you look like a cool older sister." Noelle laughed. "I need you, Lumi."

The two friends stared at each other for a long moment. Noelle had found her family—it wasn't by blood, but it was by a bond, unbreakable. Whether fate or not, she had found her family, and she would do whatever she could to protect them. And she knew that they would do the same.

Eden, who had pretended not to listen in the corner of the room, smiled. "Not to interrupt, but the party is waiting on you both. Shall we get you dressed?" Eden looked over Lumi's disheveled clothing.

Eden had crafted Lumi a deep, royal blue gown and a cocktail hat that matched along with long blue gloves. Lumi opted for a tight fit gown with a slit, optimal for dancing. She looked regal and beautiful. Noelle was certain Marko would like the dress, if he wasn't tied up somewhere from betraying his alliance in the arena. Of course, she would go fetch him if he didn't turn up in the dance hall.

A knock at the door sounded, and behind it was Luis. His hair was combed, and he wore a black leafy ensemble that looked much like a Naturei uniform. Blossom wrapped a dainty hand around his arm. She wore a pink petal dress with long flowing petals that dropped from her waist to the dirt floor.

"What do you think you're doing?" Noelle asked.

"Enjoying myself. Let's go," Luis said.

Noelle and Lumi exchanged glances, then followed too.

"I need you to know that Sage—"

"We know." Lumi wiped her nose. "They said she fell down the stairs. But we knew once you emerged in the arena with Sage's blood on your hands. They killed her. They'll pay for that. For all of it. I personally guarantee it."

They walked in silence to the ballroom.

The dance hall glowed with candles all around, and the massive hall contained Leizei and Naturei everywhere, donned in gorgeous attire. Noelle marveled at a Naturei woman whose skirt was made entirely of violet flowers that flung into the air every time she moved. They faded and disappeared once they flew into the air in a peculiar fashion.

As Noelle entered the dance hall, everyone turned to her and began to cheer wildly. Leizei saluted her with fire, and almost all of them praised her. She had never expected this to happen—but she had saved their heir. The Naturei around the room bowed to her with a greeting reserved for only fellow Naturei. Noelle eyed the Leizei and Naturei king, and they both clapped for her entrance. Though it had been fake, it pleased Noelle. Even they were beholden to their people, and she had managed to win over some within the realms. They wouldn't be able to do away with her easily.

Despite the warm greeting for Noelle, most of the Leizei and Naturei still kept their distance from Lumi in the grand Naturei dance hall. She was arguably the most dangerous one there, and she was still credited with being a murderous villain—whether it were true or not.

After a moment, the entire dance hall went back to their usual business. Gold goblets were filled to the brim with deep maroon liquid, and their plates and drinks clinked as they danced. Several royal Naturei musicians played in the corner of the room, and many people danced on the dirt floor in the middle.

Luis and Blossom found their way to the dance floor, and Noelle sighed.

A loud roar from all the Leizei told Noelle that Marko had entered. He was entirely healed, but when his eyes met hers—something was wrong. He didn't smile back, nor did he make his way toward them. Instead, Yuri, his fiancée, glared in their direction, and she wrapped her arm possessively around him.

He was still acting. He wasn't Lumi's boyfriend or Noelle's brother. He had to survive, and he still had to navigate his realm's politics. They couldn't publicly be friendly or cordial. They were supposed to be enemies even though Noelle had saved his life. Despite understanding his distance, Noelle still felt the sting of his coldness, which seared her.

She turned to Lumi, who seemed just as disappointed.

"I still believe he loves you. He risked everything to protect us both," Noelle said quietly so that nobody near them could hear.

Lumi nodded. "I can feel his feelings through the bond. He cares very deeply," she said and wound her fingers around her arm-length royal blue gloves. "This fire bond is torture, Noelle. I think about him all the time—not being able to be near him is *so painful*. My soul is literally woven into his, and it craves him." Lumi looked down at her feet and then to Noelle.

"We'll figure this out. One day at a time. We have each other, and we'll get through this." Noelle wrapped a protective arm around Lumi, who seemed less like a queen and more like a wilted flower as she watched Marko dance with his fiancée. They danced on the dirt floor, and Marko spun her around. He didn't dare to look in their direction.

And then she spotted him before the crowd could erupt. Eli had descended the spiral staircase, donned in decorative Naturei leafy clothing. His entire outfit was made of black roses, and it made Noelle want to swoon. His outfit was dark like midnight, and the petals that were crafted together made him appear majestic. He wore a leafy crown on his dark hair that pulled the entire look together, and when he saw her and beamed, she felt her face flush.

He survived. She survived. Now they could dance. Maybe they couldn't dance tomorrow, but today she would dance. Eli ignored the cheers of his people and made a beeline for Noelle.

In typical Eli fashion, uncaring about consequences, he pulled Noelle into his strong arms and held her against his chest. And she let him. She planned to deal with the consequences tomorrow. The Naturei people roared with cheers and seeming approval. Noelle even spotted the Naturei king, who clapped in false happiness. But his eyes gave her a message; she would pay for this. She turned her face and buried it into Eli's shoulder and sighed.

"May I have this dance?" Eli whispered against her neck. She nodded, and he led her by her hand to the dirt dance floor. His fingers trailed against her palm, and she was keenly aware of his every touch because it sent electricity up her skin. She smiled at him as she saw the healthy numbers in red above his head, large and numerous.

Eli pulled her close to his chest, and as the music began, he twirled her. His hand found its way to the small of her back. His other hand clasped hers. He pulled his hand away momentarily and flicked his fingers together and produced an alanis flower, which he placed behind her ear. The curse was broken, so now that the necklace was used, he could use all his abilities around Lumi.

"You look beautiful, Elle. You're the prettiest girl that I've ever laid my eyes on."

Noelle blushed and wondered how that could be true. "You clean up pretty well, Goldner. I suppose I wore a gold dress to match your name because I like it so much," she said with a laugh.

"Careful, if you like it that much, I just might give it to you."

And then he spun Noelle and they both laughed. Noelle welcomed the warm feeling of laughter, which had seemed to elude her for so long. Real, joyful, careless laughter. It felt wild and loose, yet it had seemed so distant for so many days and evaded her until now.

"A toast to my heir, Prince Eli. To celebrate this Heirling Duel, we will have a Naturei pageant to keep with tradition, where all young women are invited to participate. The chosen winner will be Prince Eli's wife," the Naturei king said and raised his glass. Several Naturei girls cheered and raised their glasses too.

Eli frowned and pulled Noelle in closer and continued his dance. "He is getting revenge on me. That is how he and Lumi met. The pageant is a nightmare for matching. I don't suppose you would want to enter a pageant?" He grinned.

Noelle wanted to say, *not if you're the prize*, as a playful jab. But she couldn't because of the vow. Instead, she asked, "Do I have to fight somebody?"

Eli laughed. "I can't believe he is doing this to me. There is nothing worse than these pretentious pageants, where girls line up to be selected based on the stupidest things."

Noelle laughed and looked around at the numbers above everyone's heads. "You know, I'm quite upset that your ability is cool and mine is lame. I just see how long people have to live. It seems a bit like a curse!" Noelle gazed at others who danced beside her. She spotted Adam with a Naturei girl and sighed as it showed he had a mere time of 09:35:06:07.

Eli followed her gaze. "How long does Adam have?"

"Nine years," Noelle said and darted her gray eyes away. It felt too intimate to know those details about people. "But yours is really long." She hoped that would comfort him before he could manage to ask her.

Eli's face fell momentarily, then recovered. "Then we will make it an amazing nine years for Adam." He looked around the crowd. "Tell me, how long do you see for the others?"

Noelle scanned the crowd for familiar faces. She spotted the Naturei king, and to her dismay, the red letters above his head said 20:21:08:03. "Your father will live another twenty years," she said, somber.

"And how about the Leizei king?" Eli asked and spun her again. Then his fingers greedily found their way to her waist, and he pulled her close to him. She inhaled the fresh black roses that comprised his outfit and gently touched one rose's petals.

Noelle turned to face the Leizei king, who sported his regular gold hood and black armor, but when she did, her brows made a deep V-shape. Lumi stood close to the Leizei king, and the hatred in her stormy-gray eyes poured out as she looked at him, and the red letters above his head read :09. Lumi took a step toward the Leizei king, producing an icy dagger.

"Lumi! Don't!" Noelle yelled and pulled away from Eli's grasp. But it was too late. Lumi's icy dagger plunged into his heart.

Several soldiers descended upon Lumi as the Leizei king fell to the ground, dead. But she blasted all of them backward with gusts of wintry mix. Lumi's chest rose and fell, but all she did was stare at Noelle.

Noelle placed a hand over her mouth. Lumi just enacted her own version of justice for Lorelei and Noelle's grandma, but Noelle couldn't shake the eerie feeling that perhaps Lumi's ability to sense people's ill will had something to do with this sudden death.

"Kill her!" the Naturei king yelled, and Naturei all around the room scurried toward Lumi. But she held her arms out, and every time one tried to grab her, she knocked them away. Piles of bodies were strewn across the floor by Lumi, and the soldiers slowed their pace as they realized she wouldn't go willingly.

Marko emerged and broke away from his fiancée. He darted in front of Lumi and placed himself between the soldiers and Lumi.

"No, arrest her. She will pay for her crimes, and we will begin her trial immediately," Marko said, eyes wet. "I am the king of the Leizei realm now." Marko turned toward Lumi and looked crestfallen. But he had made a promise to Noelle that he wouldn't hurt Lumi, and he honored it. Lumi shook her head at Marko.

"You can't run," Marko said and pointed at her wrist. "Just trust me."

Lumi laughed in response. "Trust you?" And then many soldiers were upon Lumi, and she struggled against them.

Noelle sighed as soldiers descended upon Lumi. Eli stood at her side and wrapped his fingers around hers.

"Maybe you didn't really know her like you think you did."

"No, I believe she had a reason for doing that," Noelle said and watched as Lumi knocked down dozens of soldiers who attempted to arrest her. "I'm going to have to trust her, and Marko." Noelle sighed. "Maybe you don't know your king like you thought you did. What about Sage? And your parents?" But Eli was pulled away before he could answer.

Noelle caught a glimpse of something in Lumi's right hand,

which quickly disappeared from sight when Lumi closed her fist. She watched as Lumi seemingly allowed the soldiers to win, fawning weakness and lessening her blows as they came, and they restrained her with cuffs. The soldiers closest to her smiled, thinking they were stronger than the Snow Queen. But Noelle knew Lumi allowed them to do it, because she barely put up a fight. But why? What was her plan?

Noelle stepped forward to intervene, but Lumi shot her a look and shook her head. She wanted them to take her, Noelle realized. So she stopped in her tracks and allowed it. What was Lumi's plan?

Lumi, hesitant at first, went slack and allowed the soldiers to lead her into a nearby room with double doors covered in vines. Marko trailed behind her, along with his fiancée.

When the doors closed, Noelle moved forward but stopped at the sight of a bloodied body on the ground. Noelle's entire body went numb when she neared it. Her face turned white, and her knees buckled underneath her. She reached for the body to see if they might be alive with a pulse.

Noelle recognized him. It was the Naturei king's adviser that lay there with an icy dagger plunged into his heart. Next to his body, written on parchment on the ground read, *Queen Noelle Hudson*. Noelle felt no heartbeat, and the body was cold to the touch. The body hadn't been there only a moment ago, so how could Lumi have done this? It couldn't have been her.

To Noelle's horror, the Naturei king and many Naturei soldiers moved toward her.

"It isn't what it looks like!" Noelle shrieked.

"It looks very bad, Noelle," the Naturei king growled.

"Wait! Remember that I can't lie to you? I didn't do this. I found this body, and I don't know how somebody got an icy dagger, but I didn't do it. And it couldn't have been Lumi. I just found him," Noelle said. Her anxiety started to ease as she recalled she made a vow to the king to never lie.

"Everyone out! Except for my personal guards and Noelle." The Naturei king scowled.

"But, sir," a soldier protested.

"Now!"

It took many moments, but eventually everyone left the ballroom, hauling out the injured soldiers. Eli gave Noelle a look of concern before exiting.

Once they all left, the king sighed. "It looks to me like you killed my adviser."

Noelle shook her head. "What?" She opened her mouth to explain herself, but then it dawned on her that the king might be setting her up.

Noelle stood to her feet and held out her hands, prepared to attack.

"Stupid girl. Put those away. You'll only hurt yourself. Lucky for you, I'm in the mood to negotiate." The king snapped his fingers. "Bring out the boy."

Two Naturei guards turned the corner and brought a terrified Luis out and held a knife to his throat. The whites of Luis's eyes showed, but he said nothing.

"I have nothing to do with any of this. Let Luis go!" Noelle yelled.

"You are turning my realm upside down, and half my kingdom is rooting for you to take my throne. And now? Now I have a dead adviser because your followers want you in my place. You're going to fix it. All of it!" the Naturei king yelled.

Noelle kept her hands out but didn't dare strike while the knife was so close to Luis's throat. "What do you want?"

"I've crafted a great deal for you. You're going to display cordiality with me and my decrees. You will turn your supporters into my supporters by lending your allegiance to me. You'll live comfortably here in the Naturei realm or wherever you decide. But you will not sit on my throne."

"That's it? Fine—"

"There is more," the Naturei king said. Luis whimpered as the Naturei soldier dug the knife into his neck.

"Stop it!" Noelle yelled.

"You will enter the pageant to compete. And you will put on a good show, because if you don't enter, then Eli will know that I intervened. But each day, I expect you to hang out with Captain Adam. And then before the pageant commences, you will inform Prince Eli that you've fallen in love with Captain Adam. This will disqualify you from the competition, and you'll never obtain my throne. You are forbidden to tell anybody about our vow. Your friend's life depends on it."

Noelle looked at Luis, whose breath was ragged. The Naturei soldiers didn't flinch. They just stood, ready to obey their ruler.

"And if I don't agree?" Noelle asked.

"Your friend will die," the Naturei king said. The Naturei king reached out and grabbed Noelle's wrist. "What will it be? You have ten seconds."

Noelle looked above Luis's head, and her heart skipped several beats when she saw a countdown of ten seconds above his head. It was true. If she didn't make the agreement, then they would kill Luis, and her ability proved their threat to be credible. She couldn't let that happen. Noelle closed her eyes and let out a long sigh.

"Fine! Now let go of my friend!" To Noelle's relief, they let go of Luis, and he fell to the ground. A bright green ribbon of light tied around their wrists, which sealed her vow.

"Good. You will enter the pageant and simultaneously spend time with Captain Adam each day until the end of the pageant. Then you'll inform Prince Eli of your choice." The king shifted to Luis and held his wrist. "And you will say nothing of this, or I'll kill you. Understand?"

"Understood," Luis said and glared at him. The king waited for their seal to finish, then shoved Luis's wrist away as if it were repulsive. He, along with the guards, moved toward the doors.

"Aren't you going to investigate who did this?" Noelle asked.

The king stopped and turned to face her. The sneer on his face was dark and twisted, yet his eyes were the things that made Noelle want to shrink back.

"If I were you, that would be the last thing I'd worry about. I heard that people gave you a royal bow. We'll start with crushing your supporters by publicly giving lashes with the whip. Then we can move on to the others that so generously helped you survive this duel, by sending them to the pit." He sneered. "I doubt your supporters will remain loyal when they see what it costs them. Besides, you're supposed to be dead."

"I won the duel." Noelle lifted her chin.

"I'm not talking about the duel." The Naturei king faced her. "When I found out your cheating mother tried to pass off her human child as mine, I knew I had to end you. *How* did you survive the Merklei massacre, Lorelei?"

Noelle went rigid at hearing her real name. When she finally lifted her eyes to meet him, she stared at "her father", whose venomous glare sent a chill down her spine. It was time for Lorelei to take what was rightfully hers. Lorelei was going to sit upon her father's throne or die trying.

ACKNOWLEDGMENTS

I am so grateful to so many people for helping me with this book. Firstly, I'm thankful to God for listening to me ramble (I mean pray!) endlessly about this book. God answered so many prayers with this book. I also want to thank the readers and my online book community on Tiktok, Instagram, and Youtube. I am overwhelmed with gratitude for the amount of readers (and complete strangers!) who championed this book, and cheered me on in the process. I'll admit it–you guys brought me to tears on several occasions. Book people are literally the best people on the planet! I have truly found my people and I absolutely adore you all.

Thank you to Leigh Johnson for being my incredible developmental editor. I find it absolutely hilarious that despite fantasy not being your favorite genre, you always edit fantasy novels. How does this keep happening? Thank you for helping me iron out the plot holes and character issues, and thank you for taking my long phone calls to discuss potential edits. I am so thankful for you!

Thank you to Anne Victory and Annie S. from Victory Editing LLC for amazing copy edits! You are such a talented team. I am beyond grateful for your work and copy edits. You really helped me polish this story! Connecting with you was an answered prayer. Thank you to Miblart, based out of Ukraine, for the exceptional customer service and beautiful cover design. You really outdid yourself and the cover is beyond gorgeous. Thank you to Jason Buff for allowing me to use the amazing studio photo. I am so grateful to every person who shared their talents to help make this book happen.

And thank you to my amazing husband, who is so supportive. He offered encouragement and always listened to every detail about my book and offered to help in any way that he could. And thank you to my parents for their support and encouragement. And thank you to my entire family for their love and support.

Additionally, thank you to the following people on the internet who helped me name Sage: @lexy_gonzales, @teafarmguy, @the.bookcourt, @jonseylarue, @elliewebster53, @jaredt_20, and a shoutout to @poeticbookreads too!

Thank you to every person who helped make this book happen. I am beyond excited to share this with you.

I love you so much!

Keilah Jude

About the Author

Photo by Jabu Studio

Keilah Jude graduated from the University of Cincinnati with a degree in English literature and a minor in creative writing. She received a master's degree in her favorite book, which is the Bible, from Wheaton College. She is an actress and you can find some of her films on Amazon Prime and she has commercials for exciting brands. She enjoys making book content online where she rants (and sometimes cries!) over books. When she isn't writing, she is on a never ending quest to find Dunkaroos. If you know of their whereabouts, please contact her. She would love to connect with you on social media and hear about what you're reading lately!

KeilahJude is on Tiktok, Instagram, Youtube, and Facebook as @KeilahJude

www.KeilahJude.com

BONUS CHAPTER

Turn the page for a sneak peak of the second book. *The Snow Queen's Heir* series by Keilah Jude continues.

CHAPTER 1
LORELEI

Lorelei heard an explosion nearby and hurried to her feet. The ground beneath them shook, and she just knew it was Lumi. She grabbed Luis's hand and together they scurried toward the door that Lumi and Marko were in.

"Where do you think you're going?" the Naturei king yelled.

But they didn't stop. They hurried toward the double doors, where Lumi and Marko were surely fighting. Lorelei could hear what she imagined was fire and ice colliding. She threw her hands backward at the Naturei guards and the king, and crafted a massive ice shield, larger than she had anticipated. It cut them off entirely.

"Woah, you're getting better!" Luis yelled.

They sprinted and threw the doors open when they reached them. They both panted as they closed it behind them and she crafted ice that jutted upward, which sealed the door. She felt uncomfortable warmth at her backside and jumped.

When she turned to face the crazed sight, she found Lumi, nose flared, sending ice shards toward Marko. How did she get her shackles off? Marko maintained his position and stood between the Leizei and Naturei soldiers and Lumi. He held his hands up, as if he might manipulate fire at any moment.

"Nobody touches her. She will have a trial and we will see what happened, and she will be judged by guilt or innocence," Marko shouted over the huge crowd.

"Innocence? She killed the Leizei King! Kill her! I saw it with my own eyes!" a soldier shouted back. Many soldiers, both Leizei and Naturei, shouted in agreement.

Marko spotted Lorelei and examined her ice shield. "Everyone must leave, except my guards, Noelle, and Yuri. Where is the Naturei King and his heir?" Marko looked around the room, but they were nowhere in sight.

Lorelei and Luis shrugged in unison.

The soldiers filed out of the room by the back door, but many hurled insults at Lumi before doing so. Once they left, she iced the door.

Lorelei took in a deep breath and spun around the back room where gold furniture laid across the room, and not much else. It must have been a storage room of some sort, she judged by the amount of tall and odd gold furniture. Lumi stood in her elegant blue dress, with her gloves still on.

"Wrong move." Lumi produced an icy knife and lunged for Marko's throat, but he shoved her to the side. Yuri pulled Lumi off Marko and launched a fist to her temple.

"Stop it!" Lorelei yelled. She noticed there were only a small group of elite hooded Leizei surrounding them.

Marko cleared his throat. "Do not let anybody come in. We have only a few moments before the soldiers arrive. Now listen to me—"

Lumi took a step toward Marko. "I'm not listening to anything you say. You're a liar."

It was Yuri who now moved toward Lumi. Lorelei intercepted her path and put her hands out.

"Don't," Lorelei warned.

Yuri smirked. "I should be thanking you. If it weren't for the fact that you just ruined all of our plans," Yuri spoke and leaned to the side to view Lumi.

"What?" Lorelei asked, arms still out in a defensive posture.

"Lumi, how could you do this?" Marko asked, and his brows pulled together. His eyes were watery, and it dawned on Lorelei that although they had a twisted relationship, part of Marko still loved his grandfather.

"He was going to kill Noelle. And I imagine you already knew about that," Lumi spat. Lorelei twirled around to face Lumi now, and guilt weighed heavy upon her as realization set in that Lumi had struck the Leizei King to save her.

"They stopped sharing their plans with us, because of you. If you're willing to share your memories, we might be able to prove you acted in defense of your heir," Yuri said, and began to walk around Lumi.

"And why would you help? Would you like to know what your fiancé has done?" Lumi asked, and looked over at Marko with disdain.

"Yeah, yeah. I already know. The fire bond." Yuri shrugged. "Marko, you have to tell her the truth."

Lumi looked between Yuri and Marko and then to the guards. Marko followed her gaze and shook his head.

"My guards aren't threats. They're with me. We don't have much time but you should know that Yuri and I aren't really engaged."

"I don't care," Lumi said and swiped at Marko again.

Lorelei carefully considered this. Perhaps Yuri just wanted a seat on the throne, and she was after power. Perhaps she didn't care about Marko or his personal affairs. Perhaps they had made some sort of agreement or exchange—she supposed this could be plausible.

Yuri rolled her eyes. "I don't have time for this. Listen to me—Marko protected me by allowing me to be called his fiancé for many years. There is a reason we never truly got married—the entire thing was a farce. We blamed it on his spying duties and planning. In the fire realm, women stay with their families until they settle in a new relationship. Marko and I grew up together, and my father brutally beat me often over the smallest offenses. Marko offered to say we were engaged, as a cover story for me to move out. In our realm, women can move into their own place only when they're engaged to prepare for their new home."

Luis's mouth dropped. "That's terrible. Why would your realm have such awful laws?"

"We have high hopes for King Marko's reign, so that wrongs can be made right. Particularly for women in our realm," Yuri said and nodded at Marko.

The ice shield shattered and Lorelei covered her face. "Merca!"

Dread poured over Lorelei as the Naturei king entered, along with seemingly half the kingdom behind him. Soldiers filled the room, and many stood outside of it.

Lumi lifted her icy knife and aimed for Marko's heart. Lorelei's heart shuddered as the red letters above Marko's head dwindled and so did the ones above Lumi's head. What was she thinking?

"Don't!" Lorelei yelled.

She hardly slowed. "Give me one good reason, Noelle." Lumi aimed and her hand was about to make contact with his chest.

"Because my name isn't Noelle. It's Lorelei."

Lumi halted, and turned to face her. She dropped the icy knife and all the rage on her face evaporated. She simply stared at Lorelei, face unreadable.

Gasps could be heard all throughout the room and in the dance hall.

Marko quickly picked up the shackles on the floor and cuffed Lumi. She let him.

Lorelei stared at her mother, and she tried to discern whether she was pleased, upset, or offended at the truth. But Lumi's face was blank as they led her away from the room, in shackles. But her eyes never left Lorelei as she exited.

Lorelei turned to the Naturei king and smiled. "My father and I wanted to wait until after the Heirling Duel to announce it. We're so happy to be reunited. I plan to help my father with his rule." She bowed low, hoping he took the bait. Would he kill her for this? He'd cause an uproar if he did. When she lifted her head to get a good view, she saw a stunned audience. Even the king seemed surprised.

"Is it really her?" a woman asked.

"How is it possible? After all this time?" a soldier whispered.

After a long pause, the king smiled a calculated grin. "Yes, my daughter had a head injury and lost her memory. But we figured it out, slowly. We couldn't wait to tell everyone."

Lorelei grinned. She knew he couldn't resist seeing her supporters become his.

Eli emerged at the king's side and balked at Lorelei. She knew her presence could jeopardize his life, if others thought it would mean he would usurp the throne.

She swallowed. "But of course we agreed that Prince Eli would still inherit the throne! He is older, after all."

And with that, the Naturei swarmed Lorelei, greeting her, patting her on the back, and welcoming their long, lost princess home.

Lorelei looked up through her lashes at the Naturei king, who tilted his head as he watched her being embraced.

If only Lorelei's grandma were here to witness the most epic game that Lorelei would ever play. Let the games begin.

www.ingramcontent.com/pod-product-compliance
Lightning Source LLC
LaVergne TN
LVHW010307070526
838199LV00065B/5472